THE
ENGLISH LADY

Other Books by William Harrington

PARTNERS

SCORPIO 5

MR. TARGET

THE JUPITER CRISIS

TRIAL

THE SEARCH FOR ELISABETH BRANDT

YOSHAR THE SOLDIER

THE POWER

WHICH THE JUSTICE, WHICH THE THIEF

THE ENGLISH LADY

WILLIAM HARRINGTON

Seaview Books

NEW YORK

Copyright © 1982 by William Harrington.

Manufactured in the United States of America.

Seaview Books/A Division of PEI Books, Inc.

Library of Congress Cataloging in Publication Data

Harrington, William, 1931–
    The English lady.
    I. Title.
PS3558.A63E5   813'.54   81–52071
ISBN 0–87223–750–8   AACR2

Designed by Tere LoPrete

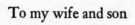

To my wife and son

PART I

—◆—

1931–34

She might have become Queen of England.

In his official biography of King George V, Sir Harold Nicolson recounted a conversation that took place in January or February of 1931 between the King and Sir Frederick Knowles:

"The Prince of Wales," the King remarked with a faint, sly smile, "seems to find something extraordinarily attractive in the younger daughter of the Earl of Edham."

Sir Frederick thought the King seemed pleased. "Well His Royal Highness might, Sir," he replied. "Lady Nancy is both intelligent and exceptionally pretty."

When Nicolson interviewed Sir Frederick Knowles in 1950, Sir Frederick made additional comments that Nicolson noted but did not elect to incorporate in the biography. "If Wales had had the good sense to remain smitten with Lady Nancy Brookeford and had married *her*, many things might have turned out much better. She was English and of good family and eligible. The trouble was, the lad never did have good sense, y' know."

On February 2, 1931, Winston Churchill wrote to David Lloyd George:

What you say you hear is no mere rumour but is true. HRH is indeed enamoured of the younger dghtr of the

Earl of Edham. Tho' HM will be pleased, I am not sure
many others will be. The old business of the Somme & 1916
still sticks in many craws, & tho' you & I know the Earl's
Toryism is emotional & superficial & contrary to his family's
tradition, many will deplore the prospect of an alliance
between Edham & Windsor. All this is shortsighted. The
girl is lovely, level-headed, & would be, in every way, an
admirable Princess of Wales. I have known her for some
years past, since she was a child, in fact, & it is my thought
she would exert an intelligent & steadying influence on
HRH.

When Lloyd George next saw Churchill, the brief affair
between Lady Nancy and the Prince of Wales was over; but the
old gentleman did not know that, and sought out Churchill to
tell him a story about the young woman he still supposed might
marry the prince.

He had been at Wickstone, he said—the country seat of the
earls of Edham—for a weekend's shooting. His daughter, Megan,
had been with him. One morning, a heavy political discussion
developed over breakfast. Lady Astor was at the table, and just
as she was delivering herself dramatically of a weighty opinion,
the young Lady Nancy Brookeford walked in. The conversation
stopped as the Countess of Edham introduced the girl, then only
fourteen, to the assembled company. The girl's late appearance
for breakfast had interrupted Lady Astor, who was annoyed. She
waited impatiently until Lady Nancy had been presented to each
guest, then dismissed her with a condescending flutter of her hand
and a curt word and resumed her interrupted declamation. The
fourteen-year-old girl allowed herself to be dismissed; but as she
sat down and picked up her napkin, she settled on Lady Astor a
look of such unalloyed contempt that Megan Lloyd George burst
into a peal of laughter. Others around the table—Stanley Baldwin
was among them—had seen all that had happened, and they
began to laugh, too. Lady Astor flushed with anger at first, then
smiled and said: "God help us when she's ten years older."

Major General Sir Henry Brookeford, tenth Earl of Edham,
was the direct descendant of Friederich Georg Heinrich von
Bachfurt, who had come to England in the entourage of King
George I and was created Earl of Edham in recognition of his

services, not to England, but to Hanover. The peerage was thus more than two hundred years old; its origins in the despised German cronyism of George I had been forgiven or forgotten; and in the frame of reference of King George V, the Bachfurt-Brookeford family was an old and honorable line. That, undoubtedly more than the young woman's reputation for beauty and intelligence, was what pleased him when he learned that his son seemed to be in love with Nancy Brookeford.

If the King was in fact pleased, Churchill was right, however, in guessing that many others would not be. The Earl, although he shrewdly extended his lavish hospitality to leading men and women of all parties, was rigidly, outspokenly Tory. "He out-Tories the Tories," Ramsay MacDonald once grumbled. Liberal and Labour politicians would have deplored an alliance between the Prince of Wales and the daughter of the Tory Earl.

"The old business of the Somme" that Churchill mentioned in his letter to Lloyd George was a reference to a desperate, costly assault on the German line in 1916, in which the brigade commanded by the Earl suffered sixty percent casualties—almost ninety percent among his junior officers. That the Earl was himself severely wounded in the first wave of the attack and was not in command during the balance of the day did not absolve him, in the minds of many, of blame for a poorly planned and foolishly ordered attack that cost many lives. His clumsy, insensitive references in later years to "that valiant day" kept his detractors' memories vivid and their resentment deep and fresh. The business of the Somme did, as Churchill had remarked, "stick in many craws."

In the autumn of 1930, when the Prince—Edward Albert Christian George Andrew Patrick David—decided he was in love with her, Nancy Brookeford was twenty years old. She was small —"just sixteen hands and seven stone," as her father put it—which was a Bachfurt family trait; the Earl himself was not much bigger. Her face was faultless: clear, smooth skin; a small nose; a small mouth with full, mobile lips; large, deep-blue eyes; straight, unplucked brows. Her light brown hair was cropped short as the fashion of the day dictated, and often it was all but out of sight under the cloche that fashion also dictated.

She had a reputation, as Sir Frederick Knowles and Winston Churchill both knew, for being pretty and intelligent. Aside from those two elements with universal acceptance among all who knew her, the remaining elements of her reputation were varied, even conflicting, depending on who reported. There were those who called her cynical and hedonistic. There were those who referred to her mercurial temperament. She remained capable of the sidelong glance of unalloyed scorn with which she had favored Lady Astor, and it was an element of her reputation. Jeremy Dudley, who suggested to the Prince that he should consider becoming better acquainted with Lady Nancy Brookeford, told the Prince she was "a girl who knows how to have fun but also knows when to stop the fun."

She had her twenty-first birthday while she and the Prince were still close. On that day her mother handed her a small package wrapped in brown paper and tied with string, saying it had been left for her, to be opened when she was twenty-one. The package contained a copy of the privately printed first edition of *Lady Chatterley's Lover*, personally inscribed to her by D. H. Lawrence. Lawrence was dead and had been for some years. The package had been in the house, waiting for this day, since a day when she was fifteen years old and had innocently told Lawrence in the breakfast room at Wickstone House, where he was a weekend guest, that she had heard much of his novel but could not buy a copy anywhere. He had laughed and said he didn't think she was quite old enough to make the acquaintance of Lady Jane.

When her father saw the package unwrapped, he guffawed. Likely he had read *Lady Chatterley*—more likely he had read a few parts someone had pointed out to him. The Earl was a lusty, hard-drinking man: small and bristly, abrupt, quick to judge, quick to err, quick to recant. His face was ruddy, and his nose was bulbous and crisscrossed with the purple lines of broken veins. His hair was white, and he wore a toothbrush moustache. He was a clubman. He rode. He shot. He sailed. He fished. He thought of himself as a retired soldier and carried himself with what he considered a military bearing. He had told a thousand people he was an Edwardian, born a bit too late. He deeply regretted, he also said often, the Parliament Act of 1911, which had so severely curtailed the legislative powers of the House of Lords that it left him, as a peer, with virtually no influence on the conduct of public affairs. He would have liked, he said, to help govern the kingdom.

The Countess of Edham, if she had read *Lady Chatterley*, or if she had been aware of the controversy about it, would not have given the book to Nancy; she would have long since destroyed it. She was a devout High Church Christian and would have destroyed the book without conscience for what she would have called its "indelicacies." The unceasing procession of guests through the dining rooms and guest bedrooms of Edham House and Wickstone was not limited to the politicians favored by the Earl or to the occasional writer or artist he tolerated because he thought it was good for his children to meet them; it included clergymen, and it was a rare Edham House dinner or Wickstone country weekend that did not include a bishop. The Countess was elated when her great good friend Cosmo Lang was elevated to the See of Canterbury. He had been at her dinner table many times over the years, and Nancy knew him well. Probably he had read *Lady Chatterley*; it was the Countess's small joke, not his, that of making many books there was no end and that reading much besides the Holy Bible was a weariness. It was her ambition, she said as often as the Earl said he was an Edwardian man, to know *everyone*—knowing *everything* was not worth the trouble.

Nancy's brother, Henry Herbert, Lord Random, was ten years her elder. He was away from home almost all the time, first at Eton, then at Oxford. When he was at home, he was a stranger; so far as she was concerned, another guest in the house. He was small like his father. He smoked cigarettes one after another. He expressed his opinions, of which he had many, in a nervous, high-pitched voice, punctuated with a girlish giggle. Nancy did not like him.

Her sister, Penelope, was four years her elder; and until 1927, when Penelope married and left home, she was Nancy's best friend. They were educated together, at home by a series of tutors hired by their father and mother. Nancy was ten and Penelope fourteen before they slept in separate bedrooms. The Countess

thought it amusing to dress them alike, as though they were twins
—although they conspicuously were not, Penelope being tall,
long-faced, and busty. Penelope was saturnine; she wrote poetry
on violet-colored paper with purple ink, and ritually burned
every poem in a brass bowl she kept on the hearth in her bedroom.

The Earl dominated his family and his homes, of course; but
in a more direct and personal sense, Edham House and Wickstone
were dominated by Mr. Dunn, the butler. Mr. Dunn (called
"Dunn" by the Earl, and "Mr. Dunn" by everyone else) ruled
with lofty and rigid dignity a household staff that consisted,
typically, of himself, an underbutler, the Earl's valet, the
Countess's personal maid and two other ladies' maids, two foot-
men, a housekeeper and three housemaids, a chef and four kitchen
maids, a hall boy, two laundresses, a night watchman, and a
telephonist. Mr. Dunn moved his principal staff—plus the girls'
tutors—from Edham House to Wickstone and back as the family
moved. He was held in awe by the Brookeford children, even
after they were old enough fully to comprehend his status as a
servant. (Nancy was eighteen years old before she discovered his
Christian name was Charles.) His studied dignity and his conspicuous efficiency in running two households earned him respect
even from distinguished guests. Neville Chamberlain once gave
him a bottle of Napoleon brandy. Winston Churchill referred to
him as "Lord Dunn" and brought him boxes of cigars when he
came to call at Edham House. The Earl joked that "Dunn smokes
Winston's damned Havanas. He hides them and won't give me
even one. Damned Winston values Dunn more than he values me,
't's plain enough."

Mr. Dunn organized the family's frequent trips to the Continent, just as he organized their moves from Edham House to
Wickstone and back. The Earl considered it a family obligation
to pay visits to the German cousins—Bachfurts and others—from
time to time. Nancy spoke fluent German before she had seen
anything of Germany beyond the immediate neighborhoods of
her cousins' homes. Her tutors made her fluent in French before
she saw anything of France. In Paris, family excursions from the
George V were more likely to be to Longchamp than the Louvre,
to Maxim's than to the Madeleine, to Chanel than to Sainte
Chapelle. Nancy was sixteen before a tutor angrily asserted her-

self and dragged her and Penelope away from a family expedition
to the racecourse and led them, startled and wondering, through
the Louvre.

Penelope was married in the summer of 1927. Three weeks later
the Earl, the Countess, and Nancy sailed on the *Mauretania* for
New York. The Earl wanted to see the States, he said. Accompanying the family were Mr. Dunn; Mr. Flesher, the Earl's valet;
a lady's maid for the Countess and one for Nancy; and a Miss
Gardner, the last of the daughters' tutors. The entire party had
first-class cabins; it was a point with the Earl that his servants
should be on the first-class deck, where he could find them when
he wanted them, rather than "lollying about" in the second- or
third-class bars. In New York he took a large suite and a group
of adjacent rooms at the Waldorf-Astoria Hotel and began to
hold luncheons and dinner parties. His actual purpose in coming
to America was not to see the country as he had said but to renew
old friendships with Americans he had met in France during the
war. He was thinking of investing some of his capital in the
booming American economy, and he wanted to explore that idea
with American friends.

With Miss Gardner, Nancy went out to explore the city, while
her father and mother spent most of their time in the hotel suite.
In company with Mr. Dunn, she and Miss Gardner took a boat
trip to the Statue of Liberty. They rode in a lift to the top of one
of the tall buildings and from a giddying height looked out over
the city and its harbor. They saw a motion picture—Greta Garbo
and John Gilbert in *Flesh and the Devil.*

After a week, when her father had made the acquaintance of a
Mr. Roth of Kuhn, Loeb & Company, Mr. Roth assigned a young
banker from his company to escort Nancy and Miss Gardner to
the theater and perhaps to a nightclub. The young man's name
was Gruenbaum, and he took them to see the Ziegfeld *Follies.*
Nancy was fascinated by an American named Will Rogers who
twirled a rope at the front of the stage and talked in a comic
accent about American vagaries. She understood little of what
he said, but his manner and appearance were in themselves entertaining. Mr. Gruenbaum arranged for her to go backstage and
meet Mr. Rogers, who, it turned out, used the same accent off-

stage as on and said he was "always glad to meet an English girl and hear them talk." Another night Mr. Gruenbaum took her to a nightclub called Villa Vallee where the principal attraction was a young redheaded man called Vallee who sang and played a saxophone.

They spent three weeks in New York. After that, they went by train to Washington, where the heat was so oppressive that the whole party spent most of the four days they were there in retreat in their hotel suite, sitting not far from the oscillating fans that were supposed to make the damp, hot air more bearable. Their embassy held a dinner in their honor. The President of the United States, Mr. Coolidge, had, it seemed, had the good sense to be away from Washington—fishing somewhere in a cool stream, someone said. Mr. Kellogg, the Secretary of State, did attend.

They went south from Washington. It seemed insanity, both to Nancy and the Countess, to plunge deeper into the caldron of an American summer; but the Earl was determined to see again an old friend, a man he had met in France in 1918. This man, it seemed, was cruising on his yacht off the Florida coast. It would be a relief from the American heat, the Earl promised, to cruise for a weekend on the Atlantic. He had telegraphed the man— whose name had escaped Nancy—and had received word in return that the Earl and Countess and Lady Nancy would be welcome aboard the *Larooco*, which would dock at Miami and wait for them. Unfortunately, the boat lacked sufficient space for servants; and, in any event, aboard the *Larooco* everyone lived what the telegram called "community life."

Placing the servants, including Miss Gardner, in a Miami hotel —and on this the Earl saved money, putting them in ordinary rooms in an ordinary hotel—the Earl engaged two taxicabs to drive the family and their luggage to the pier where he expected to find the yacht *Larooco*.

The pier was no city pier, only a long dock of weathered gray planks and barnacle-encrusted pilings, stretching along a weedy lot at the end of a sandy road on a tropical river. None of the boats moored there were yachts. The *Larooco* was a houseboat— a weatherbeaten, aging houseboat at that. It lay comfortably deep in the water, rolling gently on the swells.

"I don't think I want to go aboard that," the Countess whispered urgently to the Earl.

The Earl stood beside the taxi. He was wearing yachting clothes: a blue blazer, white duck trousers, a yachting cap. Agape, he stared at the man fishing from the stern of the *Larooco*—a conspicuously muscular, deeply tanned, handsome, middle-aged man, casually dressed in gray flannel slacks, an open-collared white shirt, a floppy white sun hat with wide brim wrinkled all around. Before the Earl could reply to the Countess, the man saw him. "Henry!" the man yelled with warm enthusiasm. "Come aboard."

A young woman emerged from the cabin and hurried toward the gangplank. "Sir Henry," she said with a wide smile as she crossed the plank toward the dock. As she came up to him, she extended her hand. She was a black-haired, erect young woman, slender, rather tall. "I'm Marguerite LeHand," she said. "I'm Mr. Roosevelt's secretary."

Mr. Roosevelt did not remain in his chair only to reel in his fishing line, Nancy discovered. He was a cripple. He was so conspicuously muscular in his upper body because whenever he moved his own weight it was his arms and shoulders that moved him, not his useless legs. His clothes were rumpled and baggy. He sat in the midst of a litter of fishing tackle, bait, cigarette packs, the remains of his lunch, and a stack of newspapers: an almost comic figure. Yet he was, she thought, the most aristocratic man she had ever seen. He welcomed her father and mother and her with perfect ease. Americans had tended to confront the Earl of Edham and his Countess with one of two attitudes: awkwardly exaggerated courtesy coupled with a grudging deference, or aggressive egalitarianism. Mr. Roosevelt treated the Earl as an old friend, certainly an equal, but without any need to demonstrate their equality. He was so comfortable, he made them comfortable.

Almost before the Countess could have protested she was reluctant to go cruising on this dilapidated houseboat, the taxi drivers were paid, the luggage had been toted on board by the middle-aged couple who constituted the crew of the *Larooco*, and the boat was chugging placidly along the waterway.

It was one of the most pleasant weekends of Nancy's life, and Frank Roosevelt was the most charming host she had ever met.

He had come close to death, apparently, from the disease that had crippled him, and he took an ingenuous pleasure from life. He directed the little boat toward nameless islands in a nameless tropic sea (they had names, of course, but she did not remember them), where they anchored off white beaches and bathed in the clear, warm waters. None of the Brookefords had brought bathing costumes, but Frank Roosevelt kept suits for men and women aboard the *Larooco* (pronounced, he insisted, like "cocoa"), and so persuasive was he about the tonic pleasures of swimming in the tropic salt waters that even the Countess squirmed into one of the knit wool suits and bared her lanky, freckled arms and legs to the sun. Roosevelt himself swam strongly, pulling himself through the water with his powerful arms, dragging his legs after. With his secretary—called "Missy" as soon as one got to know her—he taught Nancy to swim. He told her it was the world's finest exercise; he had hopes it would even restore his atrophying leg muscles. The Earl swam with the same manic vigor he gave to everything. The Countess paddled. Missy LeHand—handsome and womanly in her black swimsuit—kept near Frank Roosevelt in the water.

In the evenings they sat on the deck and Frank presided over a ritual he obviously enjoyed: the mixing of the cocktails they would drink before dinner. He put ice in a tall glass vessel, to which he added portions of gin and dry French vermouth, carefully measured in proportions of five parts gin to one of vermouth. He shook the mixture with the ice until the concoction was American-cold, then poured it into small glasses in each one of which Missy LeHand had placed a small green olive. He offered Nancy an alternative to what he warned was a strong drink, and he laughed uproariously when she said she would rather have any drink, strong as it might be, than another glass of the sweet brown Coca-Cola.

Missy LeHand sat on his lap, and Frank Roosevelt clasped her to him with his big brown arms. He talked with the Earl about the summer of 1918 when he had come to France as Assistant Secretary of the Navy. He recalled how he had met the Earl at Verdun and how they had been acquainted less than five minutes when an unexpected shift by a German battery had brought the hillock where they stood under lively shellfire and compelled them to jump fast into a muddy bunker. They had met again in

Paris. He recalled how both of them were introduced to calvados by a French colonel. Even now their memories of that night were hilariously confused. The gin-and-vermouth drinks warmed everyone as the calvados must have done, and even the Countess, who was appalled at the Spartan quarters she and the Earl shared on the *Larooco* and was disturbed by the apparently "improper" relationship between Frank Roosevelt and his secretary, relaxed and laughed.

The weekend passed too quickly. Before it was over, Nancy could swim. She had acquired a taste, as had the Earl, for Frank Roosevelt's martinis—which was what he called his gin-and-vermouth drinks. She had acquired, too, a different perspective on America. On the dock, however, the Countess sighed loudly and proclaimed herself happy to escape what she called "Mr. Roosevelt and his bum boat." Nancy looked back at the shabby little boat, pitching heavily in the wake of a passing yacht, and wished she could go back aboard for a month.

Frank Roosevelt had advised the Earl to be cautious in his American investments. ("If there were such a thing as a sure thing, Henry, we'd be cruising on a real boat, like Vincent Astor's.") The Earl had taken his advice and invested cautiously. His only flyer was in some Florida land, in which he invested two hundred pounds. By 1930 the Florida land could not be sold for any price whatever; no one would offer anything for it. The Earl had no choice but to hold it, pay the minor taxes imposed by the state of Florida, and wait. He had invested conservatively in the stock market. He bought, for example, ten thousand shares of Radio Corporation of America at 94½ and watched it rise to 505 in the bull market of 1928 and '29, only to fall to 42 by the time he felt compelled to sell it in 1930. He lost more than a hundred thousand pounds. His other conservative investments performed as badly. The trip to America, he said later, cost him almost a million pounds.

In the fall of 1930, when the Prince of Wales began to court his daughter, the Earl was in a sour mood. He spoke of disaster. He called for retrenchment, for drastic cuts in living expenses. He talked about personal sacrifices—although Nancy found it difficult to see any sacrifices he or the Countess were making. The sudden realization that his daughter might marry the Prince lifted the Earl's spirits. He looked away from his account books and began to smile quizzically. His daughter Nancy, Princess of Wales, in time Queen of England . . . Ha!

The rumors of the love affair were far more exciting than the facts. The Prince danced with her one night, then began to telephone her. He invited her to dinner, to go dancing, to accompany him on a drive in the country, to a champagne supper. His father, the King, became aware of his son's new interest when the Prince began to adjust his social schedule, sometimes awkwardly, to make occasions to be with her. When the Prince invited her on a hunting weekend at Melton Mowbray, everyone knew he was in love with Lady Nancy Brookeford.

Everyone, that is, within the confines of a group comprised of very few. The newspapers in 1930 and '31 were still following their longtime policy of treating the private lives of the royal family with complete restraint and discretion. When she entered a restaurant or a theater, one or two people might look up from their meals or their programs, follow her with their eyes, and maybe whisper furtively to companions. She was hardly conscious of it. Even her friends who knew she was seeing the Prince regularly said nothing to her but waited for her to tell them. And she didn't. She continued to see him—neither discreetly or indiscreetly. He would telephone. He would come to Edham House. She would go with him in his car, to a party at the home of some friend, to dinner, to the theater, to a club, occasionally to York House. At York House they would take dinner alone together, usually late, and then would ascend to his sitting room for coffee and brandy, sometimes for late champagne. It was there that she expected him to be bold—and he never was.

What passed between them she later dismissed in a sentence she spoke in confidence to Winston Churchill: "The trouble with David is that he is insufficiently endowed with character to carry a love affair to a conclusion, either to marriage or to a seduction."

She could have married him. The choice was hers: With him, the choice belonged to the woman. She did what he was neither clever enough to do nor clever enough to understand had been done *to* him—she terminated the affair and made him think *he* had terminated it.

He gave her a huge emerald set in white gold: a brooch he had inherited from his grandmother, Queen Alexandra. It was a gift to console her for the loss of the prospect of becoming his wife. Her father and mother, supposing she was devastated, gave her a tour of the Continent. It was on this tour, in the spring of 1931, that one of her German cousins introduced her to flying. A year later she returned to Germany to learn to fly.

Nancy tightened the belt across her lap and carefully buckled it. She leaned to each side and peered at the floor mounts, where the belt was fastened to the frame of the airplane. Yesterday Helmut had put the airplane through a string of rolls, and for a moment during each one she had hung there upside down, 2,000 meters above the earth, with nothing holding her against falling but this single heavy leather strap.

She glanced over her shoulder at Helmut in the rear cockpit. He grinned and said something the wind blew away.

Today she was to fly this airplane—the biggest, most advanced, highest-powered, fastest airplane she had ever been in. Yesterday and the day before, she had taken control, from the rear cockpit, to get a feel for the airplane. Today she was in front, sitting deep in the open cockpit, her forward vision entirely blocked by the huge round engine. She forgot how many horsepower Helmut said it was, but she knew it could pull the plane through the air at 150 miles an hour.

She began her cockpit check. The wing flaps were up, so she pulled the big wheel on the left cockpit wall through a few reverse revolutions to bring the flaps down a little. The plane would take off in a shorter distance with wing flaps extended a little. Other, smaller wheels set elevator and rudder trim for takeoff. She turned those wheels until the indicator needles showed takeoff position. She yanked the lever that opened the cowl flaps to give the engine more cooling air.

She glanced back at Helmut. He was leaning forward, trying to see what she was doing. He could not quite reach her, to tap her on the shoulder if he wanted her attention, so he carried a short baton with which he could poke her if he needed to. He could not see everything she was doing—or not doing—so if there was anything for which she needed poking, likely as not he didn't know it.

She returned his grin with a wan smile. She was ready to start the huge, threatening engine that loomed in front of her.

With her right hand, she began to work a small hand pump to raise enough fuel pressure for the start. When she judged she had enough pressure, she grabbed the primer handle and gave the engine two sharp shots. Now she put one hand on the mag switch, one on the starter switch. She pushed up the handle on the starter switch. The big engine groaned, and the propeller began slowly to turn. She shoved the throttle forward a little. She let the engine pull the propeller through one complete revolution before she flipped the mag switch. The engine fired. With booming, smoky explosions that shook the airplane, the big engine took hold and began to run.

As it warmed up, the engine ran more smoothly—although its overpowering roar ended any possibility of even shouted communication with Helmut. She leaned out to see that there was no one in front. The engine was spitting tiny droplets of oil, which the propellor kicked back into her face, so she lowered her goggles. She pulled the lever to release the brakes. The airplane bumped forward, and she planted her feet on the toe brakes to control it. She held down the right brake and released the left. The left wing swung around, and she let the plane taxi forward, out of the line. Then she pushed down on the left brake and let the right wing come around, so she could taxi toward the end of the airfield. The plane rolled along the front line of biplanes, toward the east end of the airfield.

It was a Henschel, this airplane: a high-wing monoplane. The single high wing, looming above her, obscured much of the sky. On each side the wing was braced to the fuselage with two fat struts that diminished vision to the sides. She leaned out and tried to see what was ahead of her as she taxied. Mostly, safety depended on people having the good sense not to walk in front of a taxiing airplane. A mechanic in coveralls waved at her as she taxied past the last biplane in the row. The Henschel was a new design, and Helmut was one of the designers. Pilots on the field would stop whatever they were doing and watch her take off. They would watch because she was a woman and because she was flying the most sophisticated airplane most of them had ever seen.   ·

At the end of the field, she stopped for a final check before takeoff. She pulled back the stick as far as it would go, then pushed it forward as far as it would go. In the mirror she saw the elevators rise and fall, full travel. She wobbled the stick from side to side, watching the ailerons move. She set the brakes tight again and pushed the throttle forward to run the engine speed up to 1,800 revolutions. It seemed to be running smoothly—as smoothly as it would; the airplane would still tremble under its normal vibration. She looked to the wind sock. The wind still quartered toward this end of the field.

She turned and looked one last time at Helmut. He grinned and pointed forward with his baton.

She released the brakes and turned the airplane into the wind. Tense, her mouth set grim, she shoved the throttle all the way forward. The engine roared, and the airplane began to bump over the rough field. She pressed the right rudder pedal and held it down to overcome the tendency of the airplane to turn left: the influence of the torque of the big engine. The airplane bumped faster. For a quarter of a minute it bounced insanely over the grass. Nancy could see nothing forward. Her eyes were on the airspeed indicator—like the altimeter, calibrated in metric units. When it reached 75 kilometers per hour, she eased the control stick forward. The tail of the airplane rose from the ground. The nose lowered slowly, and suddenly she could see ahead.

The open field lay ahead, with a grove of trees still five hundred yards distant. The airplane bounced wildly. She glanced again at the airspeed indicator. One hundred. The airplane was straining, almost ready to fly. One hundred twenty. She pulled back on the stick. The bouncing stopped. The airplane was flying, and in a moment it rose fifty feet. She pushed the stick forward and stopped its climb, to let it gain airspeed. One-forty. One-fifty. She pulled the stick back again, and the airplane climbed. They were above the buildings at the edge of the field. They passed over the trees at the end, well above them. The horizon receded all around. Nancy relaxed her tight, tense grip on the stick. She was flying.

Helmut Bittrich was a distant cousin of some sort; she was not entirely clear in her mind exactly what the relationship was. The Earl's family had German cousins, still calling themselves Bachfurt. The Bachfurts were related to the Bittrichs. The Bittrich family estate was a modest but very old house with lands, not far from Düsseldorf. When he was on the Continent for any extended visit, it was a point of family duty with the Earl to pay a call on Gerd Bittrich, Helmut's father. Nancy had been in the Bittrich home a dozen times over the years, but she had rarely seen Helmut. At first he had made his duty appearance and then retreated as quickly as possible, at no pains to conceal his boredom with the conversation between his father and his English cousin, the Earl of Edham. He was ten years older than Nancy and had had no patience, either, for the little girl his mother suggested he should entertain. Later he was at Heidelberg, at the university, and then in Berlin, pursuing his career; and she had not seen him.

When, however, she came to Germany in the spring of 1931, preceded by the rumor of her aborted romance with the Prince of Wales, Helmut had made a point of seeing her; he had come to Munich to find her, to entertain her and maybe to console her, and in any case to hear the story of what had passed between her and the Prince. He was a pilot and an airplane designer, and he introduced her to flying. He promised to teach her to fly if she would return to Germany and spend a month with him.

For a year, the prospect of coming back, of flying again with Helmut, of learning to fly herself, had intrigued her. It was a secret, carefully kept from her family, that she had ever been in an airplane, much less that she meant to learn to fly. Her parents were pleased she was in Germany with Helmut Bittrich. They had no idea she was flying with him—and certainly not the faintest suspicion that she and Helmut would become lovers.

The Bachfurts-Brookefords tended to be diminutive, and, no matter how distant the relationship, Helmut seemed to have inherited the family tendency to be small. Unlike the majority of the men in the family, however, who tried to compensate for shortness of stature by adopting a hailing, booming personality, Helmut was quiet, introspective, precise of movement and speech, quick to understand, slow to judge. His hair was yellow-blond, his complexion was smooth and pink, and his eyes were pale blue. His lips were full and sensuous. His lids often hung heavy over his eyes.

"I am not a romantic about it," he had said to her of flying. "It's exhilarating, of course; but more than that, it's important." (He spoke English, but not fluently or comfortably, and almost all their conversations were in German. *Wichtigkeit* was his word about aeronautics—it had weight, consequence.) He resented the suggestions he heard not infrequently: that flying was frivolous and he had chosen an inconsequential career. In spite of what he said, it was apparent to her when she flew with him that he *was* a romantic about flying. It was too obvious that he loved it. He was, also, a natural teacher. He had taught her a carefully measured mix of theory and practice, so she would know how her plane flew as well as how to fly it.

It was the spring of 1932. She had paid her mandatory call on Gerd Bittrich, and then Helmut had taken her away to begin her flying lessons. He had taken her to Berlin, where he worked and where he was supposed to be showing her the cultural attractions of the city and introducing her to people. She was scheduled to spend a month there, at the end of which time her mother would meet her in Berlin and take her to Vienna. Nancy was living in a small comfortable *Familienpension* not far from Helmut's flat. Almost every day when the weather was suitable for flying, he picked her up early in his car—she dressed in boots, jodhpurs, a shirt, and a heavy twill jacket, carrying her leather flying helmet with goggles—and they would drive to the flying field to the east of the city. On days when the weather would not allow flying, he worked at his office, and in the afternoon he would come to find her and take her to the museums and galleries she was supposed to be seeing. They spent every evening together, and some nights they slept together.

"I am not a fanatic about it," she had said playfully to him the evening he suggested they not return to their separate rooms but spend the night together. She watched his face to see if he would recognize his own words about flying; and when she saw in his smile that he did, she went on, paraphrasing the rest of what he had said: "It might be exhilarating, but I wonder if it will be important."

She had hoped it might be exhilarating. She had been taught a grim moral code, with which she had been at war for a long time. She was adventuresome, too much so to deny herself a taste of something she knew could be an essential element of a complete life. Anyway, she had long felt her carnal nature stirring within her. She had spat away a succession of groping, pawing boys, but she would have readily gone to bed with the Prince of Wales if he had asked her, and had been disappointed when he didn't. Helmut, she had guessed, was what David could never have been —whole: physical as much as contemplative, emotional as much as rational, intellectual as much as spiritual; he was not too timid to essay what he might not achieve; he was not afraid to fail. She had wanted what Helmut suggested, maybe more than he did, since he had experienced it before and she had not.

"We are cousins," she had said.

"Not within the biblical injunction."

"You checked."

"I read the Bible sometimes," he had said soberly, with a thin smile. In the bedroom, Helmut was a different man from what he was at the airfield or at the controls of a plane. His mouth-turned-down, cheeks-sucked-in, heavy-lidded self-confidence had not followed him through the door of his Spartan bedroom, where with hoarse, blushing diffidence he had apologized for his narrow bed and offered to wait outside the room until she was undressed and under the sheets. In bed he had insisted he did not want to take advantage of the difference in their ages and experience and begged her not to accept him unless she understood what they were doing and what might result. When she had yelped with surprise and pain as he penetrated her, he withdrew. When, later, he discovered his condom split and hanging in shreds around his diminishing penis, he soberly promised to marry her if need be and, in any event, to care for her and cherish her and her baby, if there were one, and in every way to conduct himself with honor.

He did not say he loved her. It was, she thought, a conscious omission. She did not say she loved him. She didn't. But she felt what must be very close to it and was not certain she wanted to feel anything more.

In time his self-confidence began to extend itself to his intimacy with her—and with it came a recovery of his sense of humor. In his car one morning, as they drove to the airfield, she heard him whistling an English tune—"I Danced with the Girl Who Danced with the Prince of Wales." "You cocksure bastard," she said to him. "You've done a hell of a lot more than dance."

A week ago—a week before the day she first flew the Henschel —she had landed a biwing on the field near the Landsberger Chaussee, and as she taxied back to the upwind end of the field, intending to take off again, she had scattered a group of men who had wandered near to her path. She couldn't see them over the nose of the plane, after all. Helmut had poked her on the shoulder with his baton and signaled that she should stop. She had pulled back on the throttle and cut the switch. With a couple of angry pops, the engine had stopped. She had looked around at Helmut. He was laughing.

The group of men on the field had stood glaring at the yellow biwing. Helmut stood in the rear cockpit and yelled: "Allo, Herr Abgeordneter!" He pulled off his helmet and goggles. "Allo!"

The three men in the group ceased to glare. One shrugged, and the others laughed and began to talk and gesture with animation.

Nancy unbuckled her safety strap and stood in the cockpit. She pushed up her goggles but left the leather helmet covering her hair. She was wearing khaki jodhpurs, tall leather boots, a tight, dark-brown jacket, a light blue silk scarf. "Who are they?" she asked Helmut. She was not pleased that he had ordered her to stop to talk with them. It was only at their own risk that they had ventured onto the edge of a flying field, where a pilot taxiing an airplane might not see them.

"They are important to my business," he said. The blending in his voice of awe and contempt was unnatural. "They are friends."

Swinging a leg over the wall of the cockpit, she stepped out on the lower wing, steadied herself with one hand on the upper wing and one on a wire strut, then jumped down to the grass. Helmut jumped after her and was beside her as the three men strode up.

"A student pilot, ha, Bittrich?" said one of them jovially. He was a heavy man, with a jowly smile. "Ha? Ha?"

"One of Helmut's test pilots, I am sure," said another of the men. This one was a solid Germanic type, with odd eyebrows that slanted down from the bridge of his nose toward his ears, a jutting chin, and thin lips.

The third man stood a little behind them and seemed to defer. Nancy only glanced at him.

"Gentlemen," said Helmut briskly, "allow me to present Lady Nancy Brookeford."

The two men stiffened, and the fat one's smile broadened into a comic grin.

Helmut spoke to her. "Herr Erhard Milch, a director of Lufthansa," he said, indicating with a nod the one with the slanting eyebrows and the pronounced squint. "Herr Hermann Göring, Deputy to the Reichstag."

Nancy pulled off her helmet and shook out her hair. It hadn't far to fall; she kept it short. "Gentlemen," she said. She spoke English. "You must never stroll about on an airfield."

Although both men laughed and seemed to understand what she had said, Helmut translated. To her he said: "They are not un-acquainted with airplanes. Herr Göring was the last commanding officer of Richthofen's Flying Circus."

The third man had not stood back deferentially, rather for lack of interest in a decrepit airplane and two pilots. He had not heard Helmut introduce Nancy. When he saw her pull off her helmet and shake out her hair, he stepped forward briskly and smiled broadly.

"I am sorry," said Helmut, "I don't believe I can introduce the third gentleman."

Göring spoke. "Lady Nancy Brookeford," he said courteously, "allow me to present Dr. Josef Goebbels. Dr. Goebbels is also a deputy."

"What party do you gentlemen represent?" Nancy asked. It was a conversational question only. She was shrugging, shaking her hair.

The three men laughed, and so did Helmut. "Herr Göring is Reichstag leader for the NSDAP," Helmut explained. "Dr. Goebbels is Berlin party leader."

She had heard of the NSDAP—Nationalsozialistische Deutsche Arbeiterpartei—called Nazis. It was a party of wild men, she had heard. She looked at the two standing before her.

Hermann Göring was a big, solid man, his body lately softened and fleshy. He was well dressed, in an expensive gray suit, but the cloth of his jacket tugged at the button. From the buttonhole in his lapel, a small gold chain ran to the breast pocket of his jacket, to his watch. He wore a gray felt hat with the brim turned up all around, and the wind just now flapped the front of the brim. He showed a fat man's jolly, smiling face, but in his eyes she could see a glint of hard, calculating sensual appraisal.

Dr. Josef Goebbels was not younger, as she had first supposed; he was just smaller—more than that, he was a pinched, weaselly little man with a look of weakness. He had, however, an engaging toothy smile and big brown eyes, which had settled on her face and seemed calmly to be begging her to like him. "*Lady* Nancy Brookeford," he said. "You are English?"

"Lady Nancy is the daughter of Major General Sir Henry Brookeford, Earl of Edham," said Helmut.

Goebbels's toothy smile widened and his eyes sparkled— literally, somehow they sparkled; she had not confronted the phenomenon before. He bowed. "I know the name," he said. "He led English forces in battle on the Western Front, if I recall correctly."

Nancy nodded. She was well aware of the controversy surrounding her father's military leadership during the world war; and she had to suppose, if Goebbels knew anything of it at all, he knew of this, too. Still, she could think of no reason why he should be sarcastic, and she accepted his comment. She returned his smile.

"Might I, Lady Nancy," interjected Göring, "enjoy your company at dinner tomorrow evening? I am entertaining a few friends." He nodded at Helmut. "Helmut, too, of course."

"Tomorrow," said Helmut quickly. "With pleasure, sir."

He accepted the invitation so quickly that Nancy had no opportunity to express any reservation. He explained to her later that Göring was an important supporter of civil aviation in the Reichstag and that it was important to his, Helmut's, career to be civil to him. "They are hooligans, his Nazis," he said to her over an aperitif later, "but Göring himself is an aristocrat."

An engraved invitation was delivered to her *pension* the next morning, and Nancy was surprised to learn that Göring's dinner party was white-tie and was being held at the Adlon Hotel. She telephoned Helmut, whose invitation had just been delivered at his office. " 'Entertaining a few friends,' " Helmut laughed nervously. "We have been honored more than I supposed."

His face was shiny pink when he escorted her into the Göring suite at the Adlon. The hotel was one of the finest in Europe, and this must have been its most luxurious suite. Furnished in Louis XV antiques accented with gold and porcelain clocks, china bowls filled with fresh-cut flowers, and gold candelabra, the rooms of the suite were redolent with the smoke of fine Havana cigars. She found herself one of only half a dozen women present, in a company of two dozen men. The party was, indeed, small, as Göring had suggested, and perhaps he *had* honored her by including her and Helmut.

Göring saw them enter. He was the gracious and ebullient host, insisting he himself would fetch their first glasses of champagne. He bustled off, leaving them with the man they had met on the airfield the day before: Erhard Milch, the director of Lufthansa.

"We are honored," Helmut murmured to Milch. "I don't believe I know many of these people."

"Money," said Milch, glancing around from under his peculiarly slanted brows. "Contributors to the NSDAP." He nodded toward a man across the room, whom Nancy did not identify. "Thyssen," said Milch. She knew the name. "The French put him in jail once," said Milch. He glanced around the room. "Grelowitz," he said, nodding once again toward a man she did not recognize. "The banker." He nodded, as if she should understand the significance of the banker's presence at this dinner party.

Helmut's heavy-lidded eyes opened wide. "That man there," he whispered to Milch, indicating only with his eyes the man he meant. "General von Schleicher?"

Milch nodded. "Not a supporter of the NSDAP," he said.

Nancy recognized the bald general. He was the *éminence grise* behind the von Papen government. (It was Schleicher who was supposed to have said of von Papen that if he was not a head, at least he was a hat.) His presence at this dinner party could have deep political significance.

Göring returned, bearing two glasses of champagne. He bowed deeply to Nancy as he handed her a glass. "Lady Nancy, it is a great honor to have you here," he said. "I want you to meet all my guests."

She noticed with some surprise that Göring wore at his throat the distinctive blue enamel cross, Pour le Mérite, the fabled Blue Max. It was Imperial Germany's highest military decoration, and even in a country fond of displaying its every decoration, the Blue Max was rare. He offered her his hand, and, with her eye frankly fixed on the medal she accepted his lead and accompanied him on a circuit of his guests. He introduced her to Fritz Thyssen, to Konstantin Grelowitz, and to Kurt von Schleicher. He introduced her to others whose names she could not remember.

He introduced her with emphasis that she was *Lady* Nancy Brookeford, daughter of Major General Sir Henry Brookeford, Earl of Edham; and he introduced her as if she were a longtime friend, not simply a young woman he had met by chance yesterday on an airfield east of the city. For all his Blue Max and his leadership of the party in the Reichstag, this Hermann Göring was a clever opportunist, using her to impress his oddly mixed group of dinner guests. She was not dismayed. He was not the first opportunist who had invited her to a dinner party to show her off to guests. At least he knew nothing of her late affair with the Prince of Wales, and that was refreshing; he meant to impress his guests only with her family name. His guests *were* impressed—some of them, at least—and she went along with his game.

"Our family name was Bachfurt until 1914," she told him. "We have German cousins. In fact, Helmut is a distant cousin."

"Ahh," said Göring, conceding a glance toward the abandoned Helmut, who stood alone looking disconsolately into his glass of champagne. "A cousin . . ."

She smiled enigmatically. "A *distant* cousin," she laughed.

Göring laughed. He was not a stupid man, she saw, and he had understood the undertone of the exchange perfectly. "I am very happy you came," he said. "You grace my dinner party."

She accepted the compliment easily. The other women at the party were wives, none of them there on their own account, as she was. She wore a pale green silk dress that hung over her slender, boyish figure, concealing and yet revealing every line and turn. Looped around her neck she wore a single long strand of pearls, matched by a three-strand bracelet on her left wrist. Helmut had offered to provide flowers, but she had gently suggested she did not need flowers. In her evening bag she carried a gold case filled with cigarettes, but she would light only one or two in the course of the evening. She did not care to smoke much. When she did light a cigarette, she noticed the lofty frowns of disapproval from the heavy German wives.

"I had hoped the Führer would be here this evening," said Göring. "Unhappily, I received word only an hour ago that he could not be with us."

"Führer?" she asked. She knew the meaning of the German word Führer but was not sure how it might apply to someone who might have come to the party.

"The leader of the NSDAP," said Göring. "Adolf Hitler."

She nodded. "I've heard and read a great deal about your Herr Hitler," she said. "I'm sorry I will not meet him."

"He would enjoy meeting you," said Göring. "The Führer is something of an Anglophile."

"I had not heard that."

"It is true," said Göring. "Would you like more champagne?" He led her toward the table where a servant in fawn satin livery was pouring champagne. "He is a great man, Adolf Hitler," Göring said, nodding. "You really should meet him."

"I would like to meet him."

"He is the victim of the most vicious slanders in the Jew-controlled press. He—"

"I understand," she interrupted, "he is no friend of the Jews."

Göring laughed. "A majority of the people of Europe are anti-Semitic," he said. "Including a majority of the English. We National Socialists are heirs to a long and honorable tradition."

"Long, I suppose," she said. "Honorable, I'm not sure."

"Our anti-Semitism might be described as reactive," Göring argued. "It is only our response to what the Jews have done to our people."

She responded with a skeptical, half-mocking smile. It was in her mind to tell him he was transparent, that obviously he did not believe what he was saying; but it was apparent to her that he would never concede a point in this argument; he was reciting his political catechism, which did not admit of any concession.

"The Führer told me he may be able to join us later, at a smaller party I am having for a few of these people," said Göring. "May I beg you to join us? You will be the only lady present, but . . ."

"Helmut?" she asked.

Göring nodded. "Of course."

She was seated at Göring's right at dinner, between him and von Schleicher. Von Schleicher worked at being gracious and at saying nothing. She recalled now that he was called "the office general." It was apparent that was what he was: a political general. She remembered, too, that he was a boyhood friend of Oskar Hindenburg, the son of the old President. He was a shallow man, she thought. He seemed relieved that she did not require much conversation of him. She was herself relieved when he turned to the man beside him and engaged him in close conversation. Over most of the dinner, she conversed with Göring.

He told her his wife had died two years ago. He was, he said, a lonely man. He said he was committed to the NSDAP, both intellectually and emotionally, and he told her she would never understand why so many men like him were committed until she met and heard Adolf Hitler. Hitler was, said Göring, "the outstanding man of our time." "You will be amazed by him," he promised.

Helmut promised her she would not be amazed. He was beside her at last, as they rode down on the elevator toward the floor where, in a smaller suite, Göring was holding his later party. "Hitler is a guttersnipe," he said—or so in her mind she translated the German word *Strassenkind*. "He is a demagogue. He appeals to the great unwashed. These men here tonight—they own him."

She discounted what Helmut said. He was understandably annoyed to have been seated below the salt at the dinner table, while she had been seated to the right of the host. Göring, he warned her, would propose an intimate, early-morning tryst. She told Helmut she anticipated that and was ready for it.

She was not ready for the midnight party in Göring's second hotel suite. In two cozy, dimly lighted rooms where incense burned and weighted the air with cloying perfume, naked girls served champagne and brandy to no more than eight or nine guests: von Schleicher and Thyssen, and six or seven others who had not been guests at the dinner party. Helmut was quick to suggest they leave, but Nancy was already laughing at Göring, who was laughing as he hurried toward the door to welcome her. "I've never seen anything like this," she said to Helmut, "and I'm not going to miss the opportunity."

Göring beamed as he bustled up and took her arm. His face was now flushed, and alcohol seemed to have loosened his broad smile,

which was by now comic and lopsided. "I do hope the—uh—
nature of the party will not offend you, Lady Nancy," he said.
"These are all distinguished men." He glanced at Helmut and
curtly dismissed him with the suggestion he get himself a brandy.
"I will introduce you to my guests, Lady Nancy."

Except for von Schleicher and Thyssen, who had met her at
the dinner party, the men Göring introduced her to now were all
surprised, and one or two of them apparently a little troubled, to
meet an Englishwoman at this party. Göring offered quiet comments about them as he led her to each conversational knot.
("They feel conspiratorial about being here. I know you are
discreet.")

He introduced her to Oskar Hindenburg, who was talking with
General von Schleicher ("The son of the Reichspräsident. Influ-
ences him greatly"). An NSDAP functionary named Frick ("A
leader of our party, one of the most prominent") was talking to
Thyssen and to a banker named Schacht. The most handsome,
most distinguished-looking man present was introduced as General
Werner von Blomberg ("A friend in the army"). He was talking
to an undistinguished-looking man Göring introduced as Joachim
von Ribbentrop ("An importer of champagne, responsible for the
good quality of what we are drinking this evening. He's a luke-
warm Nazi, but he is a friend of von Papen").

It was apparent that some of these men were uncomfortable in
the company of the others. Hindenburg, especially, stood uneasy,
glancing around, frowning nervously. The banker Schacht looked
as if he were up too late. General von Blomberg was as uncomfortable as Hindenburg, but the two naked serving girls had much
of his attention and eased him somewhat.

One of the girls handed Nancy champagne. She was small and
apparently very young. She did not seem embarrassed, but she did
look apprehensive, even frightened.

Hitler did not appear. Nancy had not expected him. She had
understood that Göring had promised him only as an incentive to
her to come to the later, more intimate party.

She talked with General von Blomberg and was able to encourage him to engage Helmut in conversation. The General
was interested in the design of future military airplanes. He asked
Helmut if the new Henschel would have a military application,
and she was surprised to hear Helmut say the Henschel was

capable of being armed with bombs or machine guns and that its high speed would make it a valuable military plane.

Von Ribbentrop was a shallow, ill-educated man, not worth a moment's conversation. Hindenburg was a sly, distant character; he reminded her of a butcher who would put his thumb on the scale.

The hour came, as she had expected, when Göring stood close beside her, put the palm of his hand gently on her backside, and suggested there was still another, still smaller party at which they might have even more fun. Fortunately he did not take her excuse with ill grace. She said she had an important flying lesson early in the morning and had already stayed out longer than she should. Göring smiled and nodded and said he understood. He hoped, he said, he would see her again soon, and he added that he hoped she would soon meet the Führer.

Berlin was a beautiful city, and to her it was even more beautiful from the air, spread out below, its lines softened by the remnants of the morning mist that lay like grounded clouds in the green parks. She flew the Henschel 500 meters above the ground. That was the altitude Helmut had told her to fly, but she wondered if the roar of the huge engine did not disturb the neighborhoods below.

Approaching the Brandenburg Gate, the wooded Tiergarten—Berlin's great central park—lay ahead. To her left—she looked for it and found it—was the Adlon Hotel at the corner of Unter den Linden and Wilhemstrasse. The domed Reichstag Building was to her right. Swinging the nose of the airplane a little to the left, she set it on the Charlottenburger Chaussé and crossed the Tiergarten east to west.

She had received a note from Hermann Göring, thanking her for coming to his dinner party. Adolf Hitler, the note said, had expressed his regret that he could not be there to meet her. The little man, Dr. Goebbels, had sent flowers to her *Familienpension*. His note was empty but gracious.

Helmut scoffed. The Nazis, he said, were in perpetual pursuit of respectability, and the appearance at one of their parties by an Englishwoman with a noble title lent them momentarily a respectability they would spend much to attain. They represented, he went on to say excitedly, the rise of the rabble in postwar Europe. There was little to choose between them and the Communists. He suggested she read a book called *The Revolt of the Masses*, by a Spanish political writer called José Ortega y Gasset. Then she would understand the significance of Göring and Goebbels—and Adolf Hitler.

She was not, she told him airily, particularly interested in understanding the political philosophy of an odd German political party.

Over Charlottenburg, Helmut touched her shoulder with his baton. She looked around, and he pointed to the east: Return to the airfield and land.

Helmut had drilled into her endlessly over the past few weeks that landing an airplane was a difficult exercise in coordination, and the most dangerous of all flying maneuvers. At or above a given speed, the airplane was a flying machine, held in suspension in the air by the pressures generated on its wings by its speed. Below that speed, it was a dead weight of steel and wood and fabric—plus human flesh seated in its cockpits—and it would surrender to gravity and fall. If she allowed the airspeed to drop below what was called the "stall speed," the plane would nose over, pulled down by the weight of its big engine, and plunge toward the earth. If, on the other hand, when the wheels touched the ground the plane were still moving at flying speed, it would not stay on the ground but would bounce off into the air again. Bouncing off, it would probably go nose-high, lose airspeed instantly, and nose over into a crash. The problem was to reduce airspeed at a controlled rate, coordinated with the approach to the field, so that the airplane ran out of flying speed just as the wheels touched. Any major deviation from that objective could be disastrous.

Complicating the problem was the fact that if the airplane lost flying speed too soon, it would probably not nose over head-on but at an angle, with one wing going down much more sharply than the other. That was called a spin.

She flew past the field to the south, turned left, then left again. She pointed the nose of the airplane at the long grassy field. She glanced at her altimeter, but the altimeter meant little on approach to landing; she would have to judge her altitude and angle of glide visually. The important instrument was the airspeed indicator.

She had learned to glance back and forth between the airspeed indicator and the landing point on the field ahead and below. Tense, sitting high in her seat, she stared over the looming nose at the field and began to ease back the throttle to increase the rate of descent.

It was little comfort to know that Helmut could take the airplane away from her and land from the rear cockpit if he had to. She would have failed if he had to do that. He had told her—as had several old hands on the field—that she had a natural aptitude for flying. She felt she did, too. She had felt confident from her first flight.

Helmut tapped her shoulder. He gestured downward. He judged her approach was too high. She peered over the nose. She did not agree. She eased the throttle back slightly, to reduce power and increase the rate of descent; but she did not ease it back as much as Helmut would have liked. Already she had developed her own landing technique: to hold the plane high until it cleared the last obstacle short of the field, then to drop quickly toward the ground. She followed that technique now. She kept the engine revolutions high and the airplane high above the ground, descending only slowly. At the proper moment she would slow down the engine and drop the airplane toward the field.

The Henschel came over a grove of trees to the east of the airfield. She held the speed constant at 150. The airplane passed through 100 meters' altitude. Now she pulled back the throttle. The rate of descent instantly increased. The airplane sank toward the ground. Fifty meters altitude. She was over the rough ground at the edge of the field. The plane sank rapidly. Twenty meters. She was over the grassy field. Ten meters. Five. She pulled back the stick. The rate of descent continued fast, but the plane slowed. She glanced at the airspeed indicator: 125. Good. She pulled the stick back more. She raised the nose and held the airplane off the ground, as if she meant not to let it land. The rate of descent diminished. The wheels were almost to the ground. She pulled the stick all the way back, as if in a futile effort to force the airplane to keep flying. It ran out of airspeed and sank gently to the ground, tail-first. The main wheels hit hard, but the Henschel did not bounce. She had landed.

❧ III ❧

She had not seen Helmut since July. They had exchanged weekly letters for five months, but she had not seen him again in Germany when she and her mother returned from southern Europe, and neither of them had had any occasion to cross the Channel since summer. This was December. The Earl and the Countess had gone up to Wickstone, where the family would gather for Christmas, and Nancy had insisted she could not leave London so soon but would join them in a week. They left reluctantly without her, but—as she assured Helmut—not suspecting he would arrive in London the day after they left.

"Hatten sie keinen Verdacht?"—"Don't they suspect anything?"—Helmut asked as he tugged the collar of his overcoat tighter around his throat and squinted into the light drizzle that had begun to fall in the gloom.

Nancy shook her head and grinned. "Nein, Nichts," she said. She, too, pulled up her collar. The Bentley four-seater was open. She had not expected rain when she chose it for the drive to the railroad station. Even the windscreen was folded down, and the fine drops swept into her face as she turned onto Westminster Bridge.

Helmut was in the bad graces of the Earl and Countess. They knew he had taught her to fly. The Earl had written his cousin Gerd Bittrich a letter, complaining of what he described as Helmut's *jugendliche Unverantwortlichkeit*—juvenile irresponsibility—in so much as taking his daughter up in an airplane, much less *sending* her up in one. He had forbidden her ever to set foot in an airplane again.

"Fine car," Helmut commented. The dark green Bentley sporting tourer slipped smartly through the traffic on the bridge and on Parliament Square.

"It's mine," Nancy said simply.

"Your father . . . ? If he finds out I am with you . . . ?" ˙

"I'll tell him you're here—after a day or so," she laughed.

"He'll return from the country with a bird gun," said Helmut.

"No. He is angry and stubborn about my flying, and he blames you for having taught me; but he suspects nothing else, and you *are*, after all, a Bittrich. He'd condemn my want of hospitality if I let you stay in a hotel."

Helmut grunted skeptically and settled more deeply into the leather seat. "I met Mitchell," he said.

"I'm glad," she said. "I'm glad your trip wasn't for nothing." She glanced at him and smiled wickedly. "Did you ask him if I could fly one of his airplanes?"

"One of the Supermarine racers?" Helmut laughed. "I wouldn't dare one of them myself."

Nancy switched on the headlamps as she drove into Birdcage Walk. It was dark except for the dim green glow of the gas lamps along the park. It was six o'clock and cold as well as drizzly. Traffic was light. London had settled down for a long, damp night.

"His airplanes are fast," Helmut said. His thoughts were still of R. J. Mitchell, the chief designer at Supermarine's. "But they are not maneuverable."

"So?"

He glanced at her as if surprised by the question. He raised his arm to wipe droplets of water from his forehead with the sleeve of his coat. "It is believed," he said pontifically, "that in combat, maneuverability is more important than speed."

"What combat?" she asked disingenuously. "I was not aware that anyone had combat in mind."

Helmut shook his head. "No. The Supermarine racers are built for speed alone and are the fastest airplanes in the world. Can you doubt, however, that your Air Ministry is thinking about a fast warplane, designed on the basis of what Supermarine's and Mitchell have learned? Imagine a warplane flying three hundred miles an hour. What could pursue it? What could interfere with its mission?"

"What mission?"

He shrugged. "To carry a bomb, perhaps. It could fly to a target, drop its bomb, and fly back to its base, and no one could intercept or pursue it. If it encountered defenders in the air, it would simply fly around them."

"Then maneuverability is not more important than speed," she said.

He looked at her. His face was grim in the faint green light of the streetlamps. "The authorities still think it is. Pursuit planes are built to twist and turn, like the ones that fought over the Western Front. I wonder, just the same, if your Air Ministry isn't thinking differently."

"Are you working on warplane designs, Helmut?" she asked, keeping her eyes on the road ahead.

"I am *thinking* about them," he said. "Germany will have warplanes again someday. The *Diktat* of Versailles is not forever."

She said nothing as she slipped the car into the traffic circling Victoria's statue in front of Buckingham Palace, circled, and turned into Constitution Hill. He had talked in Berlin about the Treaty of Versailles—always calling it the *Diktat* as he did now—and he had sometimes embarrassed her with his vehemence. There was about him a disconcerting Teutonic intensity. She remembered it too much. She had wondered for five months if she loved him. It was a negative sign that her most vivid memories were of his grim intensity.

"Are you a spy, Helmut?" she asked playfully.

"Yes," he said. "In a sense."

"Anyway, it's no secret," she said.

He nodded. The exchange had not seemed playful to him. He wiped his face with his hand and wiped his hand on his coat. As she rounded Hyde Park corner and drove into Piccadilly, then into Park Lane, he cocked his head and stared at her. The rainwater glistened on her face, and the big drops forming on her black leather coat filled with reflections. Her cheeks were high pink from the rush of cold air, and her hair was blown back. She was an exceptionally beautiful young woman. The Prince of Wales had been indeed a fool.

Edham House was just west of Berkeley Square. It was a square, stone Regency house, smaller but far more comfortable than Wickstone. Mr. Dunn and his principal staff had gone with the Earl and the Countess to Wickstone, but the underbutler and a staff of four had remained at Edham House to attend to the needs of Lady Nancy and care for the house. A footman drove the car to the garage, and the underbutler carried up Helmut's two bags. The senior kitchen maid was almost as good a cook as the cook who had gone to Wickstone, and she prepared a dinner to be served to Lady Nancy and her German cousin.

" '*Unverantwortlichkeit*,' " Helmut mused over their veal.

Nancy smiled and shook her head. "I'd fly whether he found it *unverantwortlich* or not," she said. "The trouble is, I can't find an airplane anyone will let me fly. Aside from my father's vocal opposition, which frightens companies who would like to let me fly their airplanes, there is the notion that a woman can't fly."

"I should have thought the achievements of Mrs. Putnam had settled that," said Helmut.

"Amelia Earhart . . ." said Nancy, nodding. "The first solo crossing since Lindbergh. Amy Johnson—"

"Of course," said Helmut.

"But my father talks about Frances Grayson and Beryl Hart."

"And I suppose Elsie MacKay," said Helmut.

Nancy nodded. "Yes." She shrugged. "They're all dead, I have to admit."

"I had not supposed you planned to fly the Atlantic," said Helmut dryly.

"I can't fly the Channel, Helmut," she complained sadly.

"East to west you can," he said.

"From Germany . . ."

He nodded emphatically. "You met Herr Milch, the director of Lufthansa. We will train you to fly multiengine airplanes, his Fokkers and Junkers, and we will get you a commercial license—"

"But why?" she interrupted. "Why would Milch let me fly his big planes?"

Among the facial expressions peculiarly characteristic of Helmut was a special smile: inward, ironic, humorless. He smiled that way now as he reached for his wineglass. "An English lady," he said quietly. "Of the English aristocracy. A lady of taste and refinement. Not just flying as a Lufthansa passenger—which too many people still regard as a brave adventure—but actually at the controls of a big trimotor. Everywhere you might fly, crowds would gather to see."

Nancy smiled. The thought was warming. "My father has threatened to cut off my allowance if ever I fly again."

Helmut shrugged. "You could be paid."

She grinned. "Am I strong enough? Big enough?"

"We'd have to move the seat forward, maybe put extensions on the rudder pedals. No problem."

"My father is an influential man," she said.

Helmut shook his head. "Not in Germany," he said.

She dismissed the staff. She told Helmut to go to his room for half an hour, then come to hers; the door would not be latched. She carried iced champagne and glasses to her room and waited for him.

A footman had laid a fire of coals in the fireplace in her bedroom, to warm it before she went to bed. The coals glowed, and the room had the sharp warm smell of a coal fire. She put the ice bucket on the floor between the fireplace and the sofa. She pushed aside a book she had been reading—*The Bridge at San Luis Rey*—and sat down on the dark red plush of the little sofa.

This room had been her brother's before he married and no longer kept a room at Edham House. She was not entirely glad she had taken it; it was too grand, and the dark oak and the blood-red and maroon of the drapes and wallpaper and furniture could depress her mood on nights when she was susceptible. For most of a century the room had been lighted by yellow gas flames inside frosted glass globes, and now the small electric bulbs glowing in those globes cast the same weak yellowish light. Only the white pillows on her tall bed, catching a beam of the glaring white light from her bathroom, were harshly lighted. She crossed the room and kicked the bathroom door shut. Then she parted the heavy drapes at a tall window and looked down on the street. It was filling with fog.

Inviting Helmut to come to her room, to sleep with her, was nothing final. Not inviting him might have been. In Berlin they had not used the word "love" to each other. In letters since, they had. After she received a letter from him referring to *"unser Liebschaft"*—"our love affair"—she had written him to address his letters to a friend of hers, who would receive them and hold them for her, to insure their privacy. Although neither of them ever wrote the actual words "I love you," he addressed his letters to *"Meine geliebte* Nancy," and, more than that, he referred to her often as *Liebchen.* She wrote to him the same way. He had not come to England, she suspected, to see Mitchell and his high-speed airplanes so much as to see her. To deny him tonight would have been a hard, abrupt signal. Whatever her doubts, she was not ready to give that signal.

He was no longer the diffident lover he had been at first in Berlin. Entering the room, he seized her immediately and kissed her, on the mouth, on her cheeks and eyes, on her ears and throat; and while he was kissing her, he—rather deftly, she thought—unhooked her dress in back, so that it fell around her waist as soon as he loosened his arms around her. As he led her to the sofa, he—deftly again—gave her dress a downward flip. It slid down over her hips and fell to the floor.

"Ich liebe dich," he whispered.

She sat on the sofa, dressed now in her peach-colored teddy trimmed with white lace. Her stockings were rolled just above her knees. She crossed her arms over her breasts and pulled up on the two bows on the shoulder straps of the teddy, to prevent its falling down. His hard kisses and rough beard had reddened her cheeks. "Ich liebe dich auch," she said softly, staring downward and drawing a deep breath.

"I'm glad. I—I needed your assurance," he said.

She raised her chin and exhaled the deep breath she had drawn. "Really? Why?"

"What about this Lord Euston?" he asked.

Nancy sighed. She reached for the champagne bottle, took it from the bucket and wrapped the white cloth around it, and handed it to him. She held two glasses toward him then. "My parents' heads were permanently turned by the prospect of my marrying David," she said. "Now they've set their sights a notch lower. If I can't be a princess, at least I will be a duchess. Willy's father is old, and he's rich—"

"Willy?"

"William—Lord Euston. He will be at Wickstone for Christmas."

Helmut looked up from pouring the champagne. "Is he a nice fellow?"

"He's David's age. A guardsman. He was wounded in France in 1917. Yes, he is a very nice fellow. He's unobjectionable, actually. That's what makes it so hard for me to put my foot down."

"You have not refused to marry him?"

"The occasion for refusing hasn't come. He has not asked me to marry him."

"Then what," Helmut asked crisply, "will you do when he does ask you?"

She lifted her glass in a toast and smiled at Helmut over the champagne. "I will not marry Willy, Helmut. I promise you."

"Will you come to Germany with me?"

She frowned. "I don't know. You talk about what Herr Milch will do. How can we be sure anyone will be able to do anything he promises, in Germany the way it is today?"

"You know the Chancellor," said Helmut. "You met General Schleicher at the Göring dinner and party."

"Yes," she said. "But what difference does he make? Is he strong enough to bring order? Can you promise me the Communists won't come to power in Germany in 1933?"

"I promise you that without qualification," he said. He, too, lifted his glass—but not in a toast, only to stare grimly across it, emphasizing his flat statement. "I promise you. The Communists will never rule Germany."

She shrugged, dismissing his sober certainty. "How can you be sure?"

"I have joined the NSDAP," he said. "And we will fight."

"You're a Nazi?" she asked incredulously.

He smiled. "Yes. I am. I don't suppose I am what the English think a Nazi should be: I am no ogre. I don't look like a Nazi, do I?"

"Do you have a brown uniform?"

"No. I didn't join the SA, just the Party."

Nancy shook her head. "Why, Helmut?"

"Our choice in Germany today is between communism and national socialism," he said in a quiet, pedagogical tone that suggested he had recited this explanation to a hundred others. "The other parties are too weak to cope with our economic situation. I could not, of course, tolerate communism. A man like me would be compelled to emigrate. Hitler is not right about everything, of course; but he is now our chief defense against the Communists, and his party is the only one capable of fighting them off. We have to take our stand."

"Your party lost the election in November. The talk is that Hitler is finished."

"We lost one election, but there will be another. I tell you, Adolf Hitler will be Chancellor within six months."

She chuckled. "You've become a zealot!"

He returned her smile. "Not a zealot," he said lightly. "A realist, a practical realist. Hitler and Göring are committed to a major program for German aviation. I expect to do well in an expanding industry."

She laughed. "Not a zealot, then. A cynic."

Though his smile remained, Helmut shook his head and sighed. "Who has a real choice in politics?" he asked. "Who can tailor a political movement to suit his own ideas? Only Hitler has done that, and you have to admire him for it."

"I don't have to admire him at all," she said.

Helmut refilled their champagne glasses. "Maybe you will change your mind if you come to Germany," he said. "You will see it all differently. Anyway, you can fly there: big planes, fast planes, all you want, the very newest; and you will be admired for it, respected, not scorned as you are in England. What's more, you won't have to marry Lord Euston. You and I can be together. We love each other, and we can be together. We can marry, in fact. You and I can marry, Nancy."

"Is this a proposal?" she asked.

He put aside his champagne glass and reached for her, to take her in his arms. He held her and kissed her, and he pulled the bows on the little straps of her teddy.

They did not marry. She spent that Christmas of 1932 at Wickstone with her family, and William, Lord Euston, was a guest. She said nothing to her family about Helmut, except that he had been in London, that she had invited him to be her guest at Edham House during his stay, and that he had declined to come with her to Wickstone to spend the holiday in the cousinly crowd that had gathered there. She drove her car back to London on December 28, and on the 29th she left England for Germany—leaving at Edham House a letter to her parents, telling them she was returning to Germany to resume her flying lessons, with a view toward making herself a career in the field of aviation, and saying she would send them her address in Berlin as soon as she had one.

She met Helmut at his father's house, where she spent one day, and then she and Helmut left by train for Berlin. He had already arranged for her to have a room in the *pension* where he lived. The landlady rented her a big, sunlit room facing the street, cheerfully accepting the idea that Helmut would slip down the hall at night, from his own Spartan room toward the rear of the house, and would sleep with the young woman she called *meine gnädiges Fräulein*. They lived as a couple about to marry, although *when* they would marry remained unspoken. He did not press that subject. She was grateful that he didn't. She loved him and was confident that he loved her; but if he had proposed they marry immediately, she would have said no. She was not ready to commit herself to him that fully or that finally.

She had already begun to fly again, in the big, fast Henschel, when word from her father arrived—first a telephone call from Helmut's father, Gerd Bittrich, relaying an angry call from the Earl, then a letter to Helmut. He did not write to Nancy. In his letter to Helmut he referred to her *verabscheuungswürdigem Verrat*—despicable betrayal—of her family; and he said, of course, he had stopped her allowance of two hundred pounds a month. She had emptied her London bank account before she left—which had further infuriated the Earl—and had more than a thousand pounds with which to establish herself in Germany. It was enough to live a year. She had brought, also, some of her jewelry, items she did not regard as family heirlooms and could sell if she wished for at least another thousand pounds.

Helmut was surprised at how much she had. Even so, he began immediately to talk with Erhard Milch about her flying as good publicity for Lufthansa. Milch was interested. He told Helmut to continue the flight training of the English lady; he would make a three-engine Junkers available for her to fly as soon as Helmut thought she was ready.

Happy though he was to have her with him and to be again teaching her to fly, January was a depressing month for Helmut. Chancellor von Schleicher clung firmly to his office; and, as Helmut told Nancy glumly over many dinners taken around the quiet table at the *pension*, a tight conspiracy had been contrived to keep Adolf Hitler out of the Chancellery.

She could believe it. On the streets of Berlin, the men of the SA begged on street corners, trying to rebuild the exhausted treasury of the NSDAP. "Hitler *geht es an den Kragen*, / *Dieses 'Führer's' Zeit ist um*"—Hitler gets it in the puss, / This 'Führer's' time is up"—were the last two lines of a political verse gleefully repeated in Berlin that month: repeated at the table where Helmut and Nancy took many of their meals with their fellow boarders. Responsible reporters wrote that the business community had withdrawn its support from the Nazis, that the party had peaked in 1932, that Hitler was no longer to be seriously considered as a candidate for president or chancellor. "A few marks, fräulein? Winter help for the nasty Nazis?" a sly SA man wearing a shabby overcoat over his brown uniform said to her on a frozen street one day.

Göring knew she was in Berlin, Helmut said; but he did not contact her. The little doctor, Goebbels, sent her a short note, saying he was pleased to hear she was again in Germany. Helmut promised a meeting with Hitler, but was unable to arrange it. The Nazi leaders either were busy scheming or had retreated out of sight.

Helmut's office was in a building on Potsdammerstrasse: a dusty, littered group of rooms where men in shirt sleeves kept grimly at work all day—doing what, she could not tell. Helmut was working on the design for a new airplane, but it was in such a nebulous stage that his fact sheets and drawings meant little to her. Each day when they did not fly, she came to his office sometime after noon. Usually a small office was available to her, where, at Helmut's insistence, she spent dull hours studying a succession of books he put there for her: books on aviation, airplane design, engine design, navigation, air battle tactics. When the sun set, as it did early at that time of year, the room was lighted flat yellow by the single bulb in a flyspecked globe overhead, and through the streaked window she could see nothing but a cold and sullen city street. It was on these afternoons that she had to fight back an impulse to flee to the station, catch a train, and go home, to apologize to her family, surrender to Lord Euston, and settle into the elegant, candlelit life he would provide. It was there, when she arrived a little after noon on January 30, that she was astounded to be handed a note from the sour-faced clerk who answered the office telephone—a note saying William, Lord Euston, was at the Adlon Hotel and would like for her to call him as soon as possible.

Willy begged her to come to the Adlon for lunch—bringing Helmut with her, of course. He could spend only a day or two in Berlin and wanted to spend as much of his time with them as possible. Helmut was reluctant to meet Lord Euston. He was more reluctant to have Nancy see him. He was not entirely confident, he admitted to her, that she could not be persuaded to return to England. They had better find out, she said. She told Willy they would be with him in half an hour.

"I seem to have arrived at an interesting time," Lord Euston said when they sat down with him at a lunch table at the Adlon. "The rumor is that von Schleicher may attempt a military coup before the day is over. There are crowds in the streets."

"There are always crowds in the streets," said Helmut.

"Will he attempt it?" Lord Euston asked. "I suppose you know something of these things."

"I expect he will," said Helmut. "It is another element of the conspiracy to deny the chancellorship to Adolf Hitler."

"Hitler met with the President this morning, they say."

Helmut shrugged. "Hitler meets with Hindenburg often. I wonder what they find to talk about."

"There could hardly be two different characters, could there?" remarked Lord Euston.

William, Lord Euston, was a handsome man. His hair was iron-gray. He had a square jaw and a hard-lined face. He used a monocle, which hung on a thin black ribbon around his neck and was tucked out of sight in his breast pocket when he did not insert it to scan a menu or check the time on his watch. His talk was straightforward and crisp, and he stared directly into the eyes of anyone with whom he was speaking. Unhappily, his conversation was often lifted to a level of overstated heartiness, after the caricature of an archaic English country squire.

"Well," he said with exactly that unfortunate hearty boom when their lunch was before them, "let me tell you why I have come here."

Helmut straightened his back and eyed Lord Euston with unconcealed apprehension.

Lord Euston spoke directly to Nancy. "I have unlimited regard for your mother and father," he said. "They seem, however, to have assumed a great deal, don't you think?"

"Yes," Nancy murmured uneasily.

"They've come close to putting us in a distinctly embarrassing and quite untenable position, don't you think?"

"Yes."

"Well, as for myself," he said, with a modest, chin-down smile, "I could cope with it. I would have been pleased if things had worked out as they wished—provided, of course, it was what you wished, too. On the other hand, I never assumed you would wish it, so I was not surprised to discover you didn't."

"You're a gentleman, Willy," she said softly. "In the best sense of the term."

Lord Euston blushed. "Hah!" he popped with a toothy grin.

"Weiss der Graf dass Sie hier sind?" Helmut asked.

Lord Euston frowned. "I beg your pardon?"

"He asks," said Nancy, "if the Earl knows you're here."

"Uh, yes. Forgive me," Lord Euston said to Helmut. "Yes. In fact, I asked the Earl to come with me. But of course he wouldn't."

"That's probably just as well," said Nancy.

"P'r'aps. Anyway, I am deeply disturbed by his unreasoning reaction to—uh—to your decision to come to Germany. I can't help but feel some sense of responsibility for it."

"It's not your responsibility at all," said Nancy.

Lord Euston began to push a couple of shrimps around on his salad plate, frowning over them with a concentration that suggested he had found something live under one. "I should like to believe you fled the Earl's anger, that you did not in fact flee from me."

"Of course I didn't," she said.

"Good," he said. "On the other hand, p'r'aps I encouraged the Earl and your mother too much—frankly in the hope that what they had in mind would appeal to you. I could have dashed their hopes and probably have saved you a deal of trouble."

"Don't even think of it that way," she said.

"They've cut you off without a penny, I understand."

"Yes. It's probably temporary."

"That, indeed, is really why I came here," he said. "I spoke to your father. He's adamant. I told him he is wrong. He didn't like that. He insists that he will not send you another installment of your allowance unless you return to England"—he glanced at Helmut—"—uh, unmarried."

"And a virgin, too, I suppose," said Nancy with a bitter smile.

"Wir brauchen sein Geld nicht," Helmut muttered.

"I'll have an income shortly," said Nancy.

"Ah, good," said Lord Euston. "In the meantime, however, I shall be grateful to you if you will accept a bank draft I have brought. It's for two thousand pounds."

"I wouldn't consider accepting it," said Nancy sharply.

"I should be grateful if you would, Nancy," said Lord Euston firmly. "Whatever you may say, I feel in some measure responsible for your loss of your allowance. In any event, I cannot stand by and see the Earl succeed in his vindictive purpose. I ask you to help me frustrate him."

She laughed. Helmut laughed. Lord Euston laughed; and, taking the bank draft from a pocket, he inserted his monocle and peered at it, nodding.

"Even so, Willy, I—"

She stopped, her attention captured by a disturbance that was developing at the door of the dining room. All around the room, people had turned to stare at the man who had come to the door and now held the headwaiter by the shoulders, talking intently to him, nodding violently. The headwaiter began to nod. He broke away from the man and turned to face the crowded room. He raised his hands above his head.

"Ladies and gentlemen!" he shouted. "An announcement! An announcement of great importance!"

Lord Euston, who could understand very little German, frowned at Nancy. "What is 't?" he asked.

"Ladies and gentlemen!" the headwaiter shouted again. He was breathless. His red face seemed squeezed up out of his high white collar. "A new government! We have just received word that the Reich President has appointed a new Reich Chancellor! The new Chancellor of the German Reich is—*Herr Adolf Hitler!*"

For a brief moment the room was silent. The arrhythmic mutter of conversation stopped; even the clash of silverware and the tinkle of ice in glasses stopped. Then at one table a beefy man in a gray suit raised his hands before his face and began to applaud. Others took his cue, some standing. Quickly a third of the people in the room stood at their tables and applauded. Many others, foreigners, sat and stared; and still others, Germans, sat stunned with their eyes lowered. The man who had initiated the applause reached down and lifted his glass of white wine. He held it aloft, above his head, and all around the room people reached for glasses, some only of water, and lifted them. Helmut, who had stood, looked down expectantly at Nancy. She picked up her glass of wine, stood, and joined Helmut in a first toast to the new Chancellor, Adolf Hitler.

They did not leave the Adlon Hotel after lunch. When they went out on Wilhemstrasse, they found the street filled with a surging, noisy crowd. Helmut, who had somewhere found a red- white- and-black swastika armband—maybe he had been carrying it in his pocket for a long time—and now wore it around his arm, said the Communists might riot and there might be fighting in the streets. He suggested Nancy go up to Lord Euston's suite. She said she would go only if he did, and would not go if he proposed to venture into the streets with his armband and look for the riot he was so sure must be brewing. With a show of reluctance —and real reluctance besides, probably—he reentered the hotel with her and Lord Euston and went up to the suite. There Lord

Euston ordered iced champagne and said he would toast the success of Helmut's party.

Helmut sat on the couch in the handsome suite, placing one telephone call after another, occasionally standing at the window to stare down on Wilhelmstrasse: elated, yet troubled deeply by private thoughts. Nancy thought she knew what troubled him. The sudden success of the NSDAP was as much a surprise to him as it was to her or even to Willy. No one had confided in him. He was a small man in the Party he trusted to make him big. His enthusiasm had not been called for when it had seemed the Party most needed it.

He should have been gratified, she thought, that he was able to reach his friend Erhard Milch on the telephone. The director of Lufthansa told him he had agreed to accept the position of State Secretary in a new ministry of aviation that would be created soon and headed by Göring. He was disturbed instead that Milch could give him only a moment on the telephone. He returned to the window and stared moodily down at what was changing from a milling crowd to an organized parade.

At dusk, flaming torches began to appear on the street. A march began. To the persistent rhythm of big drums, carrying torches by the thousands and singing the "Horst Wessel Lied," the Nazi storm troopers, marching from the Tiergarten and through the Brandenburg Gate, turned into Wilhelmstrasse and passed beneath the window from which Nancy and Helmut and Lord Euston watched. There must have been a hundred thousand of them, she guessed, and Lord Euston guessed more: an unending stream of torches, a forest of flags and standards, a ceaseless roar of guttural voices singing their marching song, all to the uniform rhythm of big, deep-noted drums.

"It is—surely unique," Lord Euston said quietly.

Helmut nodded soberly. "The German people wanted it," he said.

Nancy watched. She had seen nothing remotely resembling it ever before in her life—men, and some women, uncritically committed to a leader and to a cause they only vaguely understood, ready to march and sing and shout for that cause, not because they knew what this new leader would do for them, but only because they expected him to do *something*, something to relieve their chronic frustrations. At that window, looking down on Wilhelmstrasse, she watched with fascination, almost hypnotized as tens of thousands of others were, and she learned in one night what others would take thousands of other days and nights to learn: what defeated men would do to redeem themselves from defeat.

❧ *IV* ❧

For a few days Helmut spent every afternoon with her, and every afternoon they flew. His business and his life were in suspension, and he was troubled. He heard rumors that Milch was assembling the basic elements of a revived German air force, and he wanted to know what place there would be for him. He heard nothing. He could not reach Milch. So he flew. He had no access to a three-engine Junkers without Milch's intervention, and they kept on flying the Henschel. She had mastered it. She had no fear of flying it alone.

On February 10, she received a check from her father—a check only, no letter. He had resumed payment of her allowance. She sent Lord Euston his draft for two thousand pounds, with an affectionate note.

On February 13, Helmut was summoned by Milch. He came home elated. Milch had appointed him head of a department in the new Air Ministry. His office was called the Amt für Lufttüchtigkeits—Office for Airworthiness—and ostensibly would be in charge of examining new aircraft for airworthiness and issuing certificates. It was a front. In truth, he was the chief of a design group charged with designing a medium-range bomber.

For weeks after that, she hardly saw him, except when at night he came exhausted to the *pension*, wolfed a quick meal, and fell into bed. She flew the Henschel a few times, but he said nothing of the bomber, and she did not mention it. He did not come home at all the night of the Reichstag fire, February 27. Alone in her room, she listened to accounts of the fire on the radio. She believed what she heard: that the Communists had at last struck back, as everyone had anticipated. Helmut came home in midmorning the next day, bearded, smudged, smelling of smoke, wearing his swastika armband, and swearing that the Reich had been saved, narrowly, by Hitler and Göring, against a Red revolution.

A week later, the nation went to the polls again, and the NSDAP with its ally the Nationalist party won enough seats in the Reichstag to assure firm control of the government. Helmut stayed all night at Berlin party headquarters and again came home only in midmorning. A few days after that, he called her on the telephone to say his army reserve commission had been reactivated on orders from the Minister of Defense, General von Blomberg. Not only that, he had been promoted a grade: He was, he told her, a captain. Milch had arranged it, saying that the head of an important department in the Air Ministry should have military status and rank.

Nancy sat alone in her room at the *pension*, took most of her meals alone, walked the streets of Berlin alone, occasionally flew alone—a detached observer of what was happening to Helmut and what was happening to Germany. She could share only part of his elation, because she could understand only part of it. She saw exultation in the streets of Berlin and heard it incessantly on the radio. Under it, not as easy to see or hear, there was despair. She was conscious of that, too. In any event, it was not her exultation and not her despair. She was not a part of it. She told herself it was time to go home.

But on March 19 Helmut telephoned her, once again jubilant with good news. He had received from Göring a command to be present at the ceremonial opening of the newly elected Reichstag, which was to be held in the Garrisonkirche at Potsdam! What was more, she was to be there, too!

The Garrison Church was the shrine of Prussian militarism, a memorial in the minds of many Germans to the lost grandeur of Imperial Germany. The bones of Frederick the Great lay entombed in the Garrison Church, and there the Hohenzollern kings and kaisers had worshiped. Hitler opened the first Reichstag of the Third Reich there as a gesture to the army and to old Field Marshal von Hindenburg, who as Reichspräsident still had the influence to trouble him if he so chose. Bismarck had opened the first Reichstag of the Second Reich on March 21, 1871, and Hitler chose the same day to open his Reichstag.

The men who crowded into the old church were a strange mix —brown-shirted Nazi deputies to the Reichstag side by side with the field marshals, generals, and admirals of Imperial Germany: the Nazis grim yet humbled, the old officers resplendent in the gaudy uniforms of the Kaiser's day. The officers wore their swords and carried their spiked helmets; old Field Marshal von Mackensen appeared in the full regalia, including the fur-and-feathers headgear, of the Death's-Head Hussars. The old officers, as they entered the church, paused to salute the tomb of Frederick the Great. Some looked up to the gallery and saluted the vacant place of the exiled Kaiser.

Helmut's engraved invitation to the ceremony was in the name of Helmut Bittrich, Hauptmann der Wehrmacht, Erster Aussichtsbeamter der Luftüchtigkeits—the latter title one he never saw before or after but which gained him the respectful salutes of the security police officers who admitted him to the church. Nancy's invitation identified her as Lady Nancy von Brookeford, *Engländerin*. In the plain field-gray uniform of a captain, without decorations, Helmut was deferential and self-conscious in the presence of bemedaled field marshals and generals. Nancy, dressed in black, was one of the very few women present, and she was conscious that she drew more than a few curious glances. They were seated in a far corner, from which they had to strain to see and hear the ceremonies; but Helmut remarked to her, shortly after they were seated, that Göring had paid them a special and important honor in arranging for them to be there at all.

President von Hindenburg tottered into the church: in his eighties, the grim, gray personification of a Prussian field marshal, with formidable white moustache, bristling white hair, uniform, orders, medals, sword, gloves. He saluted the tomb and the empty chair before he took his place in a chair before the altar, facing the gold lectern from which Hitler would speak. Seated beside him, in cutaway coat and morning trousers, was the President of the Reichstag—Göring.

Nancy had never seen Hitler, and she did not see him until he rose to speak. She had great curiosity about him, naturally; and when he mounted the low platform on which the lectern stood,

and faced the President seated in the chair just below, she stood
for a moment to have a good look at him. He did not impress her.
He, too, was wearing a cutaway coat and morning trousers, but
he looked small and ill at ease and vaguely seedy. He grasped the
lectern with both hands and read his speech quietly. He offered
nothing of the fire she had heard in his radio speeches.

"We pay you homage," he said to von Hindenburg. "A
protective Providence places you over the new forces of our
nation."

Stiff and humble, the Hitler she saw in the Garrison Church was
not the swashbuckler of the great rallies. He was pale. A wisp of
his smoothly brushed brown hair fell across his forehead. He
looked, on the whole, more like the neighborhood greengrocer
than the Chancellor of the German Reich. When he finished
speaking, he stepped down from the platform, bowed low before
the President, then seized his hand. A hundred flashbulbs exploded
in the startled church.

Two days later she received a handwritten note from Göring:
"If you can be my guest at a small dinner party at seven tomorrow
evening, I can promise you that this time you will meet the
Führer. My driver will call for you at 6:45. The occasion will be
informal—only a very limited number of guests—and the Führer
has expressed interest in meeting you."

When Helmut returned home that evening, she discovered he
had not received an invitation. He urged her to go. It was an
opportunity not to be missed, he said, and would further both
their ambitions. He was crisp and cool. You *must* go, he said.

The black Mercedes limousine of the President of the Reichstag
came for her promptly at 6:45, and she was driven to the palace of
the Reichstag President, close to the gutted Reichstag Building.
The butler who met her at the door bowed low and led her, not to
a dining room, but to a small, richly furnished parlor, where five
places only had been set on a table before the fireplace. She was
left alone in this parlor; but only for a moment, for shortly
another door opened and a beaming Göring entered, accompanied
by the Reich Chancellor, Adolf Hitler.

An animated conversation was abruptly terminated as they
came into this room. Göring's attention turned immediately and

smoothly to Nancy, but for Hitler the transition was not so easy. For a moment he was distracted, introspective, his mind obviously on what he had been discussing with Göring a moment before. When his attention did shift, it shifted fully. In a powerful swing of concentration and mood, he fixed his eyes on her, bowed slightly, and looked to Göring to present her.

"Mein Führer," said Göring expansively, "allow me to present Lady Nancy Brookeford."

Hitler took her hand, pressed it to his lips, and bowed again. "I am very pleased to meet you, Lady Nancy," he said.

"I am honored to meet you, Herr Reichskanzler," she said.

"Göring tells me you were at the Garrisonkirche for the opening of the Reichstag. You are in Germany during some of the greatest days of its history," said Hitler.

"I am aware of that, Herr Reichskanzler."

Hitler nodded. "I am pleased," he said, "that a young woman like you, representing the highest social order in England, should be witness to what is happening here."

Surprised, and unsure of how serious his statement was meant to be, Nancy bowed slightly to conceal the moment of confusion she knew she must be showing on her face.

"This should be good champagne," said Göring, lifting an already open bottle from the silver ice bucket on a small table. "Ribbentrop promises that it is." He poured two glasses, handed one to her, and, without offering a glass to Hitler, sipped from the second glass himself.

Hitler took no notice, either that Göring had poured no champagne for him or that Nancy stood uncertainly, glass in hand, unwilling to drink. His attention was captured for a moment by the way Göring tossed off his glass of champagne in two or three gulps and immediately refilled it from the bottle. Then he smiled at Nancy and suggested she sit beside him on the couch.

He was a quiet man, anything but prepossessing, she thought. He did have an appealing, modest smile; and he seemed anxious to please, to please and be accepted and liked, as he had seemed when he confronted the old Reichspräsident at the Garrison Church. His pallid cheeks were splotched with red. They were newly close-shaved and shiny. His double-breasted brown suit fit him ill. She wondered where in this man was the ranting orator she had heard on the radio.

"You are of German descent," he said to her. "So many in England are. We are two brother nations."

"Cousins, I think, Herr Reichskanzler," she said.

Hitler laughed. "Cousins, of course! Germany is full of cousins of yours, I hear."

"And in England you have, I believe, a nephew, Herr Reichskanzler," she said.

Hitler's face darkened angrily. "No," he said.

"There has been an attempt to discredit his name," said Göring quickly, "by identifying an English wastrel as a nephew of his. It is a shameful lie, originated by the despicable American press lord William Randolph Hearst."

"Oh, I'm sorry . . ." Nancy said, confused. She had read the story that a nephew of Hitler's lived in England, had married there, and . . . There was more to the story; she had paid it only passing attention and did not recall.

Hitler's smile returned. He touched her hand. "Let me hope, Lady Nancy," he said, "that whatever opinion you form of me will be based on our personal acquaintanceship. In fact, may I be so bold as to say I hope it will be a friendship? If you believe what you read and hear of me, particularly in England and America, you will hold me in very low esteem. I would regret that."

"I will form my opinion as you suggest, Herr Reichskanzler," said Nancy. "I find you a gracious gentleman."

Hitler smiled. His teeth showed under his toothbrush moustache. His blue eyes smiled, too. "Perhaps you can write that down for me, and sign it, and I will send it to the English press," he laughed.

They sat on the couch and chatted for ten minutes before the remaining two guests arrived, and Nancy gained in that ten minutes a different impression of Hitler and some idea why he was an eminently successful politician. He showed his enthusiasm. He spoke of art and music, acknowledging himself as only self-educated in both fields but a great lover of them just the same. He said a regeneration of German culture was one of his goals as the new leader of the nation. He asked her if she liked Wagner. He mentioned artists she had not heard of and recommended she seek out some of their works. He cocked his head and listened intently to whatever she said, sometimes nodding, sometimes frowning as if she had expressed an idea he wanted to consider in depth. He touched her. He put his hand on her hand for a moment. In a minute he was touching her shoulder, then her arm. His hand moved. He even touched her leg. The touches were only for emphasis on some conversational point, or friendly; definitely they were not erotic. He was an animated talker, and his touch was part of that. She enjoyed this conversation with him and was convinced he had enjoyed it, too.

A butler brought a glass of fruit juice for Hitler. Göring, who listened respectfully to the conversation and rarely spoke a word, kept her champagne glass full and his own empty. He smiled and nodded and seemed to bless the developing friendship between the young Englishwoman and his Führer.

The other two guests were General Werner von Blomberg and a Fräulein Erica Trüst. The General, a tall, square-jawed, graying man of perhaps fifty-five, was Minister of Defense in the Hitler Cabinet. Nancy remembered two things she had read about him: one, that President von Hindenburg had appointed him Minister of Defense hastily, just before he appointed Hitler Chancellor, to head off a possible putsch by General von Schleicher; two, that his wife had died in 1932. The latter fact probably explained his bringing Fräulein Trüst with him this evening. She was a girl of not more than twenty-one or -two: blond, exceptionally attractive, overwhelmed by the company and the place in which she found herself, and totally subdued.

Hitler sat beside Nancy at dinner and continued his conversation with her. He was courteous to General von Blomberg, but said little to him. After a few initial words with Fräulein Trüst, he said nothing more to her at all. Göring busied himself with playing the beaming host. He poured the wine. He summoned the butler often, with a little silver bell. Hitler was served a special plate of vegetables, with a large glass of tomato juice. He did not drink wine or touch the rare roast beef that was served to the others. He told Nancy he was not really a vegetarian and occasionally enjoyed a glass of champagne or wine but generally abstained from meat and alcohol simply as a matter of taste. It was part of his commitment to the nation, he said.

When dinner was finished and before coffee and brandy were brought, Hitler excused himself, saying he had work yet to do in his office. He said goodnight to each member of the party individually, with a quiet private word; but he took Nancy aside for a moment, held her hand, said it had been a special pleasure to meet her and he hoped he would see her again soon.

Coffee and brandy were served on the coffee table before the couch. Göring sat down beside Nancy. "The Führer was quite taken with you, as I knew he would be," he said.

"I appreciate your arranging for me to meet him."

"I was reminded somewhat forcefully that I had ignored you since your return to Germany," said Göring.

"Oh, really?"

He smiled faintly. "Yes. By your young friend Bittrich, through Milch. I have been rather busy of late, you may understand."

"Rebuilding a nation," she said.

His brows rose. He smiled, nodded; he was pleased by her comment. "Yes," he said. "And you can have a role in that process. I can make one for you."

"I am not German," she said. "But what role did you have in mind?"

"Your friend Bittrich has the idea you can do something to promote the good reputation of German aviation."

"Yes. In fact, he brought me to Germany with that idea; but, of course, I came at a time when there was much else to think about."

Göring swirled the brandy in his snifter. "I like the idea," he said. He glanced at General von Blomberg, who was nuzzling the neck of Fräulein Trüst. "An Englishwoman—an English *noblewoman*—flying for the Reich. Yes, I think it's a good idea. Bittrich thinks you should fly a big airplane."

"Yes, a Junkers 52."

"I may have a better idea in time. But for now, why not? I'll see to it the airplane is made available to you."

"I thank you."

Göring's inward little smile broadened. "This can prove a profitable partnership," he said quietly. " I can do things for you. Maybe you can do things for me."

"What can I do for you?"

He grinned. "For now you can do me the favor of remaining here while we view a little movie. The General there has asked for it. I hope it won't offend you. It involves . . ." He shrugged. "It is the kind of movie generally not shown when ladies are present."

Nancy grinned. "I can't speak for Fräulein Trüst," she said in a low voice to Göring only; "but as for me, I am a lady by title only, not necessarily by predilection."

Göring chuckled and shook his little silver bell. The butler appeared, and was told to run the movie.

The movie, on a screen pulled down from a slot in the ceiling, run on a projector behind a small opening into an adjoining room, was grainy, poorly lighted, and often out of focus. It showed a naked man and woman, at first rolling on a bed together, with grim vigor and no apparent purpose, then copulating, then exchanging fellatio and cunnilingus. The silence in which the vague shadows performed on the screen was eerie and unnatural to what they were supposed to represent. Göring sat with his legs crossed, sipping brandy and watching with a lofty, critical eye. General von Blomberg and Fräulein Trüst stared in dead quiet. Nancy glanced from the screen to Göring, to the General and his girl, and back at the screen. She caught Göring's eye and smiled and shook her head.

"You're not offended?" he whispered.

She shrugged.

He reached for her hand, clasped it, and pressed it to her thigh so that his fingers, reaching beyond her small hand, lay firmly on the thin, smooth silk of her skirt. In a moment his fingertips were caressing her thigh.

"Hermann . . ." she whispered admonishingly.

He leaned over and kissed her under the ear. She stiffened and drew away from him.

Happily, the film was short. There were other reels to be shown, and Göring had to rise and switch on a lamp while the butler rewound the first film and threaded another into the projector. Fräulein Trüst's face was flushed and her lipstick was smeared; apparently the General had kissed her fervently just before the reel ended. Göring quietly offered more brandy, and the General shook his head. He offered more to Nancy, and she, too, shook her head, looking up at him and smiling with lips pinched thin.

During the showing of the next reel, he took her hand again, and again he caressed her thigh, until she put her other hand on his and pushed his hand away. During the third reel, he did the same, and so did she.

The butler closed the panel and came in to raise the screen. General von Blomberg rose, thanked Göring solemnly for a fine dinner, fine company, and fine entertainment, and said he and Fräulein Trüst must go.

"I, too," said Nancy.

Göring spoke quietly to her. "Please. A few minutes' talk, anyway . . ."

She allowed him to splash a bit more brandy into her glass as the butler brought coats for the General and the girl; and she stood with the glass in her hand as the General bowed to her and said he had been honored to meet her. When the two were gone, Nancy sat in a chair alone; and Göring, after pouring more brandy into his glass, sat across the coffee table from her.

"I had hoped you might see fit to spend the night," he said.

"I know."

"But you don't see fit. . . ."

"I can think of too many reasons not to."

He nodded. "I am not surprised."

"And not offended, I hope," she said with a shy smile.

Göring grinned and shook his head. "No. No. Disappointed. Not offended."

She sipped brandy. "You would have been disappointed if I had agreed to stay," she suggested.

He shrugged, then nodded. "That's a shrewd observation."

"I am in the company of a shrewd man."

He dismissed that comment with a small toss of his head, warning her, perhaps, not to go too far in toying with him. He changed the subject. "The next time you see the Führer," he said, "it will probably be a more public occasion. It will be apparent that he likes you. That will be observed. Many people will then want to be your friend. Be careful."

"Will you be my adviser?" she asked.

He nodded. "More than that, perhaps. I will make more occasions for you to see the Führer. You understand I have my reasons. They are to your advantage as well as mine. Just be careful."

The Ju-52 was a huge airplane, heavy beyond imagining; it seemed impossible that anything so big and heavy could fly through the air. From the first, she flew from the left seat, the pilot's seat, not the copilot's, because only the pilot's seat was adjustable and only from there, with the seat pulled fully forward and raised as high as it would go, could she possibly reach the controls and see out and fly the airplane. The yokes were like the steering wheels of big old cars: heavy wooden circles with scallops for the fingers. She feared at first she would lack the strength to haul back on the yoke, to jam in the big rudder pedals, to shove the throttles through their long arc—in short, to fly the oversize machine. She found her fears not justified. The only control that defied her was the huge vertical wheel that controlled the wing flaps; it required so much muscle to turn that she had to leave that to her copilots. For the rest, the Junkers responded to a light touch. It was amazing how a machine so big, so noisy, so possessed of brute strength was so responsive. It was easy to fly, in fact, once she learned how.

It was the plane's complexity that was difficult to overcome. All engine controls and instruments were grouped by three, for the three big radial engines. Three throttles stood out of the massive console in the center of the cockpit, matched by three fuel-air-mixture controls and three carburetor-heat levers. There were three fuel-flow valves, three fuel-tank selector valves, three magnetoselector switches, three ignition switches, three engine-energizer switches, three starter switches, three spark-advance levers, three oil-cooler levers, three supercharger controls, three tachometers . . . clusters of gauges for fuel volume, fuel pressure, oil temperature, oil pressure, manifold pressure, cylinder-head temperature . . . In the cockpit she was *surrounded* by controls and gauges: above and below, in front and behind her, and to both sides. But they all made sense. There was a transparent logic to them. Once she had learned to fly the Junkers 52, she would not have wanted to fly it without any one of them.

She needed everything it had on August 26, when, reluctantly, fearfully, and yet with a thrill of enthusiasm, she took off from Tempelhof Airport, Berlin, on a nonstop flight to Croydon Airport, London. She was carrying 2,400 liters of gasoline and twelve passengers; yet the 52 used only half the runway at Tempelhof and lifted confidently into the hazy morning air. She climbed to 1,000 meters, set the airplane on a compass heading just south of west—260 degrees—synchronized the three engines, and began her constant, systematic scan of the many instruments. She planned to cruise at 200 kilometers per hour, and she estimated her flight time at 4.6 hours. She had wired her father that, if he wanted to meet her, he should be at Croydon at 1:30 that afternoon, British Summer Time.

Her copilot was Kurt Spiegel, a taciturn, forty-year-old veteran of world-war flying. He had been assigned to her by Milch, to teach her to fly the Junkers 52, then to fly with her as copilot. She had reason to believe he did not like the assignment. Seated between her and Spiegel, acting as flight engineer, was Helmut. He was not qualified to fly the 52. He had flown with her and Spiegel only a few times. Helmut had, in fact, lost most of his interest in flying with her. He rarely offered a suggestion about her flying. He simply watched her quietly, sometimes nodding introspectively.

"You are helping me to establish a good reputation for German civil aviation," Hitler had told her appreciatively at a garden party on a summer's evening at the Chancellery. Helmut, standing beside her, grinned and nodded like an inane marionette, so sycophantic in the presence of his Führer that she was disgusted and Hitler himself seemed to retreat a step from him. Helmut was flattered and gratified to be invited to the Chancellery, as he had been to be invited to dinners with Göring; but Göring had said to Nancy, "I invite your cousin, you understand, to place him between you and some others who would like to be closer to you. He is useful for that purpose."

She could not discuss it with Helmut, but she had guessed Göring's idea was to insinuate her ever more deeply into Hitler's consciousness, in the hope probably that eventually the Führer would make her an intimate proposition or even might ask her to become his mistress. That would be a huge victory for Göring in the vicious, turbulent rivalry among the Nazi leaders. Hitler was an Anglophile. More than that, as a son of the lower middle class, he paid romantic deference to the old aristocracy. He paid deference to her. He was plainly fascinated with her—as an Englishwoman, as what he considered an aristocrat, and perhaps even as a beautiful young woman. Göring took pains to have Hitler perceive her as his, Göring's, protégée. He was trying to propel her—

and not very subtly, either—toward the Führer's bedroom. Or so she guessed.

So long as she knew she could stop it, it was all right with her.

Two hundred fifty kilometers from Tempelhof, she reached Hanover. She passed a few kilometers to the south of it, actually. She had overcorrected for wind drift at the Elbe, or the wind had shifted. She was one hour and twenty-three minutes from Tempelhof. She was making 180 kilometers per hour ground speed. The wind, then, was from the west more than from the south. She brought the nose a little to the right, back almost to her original 260 degrees.

The engines were running normally. Fuel flow was as anticipated. The cockpit glass was spattered with grease. That was normal: The big radial engines threw oil and grease, and what the front engine threw splattered on the windshields. In a five-hour flight it would become a problem. Her vision might be cut to twenty-five percent or less when she landed at Croydon.

Helmut rose and slammed the door between the cockpit and the cabin. He pulled back the glass to her left and let the stream of air blow violently into the cockpit. One of the passengers had used the toilet in the rear of the airplane, and the stench was sickening. Nancy smiled wryly and shook her head.

The passengers were representatives of the Air Ministry and Lufthansa. They were a delegation going to London to meet their English counterparts and discuss air transport service between London and Berlin. That she, Lady Nancy Brookeford, was flying the Junkers 52 would insure plenty of press coverage of the visit. In this, too, Göring had been anything but subtle. He had secured the cooperation even of Goebbels, his rival, in requiring every major German newspaper to publish stories and pictures of the English noblewoman at the controls of the Junkers, waving down from the cockpit, arriving at Hamburg, landing at Munich, standing on a ladder, examining an engine, at Dresden airport. When the *Evening News,* of London, published a picture of her at the controls of the airplane, Göring had the page framed and presented it to her—in the presence of the Führer.

Over Osnabrück she was a few kilometers south of course and had to make a northerly correction. Four hundred fifty kilometers from Tempelhof, she crossed the Dutch frontier at Enschede. A few minutes later she could see a bank of low-lying clouds to the north—hanging apparently over the water of the IJsselmeer. Shortly she could see the same cloud bank ahead of her. It lay over the North Sea, gray and indistinct.

She looked at Spiegel. "I will try the radio," he said; and he squirmed up from his seat, squeezed past Helmut, and went to the radio desk in the passenger cabin. Nancy advanced the throttles and eased back the yoke. She had to fly above those clouds, and she began a slow climb.

Their course crossed the North Sea between Rotterdam and the Thames estuary—some 225 kilometers and perhaps an hour and a quarter over the open water. If London was under the cloud cover, then somewhere she would have to come down through it; and if she could not come down through it safely, she would have to turn back. The Junkers 52 carried enough fuel to fly to London and if necessary return across the North Sea without making a landing in England. Returning to the Continent, she would have to find a safe landing field before long. She would then be approaching the limits of the 52's endurance.

She looked back over her shoulder at Spiegel. He was tapping the key. He stopped tapping and pressed the earphones closer to his head with both hands. She climbed to 2,000 meters and leveled there. She saw Rotterdam below and to her left, but she did not see the hook of Holland and did not know when she crossed the coastline. The clouds were gray and solid below. An overcast lay above the sea, stretching hazy and vague as far as she could see.

Spiegel returned. "London says it has only scattered clouds," he said. He sat down, glanced over the gauges, and began to play the throttles, resynchronizing the engines, which had gone slightly out of synchronization during the climb. "Since they said they had no clouds at all when we called from Berlin, obviously the weather is closing in over London."

"England . . ." Helmut complained, turning down the corners of his mouth.

Göring had advised her to rent a flat of her own, apart from Helmut. ("He can visit as often as you like, but you should not give the world the impression he lives with you.") Göring, who had shown pornographic films for General von Blomberg and had employed nude barmaids for his party at the Adlon, shared with most of the Nazi leaders a public puritanism in ludicrous contrast with his private character. It was perhaps because Hitler himself, in his public character at least, adhered to the wooden prudery of his *lumpenbourgeois* antecedents. She had heard a rumor to the effect that the Führer was impotent. Certainly some of his lieutenants were homosexuals. Only the better educated, witty Goebbels was an openly erotic man and seemed to laugh at the new standards of rectitude the NSDAP had imposed on Berlin.

Even Helmut was newly righteous, and if Göring had made the suggestion to *him*, likely he would have ceased to slip through the hall at night to sleep with her. He wore his gray uniform most days now and affected a military bearing. He told her she should call Hitler "Mein Führer," as even the most prominent Nazis did. ("It is a courtesy, and one he deserves.") He had a sense of hierarchy an Englishman would have called Teutonic, and he displayed an open anxiety about his status and yearned to improve it.

The horizon—it was not the horizon, actually; it was the top of the overcast—formed a circle around and below the airplane. She held her compass bearing, but since she could see nothing below, she had no reference marks to tell her if a wind was blowing her off course. She could only hold her bearing and watch her time. An hour and twenty-five minutes west of Rotterdam, her last clear landmark, she should cross the English coastline—assuming the winds allowed her to continue making a ground speed of 185 kilometers per hour. Then she could descend to 300 meters. If the overcast lay over England lower than 300 meters, she would probably risk going down to 200. If then she did not see the ground below, she would have no choice but to climb out and turn back.

Ahead a cloud layer was forming above. She had clouds only a few hundred meters below, and now a layer was forming perhaps a thousand meters above. Drops of water spattered the windshield, mixing with the globs of grease thrown by the number two engine. Rain. English weather. It was far worse than had been forecast.

The taciturn Spiegel sat looking ahead, showing no discomfort —and no confidence either. Helmut, peering into the gray gloom ahead, frowned, and a gleam of sweat appeared on his face.

She scanned her instruments, the chronometer especially, and swung the nose a hair to the right, to correct a slight deviation from the compass heading. She was in command, but if Spiegel did not like what she was doing, he could speak. Ahead the open air between the upper and lower cloud layers had begun to be streaked with shreds of gray—rain, heavy rain. She glanced at Spiegel. He stared ahead, jaw hard. If he had a suggestion to offer, he would wait for her to ask for it.

She estimated she had twenty minutes more to fly before she could possibly make a landfall. By that time she would be flying in heavy rain, possibly in bumpy air, and she would still have to make the blind descent through the clouds below. She wondered if it might not be safer to make the descent now, over the North Sea. She could not go lower than 200 meters looking for the bottom of the clouds and a glimpse of land; but there were no hills in the North Sea and no tall trees or buildings, and she could go as low as 50 meters looking for the sight of pitching waves. She made her decision. She reached for the throttles and pulled them back. The tachometers spun back, the engines slowed, and the Junkers began to descend.

She eased back on the yoke and spun the trim wheel to stabilize the rate of descent at 100 meters per minute. Shortly the airplane seemed to be settling into a huge soft bed. She checked the altimeter. The cloud top was at 1,600 meters.

In a moment she would be flying blind, inside the clouds, and she fixed her eyes now on a new instrument, the artificial horizon. It was a gyroscopic instrument, and the gyroscope inside it would hold the horizon line on its face parallel to the earth's horizon, no matter which way the plane tipped.

She glanced out. She could barely see the wingtips. Looking back at the artificial horizon, she saw the horizon line making a slow counterclockwise turn. She jerked the yoke to raise the right wing. The horizon line turned back through its reference marks and kept on going. Her nervous jerk on the yoke had over-corrected the right-wing-down condition, and now the left wing was down. She turned the yoke the other way. The horizon line

reversed again and slowly crept back to its marks. She managed
to hold it in place. But now she could hear her engines laboring.
She looked at her airspeed indicator: Airspeed was bleeding off
rapidly. She glanced at the altimeter: The airplane was climbing.
With her tense grip on the yoke, she had unconsciously pulled
back and raised the nose. She lowered the nose. Then the wings
were off level again, and she corrected. She checked the compass:
210 degrees. She had wandered 50 degrees off her bearing. She
slipped the nose around.

Sweat was streaming down her back. She could feel the drops
running. She was breathing in nervous gasps. She glanced back at
Helmut. He was pale. The muscles along Spiegel's jawline
twitched.

Rain began to splatter heavily on the windshield. The cockpit
leaked, and water began to drip on her shoulders and lap.

"*Tausend Meter*," muttered Spiegel.

She leaned over and peered downward. At 1,000 meters she
could see nothing. Leaning over, away from her controls and
instruments for a moment, cost her another struggle to set the
horizon line back in its marks and to restabilize the rate of descent.
Flying blind required a constant, uninterrupted scan of the instruments and a hundred tiny corrections a minute.

Spiegel was leaning to his right now, peering down, looking for
the North Sea. He glanced at the altimeter. "*Fünf hundert.*"

The altimeter had not been adjusted since they had set it on
field elevation at Tempelhof, and since the barometric pressure
had undoubtedly changed with the change in weather, the
altimeter could be off by a hundred meters or more. She tried to
remember whether the lower barometric pressure that almost
certainly accompanied this rain meant the altimeter would indicate
too high or too low. If Spiegel knew, he said nothing, and he
seemed to be relying on the altimeter as it was.

"*Drei hundert,*" said Spiegel.

Nancy advanced the throttles and raised the nose slightly, to
diminish the rate of descent.

"Ha!" yelled Helmut.

Nancy leaned over and peered into the mist. It had turned dark
and, suddenly, through a hole, she saw the dark green water. She
shoved in the throttles to arrest the descent of the Junkers, and

it settled into level flight again, with the altimeter indicating 240 meters. The sea below was pitching, as she had expected. She could see whitecaps on the waves. Shreds of cloud hung below the overcast, and blurred gray columns of rain stood between the overcast and the sea. The windshield was now so splattered with grease and water that it was difficult to see anything ahead, but she could make out gray, low land ahead. Looking around, she found she could see land to her left as well. The land was where it should be, and it was configured as it should be. She had flown off course during her descent through the overcast, but she was not far off; she was flying low over the Thames Estuary. London could not be more than 80 or 90 kilometers ahead.

She glanced over her shoulder at Helmut. He was grinning. She smiled. Even Spiegel had relaxed; he was not smiling, but he was fiddling again with engine synchronization, and his jaw was no longer twitching. Nancy scanned the panel. Her fuel reserve was adequate. The engines were normal. The airspeed indicator showed 190. Pressures and temperatures were within allowable limits. She was no more than half an hour off schedule.

"I'm going to fly directly up the river and turn south from Westminster," she said to Helmut and Spiegel.

She turned the nose a little to the right and headed directly into the mouth of the Thames. The water under her turned brown, and the gray land ahead turned green. Thinking in English terms, she was only 800 feet above the ground, and she could see the shipping on the river and the cars and lorries on the roads. Some of the lorries were running with headlamps lighted, and the yellow beams reflected up from wet pavement. Grease and water obscured much more than half the windshield, but she could see out the sides. She recognized Gravesend on the river to her left. She did not follow the curve of the river at Greenwich but flew straight across, and shortly she could see Tower Bridge. The overcast was a bit higher over London, but she held her altitude and let the city see her. She followed the river, over Tower Bridge, London Bridge, Southwark Bridge, Blackfriars . . .

People with umbrellas walked Victoria Embankment. She imagined they were looking up at the strange foreign airplane flying over the river. It was marked with the insignia of Lufthansa, but the swastika was painted large on the tail. She made the turn at

Waterloo Bridge and followed the river south, over Westminster Bridge and past the Houses of Parliament. She could see the parks and Mayfair across Piccadilly. It was home. She had not seen it for more than seven months, longer than she had ever been away before in her life. She liked this return. It was more than a little triumphant.

The airplane required all her attention again. Swinging a little east of south, she headed toward Croydon. Spiegel began tugging on the wheel to lower the landing flaps. He gave her 25 degrees at first, as she pulled back the throttles and raised the nose to slow the airplane to 130 kilometers per hour. With Croydon in sight, she eased the throttles back more, and Spiegel laboriously cranked down forty degrees of flaps. She made a low pass over the field, to look at the wind sock and study the runway. The wind was from the west, and she made a long, low turn and lined up to land east to west. She could see a small crowd around the airport building—an English delegation to meet the German delegation, no doubt, plus probably the curious come to see the phenomenal flying Englishwoman. She tugged the side window open and leaned out to have a view of the runway unimpeded by blobs of grease. The wind over the runway quartered from the north, and she lowered her right wing and put in a bit of left rudder to hold the runway heading. She did not look at the altimeter again: It was a matter of visual judgment now. She glanced back and forth between the runway and the airspeed indicator. Keeping the airspeed above stall speed was vital. The runway was a mile ahead (she was thinking in English terms again now), and the airplane was 300 or 400 feet above the ground.

"It's looking good," said Spiegel.

She nodded. Easing the yoke back, she cut the airspeed to 115 kilometers. The rate of descent was good, and she did not move the throttles. The airplane crossed the last road before touching down on the runway, and she saw a car skid and stop as the big airplane roared over less than 100 feet above. She was over the threshold of the runway. She pulled the yoke back. The nose rose, and she was looking at the runway between the exposed cylinders of number two engine. The airplane sank. The right wheel touched the pavement, then the left, and Nancy shoved the yoke forward and pulled back the throttles all the way. The

Junkers rolled down the runway, she stabbing at the rudder pedals
to keep it rolling straight. She felt the tail-skid bang the pavement.
The airplane had landed.

A government delegation did indeed await the German delegation. The rest of the crowd waiting for the landing of the big
Junkers from Berlin were reporters and photographers from the
London papers—none of them with the slightest interest in the
two delegations. They had come to see Lady Nancy Brookeford,
to shout questions, to pop flashbulbs at her, to demand a picture
and a statement.

As the government delegation left the plane through the main
cabin door on the left and just behind the wing, Nancy opened
the auxiliary door on the right, just behind the cockpit, and
stepped out on the right wing, inboard of the number three engine.
Her idea was to stand there, apart from the commotion she
supposed was for the government men, and see if she could recognize anyone in the crowd. There on the wing the reporters and
cameramen found her, and there she was compelled to stand while
they shot their pictures and yelled questions.

She was dressed in riding boots and khaki twill jodhpurs, with
a dark blue, long-sleeved silk blouse. Her hair was wet from the
rainwater that had poured into the cockpit, and her clothes were
spotted with patches of water. She stood there on the wing of the
airplane and laughed at the men below, all trying to ask their
questions and shoot their pictures and still stay under their black
brollies. The August rain was warm, and she was wet anyway, and
she confidently expected to be taken straight to a warm bath; so
she stood and laughed and let them have their pictures of her with
rainwater streaking down her face.

She was distracted finally by a pounding on the door through
which she had come out on the wing. She looked, and there inside
that door, pounding to gain her attention, was her father, the
Earl. His face was flushed. His own folded umbrella was dripping.
He shook his head.

"Well!" he barked indignantly. "This is, I must say, the most
astounding display of foolhardy bravado I have ever witnessed."

Nancy leaned against the fuselage of the Junkers and bent
double with laughter.

⚚ V ⚚

In March 1934 she found the apartment Göring had recommended she should have: in the Wilmersdorf district, on Nestorstrasse, an upper-middle-class residential neighborhood favored by officers of the armed forces, government officials, and business people. She had a large living room with parquet floors, French windows opening on a little balcony, and a view of the tree-shaded street below. She had two bedrooms, one of which she used for a library, where she served coffee and brandy to Helmut when he came, and to Dr. Josef Goebbels, who came sometimes late in the afternoon for a pleasant, gentlemanly chat. She took few of her meals in the apartment. When she did not eat somewhere with Helmut or attend a dinner with one of the many people who invited her—indeed, when she was not in fact away from Berlin or even out of Germany, flying to show the Junkers 52—she ate in one of two small cafés in the neighborhood. Her neighbors knew her. They had seen her picture in the newspapers, or they had become acquainted with her on the street or in one of the cafés.

During the summer she was visited by her sister, Penelope, and her mother. Her father arrived two weeks later. Her father, on his visit, was pleased by the way her neighbors accepted and respected her and welcomed him for a chat at a sidewalk table, over beer or over coffee and pastry. He suggested she return to England, but he did not press the point. Her mother had been more aggressive about that, saying it was not proper for a girl of twenty-four to live alone so far from home.

She saw Helmut less often. Although he spent two or three

nights a week in her apartment, often he came there exhausted, barely able to share a glass of wine and some bread and cheese with her before falling asleep. He was assigned to the Air Ministry now, where Milch, under Göring, was building a huge German air force—its existence still a well-kept secret. Helmut no longer worked on aircraft designs. He was an administrator now, charged with marshaling an element of the resources that had to be assembled and organized for the building of thousands of military airplanes and the recruiting and training of crews. Promoted to major, he wore his uniform more often. He earned more money, and he, too, had left their old *pension* and lived in a small apartment of his own. He suggested once again during the summer that they marry, but when she said she would rather wait a bit longer yet, he did not argue. He did not, in fact, seem much disappointed. He was inspired by his work. He was tense and fatigued, but he was happy. She was glad for him.

For herself, she was content. She sensed that her situation was fragile, and she formed a strict determination not to value it too much. She was busy. Lufthansa paid her four hundred marks a month for her part-time services as a pilot, and since her flight to London in 1933 she had flown three times to Vienna, twice to Copenhagen, once to Oslo, once to Stockholm, and once to Rome —as well as to London a second time. She flew regularly to all the principal cities of Germany. Among her passengers she had had Göring several times, Goebbels several times, Hess, and the strange little chief of the SS, Heinrich Himmler. She flew at night sometimes, following the beacons. Wherever she went, she was interviewed, her picture was taken, and illustrated stories about her appeared in the newspapers. Goebbels saw to that. Wherever she went, too, the leading Nazis courted her. If she flew Göring to Hamburg, she could be sure of being at his dinner table that night. Even when she flew Himmler, although he did not invite her to join him for dinner, he saw to it that two SS officers entertained her. If it was a fragile situation—and she was almost sure it was— still it provided her a busy, interesting life, much in contrast to what her mother and sister described of their lives in England. She was busier even than her bouncy, enthusiastic father—with a sense that she was witness to a chapter in history. It was not exaggeration to say she was happy.

On Saturday, August 18, 1934, she left her apartment on Nestor-strasse about 10.00 A.M. She had bought an inexpensive little Audi coupe, and she tossed an overnight bag into the rear seat. She was on her way to Tempelhof, where at noon she was scheduled to take off for Heidelberg. For the first time she would fly Hitler, in the Ju-52 specially equipped for the Führer. She had had a call from the Chancellery: The Führer had requested her as his pilot for this flight; he would see NSDAP officials this evening, but asked her to join him for lunch tomorrow, after which he would take her on a tour of Heidelberg Castle. Göring was not going to Heidelberg. He had called her to say she would be alone with the Führer on Sunday and, for God's sake, let no opportunity pass.

She saw Hitler often, but if Göring had indeed hoped that she would become the Führer's mistress, his hopes had been dis-appointed. Hitler conspicuously liked her. He sought her out at dinners, receptions, and parties, for private moments of conversa-tion with her while ambassadors waited. He talked of England. He asked her if English people did not—as he thought *she* did—recognize the affinity between themselves and the Germans. He talked to her about the burden of his position. He asked if the English did not understand anything of what he hoped to do for Germany, for the Anglo-Saxons, and for Western civilization. It was difficult to believe sometimes that he spoke as he did while stone-cold sober. She had learned to recognize that he was intoxi-cated by his enthusiasms. She had experience of that, in a milder form, with her father—which prepared her to cope better with Adolf Hitler. He was, anyway, an engaging man: a naïf in important ways, following impulses that were shrewdness and ingenuousness strangely mixed. She sensed that she was in the presence of a twentieth-century Bonaparte. Helmut told her she was a fool if she thought that. The Führer, he said, was a giant beside the pygmy Napoleon.

The drive to Tempelhof would not take an hour. She was in no hurry. The faithful Baur—Hitler's usual pilot—would have climbed all over the airplane, checking the tightness of every vital rivet, before she arrived. Like Spiegel, he would concede her the left seat in the cockpit only on orders—and would resent every hour she flew. Since he would check out the plane with such grim thoroughness before she arrived, she need not hurry.

It was Saturday, of course, and Berliners were on the streets in festive mood. The sky suggested rain would fall before the day ended, but it would not fall before midafternoon, and the people were enjoying a late-summer weekend before the onset of autumn.

She drove through streets where people were out, shopping, talking, eating ice cream sold by street vendors, sitting at sidewalk tables with small glasses of schnapps or large steins of beer. She drove slowly, absorbing the morning atmosphere. Making a left turn into Abendlichstrasse, she suddenly found the street ahead blocked by a crowd. It would have been difficult to back out, so she inched forward. The crowd was laughing; small boys were darting through, jumping up and down with excitement; it seemed likely the people would separate and let her inch her way through. At first they did. But then she found herself in the middle of milling people, and they were so absorbed in whatever had caused this crowd to gather that they did not notice her gestures or hear the light beeps of her horn. An SA man in cap and brown shirt leaned down and assured her the street would not be blocked long. He grinned and suggested she get out and see what was happening.

She did. She left the car sitting in the middle of the street and pressed her way forward between three or four ranks of people.

It was the SA—the Sturmabteilung, storm troops—that had blocked the street: Some twenty of them formed into a rough circle around which the crowd had assembled. Four others in the middle of the circle stood threatening guard over a man and woman who, apparently, were their prisoners.

The man's trousers had been taken from him, and he stood with his bare legs extending below his jacket and shirttail. He looked about forty years old, a dark man of medium build. There was a purple bruise on his cheekbone.

The woman was younger, maybe twenty-five. She was blond, slender, tall, pretty. She wore a pink felt hat with a small feather, and her high-heeled shoes were tied to her feet with thongs that circled her ankles and calves. Her dress had been taken from her, and she stood, humiliated and visibly blushing, in her slip.

"*Warum?*"—"Why?"—Nancy asked of a stolid German woman who stood beside her. The woman only shrugged.

The man and woman in SA custody were conspicuously frightened. The woman had wept and had not wiped the tears off her cheeks. Most of the crowd grinned. Some laughed. Some called coarse jokes at the man and woman. A few faces here and there in the crowd were grim, disapproving—but only a few.

An SA man pushed through the crowd and into the circle. He was carrying a huge cardboard placard, and he approached the young woman and hung it around her neck with a string. It hung from her shoulders to her knees and was neatly lettered, as if by a professional signmaker. It read:

> *Ich bin am Ort die schmutzige Hure.*
> *Ich ziehe mich nur nackt für Juden aus.*

Nancy frowned. It meant "I am the dirtiest whore around here. I strip myself naked just for Jews."

The young woman hung her head, reading the words that were to her upside down. When she looked up, she was crying. The crowd hooted and applauded.

Another SA man brought a placard for the man:

> *Ich schaue deutsche Mädchen an,*
> *In ihrer Nacktheit, wenn ich kann.*

The crowd laughed. The man's placard read: "I ogle German girls—naked ones when I can." The man stared down and read his placard. When he looked up, his face was tautly neutral.

An SA man at the edge of the crowd—maybe the one who had assured Nancy the street would not be blocked long—yelled an order to the troop around the captive man and woman, and the circle of storm troopers dispersed and began to push toward the sidewalk. Some of them wandered away, and no more than half of them cleared a space on the sidewalk in front of a pastry shop and there held the man and woman to be seen with their placards. Men and women with little cameras stepped up and took pictures of the two humiliated prisoners; but generally the crowd had lost interest now, and people were dispersing to their own concerns.

"Why?" Nancy asked again, this time of a man who stood behind her.

"His name is Ernst Leinberg," said the man, keeping his voice rigidly bland and his voice utterly devoid of expression. "He is a professional photographer, one of the best in Berlin. Her name is Trudi Fritsch. She posed for him in the nude. He is a Jew."

Nancy glanced toward her car, then stood for a moment looking at the group on the sidewalk. The young blond model's face was flushed and puffy, and the tears glistened on her cheeks. The Jew stood stoic and with an expression almost of patience—being probably rigidly cautious not to goad his SA tormentors by any look of anger or scorn. The storm troopers stood and smirked. To Nancy, their most frightening aspect was their loutish—and disgusting—self-righteousness. In their own judgment they were teaching this young German woman and this Jew—and this crowd on a Saturday-morning street—a lesson in good citizenship, of which they were very proud. She wondered if somewhere in England there were men like these, waiting to be organized and set upon the rest of the nation. Whoever did it bore a heavy responsibility.

She turned away and walked toward her car. The SA men began at the same time to lead the model and the photographer along the sidewalk—marching them apparently to another street, to display them there. They passed very close to Nancy, just at her car. "Mein Kleid . . . bitte, mein Kleid . . ." the young woman pleaded with the SA men on either side. She was begging for her dress. The SA men only grinned. They sauntered—it could not be said they marched—raggedly on down the street and turned the corner.

Hitler appeared at Tempelhof promptly at noon, accompanied by Hess and two stenographers. He was wearing his brown NSDAP uniform: cap, boots, belt, shoulder strap, red swastika armband, white shirt, brown necktie, NSDAP badges. She stood beside the special, gray Ju-52 waiting for him, and when he approached the plane, he bowed low to her and kissed her hand. He told her he looked forward to seeing her tomorrow; they would have a good time. He climbed into the luxurious cabin of the airplane and settled himself in one of the seats. As she passed by him on her way to the cockpit, he joked with her, telling her to fly safely and be careful not to deprive the German people of their Führer.

The flight was uneventful, two and three-quarters hours through generally clear skies. Baur was, as Nancy had anticipated, unenthusiastic about surrendering the left seat to her. He was cooperative just the same and pointed out landmarks along the way. The number one engine overheated; they shut it down about a hundred kilometers from Heidelberg and flew the rest of the flight on two engines. Hitler noticed and came forward to ask what was the trouble. They told him they could fly perfectly safely on two engines, and he put his hand on Nancy's shoulder and squeezed; he nodded and said he was confident of his pilots.

She watched the blobs of grease plopping onto the windshield, and she scanned her instruments; but for most of the flight her mind was on Trudi Fritsch, painfully weeping and trudging along the Berlin street in her slip, bearing her obscene sign. Only a few weeks ago, Hitler had—supposedly—forcefully suppressed the SA. The brutal Röhm—whom she had never met—was dead; and Helmut had proclaimed to her happily that the respectable men of the NSDAP, like Göring and Goebbels (and she supposed he included himself), had taken the Party away from the street thugs it had had to use to gain power. The Führer had assured the army, Helmut said, that the SA would be subjected strictly to the law. Still, the streets were not free of them.

The Jews . . . She did not know about Jews. She did not know if the things said about them were true. The ones she had known were not what the Nazis described. Still, they were clannish and mysterious; and they had a notable facility for gaining money and power and clinging to them and sharing them only among themselves. To set them back from time to time was in an old European tradition, as her father had pointed out when he was in Germany this summer. King Edward I had expelled the Jews from England in the thirteenth century, and not without maltreating them, either. It was the nineteenth century, not the twentieth, in which people believed the passage of time promised improved humanity.

The landing was normal. The Junkers was entirely capable of operating with two engines. She sat in the cockpit while Hitler was ceremonially welcomed by Heidelberg, and only when he was gone did she emerge with Baur and find a small group of local Nazis detailed to attend meticulously to her needs and comfort for the afternoon and evening. They provided. They provided well. They showed her the city and the castle and the university, and saw to it that her suite at the Schloss-Hotel was perfectly appointed and served. The hotel provided champagne. The basket of fruit and box of chocolates were from Hitler. Flowers were from Göring and Goebbels. She ate in the company of an SS Standartenführer and a Wehrmacht brigadier general—both educated, witty, and charming, and both specifically detailed by the Führer to entertain her. She telephoned Helmut in Berlin before she settled in her big bed for the night. She told him about Ernst Leinberg and Trudi Fritsch, and he said he did not wish to discuss such matters on the telephone.

It was raining in the morning when she left her hotel. Hitler's adjutant, Gottsmann, had called her at eight, saying the Führer's car would call for her at eleven. It was in fact on the street before the hotel at eleven—someone's black Mercedes, equipped today with short flagstaffs and drooping wet flags on the fenders, and with an obsequious SS driver who bowed low to her and addressed her as "*gnädiges Fräulein.*" He drove her through the picturesque narrow streets in the heavy rain, to a bridge, across the river, and up a steep mountainside. Hitler had not stayed in a hotel but was someone's guest in a villa overlooking the river and the town. Gottsmann conducted her to a library, where tall shelves covered two walls and a wide window covered another; and she stood, waiting for Hitler, looking out, judging the heavy clouds that hung over Heidelberg, watching the moving shreds that rain tore from the bottoms of the clouds, and wondering if Hitler planned to fly back to Berlin today.

It had been the original plan that they would fly back late this afternoon, after he and she had toured the castle and had shared a late lunch. He was confident, she had heard, that Baur could fly anywhere, in any weather. For herself, if this were the weather, she would rather return by train, and she would recommend the same to Hitler. She had not come to the villa in her flying clothes, rather in a Sunday-morning dress, black silk, long sleeves, a small black hat that here in the library she had put aside on a table.

"Lady Nancy . . ."

"Herr Reichskanzler."

Hitler wore a black, double-breasted suit. He came to the library alone and walked immediately to the window and seemed to focus his attention on the weather as he had found her doing.

"The castle . . ." he said. "The rain . . ."

She turned to him and smiled. "I saw it yesterday afternoon."

"Ah," he said, relieved. "Then . . ." He smiled and nodded. "I am glad you are here."

"I am glad to be here, Herr Reichskanzler."

He gestured loosely toward the window, the scene outside. "I cherish moments like this," he said, "when I can simply stand near a window and look out at a beautiful view and perhaps study the weather. My responsibilities are heavy, you know."

"I do know," she said.

"I am," he said, "the most loved man and yet the most hated man in Europe."

He had spoken simply, and she did not know how to respond, except to nod.

He turned his body a quarter-turn, away from the window and toward her, and he glanced intently over her, observing her black dress, her understated makeup, her hair, which she was allowing to grow longer. It was a prolonged, appreciative glance. He reached for her hand, and, taking it in his, he said: "You are a beautiful woman."

She might have been frightened, but his statement was so simple, his manner so unaffected, that it was difficult to take his compliment as anything but honest. "Thank you, Herr Reichskanzler," she said softly.

"Annchen . . ." he said. It was a diminutive, a term of endearment. "Please—call me something but 'Herr Reichskanzler.'"

She frowned. "What would you like me to call you?" she asked cautiously.

He drew a deep breath. "Years ago, a few of my old Party friends called me Wolf. Today, even Hess wouldn't . . ." He tossed his head and chuckled. "Call me Wolf, Annchen. If they hear you, they'll turn pale."

Nancy smiled uncertainly. "Wolf . . ."

He reached for her other hand and held her two hands between his. "I want to be your friend," he said earnestly.

"You *are* my friend," she said.

He nodded, released her hands, and turned again to the window. He put an arm around her waist. "Do you like opera? Wagner?" he asked.

She nodded. She was afraid he was going to kiss her. It would be like a kiss from one of the household servants at Wickstone or Edham House: a peccant liberty resulting from an aberrant impulse, a coarse grappling, heavy with sincerity. She was anxious to avoid it, but could see no way to escape.

"When I was a boy," he said, "often I went without a meal so I would have the money for admission to the opera."

"I have read of that," she said.

He shook his head. "Annchen," he said. "You can have no idea. . . . I was denied the opportunities others had, and I had to find my own way to understanding; I had to educate myself. I had a sense, you see, that I was destined to lead; and it was my responsibility to prepare myself. It was a hard, cold way to come to maturity. Among the things denied me were the warmth and understanding of an intelligent woman like you."

She fixed a stare on the river far below the window. She was sure he was about to ask her to go to bed with him. Suddenly she felt him slip downward. She turned, startled, and found him on his knees. He circled her hips with his arms and pressed his face to her stomach. He pulled her off balance, and she had to shift her feet awkwardly. He tightened his arms around her.

"Ahh, Annchen, Annchen . . ." he murmured against her. "If only I had a woman like you. You are so intelligent. You are of such superb quality. How you could help me!"

"Please . . ." she whispered. "Please get up. If someone comes in . . ."

He nuzzled her belly through the silk of her dress. "The burdens I carry, you cannot imagine," he said. She could feel his lips moving. She could feel his breath. "Alone, Annchen. Alone. For me, it has always been that way. All my plans, all the work . . . Alone."

"Please . . . Wolf." She seized his shoulders and pulled upward. He was of course too heavy for her to move. "Please, get up."

He lifted her skirt and began to kiss her legs where the skin was bare above the tops of her stockings. "Annchen . . ." he murmured. Then he pressed his face against her lower belly. "Think of the power I hold," he said. "With the power I have, anything is possible. I can change Germany. I can change Europe. But who is to help me? Whom can I trust?"

His breath was hot and damp; she could feel it through the silk of her panties, in her pubic hair. She was afraid. His grip on her hips was tight, and he nuzzled her crotch. She could not escape him, except perhaps by an aggressive wrench free, which would certainly humiliate him, maybe hurt him. She could not forget he was, here, *der Führer*.

"Annchen . . ." He tugged her panties down, halfway to her knees; then he kissed her thighs. Then, to her surprise, he turned her around—she, again, stepping to retain her balance—and kissed her buttocks. "Annchen . . ." he breathed. "What is that scent? What is the scent you use?"

"Only a little lavender water," she said.

"Ahh . . . An Englishwoman . . . A peer of the realm . . . 'A little lavender water,' of course." He drew a deep breath, she supposed of the faint, diminishing scent of the lavender water she had sparingly splashed on more than an hour ago. He nuzzled her bared buttocks. "You are the kind of woman I could trust," he said. "What we might do together!"

It was ludicrous. Her black silk skirt was draped over his head. He nuzzled her buttocks, her hips. "Wolf . . ." she whispered. "What do you want?"

"*Oh, my God, Annchen!*" he breathed. He stared up at her. "I need your respect, your understanding, your sympathy. . . ."

"You have all that, Wolf," she said.

He retreated, on his knees; and, looking up at her, he said: "Can we sit together?"

Stunned, confused, she only nodded; and he rose and took her hand and led her to the couch that faced the rain-streaked windows. Though her skirt fell when he released it, her panties were still down almost to her knees, and she walked the three paces to the couch with clumsy, restricted steps. When they were seated, immediately he pulled back her skirt again and pressed his face to her thighs.

"You are the Führer," she whispered. Maybe it would distract him.

He raised his head. "If I were not Führer," he said, "you would not let me touch you. Yet, because I am Führer, I am restricted to this little moment I can steal with you." He bent down and kissed her belly at the edge of her pubic hair. "A million women would give anything for a moment's intimacy with me. And I would give up all I have struggled for if only I could form a perfect union with you. It *would* be perfect, you know."

"Do you believe that?" she asked. She could not follow his reasoning—if in fact there was reasoning behind his ardent talk—and she feared where it might lead. "Might you not be disappointed?"

"I am often disappointed," he said. "Often betrayed. But I know you would neither betray nor disappoint me. If it were possible, I would make you my wife and my partner in everything I am going to do."

"But it is not possible. . . ?" she ventured cautiously.

He shook his head firmly. "No. Like a priest, I have made my vow. I belong to Germany. To Europe. To history." He paused and looked searchingly into her eyes, as if to determine whether she took what he had just said as megalomaniacal. He frowned. "If I married you and made you my partner," he said very quietly and slowly, "the jackals would fall on us. They would hate you. They would regard my involvement with you as a sign of weakness. Probably they would kill us, Annchen. You see, I am what I am partly because I have embraced the loneliness from which I suffer. It is an element of what the world has of me and expects. I cannot afford to let the jackals see I am a man not so very different from themselves. Do you understand?"

"I am trying to," she said.

"It is difficult," he said. He nodded. He shoved back her skirt, which she had brushed down a little as he talked, and once again he put his head in her lap, his cheek resting on her bare leg, his forehead against her belly.

Confused, relieved apparently of the threat that he was about to summon her to become his *maîtresse en titre*, yet troubled and still frightened by his contradictory words, Nancy looked down on his freshly barbered and meticulously brushed hair—the solid head and neat hair, indeed, of an underbutler—and realized she could not abruptly and scornfully reject the man. He was complex, and yet in a real and important sense he was an innocent, withdrawn from the realities of the world like an anachronistic monk some-how displaced into twentieth-century Europe. He was appealing.

He frightened her and he remained ominous, yet she could not hate him or even entirely fear him. By innocence or artifice, he had broken his defenses for her, and in so doing had broken hers for him.

"Wolf . . ." she whispered. "What is the end, then? What do you want of me? I mean now, immediately."

He sighed. "The moment," he said. "Only the moment. There will be others at lunch. We don't have much time."

Nancy allowed herself to relax. She felt herself soften, not having realized how stiffly she had sat.

"Lavender . . ." Hitler murmured. "And talcum, I think. You must have shaken some talcum on you, didn't you? And . . . and you have sweated a little. Just a little." He pressed closer and nuzzled in her pubic hair. "Oh, *God*, Annchen!" he cried. "If only we had the rest of our lives to spend together!"

On the return flight to Berlin, postponed until Tuesday, he asked her not to pilot the aircraft but to sit in the passenger cabin, beside him. He held her hand from time to time, and he saw to it that her glass never wanted for white wine or her plate for pâté and biscuit—facts not overlooked by the beetle-browed, buck-toothed Hess.

Hitler spoke of the Jews. He spoke—for her benefit, she was sure—of the English statute of Mortmain. The Medieval Church, he explained, never surrendered property it once got in its hand —the "dead hand" referred to in the title of the statute. It was necessary, then, for the King to limit the acquisition of property by the Church. The Jews, he said, never surrendered anything they once got in their hands. It was necessary, then, to limit their acquisition of property and power. The principle was the same.

She wanted to ask him about Ernst Leinberg, the photographer, stripped of his pants and compelled to walk the streets displaying a humiliating sign because he was a Jew and had photographed the model Trudi Fritsch. She didn't ask. He was doing what he had complained to her that people did to him: He was talking *to* her and Hess, not *with* them. It was quite apparent that when he was pontificating he did not want to hear questions, certainly not objections. Anyway, she did not trust Hess not to make trouble for Leinberg if he heard his name.

On the ramp at Tempelhof, in view of the Nazis come to welcome him back to Berlin, he held both her hands and told her he was grateful to her for coming with him to Heidelberg. He called her Annchen and told her he hoped he would see her again soon.

At her apartment she found no mail. She called the Ministry and was told that Helmut was in Frankfurt. She glanced through the newspapers—which was hardly worth doing any longer, since all of them were controlled by the Ministry of Propaganda and were no longer a source of information. Almost casually she picked up her telephone directory and began to look for a name. Suddenly, as she flipped the pages, she was no longer casual. Purposefully she looked for a name—Ernst Leinberg.

He answered his own telephone. "Leinberg."

"You don't know me. My name is Brookeford—Nancy Brookeford. I am English."

"The flier."

"Yes."

Leinberg's voice was distant, careful. She wondered if he was alone.

"I saw what they did to you Saturday morning. I called to express my sympathy."

"Thank you."

"Do you speak English?"

"Yes."

"It might be well if we spoke it, then. I called also to ask if there is any way I might help you."

"I am not sure what you have in mind," he said. His English was not perfect; it was accented; but there seemed to be more warmth in his voice when he spoke English.

"Are you thinking of emigrating?"

"No. Anyway, I think it might be difficult."

"Have they ruined your business?"

"Not entirely. Not yet."

"Are they harassing your family? Your children?"

"I have no children. I am unmarried."

"What about the girl? The model?"

"Trudi? Ah, she has decided to hate me. It is because of me, of course, that she had to suffer what she suffered on Saturday, and now she is at pains to prove to them that they need not trouble her again."

"Mr. Leinberg, will you have dinner with me?"

He did not reply for a moment. "Would it be wise?" he asked finally.

She asked him to come that evening, and he came. He was a bigger man than she remembered: taller, more muscular; it was as if he had somehow shrunk himself in the presence of his SA tormentors. He came to the apartment at seven, carrying a briefcase.

"I thought," he said, putting down the briefcase beside the chair to which she had directed him, "it might look better if I brought this. It may appear to your neighbors that I am a salesman or something. Actually, also, since you asked if you could help me, I have brought some negatives. I am reluctant to destroy them, but they are the kind of pictures that caused my trouble on Saturday, and I have to anticipate the SA will again enter my studio or laboratory, and again search for what they regard as incriminating."

"Incriminating?"

"Yes." He opened the briefcase. "I do photography for advertising. Fashions." He handed her a glossy print. "See—there is Trudi."

Nancy looked at the photograph, which was indeed of Trudi Fritsch—dramatically posed and lighted, wearing a chemise, shoes, and stockings.

"This, too," said Leinberg. He handed her another picture. In this, Trudi was nude, although the private parts of her were obscured by deep shadows. "A few of my models I have photographed nude, so," he said. "It is this that caused the trouble. I have shown my nudes at salons. Some of the pictures of Trudi have been published. The SA came to my studio. My salon prints were hanging on the walls. One of them recognized Trudi. So— the trouble. They destroyed the prints they found. I suppose they will return for the negatives when they think of it. I will tell them I have destroyed them."

"Did they have any legal right?" Nancy asked. "Any authority?"

He shrugged. "Who knows what the law is now?"

She struck a match and touched it to the jellied alcohol in the burner under a copper chafing dish. Chicken livers in a sauce were already in the dish, waiting to be warmed. She had bought them and the sauce, for her hors d'oeuvre—as she had in fact bought the rest of their dinner; she cooked but little herself. A bottle of red wine was open and breathing, and she poured two glasses.

"I should think," she said as she poured the wine, "you would consider leaving this country."

"I should think you would, too," he said. "For you it is easy."

"I am not a Jew," she said.

"You are not a German, either."

She nodded. "I will go home one day, undoubtedly."

"And I *am* home," he said. "My family have been Berliners since the eighteenth century."

Holding her wineglass just short of her lips, she studied Ernst Leinberg with open curiosity. She remained innocent about Jews, and she looked for some sign of his Jewishness, something that might in future be a point of reference that would make her recognize a man or woman as a Jew. This Jew did not have even that exotic, Oriental air that had characterized Benjamin Disraeli. Certainly he did not have the nose like a 6 or the heavy, sensual lips ascribed to Jews by Nazi propaganda. He was a handsome man. His complexion was no darker than that of, say, Goebbels. His curly dark hair was cut as short as Himmler's. His gray suit was well tailored. His white shirt was starched and clean. His black shoes were shined. He had not been subdued by his experience. He sat apparently at ease in his chair, studying her as she did him, with equal curiosity.

"Your family. . . ?" she asked.

He sipped wine. "I have a brother living in Vienna. My mother is with him. My father died in 1932. He was a surgeon, and so is my brother. I have uncles and cousins in Berlin, Vienna, Munich . . ." He smiled and shrugged. "If they want to persecute Leinbergs, they will have to assign quite a few men to it."

"Why don't you come to England?" she asked.

"My property would be confiscated, I am sure," he said. "I would go impoverished. Besides, would I be welcome in England?"

"I could arrange for you to be welcome," she said.

"Why? Why would you do that for me?"

Her glance shifted from his face down to the dark red wine in her glass, then back to his face. "I don't like what they did to you—and may do yet."

"It is not your responsibility."

"I know. I haven't thought of it in terms of its being my responsibility."

He swallowed the last of his wine; and, putting his glass abruptly and solidly down on the table with a bang, he betrayed the anger he had so far kept concealed. "I won't be driven out," he said. "If I am driven out of Germany, can I find refuge in Europe? If I am driven out of Europe, where shall I find refuge? Where shall any of us find it? No. Keep my negatives for me. I will regard that as an important favor. If something bad happens to me, try to have my work shown or published. Maybe a few will learn sympathy for the Jews from seeing the work I was able to do."

"In England you could—"

"*I will stay here*," he said grimly.

PART II

1938–40

❧ VI ❧

Her telephone rang at four on the afternoon of Thursday, September 29, 1938.

"Fräulein Brookeford?" A clipped, unfriendly, male voice.

"Ja."

"Bleiben Sie am apparat, bitte. Generalmajor Bittrich ruft Sie an."

She nodded, and lifted a bare foot to the low windowsill beside the telephone table. She pushed the curtains apart and stood impatiently waiting for Helmut to come on the line. She was wearing nothing but a silk slip. This call would postpone the bath she had been preparing to take when the phone rang.

"Nancy."

"Herr Generalmajor."

"I'm sorry." He was apologizing for having had his adjutant—or whatever the fellow was—place his call, which he knew annoyed her. "Your father?"

"He'll survive—until he has the next one. How did you know I'm back?"

"The afternoon newspapers say you are. You know we keep track of you."

"You might have allowed me to unpack."

"Before I called to welcome you back to Berlin? No. The Reichsmarschall is in Munich with the Führer, you know. Otherwise, he would have called."

"Anyway," she said, essaying a tack that might bring the call to an end, "I am back. I promised to be here next week, of course."

"The Earl, then, is in such condition you felt you could leave him?"

"He's an invalid still. Demanding. Self-pitying. Not an appealing man at all. But his doctors say he will be ambulatory again in a few weeks. After that . . . who knows?"

"Could he travel to Germany? We have excellent doctors, you know. Heart specialists . . ."

"He's being well taken care of, Helmut, thank you."

"Ah. Well, it is good to hear your voice. I would like to see you. For dinner, if possible. It's . . . important."

"Official?"

"Oh, no. I would like, though, to talk to you privately, very privately, confidentially. I was thinking of one of those small restaurants in your neighborhood, one of the ones we used to enjoy so much."

She wondered if he did not mean to propose marriage again. He had arranged a corner table toward the rear at a fine old restaurant they had indeed enjoyed, called Prinz Albrecht Haus. He wore a gray suit, with only a modest lapel pin that required a squint to announce his rank—Generalmajor der Luftwaffe. He outranked the only two uniformed officers in the small restaurant —a Wehrmacht colonel and an SS Obersturmbannführer. He sat—not entirely comfortably, she perceived—with his hands clasped on the table before him. He seemed filled with something he wanted to say, but he seemed also unready to say it.

The Prinz Albrecht Haus owned and displayed with evident pride a romanticized oil portrait of Queen Victoria's German consort. Prince Albert had hung, probably for three-quarters of a century, prominently above the immense and elaborately carved and mirrored sideboard that dominated one entire wall of the little restaurant. Of late, however, the Prince had been moved a bit to one side and now shared the place of honor with an equally romanticized portrait of Adolf Hitler.

Nancy nodded at the picture of Hitler. "He telephoned me in London, to inquire after my father and wish him well," she said. "Did you know that?"

"The Führer thinks very highly of you," said Helmut solemnly. He remained innocent of just *how* highly the Führer thought of her. Even Göring had to guess as to what passed between her and Hitler on those occasions every two or three months when Hitler summoned her to the Chancellery for a private dinner in his personal quarters or to accompany him on a trip away from Berlin. The scene at Heidelberg had been repeated many times over the past four years. She remained uncomfortable with it, but she was distinctly less uncomfortable now that she was confident he had no desire to do anything more than kiss her legs and nuzzle her belly; he had never so much as hinted at anything more.

He did not want conversation, either—as she had learned. What he wanted was her reaction to his monologues. He had told her, for example, that he did not dare marry and have children. If he had a son, he said, someone would surely insist that his son succeed him; and, since his son was unlikely to be as able as he was, that would be politically disastrous. He asked her judgment of English political leaders. What did she think of Eden? Halifax? Chamberlain? Hoare? Churchill? When he had heard her brief answer, he would expound at length on *his* opinion of the man and would study her face to read her reaction. He asked her also what the English people thought of him. What did they think of Mussolini? Stalin? The Pope? Nancy answered all his questions with great care, suspecting that what she said, when it did not encounter the wall of one of his preconceptions, was thoroughly absorbed and incorporated into his stock of opinions.

Only once did she attempt to talk to him about the Jews. He shrugged and said the Jews throughout their history had exaggerated their misfortunes and played on public sympathy.

Her visits with the Führer and her travels with him were never touched on in the German press—although they sometimes were the subject of comment in the English papers. Goebbels had arranged for her every other activity of the past busy four years to have thorough, front-page coverage in the newspapers he controlled. Stories and pictures had been published about her Lufthansa flights—which had been much less frequent the past two years; her flights in new civil and military airplanes; her visits to aircraft factories; her weekends on the Göring estate; her dress and conversation at dinners, balls, and parties; her assistance to Winter Help and other charities; but never once had any German newspaper taken notice of her visits to Hitler's mountain house in Bavaria, her presence when he traveled to make speeches, her weeklong tour of the Rhineland with him, his birthday gifts to her, or hers to him.

The inner circles of the Nazi leadership knew the Führer and the *Engländerin* were very close friends. The rest of the nation was not told.

"What are they saying in England?" Helmut asked. He was toying with his wineglass, frowning over it.

She shrugged. "About what?" she asked.

"About Czechoslovakia," he said. "About the prospects for war and peace. When I heard you were coming back to Berlin, I took that to be a good sign. You would not have come back if you thought England would go to war over Czechoslovakia."

She smiled. "If Chamberlain can come to Germany, I can. I have better friends here than he does."

"I am serious," said Helmut. "You must be confident there will not be war. Otherwise you would not have returned."

"I came back because I am committed to the Capetown flight," she said. "I haven't heard it's being called off."

"But if our two countries go to war, you'll be interned as an enemy alien."

Nancy lifted her eyebrows. "Considering the character and rank of my friends in Germany, I should think my internment would be brief and comfortable," she said. "I didn't think coming back was any great risk."

Helmut leaned across the table. "The German army will cross the Czech frontier Saturday. There is no question of that. If Chamberlain and Daladier do not come to an accommodation with the Führer tonight or tomorrow, it means war." He sighed. "Or does it? Will England fight?"

"Not on Saturday," she said. "I'll still have time to get out."

He leaned back and watched with impatience as the waiter re-filled her wineglass. He still had not taken a sip from his. "Would you consider staying?" he asked as soon as the waiter had moved away. "You are more German than English, I think, and you would be made very welcome as a new citizen."

"No," she said.

He picked up his glass at last and swallowed a large gulp of wine. "I.didn't think you would. Anyway, I had no right to ask."

"Germany has no right to invade Czechoslovakia," she said quietly, careful that diners at other tables should not hear.

"You've been reading English newspapers all summer," he said. "You don't know what the Czechs have been doing to the Sudeten Germans."

"And you have been reading German newspapers," she said.

"Woodrow Wilson spoke of the self-determination of peoples. The Sudeten Germans, a majority of the population of the Sudetenland, want to live in Germany."

Nancy shrugged. "I care less about the Sudeten Germans than I do about the peace of Europe."

Helmut nodded. "Which returns us to my original question. Will England go to war over Czechoslovakia?"

"The decision is not England's."

"But it is," Helmut argued quickly. "The Führer has announced what he will do, and he will not go back on his word. He will annex the Sudetenland on Saturday. The only question, then, is: Will England go to war over it?"

"Suppose . . ." Nancy said slowly. "Suppose the Prime Minister announced that England would definitely go to war if Germany annexed the Sudetenland. What then?"

Helmut glanced around the room. "Might he do that?" he asked.

Nancy did not think so. They talked of it in England, but the talk that counted—the quiet talk, the private talk, among knowledgeable people—was that Chamberlain was more interested in pulling off a clever political trick than in committing England to a major sacrifice. She did not want to end this conversation by telling Helmut that, so she shrugged and said lightly, "He might."

"And would he actually do it?" Helmut asked solemnly.

She nodded. "If he pledged it."

Helmut swelled big with indrawn breath. "Do you know what that would mean?" he asked.

She dropped her eyes. "I can think of a lot of things it would mean," she said quietly. "I can't believe it can happen, over—over nothing much." She shook her head and looked up into Helmut's face and smiled wanly. "Will you tell your bomber crews to avoid Edham House?" she asked.

"Don't be ridiculous."

"It's not ridiculous," she said crisply. "Will you bomb Westminster Abbey? Saint Paul's? The Tower? Not by accident even? Can you promise me you won't bomb anything but military installations?"

Helmut took another heavy gulp from his wineglass. "You have been reading too many English newspapers," he said.

"You bombed Madrid," she said firmly.

He leaned closer to her. "Yes, and we could bomb London," he said in a low voice. "Once or twice. Small raids. Not much more."

Nancy shook her head. "Why not?"

He sighed and glanced around at the other diners in the restaurant—all of them oblivious to this conversation. "The English might be less hysterical about the Führer," he said, "if they understood how remote from his mind is any notion of making war against England. We haven't even begun to build the weapons it would require. You've seen the bomber we are building: the Junkers 88. Its range is only a little more than fourteen hundred kilometers, carrying four hundred and fifty kilograms of explosives. It could reach London, drop bombs, and return. But it could not reach Birmingham or Coventry. What is more, we have no fighters that could escort it. We have not a single fighter capable of flying from Germany across the Channel and returning. The bombers would have to face the fury of the RAF unescorted. Two or three raids and we would be crippled."

"Crippled?"

Helmut's face reddened. "How many do you think we have?" he asked. "Nuisance raids . . ." He shrugged. "But major operations, calculated to win a war, are something else. If we sent a fleet of two hundred bombers and lost, say, fifty . . ." He shook his head. "We can't do it." He glanced nervously around the room once more. "English newspapers and politicians who cry that the Führer is plotting terror raids on English cities are simply hysterical. The Führer has no such idea. He hasn't even ordered the building of weapons for it."

"Then what is this Luftwaffe you've built?" she asked. "What are all those planes?"

"A tactical weapon," he said. "Not a strategic one—except for targets close to our frontiers. Even as a tactical weapon, it is not ready for a major war."

Helmut drank French brandy after dinner—more of it than she had seen him drink since he had acquired position and rank. The alcohol did not relax him. He remained tense and unhappy, and he repeated most of what he had already said: that Hitler would occupy the Sudetenland on Saturday, regardless of what was decided at Munich, and the Luftwaffe was not ready for war.

"Does Hitler know he can't bomb London?" she asked.

Helmut shook his head. "I doubt it. The Reichsmarschall probably tells him otherwise."

"Göring lies?"

Helmut shrugged. "Is it for *me* to contradict him?"

"No," she said. "No one would believe you."

"No one would believe me," Helmut agreed unhappily.

"And if you lose a war . . ."

Helmut nodded. "I might not survive it."

"We can fly to England," she said.

He smiled bitterly as he shook his head.

"Tonight," she said. "Tomorrow at the latest there must be an agreement at Munich, or the failure to reach an agreement. Tomorrow may be too late."

Helmut shook his head again.

"I am willing," she said. "I only want you to know."

He swallowed brandy. "Like everyone else in the Wehrmacht, the Kriegsmarine, and the Luftwaffe, I have sworn an oath to the Führer. Even in the absence of that oath, I would not betray my country."

"Very righteous. Very patriotic," she said.

Helmut glanced around the restaurant. Most of the diners had finished and gone; it was a neighborhood restaurant and its patrons came from their nearby homes. "Nancy," he said quietly. "It has been a long time since I spent the night with you. I hope you will accept me tonight."

"I had breakfast in London this morning," she said.

He nodded. "You're tired."

"Yes."

"I should have thought of it. I'm sorry. We don't have enough opportunities."

"We have to make opportunities, Helmut," she said, knowing he would not make them.

He lifted his glass and swallowed the last of his brandy. "Yes," he said distractedly.

In a few minutes she was in her flat, alone, standing at the window, watching him drive away. As soon as his car turned the corner, she picked up the telephone.

"This is Lady Nancy Brookeford," she said to the night officer at His Majesty's Embassy. "I must speak with Major Buxton. You must ring him up, no matter if he has retired, and tell him he must telephone me immediately. He has the number. It is urgent."

"It is only a few minutes before midnight, my lady," said the young voice on the line.

"In more ways than you know, sir," she said.

It was ten minutes before Major Buxton returned her call. In that ten minutes she paced the floor, wondering whom she would telephone if he did not call. The decision she had made as she faced Helmut across the table was firm, and all her thought now was on how to carry it out. It had been an easy decision; yet she was sick with the personal betrayal it represented. She was impatient with Buxton when he expressed reluctance to leave his home at midnight and meet her.

"I cannot talk on the telephone," she said to him. "Neither can I exaggerate the urgency of this call. You know the Michalke Hotel? I know you do. I saw you in the bar there. I will be there in thirty minutes."

Actually it was twenty minutes; but to her surprise, the Major was there, waiting in the lobby. With him was his wife, who apparently had declined to allow him to leave home alone to meet at a hotel with the slightly notorious Lady Nancy Brookeford. The Major was a short, stocky man with a fat blond moustache. His wife was a slender, dark-haired woman. Both of them were in their mid-forties.

"What I have to tell you," she said crisply to the Major, "is official business and quite confidential." She nodded to his wife. "I'm sorry. It will only take a few minutes."

The wife stepped away and sat down in a leather chair a few paces nearer the elevator. A frond of a potted palm partially obscured her from Nancy, but still Nancy could see her unfriendly, skeptical stare.

"We should speak German," she said to the Major. "It will be less likely to attract attention."

He nodded. He looked up at the white-jacketed boy who had approached and quietly asked if they wanted coffee. "Milchkaffee für meine Frau," he said, pointing to his wife. "Schwarzen Kaffee für mich, bitte. Und . . . ?"

"Schwarzen Kaffee, bitte," said Nancy.

The Major watched the boy hurry away to the kitchen; then he looked expectantly at Nancy.

"First, we need a cover story," she said to him in German.

"Really?"

"Yes. You may be asked why you left your home in the middle of the night to meet me in a hotel. I may be asked why I called you. We can't be sure they don't listen on my telephone."

"Well . . ." said the Major, with a faint shrug. He frowned. "Do you think they do, really?"

"I don't know. It's possible."

"Then why didn't you call from a public telephone?"

"It's more likely they listen to yours."

His frown deepened. "I have diplomatic status," he said.

"They place little emphasis on the niceties," she said.

"Very well," he said unhappily. "Why have I met you here?"

"I am scheduled to make the Capetown flight for Lufthansa this week. I called you to ask if we are about to go to war with Germany, whether I should refuse to fly, for fear I will find myself flying an enemy aircraft."

The Major nodded. "Very well."

She glanced toward the door through which the young waiter had gone. He was not coming. "You must," she said quietly to Major Buxton, "communicate with the Prime Minister at Munich before he signs an agreement."

"I'm afraid that is impossible."

"Nothing is impossible if the matter is of sufficient importance."

The Major stared thoughtfully at her tense, sober face. "Well . . ." he murmured doubtfully.

"I had dinner this evening with Generalmajor der Luftwaffe Helmut Bittrich—"

"Your cousin," the Major interrupted.

"A distant cousin. I've had a different relationship with him as well, as you probably know."

The Major's face was now rigidly bland. He said nothing.

"He trusts me. He speaks to me in confidence. He told me tonight that the Luftwaffe is incapable of mounting bombing raids on London; they don't have the bombers for it, and they don't have the fighters to cover their bombers. Many people in London fear bombing raids. The Prime Minister fears it, I suppose. General Bittrich tells me that Göring lies even to Hitler about the capacities of the Luftwaffe, so probably even Hitler doesn't know he can't bomb London."

"So?"

"General Bittrich says Germany would lose a major European war if it broke out now. The Luftwaffe is not ready. The Prime Minister should stand up to Hitler, *now!*"

"That's your advice?"

"That's the information I have from General Bittrich."

"General Vuillemin thinks otherwise," said the Major. "He saw their planes—fast, heavily armed, in the hundreds. He told his government, which told ours, the Luftwaffe is invincible today."

"Over Prague, perhaps," said Nancy. "But their planes don't have the range to carry bombs to London and return. Their fighters don't have the range to accompany their bombers over the Channel. General Bittrich thinks the RAF would shoot down twenty-five percent of the planes that attempted the first raid on English soil. He says we might suffer one raid or two—I mean big raids, in force—before the Luftwaffe was in essence destroyed."

"They have big bombers, four-engine ones."

She shook her head. "Prototypes only. Their present theory of air war emphasizes dive-bombing."

"General Vuillemin headed a French delegation especially appointed to investigate the strength of the Luftwaffe," said Major Buxton.

"All the more reason for Göring and Milch to make a special effort to deceive him."

The Major sighed. "Well, I—" He stopped as they received their tray and cups of coffee from the waiter. When the boy had moved on, he continued: "I suppose I can communicate your information to the Foreign Office in the morning."

"Not in the morning, tonight. By morning Mr. Chamberlain may surrender the Sudetenland to Hitler."

❈ VII ❈

On August 10, when Nancy had been in London, living at Edham House and watching her father's slow recovery from his stroke, a Focke-Wulf Condor, under the command of a Lufthansa captain named Henke, had flown from Berlin to New York, some 6,000 kilometers, nonstop. The Condor was a four-engine airplane, all metal, long and sleek and sharp-nosed. It was designed to carry twenty-six passengers. For the flight to New York, over the Great Circle route, fuel was carried instead of passengers. The world was astounded—if not dismayed. A few days later, Captain Henke flew back to Berlin, again nonstop.

Nancy had flown the Condor. She had spent the spring being trained to fly it. The Berlin-to-Capetown flights, one-stop, had been planned for months, to take place early in October, perhaps to distract some of the world's attention from the German occupation of the Sudetenland. When she heard of the New York flight, Nancy guessed the Capetown flight, now eclipsed, would be canceled. It was not.

They took off from Tempelhof on Tuesday morning, October 4. They had planned to fly on Monday; but one of the Ju-52s, making its way down through Africa with a camera crew to be ready to photograph the arrival of the Condor at Capetown, was delayed for repairs at Salisbury, and the flight was postponed one day on the personal orders of the Führer. They took off before dawn—a crew of four: three pilots and a flight-engineer–navigator —and landed at their refueling stop at Fort Valmy, on Lake Tchad, twelve hours and twenty-six minutes later. They had flown slightly more than 4,500 kilometers, and their average speed was 363 kilometers per hour.

After two hours on the ground at Fort Valmy—where they were refueled and the Condor given a mechanical check by Focke-Wulf technicians earlier flown to Fort Valmy for the purpose—they took off for Capetown. They flew the second leg, 5,150 kilometers, in fourteen hours and twenty-two minutes. Surrounded by a cheering crowd at Capetown's airport at 10:15 A.M., October 5, they were only twenty-nine hours from Berlin—including their ground time. A congratulatory radiogram from the Führer awaited each member of the crew.

The return flight, on Saturday and Sunday, October 8 and 9, was even faster. They were back in Berlin twenty-eight hours and eleven minutes after they left Capetown. At Tempelhof they were personally greeted by Hitler, who pinned on each of them the silver insignia of the *Nationalsozialistische Flugwehr*—National Socialist Flying Corps. At a private dinner that evening, he presented Nancy with a smaller version of the insignia—in platinum, set with diamonds. One of the Berlin newspapers called her *"die Deutsche* Amelia Erhardt"—ignoring in one phrase both the fact that she was English and the correct spelling of Earhart.

Among the letters of congratulations she received was one that was totally unexpected: handwritten on the notepaper of His Royal Highness the Duke of Windsor and signed "David."

It was not until November 9 that she received any acknowledgment of the information she had tried to communicate to the Prime Minister just before he signed the Munich Agreement. It was a typewritten note from Sir Horace Wilson, Chamberlain's closest adviser, and it read: "The PM has asked me to thank you for the information you sent him through Major Buxton. He was not able to act on it, since it arrived after all decisions were taken and was, besides, sharply at variance with authoritative information he had from other sources. He asks me to say, however, that he will be pleased to receive any further information you may obtain." The note came in the ordinary mail. Angry at Wilson's want of caution, she examined the envelope minutely, looking for any sign that it might have been opened. She was sure, if it had been opened, the people who did it would have been too clever to leave any sign, but she looked anyway. She tore up both letter and envelope and flushed them down the toilet.

She dined alone that evening, once again at the Prinz Albrecht Haus. She had beef and a bottle of red wine, and back in her apartment she went to bed early, taking with her a fascinating American novel she had begun to read—a story of the American Civil War, called *Gone with the Wind*. She fell asleep with the book open in her lap, her bedside lamp burning. She slept soundly for about four hours and was awakened by the ringing of the telephone.

She stumbled into the dark living room and groped for the telephone, still unsure of the hour or the day or even if the bell she heard ringing was indeed the telephone. She was naked. She stubbed a toe on the leg of a chair. She found the instrument and lifted the receiver.

" 'Ullo?"

"Fräulein Brookeford?"

"Ja."

"This is Ernst Leinberg calling."

Leinberg. She had not heard from him in six months. She had seen him a few more times after the evening when he came to her apartment, bringing his briefcase full of negatives—what he called his "salon work"—to her for safekeeping. Another time, a few weeks later, he had brought a second briefcase, also filled with negatives and prints; and he had brought her a gift, a framed photograph, *in color*, of a vase of flowers sitting on a windowsill in bright sunlight. The print hung now on her living-room wall, and the two briefcases of negatives and prints were in her bed-room closet. He telephoned occasionally, to tell her he was all right, managing somehow to cope with living as a Jew in the new Germany. She renewed at every call her offer to help him emigrate to England. She sympathized deeply with him. Also, as she looked at his work, she had learned to respect it and to think of him as an artist. He was an interesting man, and she had tried to cultivate his friendship.

That had not been easy. He had declined, after a few short visits, to come anymore to her apartment. He would not dine with her at a restaurant or take a drink with her at a café. The race laws, he told her, applied to him, even if they did not apply to her; and if the slightest suspicion were raised that he was intimate with her, it could cost him his life. He seemed to welcome telephone conversation with her; but it was plain that he was embarrassed, too, and that it was painful to him to talk with a young woman the law defined as his untouchable superior. He did call, nevertheless; and if she did not hear from him for several months, she would call him. Their friendship was reserved and distant, but it was a friendship. He was her friend.

"Ernst . . ." she yawned. "What time is it?"

"After two," he said. His voice was strained. "You—you have offered to help me. Many times."

"Yes. Of course."

"*Pogrom!*" he shrieked into the telephone. "*Pogrom!* They are killing us! They have destroyed everything! Smashed everything! My cameras—all, *all!* Everything! Now the building is on fire!"

"*Ernst! For God's sake, where are you?*"

He sobbed. "I am on the street," he said. "In a telephone kiosk. I ran—"

"What street?" she demanded shrilly.

"Abendlichstrasse," he croaked. "They are everywhere—hoodlums . . . SA . . ."

"If they catch you . . . ?"

"God knows."

"Ernst," she breathed hoarsely. Her throat had tightened. She felt sweat on her forehead, on her body. "Are you safe in the kiosk until I can get to you in my car?"

"No. They can see me here."

"What are they doing?"

He gasped. "Throwing stones . . . bricks . . ." he said. "Yelling . . . running . . ."

"All SA?" she asked.

"No. SA. SS. And people. Just people. All kinds of men and women, all insane. They have broken shops open. Looting . . . They are setting fires. I can see a fire company. . . ."

"There is a church on Abendlichstrasse, not far from—" She had started to say not far from where she first saw him, with his pants off, forced to wear a derisive poster. "A Lutheran church. Right?"

"In the next block," he sighed.

"Well, listen to me, Ernst," she said firmly. "Leave the kiosk.

Go out on the street. Make yourself seem one of them. Make
Nazi salutes. Yell 'Heil Hitler!' Throw a brick. Steal something.
And work your way toward the church. I'll be there as soon as I
can. I'll be driving a tan Mercedes cabriolet. Look for it. Make
yourself look like a Nazi until I can get to you. Can you?"

"My neighbors are on the street," he sobbed.

"Even so. In a mob, maybe they won't know you. If you are
arrested, go quietly. Cooperate. I have friends. I'll get you out."

She heard only his breath on the telephone line: frightened
gasps.

"Do you have a better idea?" she asked.

"No."

"Then do as I say. I will be there as soon as I can."

For another short moment he was silent, breathing. Then he
spoke. "Nancy . . ." he whispered.

"Ernst?"

"Whatever happens . . . *thank you.*" He sobbed. "Thank you."

He rang off. She heard the click and instantly wondered if he
had been attacked, right there in the kiosk as he was talking with
her. She put down the telephone slowly. She stepped to the
window and parted the curtains. On the night sky she could see
the glow of fires. From a fire burning only a few blocks away,
she could see sparks, bright points of angry red light, drifting
upward in the billowing orange glow of fire and smoke. My God!
It was true—the city was afire! The firelight was so intense in the
night sky that it glowed even in the tiny drops of perspiration on
her naked breasts and belly.

Gasping almost as heavily as Ernst had been doing on the telephone, she stumbled across the dark living room, fighting off the
remnants of sleep and the quick, powerful idea that she had not
spoken on the telephone at all, that Ernst's frightened voice was
only the shred of a dream. She had promised to come to him, to
save him from the insane savagery of the Sturmabteilung. But
how? How was she to inject herself into this wild maelstrom and
pluck one Jew out of their grasp? She remembered the day when
they had forced him to march in Abendlichstrasse, without his
pants, carrying a sign, beside the model stripped of her dress and
wearing an even more humiliating sign. She recalled the brutal
faces of the SA hooligans. What could she have done then? Could
she have thrown herself into their circle, yelling that she was a

personal friend of the Führer? Could she do it tonight? She
stumbled into her bedroom, disoriented, unsure, afraid.
She dressed. It was instinct with her to dress correctly. She
dressed carefully, in a black silk dress. She brushed her hair and
settled a small round hat on her head. She put on her black
cashmere coat with the small fur collar. Let the SA hooligans see
they were dealing with a lady, she thought.

Turned for the door, she stopped. A thought had occurred. She
went back to her dressing table. In a box in the drawer she found
Hitler's gift: the platinum pin, the insignia of the National
Socialist Flying Corps, sparkling with tiny diamonds. Lying
beside it was the silver pin he had presented to her at Tempelhof:
the same insignia, larger, but cast in silver. She took the time to
pin the platinum insignia on her dress: the wings above the
swastika, sparkling with fine little diamonds. She shoved the silver
pin into her pocket. It might prove useful.

The Mercedes cabriolet parked at the curb before her building
was the gift of the Reichsmarschall—actually, of the nation,
Helmut had said; any gift of Göring's was paid for from public
funds. Nestorstrasse was quiet enough. Only a little to the east,
however, in the direction of Kurfürstendamm, fires were burning.
She could hear the roar of big engines: the pumps throwing water
on the fires. She could smell the heavy, acrid stench of fire. It was
2:20 A.M., and the houses on Nestorstrasse were tightly closed and
dark; but at the corner a small knot of people were gathered,
apparently talking, tense and hushed.

She was afraid. It had been, maybe, only a sleep-sodden impulse
that had made her tell Ernst Leinberg she would drive to
Abendlichstrasse and find him and help him. No matter. She was
committed to him now. It was no exaggeration to say his life
might depend on her. She drove with grim purpose and fast. The
people in the knot at the corner gaped in wide-eyed astonishment
as she sped by.

As she drove nearer Abendlichstrasse, nearer Kurfürstendamm,
she saw more people on the streets. She saw men and women
running, carrying armloads—whether looters running with what
they had stolen or Jews running with what they had saved, she
could not tell. Everyone on the streets was tense, furtive. The
noise was louder, the individual sounds now distinctively shouts,
horns, screams, the crash of shattered glass, all rising out of the

pulsing roar of the engines pumping water on the fires. When she crossed Kirschnerstrasse, she drove through a wide stream of running water—water running down Abendlichstrasse, carrying a thick burden of gray ash, together with some floating chunks of charred wood. She could see the fire burning, three blocks away. Fire flashed with eerie brilliance inside the huge column of gray-white smoke that rose above the rooftops.

. She turned into Karmeliterstrasse, and there a policeman ran into the street and opposed her with a peremptory upraised arm.

She stopped, rolled down her window.

The policeman approached, shaking his head, telling her to go back.

"I must go to Abendlichstrasse," she said, leaning out the window to speak to him.

"No. It's forbidden."

"My friend called," Nancy said. "Her apartment is filling with smoke, and there are sparks falling on the roof. She asked me to come and help her, to take her and her child home with me, where they will be safe."

The policeman was an apparition of exhaustion. His face was coated with the gray ash that floated in the air and clung to his sweat. The ash was streaked around his eyes, where he had rubbed at it with the backs of his hands. He stood looking at her, breathing heavily. "A Jew?" he asked suspiciously.

"No, of course not!" Nancy snapped, pretending anger.

He stepped back shaking his head. "Be careful," he said.

She had to drive slowly now. Choking clouds of smoke rolled down and hung in the street. The air was wet, filled with the mist off the streams of water flung into the air and into the fires by the laboring pumps. People ran through the thick smoke and mist, careless of the moving car.

When she turned left into Abendlichstrasse, she drove into a nightmare from the *Inferno*. In the center of the block, opposite the church where she had told Leinberg to look for her, a building was burning. The flames stood from the windows, and mist and smoke hung thick over all the street. Great white streams of water shot high in the air and fell into the fiery cloud of smoke that billowed over the roof. A broken crowd milled in the street, keeping a little distance from the fire and watching the firemen working to save adjoining buildings. Shops all along the street were broken open. The broken windows gaped on the scene of hell.

She could drive no closer to the church. Sitting in the Mercedes, with the windshield wipers running against the heavy mist off the fire hoses, she was reluctant, and afraid, to leave the car. Could not Leinberg see the car? Could he not run to it? She sat, peering through the streaked windshield, through the mist and smoke, toward the Lutheran church.

The church was silent and abandoned. The light of the flames flickered orange on its black old stones. Through the spiked wrought-iron fence, she could see the ancient gravestones in the churchyard, alternately in light and shadow, looking as though they moved, danced, in the arrythmically pulsing firelight. She stared hard. She could see no one inside the fence.

The firemen were the only uniformed men on the street. She saw no police, no SA, no SS, none of the uniforms that ordinarily were so conspicuous in any crowd. She saw some armbands, that was all. With nervous fingers, she pinned the silver Nazi Flying Corps insignia to her coat. If she had to get out on the street, a swastika on her coat could be useful.

She did have to get out. If Ernst was alive and cowering in the church or churchyard, he had not seen her—or, if he had seen her, he was afraid to move. She would leave the engine running in the car, and the headlights on. Something about that was bold, decisive, purposeful. Anything like that might help her organize decision and courage, might even make some kind of impression. Pressing her hat down more firmly on her head, she opened the door of the Mercedes and stepped out onto the street.

Half a dozen men turned and stared. She shot her arm up. "*Heil Hitler!*" she yelled. They returned her salute and stared after her as she walked quickly across the wet street toward the church.

The pavement was awash in ash and debris. The pungent mist immediately wet her face and clothes, and in a moment she stank of burned wood and fabric and plaster. The smoke stung her eyes. She stumbled on bits of broken glass, slippery on the wet street. All around her people stared. Some of them, she saw now, were drunk. Some of them were laden with loot. Few of them would meet her eyes with theirs. Behind her she heard a yell. She turned and saw a man run past her car, pursued by two others, all three of them running hard. Why? She could not tell. Nothing around her was rational.

At the churchyard fence she grasped the wrought iron and peered in. She worked her way along the fence, looking in, avoiding men who hung on the fence, drunk. She could see no one in the churchyard, and she moved on until she came to the gate. She opened it and slipped inside. A man stared after her, but turned his eyes away when she swung around and glared at him.

The churchyard was no refuge from the unreality outside. The bare trees dripped smoke-stinking water. Smoke drifted through the fence and lay in ghostly layers over the graves and grave-stones. Looking back at the street and the fire through the smoke and the fence, the figures on the street were half obscured and moved like dark apparitions in a dance of death. She shuddered.

"*Ernst!*" she whispered hoarsely.

No one answered. She stumbled in a sodden spot on the ground and fell to her knees. She could feel the water soaking through her stockings, and she scrambled up. Her eyes were momentarily blinded with tears, from the smoke, from her anger and fear.

"*Ernst!*"

Smoke and mist swirled around her on a breath of wind, and with the tears in her eyes she was disoriented, separated from the churchyard and the street and the fire. She choked.

"Nancy . . ."

The whisper was small.

"Ernst?"

"Here."

"Help me, for God's sake!" she demanded.

He appeared out of the smoke, an ominous figure in a black overcoat, a black hat; she could not see his face. "Nancy," he said. He reached for her and took her by the shoulders and steadied her. "You've come," he whispered. "But it is dangerous. It is very dangerous."

"Drunks, hooligans," she muttered scornfully, tossing her head toward the street where they could see the men on the fence, shadows through the smoke.

"Gestapo!" he said. "I saw them take Max Kreitzer. They beat him and shoved him into a car. They're out there. And SS—out of uniform."

She glanced around, reorienting herself, gathering her thoughts. "Are you carrying anything?" she asked.

"I've got some money inside my clothes," he said. "Otherwise, nothing. They stole everything, burned everything."

She could not see his face. She could hear the despair in his voice, the defeat. She wondered how strongly he was motivated to escape this churchyard, this street.

"Here," she said decisively. She unpinned the insignia of the National Socialist Flying Corps. "Pin that on your overcoat. Quick! I left the car on the street."

They left the churchyard easily enough, through the gate. No one stopped them. But at the car, two men were waiting, one with his head inside, looking around. One stood looking for the driver.

"Walk straight," she said to Leinberg. "You've got a swastika pinned to your coat. You've got as much rank as they've got, whoever they are."

"Heil Hitler," she said perfunctorily to the man standing beside the car. "This is my car."

The man nodded. The one poking around insiue emerged. He had extracted her passport from her handbag on the seat, and he looked at it, then at her.

"Nancy Brookeford," he said. "*Engländerin.*"

She nodded.

He nodded. "Gotthard Richter," he said "Kriminalinspektor, Geheime Staatspolizei. What are you doing here, fräulein?"

She shrugged. "We came to see what's happening," she said. "My apartment is on Nestorstrasse, and we were wakened in the night by the fires."

He looked down at her knees. "You have fallen?"

"Yes, on the wet glass on the sidewalk."

A flare of skepticism showed on his face. "Have you come here to stare, fräulein, and to report back to the lying English press?"

"Do you know who you're talking to?" she asked, feigning anger the best she could.

"No, fräulein," he said with an easy smile. "Who am I talking to?"

She pulled back her coat, showing the platinum, diamond-studded pin on her dress. "See that?" she said in a shrill voice. "It was presented to me and pinned to my dress by the Führer—

personally. *Nationalsozialistische Flugwehr*," she said, nodding at
the pin. "I fly the Führer's airplane. I flew the Condor to Capetown. Have you heard of me, Herr Kriminalinspektor?"

The Gestapo man slowly filled himself with breath as he looked
at her, still skeptical. "The German Amelia Earhart, hmm?" he
asked.

"If you are unsure of me, you can call the Reichskanzlerei,"
she said. "Or Reichsmarschall Göring. The car you are leaning
on was his gift to me."

The Gestapo man stood away from the Mercedes. "Whoever
you are, Fräulein," he said, "this is a bad place for you to be."

"So I have discovered," she conceded.

He nodded. The ghost of a bitter smile crossed his face. "The
gentleman who does not talk?" he asked. "He is English, too?"

"Herr Kriminalinspektor," she said, "you should read the newspapers, watch the newsreels. Then you might recognize me, and
you might recognize Captain Henke. His insignia was presented
to him personally by the Führer, too."

The Gestapo man nodded crisply at Leinberg. "Captain Henke,"
he said. "I strongly suggest you take the lady home."

Leinberg nodded. "A good idea, Herr Kriminalinspektor," he
said smoothly.

The Gestapo man handed Nancy her passport, bowed, and
stepped a few more paces back from the Mercedes.

She stood at the tall French window and watched the dawn.
Leinberg was asleep at last, on her couch. His last cup of coffee
sat on the table, untouched. She sipped hers. The dawn was gray.
It was difficult to distinguish the wisps of cloud over the city
from the wind-broken columns of smoke that still rose from some
of the fires.

She would have to open the windows soon and bring in the
clothes she had hung out to air. She could not allow a man's
clothes to hang in the light of dawn outside her window. The
clothes reeked of smoke. His did. Hers did. Their bodies stank.
Their hair stank. Now that he was asleep, she would bathe. He
would bathe when he awoke. The apartment reeked of burned
wood and burned cloth and plaster and roofing. The stench hung

on the air of the city, but they had brought it home in the dampness from the fire hoses, and it stank here more than it did on the morning air.

Ernst was dead asleep. He was wrapped in a gray woolen robe of hers. It had been all she had to give him; she did not keep men's clothes in her flat.

"He is in Dachau," Ernst had said of his brother, a surgeon who had lived in Vienna. He had explained that the phrase "in Dachau" did not mean a person was in fact confined to the concentration camp at Dachau; it meant simply that the person had been arrested and was unlikely ever to be seen or heard from again. "After the *Anschluss*, they would not let him operate in a hospital anymore. He could not admit patients to a hospital. Then they ruled he could not treat any patients but Jews. He decided to leave Vienna. He had a friend in Switzerland, and this friend had told him he could come there and practice medicine. He was, after all, a fine surgeon. When the authorities learned he intended to leave Austria —leave the Reich—they arrested him. That was a year ago."

"You said your mother lived with him, as I recall," Nancy had said.

"She died in 1936, thank God."

From the bowl beside his coffee cup, he had eaten the canned soup she had heated for him. He had eaten cheese. They had shared half a bottle of French brandy. They had left the room dark, and through the windows they had stared at the orange glow on the sky.

"It is not just hoodlums," he had said. "It is organized. They are out of uniform, but it is the SA and the SS. I saw them take Max Kreitzer. He was selling shoes for a living, but he used to be a lawyer. I saw them throw him in a car. He was naked, with his hands handcuffed behind his back, and he was staggering, bloody. He has a fifteen-year-old daughter, Margarethe. I saw her in the doorway, screaming as they took him away. I should have gone to her. I was afraid. I was across the street, watching my cameras falling from my windows to the sidewalk, smashing to bits on the pavement. I saw her about the same time I first saw the fire inside my windows. I was afraid to go to her."

"There is no question now," Nancy had said. "You have to leave Germany."

"After tonight there will be thousands wanting to leave. The Nazis will close the German frontiers to keep us in, and all the other countries will close theirs to keep us out."

"No . . . I will take you to England."

"The English visa officer is very polite. 'You really must understand,' he says. 'If we issue visas to all of you, soon England will be utterly *overrun* with Jews.' At that, he's more polite, more sympathetic, than the French, the Swiss, the Americans. I wonder what they think we might do in their countries. Make photographs? Sell shoes? Write books? Lend money? Maybe that's it. If we knew what they are afraid we might do, we would promise not to do it. If we knew what we do that makes them hate and fear us, we wouldn't do it."

He had aged since she had first seen him in 1934. He was gray at the temples, and his face was more lined. Still, he was a handsome man—if anything, even more handsome. He had come to her flat shaken and defeated. He had sat slumped and disconsolate, holding his knees close together to preserve his modesty in her little gray robe that barely covered him. As the hours passed, he stiffened. He grew angry. He recovered dimensions of his personality, and before he went to sleep he confessed to seeing even a bitter humor in his situation.

"If they came here now," he had said, "and found me sitting here in the dark, with my feet and shanks bare, they'd laugh at me before they threw me out the window."

She brought in his clothes. They were still damp, still stank of smoke. She spread them on the floor. She would have to find him others. She would have to feed him. She would have to hide him here until she arranged to get him out of Germany.

Whom would she talk to first? Helmut? What would happen if she spoke directly to Hitler? Or Göring? A personal favor. One personal favor: Let me help one Jew to get out of Germany. How would she answer when one of them asked her why?

❈ VIII ❈

Nancy caught a glimpse of Eva Braun. Not everyone in the cars arriving at the Berghof knew who she was; but Nancy knew as soon as she saw her: a blond young woman with the face of a child, gaily smiling and waving at the guests coming for the weekend. Suddenly she had stopped waving and smiling, and with a petulant grimace had spun on her heels and retreated into the house. Probably she had spied the formidable Emmy Göring and Magda Goebbels in the third car. Hitler himself had told Nancy he required Eva to keep out of sight when certain guests—Frau Göring and Frau Goebbels among them—came to the Obersalzberg.

An hour after their arrival, Nancy stood alone at the edge of the terrace, her mind elsewhere but her eyes fixed on the spectacular Alpine scenery. She was aware suddenly that somone had edged up beside her. It was Josef Goebbels.

"Do you know the legend?" he asked. "It is said that the spirit of Charlemagne sleeps on the Untersberg—there—and will someday rise to restore the past glories of Germany."

She nodded. "The Führer told me that the first time I was here."

"Ah," said Goebbels. "Well, anyway, we won't need the spirit of Charlemagne. Adolf Hitler will restore the past glory of the Fatherland."

She nodded again, unsure if he meant his bland statement as soberly as he had made it or if he invited a riposte. Among the chief Nazis, he alone seemed to have a sense of the ridiculous. It was hazardous, though, ever to assume he saw the ridiculous in anything he said. He did not allow his sense of humor and of the ridiculous to condition his philosophical and political commitment; and although he had let her understand he did not believe everything he said, she found it impossible to judge what he did believe and what he didn't.

"I understand the Führer is still asleep," said Goebbels.

"Yes," Nancy said. She glanced at her watch. It was past two, well past lunchtime, and Hitler's twenty Friday-afternoon guests stood about on the terrace, most of them huddling together against the sharp mountaintop wind, waiting for the Führer to appear and lead them inside to their midday meal. Most of them knew his routine. They did not expect to see him much before two. They did not expect to eat until as late as four. Hitler did not go to bed before dawn and did not rise before noon. Then he read his dispatches and dictated letters and memoranda before making his first appearance of the day. "For myself, I'm hungry," she said.

Goebbels showed a toothy grin. "So am I."

"What's more, I'm cold," she said.

Goebbels chuckled. "Annchen," he said, using the diminutive that only Hitler used for her, "nothing keeps you out here. You can go inside. Magda is inside and would be glad to talk to you."

It was his little joke. He knew very well she would not go inside and attempt conversation with his wife.

"Thank you, Herr Reichsminister," she replied with a smile.

"Perhaps you can even find Eva and talk with her," he suggested, still grinning.

"Josef . . ." she laughed.

"Unofficially, of course," he added. "Officially, there is no Eva. As Minister for Propaganda and Public Enlightenment, I deny there is an Eva."

"Eva?" she laughed. "Who is Eva? I never heard of anyone called Eva."

With his grin undiminished, he lowered his voice and said: "We are about to be visited by someone who indeed may not know."

She glanced over her shoulder. Ribbentrop was approaching, snapping a brisk Nazi salute in response to the one he received from Goebbels, then extending his hand. Though Goebbels made animated conversation with the Foreign Minister, he made it brief, and in a moment he had slipped away, leaving Nancy with Ribbentrop and an uneasy moment with little to say. Ribbentrop was unequal to the moment and talked with her only as long as courtesy required. Pretending his presence was required across the terrace, he excused himself and walked away. He left her alone and pleased to be alone. She wrapped her coat more tightly around her and turned to gaze again at one of Europe's most beautiful mountain views.

Ernst Leinberg was alone in the apartment in Berlin. She'd had no choice but to leave him there. He could not go out, and she could not decline the invitation to spend the weekend on the Obersalzberg.

"*My God!*" was all Helmut had been able to say initially when she told him Ernst was in the apartment.

"I want to get him out of Germany. Will you help? Do I talk to the Reichsmarschall? Will it be difficult?"

"A Jew, for God's sake! A Jew!"

"He is guilty," she had said with icy scorn, "of witnessing the destruction of his home and business. By thugs." (*Strassenlümmeln* was the word she had used, knowing full well she was talking about the SS and SA.) "Is he, therefore, the criminal, who has to hide in fear, who is a prisoner in his own country?"

"For God's sake, *he is a Jew!*" Helmut had said; and she had been able to tell, even though he spoke across the telephone line, that he spoke through clenched teeth.

"When did you learn to hate Jews, Helmut?" she had asked.

"Nancy . . . Do you know what you risk? Do you know what you ask *me* to risk?"

"You have answered my question, Helmut, and I won't ask you to risk anything," she had said, and had hung up.

He had called back, even so, to say she should realize that harboring a Jew was hazardous, even for her, and that she should be extremely careful. He would think about the situation, he promised, and be in touch in a day or two.

Then the invitation to the weekend on the Obersalzberg came.

* * *

Everyone wandered aimlessly about the terrace, through the main rooms, waiting for the Führer. Everyone was hungry, but only Göring had the temerity to ask for food and drink. He alone stood beaming before the fireplace, his face flushed, a huge stein of beer in his hand. He wore an odd costume, his uniform as Chief Forest Ranger of the Reich: boots, breeches, a vest, a loose jacket with voluminous pockets. When Nancy entered the room, he brusquely dismissed a gauleiter who had been talking with him and came across the room to meet her.

"A word," he said. "Alone." He took her arm gently in his meaty grip and led her toward the door to the terrace. Outside, he glanced around, spotted a corner not occupied, and by forbidding glances discouraged anyone from joining them as they walked toward that corner. "The Führer's damned dogs," he complained as he stepped around something dropped probably by Blondi. "On the other hand, I suppose we should be grateful to the ones who leave their messes in neat, visible little piles."

He took a station for them in the corner and stood with his back to the Alpine view. "The Führer has a police report with your name in it," he said. "He is disturbed, and I am sure you will hear about it before you return to Berlin."

She supposed he meant they knew Ernst Leinberg was in her apartment, and she lifted her jaw defiantly; she meant to be uncompromising about that. "So," she said. "What crime am I supposed to have committed?"

"I want you to have an opportunity to rehearse your answers to the questions he may ask you."

It was loyalty she had not expected from Göring. She frowned. "I—appreciate that opportunity, Hermann," she said.

"The report is from Count von Helldorf," said Göring.

"Should I know the name?"

"Polizeipräsident, Berlin," said Göring ominously.

"Reporting that I've done what?" she asked.

"Nothing, actually," said Göring. "But the implications are seriously disturbing to the Führer. He places great emphasis on loyalty, as you know."

"Loyalty?" she asked. She shook her head. She had no idea what this meant. "Can you tell me what the report says?"

"It has to do with the Lida Baarova affair," said Göring. "How much do you know about that?"

"The actress?" Nancy asked. "I know nothing about anything involving her."

Göring glanced around the terrace, as if to be sure no one were close enough to overhear—although plainly everyone who might have come near them had been discouraged by his obvious wish to have a private conversation with the Englishwoman. "There has been a confrontation between Goebbels and his wife, in the presence of the Führer," he said quietly. "Goebbels wanted a divorce. Magda wanted one. The Führer demanded a reconciliation. He told them he could not have a scandal in a marriage as close to him as theirs. He even spoke to Baarova and forbade her ever to see Goebbels again. It came close to becoming a crisis."

"Lida Baarova . . ." Nancy mused. "The Czech actress . . . But she lives with Frölich. She's young, too."

Göring nodded impatiently. "Nevertheless, she and Goebbels— he was in love with her, probably still is. The Führer was enraged. Probably still is."

"And what could that possibly have to do with me?"

"When the rumors first reached the Führer, he ordered von Helldorf to put a watch on Goebbels and Baarova. Both of them have been watched, for months, and the report contains accounts of more than a few trysts between little Josef and the charming Lida. Unfortunately, the report also says Goebbels was your guest, alone with you in your flat, half a dozen times during the period when he was watched. He visited you in the evening and stayed a minimum of two hours on each occasion. The Führer wants to know the nature of your relationship with Goebbels."

"Has he asked *him?*"

Göring shook his head. "I don't think so."

"Am I to understand I have been under surveillance?" she asked.

Göring shook his head easily. "I am certain you have not. Goebbels and Baarova have been. You are one of the people he visited."

She drew in a breath. "Suppose I were to tell the Führer it is no concern of his whom I see?"

Göring shrugged. "You can do that. It might be to your advantage to do otherwise."

"I see no advantage to me in any element of this."

Göring smiled. He had become grotesque in the past year or

so. His cheeks were rouged—subtly but visibly—and his eyes were unnaturally bright, as if he put some kind of drops in them or maybe used some drug that dilated his pupils slightly. He was obese. His costumes were ludicrous. Hitler himself had spoken scornfully of him to her. "You have the Führer's personal confidence," Göring said. "His personal affection, I might add. That is why I mentioned the word 'loyalty' at first."

"He has not been betrayed."

"Your assurance to that effect will probably satisfy him."

She looked past Göring, out at the mountains in the distance. "It's distasteful, to think I have been spied on, suspected. I have a different sort of idea of what policemen are supposed to do."

"It would be to our advantage," Göring said, measuring his words thoughtfully but speaking with a sly, half-amused tilt of his head, "if you suggested to the Führer that Goebbels has—how shall we say?—that Goebbels has for a long time wanted to make love to you and has embarrassed you with his indecent importunities."

"I can see," she said, "how that might be to *your* advantage. I fail to see how it could be of any advantage to me."

His eyes narrowed. "What is of advantage to me," he said coldly, "is of advantage to you, at least potentially."

"I am not involved in your politics," she argued, "I am English. I am not a German, and I am not a Nazi. The Führer's mind is clear about that."

Göring chuckled. "Yes, of course," he said. "You are the Englishwoman, and you can always go home." He nodded, and his smile faded. "But for five years you have elected to live in Germany, and you are a principal beneficiary of our new order. With us—*with my sponsorship, let me remind you*—you have done what you most love to do, and you have been rewarded and honored. What would you be if you lived in England, Lady Brookeford?" He shrugged. "Do you want to go home? No one stops you. But if you live here and take every advantage of the Third Reich, then you are a part of it. You are involved in our politics. You are a Nazi."

Hitler appeared at last, accompanied by his personal assistant, Martin Bormann. All the guests stood respectfully, at a measured distance from him—not to seem to presume by standing too close, yet not to seem insufficiently drawn to their Führer— and smiled blandly. He began a circuit of them, shaking each one's hand, exchanging Nazi salutes with some—notably with Goebbels. To the women he bowed slightly, stiffly, from the waist. Nancy saw his eye pass over her. It did not pause. He gave his undivided attention to each guest. She stood waiting for her turn, her moment of his attention—like everyone else, she realized; just like everyone else.

"You are a Nazi." Göring's words. *"If you live here and take every advantage of the Third Reich, then you are a part of it."* Goddamn him!

Every day she thought of going home to England. But, as Göring reminded her, she had found advantage in the Third Reich. She flew the Ju-52 and the Condor, their new Messerschmitt fighter, and even the marvelous little Storch reconnaissance plane. He had asked her one evening if she supposed the English would let her fly the Hurricane or the new Spitfire that Mitchell of Supermarine's had designed before he died, or the Albatross, or the new Avro Lancaster? She knew they wouldn't. Here she knew the elation of commanding a big, powerful machine as it rose, roaring, from a runway and entered a majestic climbing turn toward the clouds. Her sister's life—from her letters—revolved around dresses and shoes and scents, who had worn what to so-and-so's luncheon and who had come dressed wrongly—and so amusingly—to such-and-such garden party. Something like that was what they expected of her at home, she was sure; and she was not certain she could break loose from it.

Anyway, here she had something more. Here, for better or worse, was a witness at least—Göring insisted more than a witness—to the unfolding of ever more grotesque scenes in a developing drama of immense importance. A few reckless, ill-educated fanatics were writing the history of Europe for the twentieth century, and it was remotely possible she might be able to influence them. Hitler in particular was shrewd and decisive but fundamentally ignorant, and he was subject to oddments of influence from unsuspected sources. He listened to her. Who could tell how much—if anything at all—he absorbed of what she told him? How many ideas of hers had he made his? It was a

strange thought, but she thought the most important thing she
might do in her life might turn out to be someday to tell the right
lie to Adolf Hitler.

"What would you be if you lived in England, Lady
Brookeford?"

The fat bastard. He knew.

Hitler was wearing his brown, pinstriped suit, the one she
thought most resembled the Sunday suit of an East End coster-
monger. His necktie looked as if it might be permanently knotted
and slipped on and off over his head.

"Good afternoon, Lady Nancy," he said with his little bow.
He took her hand loosely. "Welcome once more."

"Good afternoon, Herr Reichskanzler," she said.

He loosed her hand. "We will talk more later," he said, and
he moved on.

As she measured the depth of warmth in her greeting from the
Führer—the shallowest she had received in years—she looked
around and saw that others were measuring, too. Fawning syco-
phants all of them, they lived by their relationship to this man.
How warmly he greeted, how long he stood with each one, the
exact dimensions of his smile, the tightness of his grip—all these
were the things life revolved around for these people. Even for
Göring. It was a competition.

She should get out of it. The time had come to get out of it.
She was drawn in too much already. Standing there, watching
Hitler move on, watching the others watching her, knowing they
judged her a part of their competition—knowing in fact they
were not wholly wrong—she decided to go. She would go.

Except that Ernst Leinberg was hiding in her apartment, his
life dependent on her. . . .

Not once had he been out of the flat, even to stand on the
landing at the top of the stairs. He stayed away from the windows
except when he pulled back a curtain with great care and peered
cautiously down toward the street.

They were looking for him. She had no more direct evidence
of it than he did, but she had learned they were rounding up the
Jews dispossessed on *Kristallnacht* and sending them to . . . Ernst
would say to Dachau.

Her embassy talked to her exactly as Ernst had said it would: "Of course. Of course. . . . Yes, but I've got a thousand such requests on my desk at this moment, you must understand. And, my dear Lady Nancy, they are *all* urgent."

She had bought him clothes: trousers, a turtleneck sweater, a jacket, shirts, shoes, underwear. These and the extra food she now had to buy she bought in distant neighborhoods, so her neighbors might not wonder why she bought men's clothing or why she bought more food than she had bought before. Suddenly every friendly German who smiled at her on Nestorstrasse was potentially the enemy who would betray Ernst to the Gestapo.

She was distressed to see how ashamed he was of his dependence on her. He tried in some small measure to compensate for it by preparing their meals, tidying up the rooms, washing clothes in the kitchen sink. He tried also to keep out of her way in the small flat. It distressed her, too, to see him demean himself: to see him scurry into another room to avoid intruding on her privacy, to see him replace a book on a shelf with elaborate care so she could hardly notice it had been taken out to read.

"Ernst," she had said to him, "maybe I don't personally owe you anything; but mankind owes you something, and you needn't be grateful to me if I choose to repay a little of it."

Toward the end of the week, just before she had to leave for her weekend on the Obersalzberg, he said something she found encouraging. He asked her if she had a pistol or if she knew how he could get one.

Führer though he might be, Adolf Hitler's life was so elaborately circumscribed with customs and rituals of his own making that he found it difficult to vary the routine sufficiently to find a quarter-hour to be alone with Nancy. After their extended afternoon meal, he led the company on a long walk to the teahouse, where they stood around aimlessly, spoke banalities, and partook of cakes and coffee. Hitler himself fell asleep in his chair in the teahouse, and all conversation was reduced to whispers so as not to chance wakening him. At six the company returned in cars to the Berghof. Guests had two hours to rest and perhaps bathe before gathering again for supper and the three or more movies that would occupy the evening and night. Nancy had spent weekends here before and knew the routine. She knew if Hitler wanted to talk to her alone, he would do it during the two hours between teahouse and supper. She would be ready.

She did not anticipate he would come immediately, so she was in her bath when her telephone rang. She had only managed to wrap her damp body in a terry-cloth robe when he arrived at her door; she was barefoot, and she had put on no makeup, and her hair hung in uncombed strands. He sat down in the only chair in her bedroom, and she sat on her bed. He faced her for a long moment of silence. His face was pink, and his eyes glittered oddly, unnaturally.

"What is the relationship between you and Goebbels?" he asked abruptly.

Anger stiffened her, and perhaps he saw it on her face; but she had decided not to defy him—not yet, anyway. She composed herself. Consciously she made her face bland. "He is a friend," she said. "The same as—Göring."

His chin rose. "An intimate friend?"

She could not tell him what Göring had told her. She had to pretend she did not know what von Helldorf had reported. "I am not sure what you mean by 'intimate,' Herr Reichskanzler," she said—and she saw him almost wince at her use of his formal title. "If you want to know whether we are *good* friends, I would say yes, we are. The Reichsminister is a witty, amusing man. I enjoy his conversation."

"Does he visit you in your home?"

She nodded. "Occasionally."

"At night?"

It was an absurd contrast: his megalomania and his stumbling inability to ask the question he had in mind. She was too resentful to help him. She would let him struggle through his circumlocution to the end. "Uh—evenings, usually," she said. "For brandy and coffee. I have no household staff, and I don't cook much, so I don't serve dinner to guests."

"Ah . . ." said Hitler, nodding, lifting his brows, as if her answer entirely satisfied him and resolved all his doubts. He glanced around the room.

"Do you ask for some particular reason?" she inquired ingenuously.

He shook his head quickly. "Well . . ." he said uneasily. "My friend Goebbels has an unhappy reputation for—for working his way into the confidence of attractive young women, then taking advantage of them, then betraying them. Something he said the other day suggested to me he might be trying to do something of the kind to you. I was concerned, Annchen."

"I appreciate your concern," she said. Here was her opportunity to do what Göring wanted. She smiled at Hitler. "Actually, Dr. Goebbels has been a gentleman. I've had subtle hints from him, I suppose, but when I did not take them seriously, he did not press them."

"You—uh—should tell me if he becomes the source of any embarrassment," Hitler said stiffly.

"Of course."

His eyes wandered around the room, then settled on her: on her bare feet for a long moment, then on her freshly bathed, damp face. "Do you plan to marry Bittrich?" he asked.

She was startled. She shook her head. "No, I don't think so," she said quietly.

"It would be well if you did, you know," he said.

"Why?"

"An unmarried woman will always be the subject of speculative talk," he said.

"Better to be the subject of talk than to be unhappily married," she said.

"Ah . . ." he said distractedly, obviously sorry for the conversational gambit and not interested in pursuing it. He licked his lips. He dropped to his knees and gently kissed each of her bare feet. "Annchen . . ." he whispered.

"Wolf," she said softly. She touched his head. Maybe she would dare ask him to let Ernst Leinberg leave Germany. "Wolf, is there any reason why—"

He stood. He seized the shoulders of her robe and gently, slowly—offering her the opportunity to stop him if she wished— he pulled it off her shoulders and pushed it down, until she was naked to the waist. "Oh, Annchen!" he whispered. He stared at her small breasts. "Would you let Ziegler paint you for me . . . so?"

"You mean nude?" she asked, unable to conceal her surprise.

He nodded. "He painted Geli for me. But only after she was dead, only from photographs. If I had a portrait of you, so . . ."

Even the words "nude" or "naked" he could not bring himself to utter. "I would cherish it, Annchen."

"Where would you hang it?" she asked. She knew the work of Adolf Ziegler. He was a painter of slick, photo-realistic, erotic nudes. Goebbels joked about the Führer's fascination with the work of Ziegler. "I am—not sure I would enjoy seeing myself naked on the wall of—"

"No," he said. "I would have it built into a case, and I would hang it only in my private quarters and close the doors over it except when I was there to admire it."

She smiled. The smile was genuine; it was difficult not to smile in the face of such a boyish invitation, from such a man. "Let me think about it, may I?" she said. She lifted her robe over her shoulders and closed it. "I—"

"May I speak to Ziegler?" he asked.

"Well . . . You don't have my promise. Please allow me to think about it."

She stood and kissed his forehead, then his cheeks. Adolf Hitler blushed.

❧ IX ❧

The Fieseler Storch was a splendid little airplane. Though called a stork, it might have been called a grasshopper. Small and light, it was powered by a 240-horsepower inverted V-8 engine; and although its top speed was only 175 kilometers per hour, it was capable of taking off and landing on a field no more than 50 meters long. What was more, it could stay in the air while flying as slowly as 40 kilometers per hour. With a little headwind, it could almost hover. Generalmajor Bittrich had one personally assigned to him. Flying the Storch himself, he could drop in unannounced for a quick inspection at almost any factory in Germany. Nancy was with him one day when he landed on a soccer field. Another day he put his Storch down on a test track for armored vehicles—for the Storch, with its landing gear on long, springy struts, could land on rough fields as well as short ones. He left orders at the hangar that the airplane was to be available for Fräulein Brookeford whenever he himself did not want it. It was the plane she flew for pleasure.

This morning she was not flying for pleasure. An early-December snow was whirling on a cold wind, and the Storch was pitched roughly by gusts as it flew from open sky where the sun shone weak and white into and out of snow showers where visibility fell almost to zero. She was flying a circuit of the Berlin airports—Tempelhof, Gatow, Schönefeld, Tegel—landing at each. At each she made a point of exchanging a few words of aviation banter with the men on duty. She wanted them to know her, to give them something to talk about at home—that the *Engländerin* had landed there this morning—to welcome her, maybe even to like her.

"A cup of coffee, *Gnädiges Fräulein?*" an elderly mechanic at Schönefeld offered. "On a morning like this . . ." He stood under the high wing of the Storch, watching her unbuckle from the cockpit, ready to offer her a hand as she stepped down. Dressed in coveralls with a wool cap, he patted the fabric-covered fuselage of the Storch and murmured, "Beautiful machine, beautiful. . . ."

Inside the heated shack adjoining one of the hangars, the air was pungent with the clean smells of oil and steel. She sat on a bench and watched him pour black coffee into a heavy mug. Another mechanic, a younger man, came in from the hangar. "Fräulein—uh, Brookeford?" he asked.

She nodded. It was good. They recognized her. Well they might. What other woman flew a Storch marked with Luftwaffe crosses? They were deferential.

"Where are the police?" she asked.

The old man shrugged. The young man spoke. "They don't trouble people who fly those," he said, nodding toward the door and the Storch they could see through the glass. He referred to the fact that the Storch was often commandeered by high-ranking men for personal use. Helmut was not the only general who flew his own Storch.

His answer about the whereabouts of the police was encouraging. At Tempelhof they were much more careful. There the police checked every plane that landed or took off. Here, on a cold morning when they did not want to trouble themselves to check a Storch, she could maybe land, pick up Ernst along the hangar line, and fly out with him without anyone noticing. She might even drive him here someday, let him be seen with her, and let the people around the airport become accustomed to him as a friend of hers. On the day when she picked him up for their flight, he might not have to cower in the cold between two hangars or in a ditch along a runway—another possibility they had considered. He might be able to sit right here, enjoying a mug of coffee, making small talk with the mechanics, warm and comfortable.

Denmark would be the easiest flight—only 320 kilometers or so, all over land. But she could not be sure the Danish government would not feel obliged to return Ernst and the airplane, even assuming they did not return her. Sweden was 400 kilometers, 150 of it across the waters of the Baltic. Most appealing but most difficult was England. She had studied the charts a hundred times. She would fly northwest across Germany and would have to refuel the Storch at Bremen or Bremerhaven or Wilhelmshaven. (She would have had to rehearse this, to make the refueling crew accustomed to her flying in and out in Generalmajor Bittrich's Storch. If she had Helmut with her once when she refueled there, it would be helpful; and she had been trying to find a reason to induce him to fly with her to one of those cities. With Ernst in the plane later, she would perhaps have to hide him in the fuselage behind the rear seat, so the refueling crew did not see him.) Slipping across the coastline at Norden or thereabouts, she would turn southwest and fly the line of the West Frisian Islands, keeping them in sight on her left. Reaching the southern end of Texel, she would head directly across the North Sea, 200 kilometers over the water, to make a landfall in East Anglia.

All would depend on just two factors: a smooth deception and friendly weather.

"They say our country has the fastest and slowest airplanes in the world," said the old mechanic. "The Me-109 and the Storch."

"I've flown both," said Nancy.

"Ah," said the old man, sipping his coffee. "I worked on airplanes in the war and have ever since, and—would you believe? —I've never been off the ground." He nodded.

"I'll take you up now."

"Ahhh. In this weather. Thank you, fräulein, but if I ever go, it will be on a better day than this."

She flew from Schönefeld to Gatow, which was on the west side of the city, just west of the Wannsee. She kept low, not above 500 meters, staying out of the way of heavy transports approaching Tempelhof, keeping below the worst of the winds, but, even so, passing in and out of snow showers as before. She was kept busy controlling the pitching airplane and could give

little attention to the eerie beauty of the weak sun shining through
the broken clouds on the fresh snow, the snow showers standing
like vague gray towers reaching from the ground to the clouds,
the eddying, glittering snow falling through the sunlight. She
crossed the Wannsee and could see Gatow Airfield ahead, gusts
of wind whipping waves of snow across the ground. She turned
north of the field and entered a left circle of it, preparing to land.

Gatow offered plenty of landing distance for the Storch. She
would keep the flaps up and make what would be, for the Storch,
a high-speed landing. That would be safer in this gusty wind. She
watched the field as she circled to the south of it, parallel to
what would be her final landing course. It looked deserted. On
a winter day like this, it might be an alternative to Schönefeld.

Over the shore of the Wannsee, she turned left again. Now the
field was to her northwest, and one more left turn would put
her on her final approach. Her altitude was about 200 meters. She
pulled back the throttle to increase the sink. Keeping her eyes
generally on the field where she was about to land, she glanced
around once or twice a minute to be sure no other airplane was
approaching Gatow. It was not likely in this weather.

Ready to turn on final approach, she glanced around one last
time. *God!* Over the Wannsee, on its own final approach to the
field, was another airplane, coming straight toward her. It was
another Storch, and the pilot was making a long, straight-in
approach, rather than circling as she had done. It was to her
right and just ahead, no more than a hundred meters distant,
and the two airplanes were closing at probably 30 or 40 meters
per second.

She hadn't time to calculate. Instinctively she shoved the stick
forward, hoping she could dive under the other plane, and hoping
its pilot would not attempt the same maneuver. At the same time,
she threw her airplane to the right. That was the rule: Avoid
collision by turning right—although this time just turning right
would have been fatal; the dive was her hope. The other pilot
followed the rule. The other Storch banked hard right. Looking
up through the glass top of the cockpit, she could see nothing but
the other Storch; its left wheel, on the end of its long strut,
whipped by no more than a meter or two from her cockpit, and
an instant later the tail skid almost grazed her banked-up left
wing.

The other Storch had missed her, but she had put her own airplane into a diving turn only 200 meters above the ground, and now the treetops were coming up fast. It would spin if she tried to jerk it out. She jammed in left rudder. The Storch responded instantly. It stopped turning. She shoved the stick left to raise the right wing. Now in a flat dive, she was less than 50 meters above the water of the Wannsee. She hauled back and the dive flattened, but the airplane continued to lose altitude. She shoved the throttle all the way in. The Storch was level and beginning to climb, but she was below the treetops. She banked into a sharp left turn to stay over the water. She saw her wingtip seem to reach for the gray water of the Wannsee. She lifted it. Now flying north over the Wannsee, she kept the Storch over the center of the water as the Wannsee narrowed into the Havel River. Ahead was a bridge. She eased the stick back, then back more, and the Storch climbed as only a Storch could. It rose above the level of the treetops of the Grünewald. The stadium appeared on her right, and she turned into a shallow climb over it. She had survived.

Men were running on the Gatow field. She could see the other Storch on the ground as she turned again over the Wannsee and set up another final approach. Her hands were firm on the stick and throttle. The weakness was in her chest and shoulders, and she felt sweat on her face, even in the cold cockpit. She breathed hard. Her leather flying jacket and her jodhpurs and boots seemed to tighten on her body. She had never come so close to death before and had never been so afraid. They were excited on the ground. One Storch had landed, and they had not expected to see the other one. They had supposed she had gone down in the Wannsee.

She landed. She taxied toward the hangars and drew her airplane up alongside the other Storch. The other pilot was still in the cockpit. He stepped out and hopped to the ground only as she cut her switch and stopped her engine. With the men around him, he strode toward her plane, apparently angry—a tall, blond man, thin, with a sharp nose and a long chin and thick lips. She jerked off her flying cap, shook out her hair, and loosed her belt. She opened her cockpit door as he swung around the front of the Storch and stalked toward a confrontation.

He stopped a pace short. A frown of surprise flickered over his angry face. Then abruptly his face softened, and a forced smile appeared. "Ah," he said. "Die Engländerin, nicht wahr? Fräulein Brookeford?"

She nodded.

"Sehr angenehm!" he said with a short bow. His voice was surprisingly high for so big a man. "Ich bin Reinhard Heydrich."

"Heydrich, for God's sake!" Ernst exclaimed when she told him, in the apartment that afternoon. "My God, do you know who he is?"

He spoke to her through the bathroom door. She was lying in a tub of hot water, soaking the cold out of her body, and she had asked him to sit down outside and hear what she had learned about flying out of Germany and how she had encountered Heydrich.

"He's head of the Gestapo, I understand," she said.

"No," said Ernst. "Worse that that. He's head of the SIPO —Sicherheitspolizei—and the SD—Sicherheitsdienst. Internal security. Counterespionage. Political police. He's answerable only to Himmler—and to Hitler himself. He's one of the most powerful men in the Third Reich. Certainly he's the most ruthless."

"Have you ever see him?" she asked.

"Pictures," said Ernst. "I've never seen any of the big Nazis in person."

"He's a curious man," she said. She splashed warm water over her shoulders, to run down over her back. "His eyes are narrow and slanted, like an Oriental's; but they're blue, ice-cold blue. He's the only one of the big Nazis who's the blond, Nordic type they're supposed to admire so much; but even so, he looks Oriental—Mongoloid."

"Ugly?"

She considered. "No."

"He could give me an exit visa if he wanted to," said Ernst. "He has the power. Exit permits for Jews are issued by the Gestapo now; and Müller, who's the head of the Gestapo, is a subordinate of Heydrich's."

"He's going to invite me to dinner," she said. "Maybe I should go."

"No. He's extremely dangerous."

"More dangerous if offended, I should think. Anyway, he knows I'm a personal friend of Hitler's, so I doubt he's any threat to me."

"They sell the exit permits, you know," said Ernst.

"Really? For how much?"

"For more than I have. Anyway, I'm no longer just an anonymous Jew who wants out of the country. If I tried to buy a visa, I'd be asked where I've been living since I was burned out, and they'd find out . . . You don't dare take the matter up with Heydrich. He's treacherous."

"I won't mention you, Ernst," she said. "But I think I will have dinner with him if he asks me. After all, the more powerful friends we have . . ."

"Well . . ." he said. "I might tell you also, it is an element of his reputation that he is an extremely sensual man."

When she came out of the bathroom, Ernst had hot coffee and brandy for her. She had rubbed herself with a towel until her skin was pink, and she wore the gray woolen robe Ernst had worn on *Kristallnacht.* As she accepted the coffee and brandy from his hands, she stood high on her toes and kissed him lightly. He caressed her cheek, then her breast through the rough wool of the robe. They went to the living room and sat together on the couch. She sat close to him, her hip touching his.

They had not slept together. Their intimacy had not yet come to that. It had developed slowly and was still exploratory and inchoate. She was not surprised that she found him sexually attractive—she had always thought of him that way, since the evening when he came to her apartment with his negatives, almost five years ago—but she was surprised that she was emotionally drawn to him, because he was so many things that were alien to her. She was quite unsure of herself. Rationally she resisted the impulse to kiss him and to let him kiss and touch her—and she knew he resisted his own impulse—but emotionally she wanted even more. His warmth was something she had never experienced in anyone before.

He had the chart of Friesland and the North Sea spread out on the table before the couch. "I will want the pistol," he said. "If

I am discovered hiding in the airplane when you refuel, I will need it."

"For what?" she asked.

He shook his head. "I won't be taken," he said. "I won't let them do what they did to my brother."

Nancy shuddered. "Don't even think of it," she said thinly. "We won't go until everything is worked out."

Ernst sighed. He lowered his eyes, and his shoulders slackened. "The risk . . ." he said very quietly. "You are risking your life, Nancy. You could have been killed this morning even."

She touched his shoulder. "Everything will be well planned," she said. "The risk will be small."

"Why should you take *any* risk?" he asked. "How can I let you?"

She stopped her brandy glass just short of her lips. "What is it you want me to say?" she asked. "Anyway"—she sipped brandy—"the decision isn't yours."

The restaurant was on Kurfürstendamm, and it was very small and very elegant. The tables were few, each one covered with a heavy linen cloth and set with antique silver. Candles burned in a complex crystal chandelier; and they, with the candles on the tables, gave the room its only light. The walls were hung with oil paintings in gilt frames—landscapes and eighteenth-century portraits. A pianist and a violinist played in a corner at the rear of the room. Although she knew Kurfürstendamm, Nancy had not been aware of this restaurant, and she had not noticed its name as they entered.

She stood beside Heydrich as he allowed the obsequious maître d'hôtel to take their coats and hand them to the woman from the checkroom. Heydrich was wearing black tie, as were all the other men dining at the tables—with the exception of one Wehrmacht general in dress uniform. Nancy had worn a floor-length black silk dress. It was fluid, and her shoulders were bare except for the four thin strings that held the dress from falling. Heydrich had brought her an exquisite little orchid, a rare variety, yellow with red-brown spots, and she had attached it to her beaded black evening bag.

Everyone looked at them as they stood in the entrance. She

noticed that everyone looked once, briefly, then looked away self-consciously and did not so much as glance at them again. Heydrich, with a cold, regal air, glanced around the room. He offered Nancy his arm and let the maître d'hôtel lead them to their table.

As they passed the uniformed officer, he looked up. "Guten Abend, Herr Obergruppenführer," he said to Heydrich.

Heydrich nodded. "Guten Abend, Herr Generaloberst."

Nancy recognized the man then. He was Walther von Brauchitsch, Commander in Chief of the Army since April when von Fritsch and von Blomberg had been forcibly retired. Helmut had said the SS had had much to do with forcing the two generals into retirement, and maybe Heydrich had been involved. The two seemed compelled to acknowledge each other.

Their champagne was at their table when they arrived there. The maître d'hôtel poured and withdrew.

Heydrich raised his glass. "To the Queen of England . . ."

Nancy raised her glass and nodded. "The Queen," she murmured, surprised at this toast.

". . . which would have been you if His Royal Highness the Duke of Windsor had had the slightest intelligence or taste," Heydrich continued. "The toast is to you, Lady Nancy."

She sipped the champagne. "Few people know about that," she said.

He smiled. "But I do."

"I understand it's your business to have a dossier on everybody," she said.

He nodded. "Everybody."

"Did you find anything else interesting in mine?"

"Only that everyone who knows you finds you as charming as I do."

He may have referred to the puritanism of the Third Reich. She had learned—through experience that was not painful to her but had been to others—that dresses like the one she was wearing were regarded as more than slightly scandalous in Hitler's Germany. Lipstick, indeed, was condemned as "paint" and proscribed for proper Nazi matrons. Helmut had pronounced himself embarrassed by dresses she would have worn without notice in London—or, for that matter, in Berlin five years ago.

She had told Helmut she was English, not a German and not a Nazi, and would dress like a woman of the twentieth century, whichever totalitarian bluenoses disliked it. She knew she was *die Engländerin* not just for her flying but for her independence and feminism, contrary to the standards fixed for the Third Reich by the likes of Heydrich's superior, Himmler.

She took a moment to glance around the restaurant, at the diners studiously keeping their eyes away from the table where she sat with the chief of the SD and SIPO. She wondered where he had learned of her long-ago affair with David. She wondered what more his file—which obviously he had reviewed before tonight—contained about her.

Their meal, it seemed, had been ordered in advance. The appetizer was brought now—delicate meats in garlic butter, not *escargots* but something like that she could not identify: not periwinkles either, but something lighter, probably the meat of some small bird. Whatever it was, it was delicious and was served with respect, not just for Heydrich but for the dish. He watched for her reaction. She measured it carefully. She showed him appreciation, but not too much. She could more willingly have shown appreciation if he had been more subtle in his anticipation of it.

"The stories about your flying don't do you justice," he said. "You are a skilled and cool-headed pilot. Otherwise one or both of us would be dead."

"Thank you," she said. "Your own maneuver was quick and correct, too."

"Why were you flying in such weather?" he asked. "I wonder if it was not for the same reason I was: because flying through lines of snow showers, some of them in patches of sunlight breaking through the clouds, is like flying between the columns of some huge Grecian temple, and, if there is no such thing as heaven, at least you can know the beauty of it." He stopped, grinned. "Or do I assume too much?"

She shook her head. "I often fly for the sheer pleasure of it."

"Ah, I too. I can only be scornful of these—these mechanics of the air who fly and don't see, don't feel." He lifted his glass to her. "You and I are kindred spirits," he said.

As they ate their meal, they talked about the planes they had flown and where they had flown them. He, too, had flown the

Me-109, but he had not flown the Condor. He spoke of mountain flying. He was enthusiastic about the Storch: It was able, he said, to drop into a meadow near a chalet of his in the Bavarian Alps, which made it possible for him to go there much more often. He would like to show her that chalet sometime, he said.

Several times he mentioned things he would like her to share with him. He played the violin and would like to take her to a concert of the Berlin Philharmonic. He fenced and would like for her to see a fencing match, perhaps even one where he took part. He mentioned the Alpine chalet a second time. He said he wanted to show her where the meadow was and how to land and take off there. An assumption threaded through all his talk that this was only their first evening together, to be followed by many more.

He was not an unpleasant dinner companion. He was hand-some. He was the sensual man of which she had been warned—his narrow eyes wandered over her like exploring fingertips; but he was honest and unembarrassed—almost ingenuous, in fact—in his sensuality. She had no doubt whatever that he would ask her to sleep with him. She knew she would refuse, but as the evening went on she decided she would refuse gently. The invita-tion would simply be the expression of another of his enthu-siasms, and she doubted she would be offended. He liked to fly, to fence, to play the violin, and to make love to beautiful women. This was the positive side of his personality. He showed a dark negative in the performance of his official duties, she supposed. Maybe she need not see that side.

The invitation came as they sipped their coffee. "I am most reluctant to see this evening end," he said.

"I am afraid it must," she replied.

He smiled and laid his hand on her. "Not necessarily," he said.

She returned his smile. "I am afraid it *is* necessary."

"Let me assure you of something," he said. He spoke quietly, a little smile still on his face. "Whatever time you and I spend together—whatever we do—no report will go to the Führer."

"That dossier of yours is detailed and complete," she said thinly. She withdrew her hand from beneath his.

"There is nothing ominous in that," he said. "Of course we have a dossier on you. You are a prominent foreigner living more or less permanently in Germany. You fly our military aircraft.

You have personal access to our most important leaders, including the Führer himself. We would be derelict if we did not have a dossier on you." He paused, and his bluish lips turned in a sly smile. "And of course I looked into it. Wouldn't I be oddly deficient of curiosity if I hadn't?"

Nancy sighed. "All right," she conceded. "But I can't be comfortable about it."

"Don't you suppose British Intelligence maintains a file on you?" he asked. His smile disappeared and he spoke crisply. "It is naïve to imagine they don't. So, for that matter, does the Deuxième Bureau in Paris and the GPU in Moscow." He stopped. His smile returned. "So probably does the American FBI." He chuckled. "Even they. I wouldn't be surprised."

"I never thought about it," she said.

He put his hand again on hers. "Think of it as a compliment," he said. "After all, we regard you as someone worth watching."

"Just how closely do you watch me?" she asked.

Heydrich shrugged. "Oh, we don't actually *watch* you," he said. "We just keep track of you. We need to know what kind of person you are, after all."

"What kind of person *am* I, in your estimation?" she asked coldly.

He closed his hand over hers. "You are a very fine person," he murmured intimately.

"Still, one to be watched," she said soberly.

His lips hardened. "A little naïve, too," he said.

"Naïve," she repeated.

He nodded. "Politically."

"I think of myself as apolitical," she said. "German politics, anyway, are none of my business."

"Then you should sever your alliance, if you'd care for a word of advice," said Heydrich.

"Alliance?" she said with a scornful toss of her head. "With whom am I allied, do you think?"

"Mit unserem dickbäuchige Reichsmarschall"—"With our pot-bellied Reichsmarschall"—Heydrich sneered.

Nancy laughed. "That's ludicrous."

"He calls you his protégée. He implies that he sleeps with you."

"He doesn't say that in the presence of the Führer, I venture to guess."

Heydrich's hand remained closed around hers, and now he tightened his grip. "He wanted to make you the Führer's mistress. Fortunately for you, that scheme failed. I say fortunately for you because I doubt you have any idea what it would mean to be the Führer's mistress. He encourages the Führer to remain interested in you. He still has hopes of insinuating you into the Reichskanzlerei. The Führer's gratitude would be only one of his rewards. . . ."

"You are not very well informed, Herr Heydrich."

Heydrich smiled coldly. "Does the Führer kiss your feet?" he asked.

Her jaw dropped. She could not recover before he had seen her surprise and dismay.

"The Führer holds you in high regard, I have no doubt. Fräulein Unity Mitford would sell her soul—or, what's more important, England—to have shared the intimacy you have shared with Adolf Hitler. I am sure the Führer expresses his affection for you in fervent words. Let me assure you that, when he expresses it, he means it. Unhappily, the Führer's love for a woman is not a coin she can spend. He does not love you. Indeed, when he has finished lavishing his love on himself, there is none left for any woman."

Nancy could not conceal her confusion. She shook her head. "That's dangerous talk, isn't it—for you?"

Heydrich shrugged. "I trust you," he said. "I had evidence the other day of your intelligence and courage."

Still holding her hand in his own right hand, now he turned her hand over and began stroking her palm with the fingers of his left.

She sighed. "I didn't suppose," she said, "you invited me to dinner tonight to talk about airplanes."

Heydrich, conscious apparently of at least a minor victory, relaxed. His face softened. "Göring . . ." he said quietly. "Goebbels . . . Hess . . . The old Party fighters, as the Führer calls them. He keeps them around out of loyalty. But their squabbles are petty. Power has passed to others. They are grotesque. Look at the Reichsmarschall! Bloated, drugged . . . Goebbels—a satyric, crippled dwarf. . . . Hess hasn't the brains God gave a mouse. They're not your kind."

"But you are," she said flatly.

He nodded. "I am."

"The 'new man' the Third Reich produces," she said loftily.

Heydrich laughed. "Not at all. There has always been my kind. And their kind. And yours. The question is, do you wish to ally yourself with Talleyrand or—"

"Or Fouché," she interrupted.

"*Talleyrand*," Heydrich insisted. For an instant his newly confident mood was broken. "Talleyrand," he repeated softly, recovering himself.

"And what does Talleyrand want?" she asked.

His forefinger traced circles on her palm. "To take you to bed, of course," he said. "The moment I saw you and knew who you were, I knew I wanted that. But of course I could sleep with a million women. With you, there would be more. An alliance . . ."

"Against the Reichsmarschall?"

"Against the world," he said smoothly. "We will start with him."

Nancy breathed deeply, stiffening her back. "I hear you are the most powerful man in Germany."

"Of course I'm not," he said solemnly.

"But you want to be."

Heydrich shrugged.

She lifted her final glass of the red Bordeaux they had had with their dinner. She stared thoughtfully at Reinhard Heydrich. What Ernst said was true: If he was not the most powerful man in Germany, he might become so. He was younger than most of the top Nazis. He was not an old street fighter, obviously; he bore himself like an aristocrat, even if he was not one; and it was impossible to visualize him in a sloppy brown uniform, bullying Jews on the street. He was a far more subtle man than Hitler. He had depth that Hitler did not have—and to which Göring or Goebbels did not even aspire. It was not difficult to see, too, that Ernst had been right in warning her that Heydrich was the most dangerous man in Germany. He was intelligent. He had courage. He was utterly amoral.

"See them looking at us?" Heydrich said. "In here? Only glances. Furtive. They're afraid of me. But they want to look at you. Think of it—Chief of the SIPO . . . and *die Engländerin* . . . together. They want to stare. And some of them are powerful people themselves. You and I are an interesting combination."

"The Reichsmarschall will know we are together before the night is over," she said.

"Yes," said Heydrich with a grin. "And he'll tremble."

"What will he do?"

Heydrich shrugged. "Eat another chicken. Drink another liter of beer. Take another shot."

She laughed. "You're right. But he'll complain to me."

Heydrich shook his head. "No, he won't."

"Well, that will be some kind of test, won't it?"

He grinned. "Agreed. And tonight. . . ? Will you come with me to a flat I have?"

She sighed. "Not tonight." She shook her head. "No. Not tonight."

"If I call you again in a few days?" he asked. His voice was thinner, harder. His narrow eyes narrowed to slits. "Then . . . ?"

"Then perhaps," she said. "Perhaps. . . ."

❧ X ❧

At 2:00 A.M. on Thursday, December 29, 1938, Nancy and Ernst were wakened by pounding on the door. Ernst was in her bed. He wakened faster than she, and by the time she had sat up and found the little chain to switch on the bedside lamp, he had retrieved Helmut's pistol from its hiding place in a shoe box in her closet and was grimly cocking it. She went to the door. Ernst slipped into a dark shadow in the living room and waited. The man at the door had brought a telegram.

REGRET TO ADVISE FATHER DIED THIS EVENING STOP WILL YOU
RETURN FOR FUNERAL STOP PLEASE WIRE STOP HENRY

She telephoned Helmut. He promised to stop by the flat every two or three days, to bring food for Ernst. He offered a Luftwaffe plane to fly her to London; but she caught an early-morning train for Paris and from there the boat train.

Sir Henry Brookeford, tenth Earl of Edham, lay in state in Westminster Abbey, where his funeral service was conducted on Tuesday, January 3, by Cosmo Lang, Archbishop of Canterbury. At noon the body was placed on a private train at Victoria Station for the journey to Wickstone. It was dark in the church-yard of Wickstone Old Church by the time the body and mourners arrived there and the commitment service could be read. It was read by torchlight, and the coffin was lowered into the grave under starlight. Someone remarked that the Earl would have been pleased that he was buried in a way so much like the old tradition for the Kings of England.

William, Lord Euston, took Nancy's arm as they walked slowly out of the churchyard, along an ancient curving walk, some of the stones of which were eighteenth-century gravestones, frugally removed after they toppled and set in the walk to keep dry the feet of another century's parishioners. "I have been concerned about you," he said softly to her. "Many have been, all week. Can we help you?"

She looked up into his sober, genuinely caring face—now almost obscured in the shadow of a yew that stood between them and the flickering torches around the grave. She nodded. She would accept help.

"I think I want to come home," she said.

"I think you should."

She stopped near the wall of the church. "Look," she said. "The old stones are all worn and stained. Wickstone Old Church. How old? Six hundred years?" She sighed. "I've been living in a stage setting, a vulgar stage setting. You walk around behind, you see the props are flimsy."

"I understand," he said.

"It's what they want: a lot of settings where they can pose and strut. They talk about a thousand years. . . ." She shook her head. "They don't know what a thousand years is."

"You'll be welcomed home."

"I know." She glanced around, at the people huddled in their heavy coats, trudging away from her father's grave, dozens of them who had come from London to be with her family, to show respect, to offer comfort: stodgy, decent English people—in startling contrast to the flamboyant, coarse new men of the Germany she had just left. She sighed. "I've been afraid to be bored," she said quietly.

"We spend most of our lives bored, I suppose," said William. "But not these next few months and years, I suspect. I'm afraid exciting times may be in store for all of us."

Neville Chamberlain stopped. "My deepest sympathy, Lady Nancy," he said.

"Thank you, Prime Minister," she said. "Thank you for all your kindness."

Her eyes followed Chamberlain as he walked on toward the churchyard gate. When he was out of earshot, she looked up at William and said: "The contrast . . . You know what I mean?"

The German Ambassador, Herbert von Dirksen, had attended the funeral at Westminster Abbey. But that had not been enough for Adolf Hitler; he had sent, too, his personal representative, a Wehrmacht colonel named Rommel; and it had been obvious that he had not sent Colonel Rommel as a mark of his respect for the deceased Earl but as a clumsy public token of his affection for the Earl's daughter. She had been embarrassed.

"You need a holiday," said William. "You look tired and—anguished."

They walked on, toward the gate and the automobiles waiting beyond. "I expected my father's death," she said. "I was ready to cope with it. I guess I wasn't ready for the sympathy and warmth I've had from so many people. I've been stunned by it, Willy. You can't imagine."

"I can't imagine you'd expect anything else."

"That's just the point. I've even been scornful, you know; I mean scornful of their English provincialism—more than that, their introversion. But they've been so decent to me this week. It's made me understand, Willy, how damned cruel and vulgar Germany is now. You have to understand, I've admired a lot of what Hitler's done. I've been looking at the surface of it."

"Well . . . you *can* come home," said William.

She wondered that night at Wickstone, where her brother, Henry, had already emphatically assumed his station as eleventh Earl. She had decided, of course, to bring Ernst to England. Looking at her brother, holding his cigarette delicately between two fingers and yet inhaling the smoke deep into his lungs like an addict, looking at her widowed mother and her hugely pregnant sister, she had to wonder how she would present Ernst Leinberg, a refugee Jewish photographer and her lover, maybe even her husband.

It had come to that. They had talked of it. Could they marry? There had not been time to think much about it. Their tentative, almost timid, affection had exploded into passion. They were marked by it. It had been maybe inevitable; it was also maybe temporary—that they had yet to learn. For now it was real, exploratory, intense. She wanted to return to it. She wanted to bring it home to England.

"How many have you seen?" he had asked her after she had gasped at the sight of his penis.

"Only one," she had whispered, staring wide-eyed.

They were lying together in her bed. A winter storm blew outside and rattled the windows of the flat. "It is a token of the covenant between the Jews and God," he said to her, smiling. "You should know that. Don't your English priests teach you anything?"

"God's covenant with Abraham," she said. "I know. I've heard of it since I was a child. I never—visualized it."

Ernst had laughed. "When I was a boy, we heard that Christian girls did not know how to copulate, were never taught, and had to be shown how, at the very last moment."

Nancy had guffawed. "That's true! Absolutely true! How very lucky for you I'm not a virgin."

"How very lucky for you I'm a Jew," he had laughed.

Her eyes had settled again on his naked glans. "How very different, anyway," she had murmured.

How very different they would be. Oswald Mosley, an old friend, was leading an anti-Semitic campaign in London, and she had heard his hoodlums broke the windows of Jewish shops. She could not imagine his being behind anything like that. Yet, it was true; she had heard the tale from too many sources for it to be a lie. Was it a universal, to hate the Jews, or had Hitler managed to export his hatred even to England? She would risk whatever she must risk to help Ernst flee Germany. Would they someday have to flee England, too?

What was it? He *was* different, beyond question. He was different, as Disraeli had been different from Gladstone and Salisbury and Balfour and Asquith. Ernst was different in his odd, Semitic mix of rational and mystic, analytic and passionate, skeptic and believer, European and Asiatic. He was an artist, yet she could see in him the cool calculator of advantage and disadvantage. He was a liberated man, yet she could see on his back a burden he carried, of tradition he could not ignore. It was subtle, the difference. Still, it was real. Henry, the eleventh Earl, would not miss it. Neither would a lot of other people. And she was not confident of how they would receive it.

Was "love" the right word to describe what they felt for each other? Ernst said they could not know, except after a long time. It was foolish, he said, to believe love happened instantly and was irrational. He said he doubted children were capable of it. Only mature people could love, because it was a mature emotion: complex and subtle and lasting. For her it would have been easier to say yes. She had lived in a more romantic tradition. Galsworthy's heroines fell in love, and so did Lawrence's; they did not wait endlessly for emotion to ripen. But that is what he asked her to do.

She was impatient. She wanted to return to him. She wanted to bring him back to England, too; but now she wondered if she should not pass straight through England with him, to America. Americans had no traditions, good or bad, and maybe they could live together there without generating hostility.

Her brother would be a problem. "They're yours, of course, as much as mine," he said to her of Edham House and Wickstone; but she knew he meant to move into Edham House with his wife and children, and Nancy's mother would live there, too. There would be room for her, but Edham House would never be her home again; she would be a guest there from now on. What was more, although Henry assured her he would continue her allowance as her father had done, an allowance from a brother was not the same as one from a father. Henry had made it plain he was head of the family now; and, as her father had cut off her allowance when she went to Germany with Helmut, her brother might do it again if she brought Ernst home as a lover or husband.

The next morning she sat in the conservatory alone, drinking the coffee that Mr. Dunn kept fresh and hot in her cup. William, Lord Euston, had promised to call for her in midmorning, to drive her back to London. She had tried to reach Helmut by telephone, but he was not in at his office in the Air Ministry. She had not dared try to telephone Ernst. She had no illusions about the privacy of a call from England to Germany.

Mr. Dunn stepped in. "Mr. Churchill is here, my lady," he said. "He expresses a preference to see you."

She nodded. "Yes. Bring him in here, please."

"Shall I serve more coffee, my lady?"

"Please."

Winston's face was ruddy, and he was unnaturally hearty, probably from the minute or two he had spent in the bitterly cold wind outside. He took her hand between his—his hands *were* cold. "My deepest sympathy," he said. He sat down in a chair facing hers. It faced, too, the windblown snow outside, a gray, threatening day. He frowned at it. His pudgy body seemed to settle into the shape of the chair that surrounded him. "I hear you're going back to Berlin directly," he said.

"Yes. I have obligations there."

He nodded. "Indeed," he murmured. He clasped his hands on his belly, and one of his fingers toyed with his watch chain.

He was older than she had realized. She remembered being taken to his mother's house in Westbourne Street: a little girl taken to tea with the great lady, Jennie, Lady Randolph Churchill; and somehow, apparently, it had remained in her mind that if she knew Winston's mother, he must be more nearly a contemporary of hers. He was, in fact, well into his sixties, older than her father had been. His sandy hair was thin. His face was lined and jowly. His lower lip was thrust forward of his upper.

"I have been told," he said, "how you tried to communicate with the Prime Minister at Munich."

"Much good did it do me."

He shrugged. "Well . . . an act of loyalty and patriotism may be—amending the cliché—its own reward."

"I wasn't expecting a reward," she said. "But I couldn't make them understand. . . ."

"No more could I," he said glumly. "And so—disaster."

"Yes," she said. "Disaster."

"You know Hitler," said Winston. He nodded. "I am told you know him quite well. Do *you* think Munich saw the last of his demands?"

"I don't know," said Nancy. "I can tell you this: He's a *little* man, ill-educated, unstable—"

"Unstable?"

She nodded. "Mentally unstable."

Churchill frowned over his watch chain for a moment. "Is it an offensive question," he asked, "if I inquire just how intimate you are with Herr Hitler?"

Nancy smiled. "I haven't slept with him," she said crisply.

"Perhaps I should not have asked—"

"I don't mind if *you* ask," she interrupted. "Your motive is better than morbid curiosity, I suspect."

Churchill took a silver cigar case from the inside pocket of his coat and extracted a fat cigar. He held it between two pudgy fingers and then ignored it. "You've heard what *I* think, I'm sure," he said. "I thank God we're building aircraft now, though I know Hitler is building them, too. It remains to be seen which of us will use our time better. I'm Britain's chronic Cassandra, you know; but I tell you, Nancy, within the year we will be at war, and it will be a great, desperate, life-and-death struggle. I'm not certain Hitler himself can prevent it."

"Are you suggesting I should not go back to Germany?" she asked.

"No," he said. He looked up and paused while Mr. Dunn came in and poured coffee. He lifted his cup and watched the butler leave. "I want to suggest the contrary."

"The contrary?"

He nodded. "The contrary. There are those in this country who doubt your loyalty, you know. I have never, not for a moment; but your intimacy with the German Führer and his satraps, your apparent enthusiasm for them, theirs for you—all that combines to raise the vilest suspicions."

"Wicked," she said.

He lifted his brows. "Maybe the really wicked think so, too."

"What?"

"Hitler," said Churchill. He sipped from his coffee. "Maybe he thinks you are more loyal to him than you are to the King. Maybe Göring thinks so. You sent word while the Prime Minister was at Munich, about their aircraft, their capabilities. Someone entrusted you with that information. It was correct, you know. Someone trusted you with a military secret of the highest importance."

"Helmut Bittrich," she said.

"Yes. Has he told you more?"

"I know more," she said.

"Have you made it a point to learn all you can?"

Nancy shook her head.

"If you did, who knows what you might learn?"

"You're suggesting I become a spy," she said in a thin voice, almost a whisper—the idea having struck hard.

"As I told you, I believe we are going to have to fight for our lives," said Churchill. "You can do something immensely important. You may have a unique opportunity."

Nancy put down her cup. She looked away from Winston, out the window at the forbidding snowstorm. Her stomach was stiff; what he was saying had a physical impact. "Who is asking me?" she asked. "Is it the Prime Minister?"

"No. It is I. Only I."

She looked at him. "You're not in the government, Winston."

"If there's war, they'll have to call me. Maybe I'll have the admiralty again." He could not suppress the smile this thought brought. "In any event, I can make the necessary arrangements."

"And what would those arrangements be?"

"Let me be emphatic," he said, frowning. "You should go back to Germany. Live as you have. Cultivate your friendships. Do not do anything different. Do not again call the embassy. Unless you learn something of vast importance, do not attempt to communicate it. Let us contact you. We will set up a way of talking to you. Don't trust to any other way."

Nancy shook her head. "Winston, if war breaks out, I'll be interned, deported."

"Not necessarily. Not if they still think of you as their *Engländerin.*"

"I'll be an enemy alien."

At last he took a lighter from his pocket and lighted the cigar he had until now only turned in his fingers. "When you went to Berlin in 1933," he said, "it was, as I've been told, to marry your distant cousin Helmut. You remain unmarried. General Bittrich remains unmarried." He drew on the cigar, then held it and contemplated it with satisfaction, though whether his satisfaction was with the cigar or his clever idea, she could not tell. "If you were to marry now . . ." He shrugged. "Maybe it's too much to ask."

"It's a great deal too much," she said coldly.

Churchill drew himself more erect in his chair. "We may be in a desperate fight for our lives, for the life of our country, even for the survival of civilization," he said ponderously. "All of us will do what we can, give what we can. Many will give their all."

"You are trying to shame me."

He shook his head. "No. To enlist you."

She lowered her eyes. "I cannot, of course, refuse," she said quietly.

❊ *XI* ❊

The airplane was a single-engine Heinkel, marked with the insignia of Lufthansa but configured like a small bomber. The airspeed indicator read 450 kph, the altimeter 4,000 meters. Heydrich was flying in the left seat, and Nancy sat in the co-pilot's seat to his right. Both of them wore heavy, fleece-lined leather flying suits against the extreme cold at that altitude, and they breathed oxygen from rubber masks strapped over their mouths and noses.

"Gross Glockner," said Heydrich, pointing with his gloved hand toward a mountain directly ahead and no more than 60 or 70 kilometers distant. His voice was metallic and guttural, coming to her earphones through the small microphone strapped to his throat. "Italy," he said.

He was flying south, and the mountains spread out to the east and west ahead of them as far as the eye could see. They rose threateningly to meet the tiny airplane rushing toward them. They were beautiful, exceeding in their unworldly grandeur anything else she had ever seen; but she knew also they were dangerous. Winds whipped long plumes of snow off their crests, sometimes obscuring their sharp lines for as much as a minute. Winds like that, thrown upward by the mass of a mountain or burbling violently over a ridge, could throw an airplane like a ball, wrenching off its wings even. Violent updrafts and turbulence could rise a thousand meters and more above a mountain ridge. Their 4,000 meters was not a safe altitude at which to approach the Gross Glockner. Even so, she stared, transfixed by the cold white beauty that swept from one horizon to the other.

"Salzburg," said Heydrich, gesturing to the left. "Salzkammer-gut. Obersalzberg. Berghof."

She nodded, but she could not hope to pick out Hitler's mountaintop retreat from this altitude. Ahead was the former Austrian border, now meaningless—as had been the Czech border they had crossed twice on their flight south from Berlin. Munich was to their right and behind. All the mountaintops were snow-covered now, in January, but not all the valleys were. Some of the green slopes—black-green with pines and firs—edged sere brown valley meadows on their low sides.

Heydrich pulled back the throttle and began a fast but level descent, turning to the right until the airplane was on a westerly heading. "Ahead," he said.

He was going to show her the mountain meadow where he said he had landed a Storch almost at the door of his Bavarian chalet. He had called two days ago and said he wanted to fly her there, to show her the mountains and his chalet and the meadow, where they could come in the spring when they could land on the grass. He wanted her to see the Alps as they were seeing them now. He would commandeer an airplane they could fly high and fast. They would have time to land for lunch in Salzburg and still be back in Berlin before sunset. His unrestrained enthusiasm on the telephone had not moved her to agree to the flight. She had other reasons.

"There is no more dangerous man in Germany," Ernst had said. His statement had been half fearful, half-sullen. "I fail to see why you insist on seeing him."

Other reasons aside, she had wanted to fly the airplane Heydrich had promised. The Heinkel, although this one was equipped with seats and could fly five passengers, was designed as a reconnaissance bomber. Not only was it capable of flying 450 kilometers an hour, its range was 1,600 kilometers. She could fly Ernst to England on the route she had planned for the Storch—Berlin to Wilhelmshaven, out over the Frisian Islands and the North Sea, to a landfall probably in East Anglia—without a refueling stop and in less than two hours. If she flew solo, it would be easy to sneak Ernst aboard. Even if she could not take the airplane alone, it would not be impossible. She had wanted to familiarize herself with this airplane, to be ready to fly it if she could get her hands on one. And maybe she could explore with Heydrich the possibility of flying a Heinkel 170K2.

"Inn," muttered Heydrich, pointing at a river below.

She nodded.

"Rosenheim," he said.

The altimeter spun steadily backward. They had descended 2,000 meters, and were flying below the peaks of the mountains now to their left. She turned off her oxygen and unstrapped the mask. Heydrich did the same.

"Very few people know I own this place," he said. "It's small. It's my retreat from the world. I wish we could land there today."

The air was rough below 1,500 meters, and the airplane bounced and shook. Heydrich raised the nose and reduced both their speed and rate of descent.

"Tegernsee," he said, pointing to a lake. "Wendelstein." That was a peak. Easing in his throttle, he stabilized the airplane at about 1,000 meters. Even lower peaks now rose above them, and he guided the small airplane through the valleys between them. "The Storch is made for this kind of flying," he said. "You can drop down much lower and really see."

She was uneasy. The air remained turbulent. The airplane pitched in a tangle of winds. She could only hope he knew what he was doing and was not flying them into a box from which a Storch could climb out and the Heinkel couldn't. He expected her to see the landmarks, to be able to fly here someday alone. They passed over villages, over a river in the bottom of the valley. It was remote, picturesque country—not spectacular like the mountain country surrounding the Berghof, but modestly beautiful. Only patches of snow lay in the valley. She could see cows close to stone barns. A man on a bicycle rode along a narrow road.

"Ah!" said Heydrich. He pointed ahead.

At first she could not see what he meant. Then she saw: a small, timbered house built on the high slope of a low mountain, probably not a ski lodge, probably a shepherd's mountain cottage once, converted to a rural retreat by some prosperous later owner. And she saw the landing field he had spoken of. The house sat at the edge of a pine forest, below which there was a mountain meadow, and that meadow was, in fact, just big enough for a Storch to land and take off on ground almost level. It was covered now with shallow snow, with brown grass showing through; but she saw no rocks and no fences, nothing to impede a Storch. A wind sock hung from a flagpole atop the house.

"You see," said Heydrich with intense, almost breathless, enthusiasm. "I've landed even by moonlight—though a few lanterns properly set will serve as landing lights. Under melting snow it's too soft. It's soft just after a rain. Any other time . . . There's room for two planes. You and I can meet here anytime we want. I'll give you a chart."

He shoved in his throttle and lifted the nose, and the Heinkel began to climb.

She liked the way Heydrich flew an airplane—with easy confidence and practiced competence. It was apparent that he was no sportsman flier, that he had taken flying seriously and had applied to it that intensity that so much characterized him. It was obvious, too, that he was proud of the way he flew and had wanted her to see him fly. Climbing out of his mountain valley, he glanced at her and smiled. She could not but return his smile.

When she had returned to Berlin from her father's funeral, she had written a note to Winston Churchill:

Dear Winston,
    Thank you so very much for your kindness at papa's funeral and at the house afterward. I shall not forget the words you spoke to me the morning after the funeral.
    If your young friend does elect to make a visit to Berlin, I hope it will be soon and that he will make a point of calling on me.

Affectionately,
Nancy

In the thought the note would be opened and read before it left Berlin, she had written several more in similar terms, to others who had come to the funeral. In two other notes she mentioned anticipated visits to Germany by mutual friends, and those were real visits, actually anticipated.

She had not mentioned Ernst to Winston. She had not been

able to think things through sufficiently that morning at Wick-stone; and she had not then realized the formidable complication Winston was throwing in the way of her plans to fly Ernst to England. The commitments she had made were inconsistent: to fly a Jew out of Germany, to England, to save his life; and to remain in Germany in the event of war, to serve as an agent of British Intelligence. The inconsistency could be worked out, maybe, if Winston were made aware of it and helped. Otherwise she was faced with a choice, and the choice for now was difficult but definite—she would save Ernst from the certain death the Nazis had in store for him, sacrificing the possibility of serving England in a war that might not happen.

Between her and Ernst, the first ardor had cooled. They were better friends now, capable of loving and quarreling, living to-gether and coping with each other, accommodating each other and stepping on each other, and finding it always not just possible but urgently necessary to forgive. That was love, she told him. He agreed, but he insisted she not talk of love too readily. He was calm and wise—too calm and wise sometimes—and said they could talk of love more realistically when they were in England.

"Love should be happy. I'm afraid it can be a major impedi-ment when you are fighting to survive."

Heydrich landed the Heinkel at Salzburg. An SS car was wait-ing. The driver saluted but kept his silence in front as he drove them up the Mönchsberg to an exquisite small inn high above the city. The inn was closed for the season, but it had been opened for the Obergruppenführer SS. A stiff, proper, gray-haired man—the proprietor, she judged—conducted them to a small suite of rooms where a fire burned in a tiled fireplace and a table was laid for lunch. Heydrich showed her to a bedroom, where he suggested she would find something more suitable to wear for lunch than the rough flying clothes she had worn under the fleece and leather in the airplane. On the bed she found a light-blue silk dressing gown, tasteful and modest enough, and she changed as he had suggested. When she returned to the parlor, she found him—to her surprise—wearing field gray, with the insignia of his SS rank. His staging was exaggerated but probably harmless in midday.

He offered her a glass of champagne, then a toast. "To you, *Engländerin*," he said. "To the most exciting woman in Europe."

She tasted the champagne. It was very old, very dry, the best she had ever tasted. "To the most interesting man in Germany," she said.

Heydrich put down his glass. He stepped close to her, put his hand firmly on her back, and drew her to him for a quick but emphatically erotic kiss on the lips.

They sat down at the table. "I have no commitment to return to Berlin tonight," he said.

"You have to me," she said.

He nodded. His smile was conceded, dry. "Then we must drink sparingly of the wine," he said. "We have a return trip to fly."

She glanced around the room. It was old; the ceiling was low, the windows were leaded, the floorboards were worn. It was also warm, comforting. "You do everything well," she said to Heydrich.

"My lodge is like this, in its small way," he said. "A contrast with the Berghof, hey?"

She nodded. "A contrast. The owners' contrast. But why do you emphasize that?"

"The purpose and glory of the national socialist revolution is to preserve things like this, and the people who appreciate them, from the destructive fury of the Bolshevist mob," he said blandly, as if instructing her in the obvious. "It would be a tragedy if Nazi Philistines themselves destroy what we fight to save from the Bolshevist Slavs and Jews." He grinned. "What an irony!"

"There is that danger," she remarked.

He lifted his champagne. "The good life," he said. "It is always at hazard in a revolutionary period. Art. Music. Literature." He smiled and shrugged. "Good food, good wine, for that matter. It taxes one, does it not, to respect a teetotaler and vegetarian?"

"Could you have made your revolution without him?" she asked.

"No. You couldn't have Christianity without Christ, either; though he's acknowledged the most grim and repulsive element of it. Who'd remember the ugly Jesus after two thousand years if you didn't have warm-lit churches smelling of old stone and incense, where they worship all the friendly saints and especially the Virgin? Who'd think of God, that vague and distant figure? Anyway, we have to save what's worth saving and preserve it through the temporary excesses. You know what I mean."

"What about war?" she asked.

Heydrich shrugged. "Your countrymen must leave it to us to deal with the Jews and Slavs our own way. We'll create a better Europe."

"What would you say," she asked, "if I told you I have a friend who is a Jew?"

Heydrich pursed his bluish lips and regarded her speculatively for a moment. "The Führer's mother," he said, "was treated in her last illness by a Jewish doctor. The Führer regards the man very highly. I myself know Jews I can respect. I suppose there are a few smallpox bacilli that are capable and personable, which we might want to exempt from a general antisepsis; but we would not, I suppose you would agree, elect to allow smallpox to rage unchecked for their sake."

She dropped the subject as the innkeeper and an assistant wheeled in their lunch.

"I have bought you a gift," Heydrich said after they had tasted the oysters. A package wrapped in brown paper was within his reach on a side table, and he picked it up and began to tear off the paper. "I had it delivered here so you could have it over lunch."

He unwrapped and handed her a framed drawing. It was behind glass, on old paper, yellowed and fragile: the pencil drawing of a dark-haired young woman, draped in a diaphanous flowing gown through which her breasts were clearly visible. The young woman was smiling; her teeth showed; and her hair flowed behind her head as if blown by a sudden gust of wind. The drawing had been done by an artist of modest skills. It had the appearance of a study done by some long-ago student in a life drawing class.

"See the signature," said Heydrich.

Smiling quizzically, Nancy shook her head over the faintly penciled signature: "George B."

"George Bachfurt," said Heydrich. "Later the fourth Earl of Edham. A direct ancestor of yours."

"The fourth Earl . . ." Nancy mused. "Yes. I've seen his sketches before. There are some at Wickstone. He was the family collector. He bought the Titian that hangs at Edham House, also of course all the Gainsboroughs."

"The young lady is reputed to have been Lady Hamilton, later the lover of Admiral Lord Horatio Nelson," said Heydrich. "You remember she is supposed to have been for a time a figure model at the Royal Academy."

"Yes . . ."

"She looks like the authenticated portraits of the lady, does she not?" Heydrich asked.

Nancy tried to recall the pictures she had seen of Emma, Lady Hamilton, Nelson's mistress and great love. She could not recall the lady's face, but she smiled and nodded to Heydrich. "Wherever did you get it?" she asked.

"It once belonged to Admiral von Tirpitz," said Heydrich. "It amused the old man to think he possessed a drawing of Nelson's great love with her breasts showing. Your ancestor, you know, lived for some years in Germany before he succeeded to the earldom. The story is that he left his drawings—including this one—with his mistress in Heidelberg when he went home to England to be the fourth Earl, and she sold them for a few pfennigs each to men she thought might find them interesting. He had told her this one was Lady Hamilton, so she held it and sold it for more, many years later."

Nancy stared at the drawing. "It's thoughtful of you," she said. "I am grateful."

"I would like to believe something that is, of course, not true," said Heydrich. "I would like to believe that somehow she bore his child and that you are descended of her as well as of him. I see a resemblance."

"I am flattered, Reinhard," Nancy said softly.

"I'm a romantic," said Heydrich.

He was erotic as well. An hour later, when she was about to return to the bedroom to change back to the flying clothes she would wear on the high-altitude return flight, he seized her before the window and embraced her for a fervent kiss. As he kissed her, he ran his hands over the slippery silk that covered her buttocks, caressing, intimately exploring the valley between them. He fed on her with his kiss, drawing her lips between his and nibbling them hungrily, shoving his tongue then into her mouth and stroking her tongue roughly with his. She prevented his opening the dressing gown by throwing her arms around his neck and pulling him tightly to her. He asked her again to spend the night there with him, and again she refused.

"Maybe another time, Reinhard," she whispered in his ear. "There are so many things to think about."

"I have thought them through, Nancy," he said firmly.

"You must let me think them through, too."

She flew the return flight. Lifting off the southbound runway parallel to the Salz River, she climbed as she followed the river valley until she cleared the crest of the Tennengebirge, then turned left and continued climbing for the altitude at which they had flown from Berlin. The forecast was for clear weather on their approach to Tempelhof, but they would fly over a long, east-west cloud bank between Pilsen and Dresden.

Shortly north of the Danube, those clouds closed under them. Heydrich began to talk to stations within radio range—Nuremberg-Fürth, Chemnitz, Dresden, Erfurt, Leipzig—obtaining repeated assurances that the cloud deck did not extend as far north as Berlin, that they would not have to descend through it to make their approach to Tempelhof. The sun was to their left now, and low. The cloud tops were red. The valleys between clouds were deep purple. Nancy tuned the radio compass to Berlin. The needle wandered for a moment, then settled decisively 10 degrees to the left of the airplane's nose. A wind had blown them a little east of their course. She eased the nose over, pointing it a few degrees to the left of the needle's indication, to correct for that wind. Then she tuned Chemnitz. The needle swung sharply to their left. Good. They were passing to the east of Chemnitz. She tuned Dresden. The needle swung right. So. They were between Dresden and Chemnitz, a little east of course but not much, and only 150 kilometers or so south of Berlin. She slowed the engine to 2,000 revolutions and let the airplane begin a gradual descent.

Heydrich had stared at her as she calmly tuned frequencies and satisfied herself of her position. *"Formidable,"* he remarked, using the French word and using it in the French sense.

"I'd like to fly this airplane to England," she said to him, directly, bluntly.

"Fly it anywhere you wish," he said. He pulled off his oxygen mask. "I'll make it available to you. Call me and tell me when you want it, and I'll see to it that it is serviced and fueled for you."

She pulled off her own mask. "Is it yours?" she asked.

"It is when I want it."

"It is a beautiful airplane," she said. She glanced at Heydrich. He was peering ahead, looking for the lights of Berlin, still too far away for him to see. He did not see her smile. She was thinking. She would deliver Ernst Leinberg to London in the personal aircraft of the Obergruppenführer SS. "I appreciate your offer of it, and I *will* call you. I need to go to England."

"The telephone has been ringing," Ernst told her as soon as she entered the Nestorstrasse apartment. Of course he had not answered it, and the ringing had made him nervous. "Three times. It could be—"

"I hardly think so," she said cutting him off. She did not express the rest of her thought: that the Gestapo could hardly be calling when she was spending the day with Reinhard Heydrich.

Ernst kissed her. "I worried about you," he said. "Was he—difficult?"

"No." She softened and let her body fit itself to his, in the grasp of his arms. She did not feel an erection between his legs, as she had nervously felt Heydrich's when he kissed her the last time in the suite in Salzburg. Ernst held her to himself as if she were a child, not a lover, returned from a threatening day. "I think he is going to help us fly you to London."

"You didn't tell him anything?" Ernst asked anxiously.

"No, I—"

The telephone rang again.

"Ah, Lady Nancy? Freddy Binghamton here." A high young English voice. "Friend of Henry's, you know. I've got a package from your mother. Wonder if I might bring it 'round?"

"When?"

"Now. This evening. In fact, could you have dinner with me?"

"Dinner? No, I'm afraid not. I've just flown in from Salzburg. Perhaps—"

"Well, I could just pop by with the parcel."

"Yes," she said. "Seven? Eight?"

The youthful voice broke into a giggle. "Make it 'alf-past seven, all right?"

"Yes. I shall look for you then."

Ernst stood gaping, reluctant to believe he had heard her invite someone to the flat.

"He says he's a friend of my brother's and has a package sent in his care by my mother."

"Yes . . ." Ernst breathed. "And he could be from the Gestapo."

She nodded. "He could be, yes, and he could be from the SD or SIPO. And what suspicions would I raise if I refused to let a man who says he's from England, bringing a package from my mother, stop by here to deliver it?"

They ate; and while she bathed, Ernst worked through the flat, trying to eliminate the few visible signs that he lived there. By the time the man who called himself Binghamton was at the door, Ernst had taken refuge in the locked bedroom.

Binghamton was as young as he had sounded—a thin, pallid, blond young man, wearing a bright, nervous grin. He shed his houndstooth overcoat and his matching cap and then had to retrieve the overcoat from her closet to extract her parcel from the pocket.

"Ah, lovely flat, charming," he said, glancing around. He rubbed his hands together. "Gets damned cold in the middle of the Continent, doesn't it?"

"Would a little brandy restore you?" she asked. She had put on a bulky-knit white turtleneck sweater and a black skirt. "And coffee?"

"Yes, indeed, and I'll be grateful."

As she was in the kitchen pouring the coffee, she could see him walking around, peering here and there. She thought she saw him shudder and wondered if he was in fact deeply chilled or if he was shaking with nervous tension.

"I should appreciate it," he said when he had taken a sip of brandy, "if you would open the parcel from your mother."

She opened it. Her mother had sent a bracelet of white gold set with small emeralds. It had been her mother's as long as Nancy could remember, and she remembered borrowing it to wear to parties when she was a girl.

"Do you recognize it?" Binghamton asked.

Nancy nodded. Then, suspecting that Ernst was listening at the bedroom door, she said firmly: "Yes, I do. I can't imagine why mother would send it."

Binghamton's eyes settled for a moment on the radio, on the table between the windows. "Would you mind If I switched on the wireless?" he asked.

"Uh—go ahead."

He tuned the radio to a Berlin station playing a Schubert symphony, and he set the volume up. When he sat down again, it was on the couch, directly beside her. "You asked Winston to make a contact immediately," he said.

Nancy grinned. "Now that the bracelet has served to identify you, does mother want it back?" she asked.

"When Winston spoke to you at Wickstone, he said something to the effect that patriotism is its own reward," said Binghamton soberly. "He called himself the English Cassandra."

"Yes," she said. "I believe you're from Winston. I'll talk to you."

"When in future you have a contact, don't acknowledge any of the cloak-and-dagger stuff, such as that bracelet's identifying me. I might have been an SD man, trying a stolen bracelet to see what reaction it would produce. Your first reaction was correct—'I can't imagine why mother would send it.' That's noncommittal. Never commit yourself to a contact until he's established all his proofs, and don't commit yourself even then unless you are entirely satisfied."

She frowned quizzically. "Is it all that grim?" she asked.

"It is for me," he said curtly.

"I see."

"Do you?" he asked. "I don't know if you do or not. I'm not sure—though Winston's confident of you—if you understand what's happening and what you're doing, or if you are just playing a society girl's game. If it remains the latter, Lady Nancy, I urge you to get out of Germany as quickly as you can. You know you're involved with dangerous men. I tell you more: They are vicious. Your name and reputation protect you not at all. They have a thousand secret ways to kill you."

She glanced at the bedroom door. Ernst could not hear what they were saying, not over the music from the radio. She hoped he was calm enough not to burst out, pistol in hand. She sighed. "I have a commitment here," she said. "One to Winston, and another one besides."

"Is there someone in the room behind that door?"

"Yes. But don't worry. He's harmless to you. I'll tell you who he is in a moment."

"Someone you've trusted?"

"No. And I'm not altogether naïve, Mr. Binghamton. I wouldn't have let you say what you've said if you hadn't switched on the wireless. He could have heard through the door. But of course he can't now."

"Who is he?"

"A Jew. His name is Ernst Leinberg. He's a photographer and a very good one. They burned his home and business the night of the broken glass, and I've hidden him here ever since. I have access to a small airplane, and I was going to fly him to London. That was going to be my farewell to my Nazi friends. Then Winston asked me not to leave, but to stay. Now I have to find another way to get Ernst out of Germany. That's why I wanted an immediate contact. I think I have the way. I'll need help."

Binghamton pressed his forehead with the fingertips of both hands, and he shook his head. "Are you in love with this man?" he asked.

"Whether I am or not, I will not let them have him. They would kill him. I have promised to help him."

"Do you put this ahead of the service Winston has asked of you?"

Nancy sighed heavily. "If the Nazis get their hands on this man, beyond question they will kill him. I will not sacrifice his life for the prospect of *perhaps* being able to serve England in a war that may not happen for a year and may not happen at all. Anyway, I think I can do both: fly Ernst out of Germany and return here to wait for the chance to do what Winston asks. But that will require Winston's help."

"I am a messenger boy," said Binghamton coldly.

She glanced again at the door where she knew Ernst was straining to hear at least the tone of the conversation. "I can make a public flight to London," she said. "With their blessing. You'd shudder if I told you who is providing the airplane."

"Heydrich," said Binghamton with a sneer. "We are at least as clever as he is. We keep an eye on what you do."

"All right, Heydrich," she said, her cheeks flushed. "I can fly Heydrich's plane to London. I can arrange to sneak Ernst aboard here. I can take care of that. That's my problem, and I have a solution. I need arrangements at the other end. I want to make a quick, secret stop on an English airfield short of London. I suppose that will have to be a military field. Ernst pops out, and I fly on to London. That's one element of the arrangement. The other is for Ernst to be received, given refugee status—permanently—and settled into a home, with permission to work in his profession, and so on. All this has to be done, of course, with no reference whatever to me. Then I can fly back to Berlin and wait for war to break out."

Binghamton's cheeks were drawn in between his teeth, and he looked at her from under frowning brows. "I will take back the message," he said. He glanced at the bedroom door. "In the meantime, tell Ernst Leinberg to start bathing with *your soap*. If your friend Heydrich visits you here, he may be curious as to why there's an odor in this flat of a soap I doubt very much that *you* use."

❧ *XII* ❧

To be casual: That was the essence of the venture—to seem un-hurried, relaxed, even carefree. Heydrich had come to Tempelhof to bring her a silver-bound thermos of hot black coffee to have beside her in the cockpit during the flight. He showed her how she could drink from the narrow throat of the flask, pushing down her oxygen mask for a moment for the purpose. At the very last moment, he dropped a chilling word.

"I see the little doctor paid you a visit."

Goebbels had come to the flat only last night, Sunday night, to drink brandy and chat. "I thought I wasn't watched," she said archly to Heydrich.

"You're not. *He* is," said Heydrich.

Everything depended on that being true. If he had her watched, then he knew, not just that Goebbels had visited her last night, but that this morning, before daylight, she had driven Ernst to Schönefeld Airfield. He would know also that she had driven Ernst to Schönefeld twice before and had introduced him to the elderly line mechanic she had befriended. The old man believed Ernst was a photographer who took pictures from the air during her flights. That was how she had introduced him, with the unstated implication that he was an intelligence agent who photo-graphed foreign military installations over which she flew on some of her publicized flights. She had left Ernst this morning in a tiny café, where they had taken early-morning breakfasts together four times in the past two weeks so he would be a familiar face there. He was there now, presumably, and in a few minutes he would pay his bill and leave and walk toward Schönefeld Airfield.

Heydrich smiled. "The little doctor is harmless." Then he grinned. "At least I suppose he is. He has been a notorious womanizer at times."

"I used to see him more often," said Nancy. "He is a charming, witty man, and he has never made the slightest improper suggestion to me."

Heydrich offered a hand to help her buckle into the fleece-lined leather flying suit. "What did he talk about, if you don't mind my inquiring?"

Nancy forced herself to smile. "He talked about Bobo Mitford, for one thing," she said. "That might interest you."

"Lady Unity?" asked Heydrich. "Yes, she is called Bobo, isn't she?"

"I've never called her anything else."

"Goebbels's interest?" asked Heydrich.

"He wanted to know if I think she's mentally unbalanced. She follows after the Führer like some kind of daft schoolgirl. The Führer is flattered and listens to some of her talk. Goebbels has a superstitious notion that Hitler ought not to be exposed to people whose minds are off-center."

Heydrich laughed. "And you dined with the Reichsmarschall Friday," he said. "Did he mention me?"

She shook her head. But it was not true. Göring had told her she was making a dangerous error in associating her name with that of Reinhard Heydrich. The Führer would be angry, he had said.

Heydrich walked across the ramp with her, to the Heinkel that was fueled and checked and ready. It was a blustery February morning and she was glad for the flying suit, even on the ground. Ernst would be shivering in the black overcoat she had bought him. The wind drove Heydrich's long field-gray coat around him, and he reached up to settle his cap more firmly on his head. He climbed into the plane with her, even up to the cockpit. He looked at her luggage, strapped down in the cabin by the airport crew. He showed her where the thermos would ride handily on the floor within her easy reach. When she was seated and had reached for the end of her belt, he bent over, lifted her chin firmly with his hand, and kissed her.

"Have a good flight," he said. "Think of me. And come back as soon as possible."

She touched his face. "I am grateful to you for arranging the airplane, Reinhard," she said. "It is a very great kindness."

Heydrich beamed. "Enjoy it," he said, and he backed out of the cockpit.

He closed the door. She looked down and waved at him as' he strode back across the ramp. She fastened her belt and began the engine-starting sequence.

Binghamton had conveyed her message to Churchill very fast, and the response had been immediate. Binghamton met her for lunch and told her everything was arranged at the London end. The government had agreed to political asylum for Ernst Leinberg. She was to land at an RAF fighter base at Manston, near Dover. A car would pull up to the airplane on the runway and take her passenger, and she could be in the air again and on her way to London within two minutes. They would do everything they could to guard her secret.

It would be an easy flight, she thought. She would fly the same direct route over which she had flown the Ju-52s to London, deviating from that course only after she had crossed the Dutch coastline and was over the North Sea. The secret landing at Manston would delay her arrival at Croydon Airport for twenty minutes, not the two Binghamton had suggested, because of the deviation off a direct course; but that could be explained easily, if need be, by an error in navigation, contrary winds, or simply a decision to fly through light turbulence at a reduced speed.

The Heinkel was powered by a Mercedes-Benz engine of 900 horsepower. It started smoothly, and she taxied down the line toward the end of the runway, talking to the Tempelhof tower, receiving a clearance for immediate takeoff. Quickly finishing her final checks, she swung into the runway and took off, west to east.

Climbing only to 300 meters, she turned southeast at the Spree River, then due south where it met the Dahme. Schönefeld Airfield was to her right, and she turned west to set up an approach. Tempelhof was still in sight; and although she knew Heydrich could not possibly see her and know she was heading into Schönefeld, not directly for London, still she felt the Heinkel must be conspicuous and someone on the ground must realize that its approach to this little airfield was wrong. She wondered if Ernst could see her. She had shown him photographs of the Heinkel. She had told him it was marked as a Lufthansa plane, not as a military aircraft. She had told him this morning that she would land west to east. She had told him she would taxi to the hangar line. He could enter the little shop in the hangar, where her old friend the mechanic would be glad to see him, or he could wait between the hangars until he saw the Heinkel taxi up. She was only ten minutes later than she had told him she would be.

She let down the Heinkel's landing gear, turned for the runway, and landed. The plane rolled out, she braked to a stop, and turned into the taxiway. She could see she was attracting more attention than she had hoped. A Heinkel 170K2 was a novelty on this field. It was obviously unexpected. An unscheduled landing by a Lufthansa plane suggested mechanical trouble, maybe an emergency. Half a dozen men collected at the ramp before the hangar line, where she was taxiing. Two policemen at the fence beside the airport office stared fixedly at her. A functionary from the office hurried out, buttoning his coat, and approached.

The functionary opened the door. She looked past him and waved at her old friend. "Wilhelm!" she called.

The old man moved hesitantly to the side of the functionary, deferentially nodding at the man before he responded to Nancy. "Guten Morgen, Fräulein!" he exclaimed.

"Wilhelm," she said. "I just took off from Tempelhof. My gear seemed slow to retract. Maybe just some cold grease. Anyway, could you check the fittings? I'm on a flight to London, and I wouldn't want to skid a fine airplane like this in on its belly."

"Of course, Fräulein," the old man said.

She glanced around the area, still looking past the functionary. She saw no sign of Ernst.

"I'll warm myself in your shop while you look at the gear," she said to the old mechanic. She extended a hand to the functionary and let him help her down to the pavement.

"May I ask who you are and what this plane is and by what authority you land here?" the functionary asked stiffly.

"My name is Lady Nancy Brookeford," she said crisply to him. "The airplane is assigned to me by Obergruppenführer Heydrich. I have landed for a mechanical check and will be taking off again immediately, for London. If you have any questions, you can call him. The Obergruppenführer saw me off at Tempelhof, but he will be in his office shortly."

Ernst was not inside. He was somewhere between the hangars, undoubtedly, reluctant to show himself while so many men stood around the airplane. She leaned against a workbench and watched the old mechanic through a fogged window. The functionary had returned to the airport office—maybe to call Heydrich, but she doubted it. Others drifted away. It would be safe enough for Ernst to emerge by the time Wilhelm had finished.

She found herself weak with anticipation and anxiety. Within five minutes she could have Ernst inside the Heinkel. Within ten they could be out of sight, on their way to England in an airplane so fast it would be almost impossible to track it down and stop them, even if Heydrich learned the truth the minute they took off. She wondered where Ernst could be hiding. She found herself annoyed by his excess of caution. She was looking forward to knowing him in England, where he would not be a fugitive, not constantly under threat of capture and death. How different that would be!

Wilhelm was thorough. She decided to walk out to the airplane. Maybe Ernst was waiting to see her beside the plane. It was inconceivable that he did not realize this *was* the Heinkel, this was their escape plane. When he saw her—

"*Ach, Fräulein,*" said the old man, "I find nothing wrong with your landing gear. Maybe you were right, the cold grease slowed the action. It came down correctly?"

"Yes," she said distractedly. Her eyes searched the hangar area. Ernst . . . What would she do? How would she start to look for him? She looked inside the airplane, thinking he might possibly have gotten inside without her noticing. They would laugh!

Wilhelm was refastening a cover plate. "A well-built airplane," he said. He slapped the aluminum fuselage and nodded. "A beautiful airplane."

"I—appreciate your help," said Nancy. She shuddered.

"It's ready. You can go when you wish."

"Yes . . ."

"This is the day I would fly with you, if you were not going so far," the old man said. "I would like to be away from here for a while. This is a bad day."

"Uh—why?" Nancy asked. She was seized with dread.

"A Jew killed a policeman." The old man nodded toward the hangars. "Not far outside our shop. A good young man, too— father of two pretty little babies. And this Jew shot him dead! Skulking around the airport, probably meaning to sabotage something. Filthy damn Jew!" The old man's voice trembled and he shook his head. "The boy's name was Albrecht. He would stop by and drink my coffee sometimes. A good young man . . . *Damn Jew!*"

"Did they catch the Jew?" Nancy asked hoarsely.

"They took care of him all right! Shot him full of holes!"

Nancy's knees weakened. She braced herself against the airplane, touching the fuselage with her bottom and shoulders. She controlled her voice rigidly. "What kind of looking fellow was this Jew?" she asked.

The old man shook his head. "We only saw the body from a distance. His face was down, in the snow. Black overcoat. Black hat. They tossed the body on the trash truck. Which was right. It wasn't a man. Not even an animal. Just a damn filthy Jew! Oh, it's lucky for you, fräulein, it was all over before you landed."

Level at 4,500 meters, she could fly with the throttle almost fully advanced, and the Heinkel exceeded its rated maximum speed. Her tears froze at the edge of her oxygen mask.

Last night, beside her in bed, he had caressed her and nuzzled her neck and cheeks and told her he loved her and that she was his salvation. She had not told him she was committed to return to Germany, to await the outbreak of a war, to serve England as a spy. He talked about the studio they would open and the work they would do together. They should move on, to Canada or the United States maybe, he said. He would do portraits. He would do hers. He would do her nude. He wanted to photograph her nude, against the background of a woodland stream in Canada, he said. He wanted to photograph Winston Churchill, who he said had a fascinating cherubic face. He wanted to photograph her friend Franklin D. Roosevelt. It was an interesting fate life had dealt him, he said, to give him in his middle age a woman who proved to be a mover of mountains and the friend of minor gods and major demons. He would thank the gods by loving her.

The dead policeman, Albrecht, was only perfunctorily a Nazi, Wilhelm had gone on to say. He only did his job; and when he found a Jew in a Jew's long black overcoat sneaking onto the grounds of the airport, he had challenged him. Or apparently that had been the way it was. And the Jew had pulled a pistol and shot him. Others, with Schmeisser machine pistols, had shot the Jew to pieces.

He had killed the policeman with Helmut's pistol. He had looked like a Jew to Wilhelm because he was wearing a long black overcoat. If she had bought him a gray overcoat, maybe he would be alive.

His negatives were in her luggage. She had saved *them* at least. Last night she had watched him as he packed them between her dresses and underwear—holding some of the negatives up to the lamplight and murmuring over them. He had talked about an exhibition in London, of his best work. That would introduce him to England, he said, and show the English she had not just brought out a worthless refugee Jew. It would be again as it was before '33, he said. "There may even be people who remember my name," he had said. He had shown her a negative—a picture, as nearly as she could tell, of a ballerina dancing on a rooftop, through a tangle of clothes drying on lines. It had won a prize in London, he said.

What choice had she but to fly on to London? How would she explain a decision not to go on? Helmut's life, too, was at hazard if they connected her with the Jew shot to death at Schönefeld Airfield. She had staggered up to the cockpit. She had lifted off Schönefeld almost blind. By the time she leveled off at 4,500 meters, Hanover was clearly in view ahead of her. The Heinkel was flying at least at its maximum rated speed, and the North Sea was only an hour ahead of her.

She wept. No one could hear. She wiped the tears with her gloves, but they froze on her cheeks and reddened her skin. She let herself shudder and sob. The Heinkel wandered off course and altitude. She jerked her corrections. She was not sure she cared if she landed or not. A plunge from this altitude would be a quick, dramatic death.

Flying at 400 kilometers per hour, she was inside a long silence. Her earphones deadened the sound of the engine. The world outside was an unreal picture of dead-white blue sky and black-and-white earth, separated by a vague gray horizon. It was a proper place for lonely anguish. It was not until she passed over Osnabrück that she activated her radio and called Enschede to advise the Dutch she would be overflying Dutch airspace. The Dutch voice on the radio acknowledged her transmission and gave her the Enschede barometric pressure. She adjusted her altimeter. He had wanted to have children. He said his brother had had none. The Nazis, he said, bred large families, as a matter of duty, and indoctrinated all their children with the Nazi catechism. It was her duty, and his, to have children. It was the duty of civilized people, lest the proportion of beasts in humanity grow out of bounds. When she said she was not certain she wanted to bear children as a matter of social policy, he laughed and asked her if she would bear them out of love.

With the airspeed indicator showing 450 kilometers, she crossed Holland in less than thirty minutes. Over Rotterdam she turned 10 degrees south and retarded the throttle to initiate a descent. She made a long shallow dive across the North Sea, to descend 3,500 meters by the time she made her English landfall. The airplane steadied in the dive at a speed of 520 kilometers per hour. The English coastline was in sight twenty minutes after Rotterdam. Nearing the coast, she could see she was approaching Ramsgate, not Dover, and she turned another 10 degrees south. Descending to 750 meters, she followed the coastline, spotted the landmarks Binghamton had described for her, and, turning inland, shortly identified the RAF base at Manston. She kept radio silence. Binghamton had told her the RAF would know when she neared the English coastline, and the field would be cleared for her. It appeared to be. She saw no traffic in the air. The runway was open. She lined up and made a straight-in approach. When she was very low and close, she saw a black automobile dash out on the taxiway and stop at the edge of the runway.

Binghamton drove the car. He sped down the runway after her and pulled up alongside the Heinkel when she stopped. He was at the door when she opened it.

"Ernst Leinberg is dead," she told Binghamton. She knelt in the doorway and spoke dully. "I failed. They shot him when he tried to get onto Schönefeld Airfield."

"Did they associate him with you?"

She shook her head. "Apparently not," she told him, raising her hoarse voice to be heard in the wind and over the sound of the idling engine. "They didn't try to stop me."

Binghamton frowned thoughtfully. He stood in the melted snow on the Manston runway, wearing once again his houndstooth overcoat and cap and once again looking immature and purposeless. "Well . . ." he said hesitantly. "Fly on to London. Act out your cover story. Someone will be in touch with you."

It was curious to see how two men could smoke the same cigars and drink the same brandy in the same company after the same dinner—and the one appear conspicuously the shallow, self-centered ass and the other the confident statesman. Her brother had been told that Winston Churchill would come to Edham House for dinner, probably bringing associates with him, to discuss European events with his sister. He had been told he should find dignified reason to retire from the dinner table at a proper moment, affording Churchill and his associates opportunity to discuss European affairs with Lady Nancy. Henry sucked on his cigar like a child sucking a rubber nipple, glancing every moment at Churchill and, between those glances, at the two men who had come with Churchill: Sir Horace Wilson and Alfred Duff Cooper. Churchill savored his cigar and his brandy—heavy-lidded, relaxed, patient. At length Henry reluctantly led his wife and two other couples, their friends, from the table and the room, leaving Nancy with the men who had come to talk with her.

"The Prime Minister," said Sir Horace ponderously, "asked me to tell you how sorry he is that your friend Mr. Leinberg was killed."

"Thank you," said Nancy very quietly.

"To which let me add my personal sympathy," added Sir Horace.

Nancy nodded. She could let these three men see she was mourning the death of Ernst Leinberg; her family did not know why she spent hours alone or why she kept her face and voice tightly controlled. "I am grateful for all that was done," she said, glancing into the eyes of each man.

Sir Horace Wilson was Neville Chamberlain's confidant. He served the Prime Minister with steely devotion, and she had no doubt that the government's agreement to offer political asylum to Ernst had been arranged by Winston through Sir Horace— with his knowledge and acquiescence at least, if not with his support. He was an undistinguished small gray man, but he was shrewd and unprincipled in his devotion to Chamberlain. Chamberlain relied on him.

"Sir Horace knows what I have asked you to do," said Winston.

"Alfred knows."

"The Prime Minister knows," said Sir Horace.

"And that is enough," said Duff Cooper.

She had known Alfred Duff Cooper since she was a girl—and his beautiful wife, Diana. He had resigned from the Chamberlain government in protest over Munich. He was a handsome man, with a small brush of moustache. She was surprised to see him here with Wilson. They could not be friends.

"You've had telephone calls from Germany since you have been in London," said Sir Horace.

"Yes," she said. "Hitler, Heydrich, and Helmut Bittrich."

"Does Bittrich know about Leinberg?" asked Winston.

"He knows every bit of it," she said. "Including the fact that Ernst was shot and killed at Schönefeld."

"Is he satisfied that they have made no connection between you and Leinberg?"

"Apparently—from all he could say on the telephone. He asked if I was all right and when I expected to return. He would have warned me somehow if I were in any danger on returning."

"You've that confidence in him?" asked Duff Cooper.

Nancy nodded.

"And Hitler?" asked Sir Horace.

Nancy looked at him for a moment. "Doesn't British Intelligence listen to a call like that, Sir Horace?" she asked. "Don't you really know what Hitler said to me?"

Sir Horace raised his chin high. "I assure you, Lady Nancy, the government does not intercept and eavesdrop on private conversation."

"Perhaps then you should," said Duff Cooper.

"Herr Hitler," Nancy interjected forcefully, heading off an argument, "called simply to compliment me on a quick and successful flight and to urge me to return to Germany soon."

"Heydrich?" rumbled Churchill.

"Heydrich . . ." she said. "Heydrich wants me to accept his invitation to establish an intimate relationship. He provided the airplane. He telephoned to say—friendly things."

"A ruthless, highly dangerous man," said Duff Cooper, shaking his head.

"Yes," she said. "And possibly the one most likely to produce useful intelligence for us."

"Why so?" asked Sir Horace.

"He's privy to everything," said Duff Cooper. "He's their chief of counterespionage."

"He's a satyr," said Nancy. "He utterly slavers for me, and both his reserve and his judgment may be overcome by his lust."

"Well . . ." said Sir Horace with a nervous grin. "We could, I should judge, hardly ask you to . . ."

"You've asked me to marry," she said, glancing at Winston.

"What?"

Churchill spoke. "Yes. I have suggested she marry Generalmajor Bittrich. It is understood they have the necessary relationship already. As his wife, she could remain in Germany after the outbreak of war—with a reason and not as an enemy alien. Bittrich is highly placed in the Luftwaffe—"

"Air Ministry," Nancy corrected him.

"But is he—would he betray them? Become loyal to us?" asked Sir Horace.

"No," said Nancy.

"But he affords you contacts," suggested Duff Cooper.

"I have my own contacts," she said. "Better ones."

"Such as Heydrich," said Churchill.

She nodded. "Such as Heydrich."

Duff Cooper spoke. "I have spent some time," he said, "since I left the Admiralty, considering what intelligence resources we need for the coming war. What we have"—he nodded toward Sir Horace—"is terribly inadequate. We must build. We must recruit. You have unique contacts, Lady Nancy. You have their confidence. You have an opportunity to be of great service."

"At great risk," added Sir Horace. "But I am authorized to say that if you elect to remain in Germany in the event of war, your apparent treason will be understood by the government. After the war, we will do what is necessary to restore your reputation.

During your service, we will do all we can to—to preserve your safety. We will do everything we can to—"

"To exploit you," said Churchill. "That may as well be understood."

"Oh, I—" stuttered Sir Horace.

"It must be understood," said Churchill, thrusting his lower lip forward. "You have extraordinary contacts with the Nazi leaders. We must exploit those contacts. They can become more important than your survival."

"Oh, I *say!*" protested Sir Horace.

"Let us be realistic," Churchill insisted.

Duff Cooper nodded emphatically. "Intelligence agents are always in danger. And sometimes their lives must be sacrificed for their country, as the lives of soldiers are sometimes sacrificed. It would be foolish to enter this kind of service without understanding that."

"This assumes there will be war," said Sir Horace Wilson. He grimaced. "There may be none."

Duff Cooper shrugged. "A different question. But we are building our defenses now, on the assumption there *will* be war."

"Assumption . . ." muttered Sir Horace scornfully.

"I think there will be war," said Nancy suddenly, forcefully. "And maybe I know more about it than any of you."

"Hear, hear," said Duff Cooper quietly.

"I sent you word at Munich, Sir Horace," she said, "that Germany was incapable of mounting an air attack on England. It still is."

"The Heinkel in which you came here," said Duff Cooper, "flew all the way from Berlin without refueling and landed with its tanks still one-third full."

She smiled. "You checked. I'm pleased. You understand, too, it's a bomber. They can refit it as a bomber in twenty-four hours. But it would carry only a very small bomb load, and they have only a few of them. Their chief bombers still could not fly much beyond the English coast and return to Germany. It will be two years before they have a bomber that can fly from, say, Wilhelmshaven, bomb English cities, and return. They may not have them then. Hitler places little emphasis on developing long-range bombers."

"If they seized airfields in Belgium or Holland, a hundred or two miles closer, it would make a world of difference," said Churchill.

Nancy nodded. "Yes, certainly."

Sir Horace smiled. "Assuming the French and Belgians and Dutch could not defend their own airfields," he said. His smile widened. "If they acquire an airfield at Calais, they could bomb Cornwall."

Duff Cooper glowered. "Knowing they couldn't, you nevertheless made the Munich concessions."

"We didn't know," said Sir Horace. "Lady Nancy's information came too late and, besides, contradicted what we knew from other sources."

"If you won't believe what I tell you, why should I risk my life to spy for you?" asked Nancy.

Sir Horace lifted his brandy. "Another time we will take you more seriously. Far more seriously." He studied the back of his hand as if he did not want to meet her eyes. "The Prime Minister will take you very seriously. He joins these two gentlemen in asking you to undertake this mission."

"You must have your own motives," said Duff Cooper.

Nancy nodded. "I am as much a patriot as anyone," she said softly. "Also, I have learned to hate. . . ." She stopped, shook her head.

"They killed the man you loved," suggested Duff Cooper quietly.

She shrugged. "I did love him," she whispered. "I don't know how much; I don't know what would have happened between us if I could have brought him to England. I know he was a fine, gentle man, and they wanted to kill him—for no reason. He was an artist. He was an intelligent, sensitive man; and all they could think of was to kill him because he was a Jew." She touched the tear below her eye. "We *must* stop them. Some way—we must confront them and destroy them. I—I am ready to do what *I* can."

✖ XIII ✖

She expected some form of training in intelligence work. She received none. She expected detailed instructions. She received none beyond what she was given by Churchill and Duff Cooper and Wilson over her brother's dining table: to do all she could to solidify and if possible to deepen her relationship with Hitler, and to wait for instructions. She spent only three days in London and flew the Heinkel back to Berlin, still in February. She saw neither Hitler nor Heydrich during the next three weeks. On March 15, Germany occupied Bohemia and Moravia, the remaining provinces of Czechoslovakia. She saw Hitler a week later, over a candlelit dinner for two at the Chancellery. She told him over that dinner that she had accepted Helmut's proposal of marriage. He was very pleased. She did not see Heydrich until the first week in April, in Munich.

"Besides being the cleverest woman in Europe, you are breathtakingly beautiful," Heydrich said to her, stopping as he crossed the room toward her, drawing back his shoulders, and settling on her an intent, unembarrassed stare.

She was naked. He had walked boldly—no one would have dared oppose him—into the closed studio of Adolf Ziegler, where she was posing for the nude portrait Hitler had so long begged of her. She sat on an antique chest Ziegler had draped with a length of deep red velvet, holding a pose Ziegler said the Führer had specifically asked for—leaning a bit to the left, with some of her weight supported by her left hand resting flat on the top of the chest, her body twisted a little at the hips, her right leg and foot extended to the floor, her left leg bent at the knee and crossed behind her right, her right hand loosely draped over her right leg. The pose was wooden and somehow subtly modest; yet it displayed every intimate part of her front-on. Ziegler said the Führer had admired this pose in another painting of his.

Heydrich, smiling and nodding, stood at the foot of the small wooden platform on which she posed. Ziegler rushed forward with a chair for him, and Heydrich sat down—close to her, close enough to talk to her without Ziegler, back at his easel, hearing.

"I was supposed to have complete privacy for this," she said.

"I'll leave if you want me to," said Heydrich.

She shrugged. "Just don't stare."

He glanced at Ziegler, who was painting busily, holding one brush in his mouth, another in his hand. "It's shrewd, what you're doing," he said quietly to her. "You change so many things—at a stroke."

"Maybe I have personal reasons," she said.

"Of course you do," he said sarcastically. "All the benefits are only fortuitous."

"I *do* have personal reasons, Reinhard," she said. "I couldn't do it otherwise."

"I won't inquire in what proportions personal and practical considerations are mixed," he said. "I am a little curious about the motives of Generalmajor Bittrich. Is he looking for ways to squirm out from under Göring's thumb?"

"No," she said. "No, not at all."

"He will remain loyal to the Reichsmarschall?"

Her pose required her to stare at Ziegler—at the back of the canvas on his easel, actually. She turned her head for a second, to glance at Heydrich and smile. "Well . . ." she conceded. "He is thinking only in indirect terms, you should understand."

"He's not thinking of me?"

"No, not yet. It would be premature for me to raise that subject with him until—"

"So," said Heydrich. "Your judgment is probably right. All he's thinking, then, is that marrying the beautiful *Engländerin* will raise him a notch in the estimation of the Führer."

"He has personal motives, too, damn it."

Heydrich laughed. "Of course. Forgive my cynicism. I am so intrigued with the political consequences of this marriage that I do overlook the romantic aspect." He touched his chin with his finger, and his eyes narrowed in a slight, thoughtful frown. "You are not, I suppose, suggesting this is one of the great romances of 1939."

"I am not marrying a man I do not love," said Nancy stiffly.

"No, no, of course not," said Heydrich, briskly dismissing the subject. "Neither did my wife." He rose from his chair and walked to the other side of the model platform, where he stood for a moment with his head cocked, eyeing her from that angle. "You have pleased the Führer immensely," he said. "He likes you, but it troubles him to be seen as too close a friend to an unmarried woman. The wife of a Luftwaffe general—ah, that's another thing altogether. You will see the Führer a great deal more often in future." Heydrich returned to his chair. "I must say, I am surprised you have consented to pose for this—uh, portrait."

"The Führer wants it," she said. "He has asked me for it several times, and his last request was very close to a demand." She turned her face toward Heydrich. "If I'm marrying a German and becoming a citizen of the Reich," she said with mock ingenuousness, "I can hardly continue to refuse a request of my Führer, can I?"

Heydrich laughed. "Nor would you want to refuse the very special status it gives you with him. When I called you the cleverest woman in Europe, I did not exaggerate."

Nancy raised her voice. "How much time, Herr Ziegler?" she asked.

"Another five minutes to a break, gnädiges Fräulein—unless you want to take a break sooner."

"No. Thank you." She lowered her voice and spoke to Heydrich. "Seriously, I was under some pressure to pose for this painting," she said. "I could have refused, but . . ." She shrugged.

"Göring, too, is pleased that you are marrying Bittrich," said Heydrich quietly. "He has described it as a reaffirmation of your loyalty to him."

"If he believes that, he is more naïve than I think he is."

"He doesn't believe it, of course. But you should understand his star is rising since he played so prominent and successful a role in frightening old man Hácha into surrendering the remainder of Czechoslovakia without a fight. He—"

"It's well for him that he did," she interrupted. "The Luftwaffe was grounded by weather and could not have helped the army if the Czechs had resisted. What of his star if the Wehrmacht had had to fight its way to Prague with no air support? They've failed to develop all-weather abilities."

"Bittrich told you this?" Heydrich asked with cautious skepticism.

"Each time there's a possibility of war, the Luftwaffe staff quakes with fear—fear that the Führer will call on the Luftwaffe and learn how weak it is." She glanced at Heydrich and raised an eyebrow. "I suspect the Reichsmarschall's star will fall rapidly if there is war."

Heydrich's narrow stare was chilling. She looked back toward Ziegler as her pose required. Heydrich remained silent for too long; probably she had said too much. She had decided to tell him what she learned from Helmut and could not communicate to England—to strengthen a bond that could in time become more valuable than her bond to Hitler. Obviously it involved risk.

"There will be war," said Heydrich flatly.

She glanced at him again. He was staring, as she had asked him not to do, visibly aroused by her nakedness. She could see his blue eyes darting up and down, stopping on her pubic hair, then on her breasts, then on her belly and hips.

"I will take a break now, Herr Ziegler," she announced, and, so saying, stood and stepped off the platform. She picked up her robe from the screen behind the platform and pulled it around her.

"May I offer coffee?" the artist asked.

"No, thank you," said Heydrich coldly. He had stood and was beside Nancy. He touched her lightly with one hand. "Will you let him paint a second picture? For me?" he asked her.

She shook her head. "No."

She walked around Ziegler and looked for a moment at the painting. It was glossy, photographic, bland. She walked on across the studio and sat down on a small, tattered couch, near a tile stove that radiated warmth. Heydrich followed. Ziegler painted busily, and they were beyond his earshot.

"You've been in Prague?" she asked Heydrich.

"Yes. All is peaceful there."

"The Führer asked me how England would react to his taking over Bohemia and Moravia. I told him England would do nothing."

"Except to place new emphasis on its armaments-building program," said Heydrich. "England is preparing for war."

She had known two weeks before the Wehrmacht crossed the frontier and took the remaining provinces of Czechoslovakia that it was going to happen. She could not communicate it back to Churchill. Her instructions were to live quietly in Germany, prepare the Germans for her feigned defection when war came, and do nothing to cause them to suspect she might become the most important British intelligence agent in the Third Reich. When her instructions came, they would involve a vital mission, not merely the gathering of intelligence that England might obtain from other sources. She might not receive her first contact for several months.

Helmut had repeated his proposal of marriage immediately on her return. She had accepted with troubled conscience. He was a good man. He had risked his life in the Ernst Leinberg matter. If the Gestapo had discovered the *Engländerin* was hiding a Jew in her flat, then they would have discovered, too, that Generalmajor Bittrich went there when the *Engländerin* was away and brought the Jew food. The pistol with which Ernst shot the policeman had been supplied by Helmut. He had telephoned her in London and given her the signal they had arranged, to tell her no one seemed to suspect her of trying to fly a Jew out of Germany. When he urged her to return to Berlin as soon as possible, she could hear in his voice more than sympathy. When she returned he showed her more than sympathy. She did love him—but equivocally. The thought that he deserved better than a equivocal love and an equivocal marriage drew her closer to him. Churchill had understood what her feelings might be. He had talked with her alone for a while. The senseless death of Ernst Leinberg, he had said, was only one of many—and of God knew how many more to come, until Hitlerism was eradicated. Her commitment was not just patriotism, he said; it was a commitment to humanity. She believed that. Still, it hurt her that she was subjecting Helmut to a profound betrayal.

She stepped up on the platform again, tossed her robe over the screen, and sat down on the chest to resume the pose. Heydrich stood behind Ziegler for a moment, critically eyeing the painting; then he returned to the folding chair at the edge of the platform.

"Has the Führer ever seen you naked?" he asked.

She gave him a hard glance and shook her head.

"Uhmm . . ." He nodded.

The question was not casual or fortuitous, any more than Heydrich's presence here was a coincidence. He had learned, somehow, that she had consented to pose nude for Ziegler; and, satyr and voyeur that he was, he would have been here if he had been compelled to move a mountain out of his way. He had been denied until now a view of her sleek, boyish body; and now that he had come to see it, his appreciation was embarrassingly evident. He cocked his head now, studying with a practiced eye. There was not a gram of excess on her. She was not thin, as David's new wife, so-called the Duchess of Windsor, was thin; she was fully fleshed where she should be, but there was no place on her where two fingers could have pinched fat. Her mother was the same way, and so was her sister, and many women envied them.

"I flew over my mountain house the other day," he said. "The landing ground is soft now, but in two weeks it won't be."

"I'd hate to hear you had broken a stork's leg," she punned.

"Maybe Bittrich will give you his Storch for a wedding present. Or, if he won't, maybe I will. Better yet, maybe the Führer will."

"That would be a test of your influence with the Führer, Reinhard," she said. "If *he* gives me a Storch, then I'll know you can do anything."

"And if he does, you will fly it to my mountain meadow and spend a spring weekend with me, hmmm?"

"A new bride, betraying a new husband so soon . . ." she laughed brightly. But she glanced at him and saw Heydrich's face, grim and pallid. She drew a deep breath and looked away from him, staring again toward Ziegler as was her pose. She tightened with a sudden dread knowledge that in fact Hitler would give her a Storch. Heydrich would arrange it. She had set him too easy a test. "If he does," she said quietly, "I will test my mountain-flying abilities."

Her marriage to Generalmajor der Luftwaffe Helmut Bittrich was witnessed by Adolf Hitler, Hermann Göring, and—to her surprise—Heinrich Himmler. It was a quick civil ceremony, before an obsequious Nazi functionary at the Registry Office. Himmler took the occasion of the ceremony to present his gift: a silver saltcellar and silver bread dish, heavier and more valuable versions of the gifts presented to every SS officer and his bride, symbols of domesticity and purity. At the wedding party given by Hitler that evening at the Chancellery, Göring offered his gift: a silver-gray Mercedes sedan; and Hitler presented his: a Fieseler Storch, a Luftwaffe airplane to be at the personal disposal of Frau Bittrich.

Hitler found occasion to lead her away for a moment to his private quarters. He showed her the nude of her by Ziegler, hanging in his bedroom and enclosed as he had promised inside a wooden case, like a shrine, which only he could open, with a tiny key. In public she now called him *Mein Führer*, which she had never called him before; but when they were alone, he asked her to promise always to call him Wolf in private and always to think of him as Wolf, who loved her.

At the wedding dinner, he toasted her with champagne—for him a rare sip of alcohol—and presented her with the gold-silver-and-red-enamel medallion representing the German National Prize for Art and Science, for "her many accomplishments in dramatizing to the whole world the power and glory of German aviation." Then he announced the promotion of her husband to the rank of Generalleutnant.

Even the candles on their table were red, with black swastikas in white ovals. Hitler wore white tie and tails. Goebbels spoke at length on *die Engländerin*, an English aristocrat who had chosen to become a citizen of the Third Reich. She had in her evening bag her brother's telegram announcing he was cutting off her allowance from the family estate. Helmut beamed and only twice did she see a flicker of troubled doubt on his ruddy face. When Hitler

announced the promotion to Generalleutnant, she saw Milch
wince, and she saw that Helmut noticed, too—it had not been
within Milch's organization plan. Heydrich did not appear. The
British Ambassador, though invited, did not come either.

They spent their wedding night in a suite in the Adlon Hotel.

"Do you remember," Helmut asked her softly when they were
in bed together and the lights were dimmed, "the first night we
spent together, in a hard, narrow bed in my little room in that
squalid *pension*?"

"In 1932," she whispered. "Of course I remember."

"You were my bride that night," he said. "More than you are
now."

She put her head on his chest and wept.

She had had her first contact from MI-6. Walking in the
Tiergarten, she had been approached by an elderly man, who had
spoken quickly, nodding all the while as if palsied, and had
shuffled off before she could speak a word to him. "That your
commitment has gone so far as marriage has been noted and
appreciated," he had mumbled. "Cultivate Heydrich. Heydrich is
corruptible."

"Cultivate Heydrich." She could hardly, then, refuse his invitation to fly her Storch south for an Alpine weekend with him.
Flying a Storch, you saw the country. She kept between 500 and
1,000 meters above the landscape, flying only 160 kph. South of
Berlin she began to see yellow-green in the groves of trees—the
new buds. Helmut was in Dortmund and Düsseldorf for the weekend, inspecting aircraft factories with Milch. She was flying to
Munich—where actually she would only refuel before taking off
again for the Tegernsee and Heydrich's mountain house.

Even without that word from London, she might not have
found it possible to avoid this weekend with Reinhard Heydrich.
It was likely that his influence extended even to Milch, that Milch
had required Helmut to accompany him to Dortmund and Düsseldorf at the suggestion of Heydrich. She had let him come too
close. To turn him away now would make him a dangerous
enemy.

It was more difficult to find Heydrich's landing field than it was
to land. It was only after she had flown up and down mountain

valleys for half an hour that she spotted his Storch, pulled up near the house. As she floated low over the field, checking the surface and the wind sock, she saw him on the terrace, waving. In a gray turtleneck, black breeches, and boots, he was an imposing, handsome man.

They spent the weekend alone. He had flown in champagne in his Storch—champagne and brandy, *escargots* and pâtés, fruit and cheese and bread. . . . The house had no electricity, no running water, and no heat except for the fire he kept burning in the stone fireplace in the main room. A heavy old couch faced the hearth, and Heydrich had covered its cracked leather with layers of field-gray army blankets of coarse, scratchy wool. It was there, in that nest of blankets, in the glow of warmth and light from the wood fire, shielded from drafts by the high back and arms of the couch, that she consented to put aside all her clothes—indeed, to let him carry them away to the bedroom—and to sit naked while they sipped champagne and nibbled of the food, talked and laughed, and while he played his violin for her. It was there, too, later, that she let him satisfy himself with her.

She had flown here knowing she would have to let him do it: determined to let him do it. She had come determined also that she would not be aroused by him.

She might not have flown here if she could have imagined how it would be. Never before had she been physically manipulated and used by a man, and never before had her body taken such an onslaught of brute energy. At first she was afraid he would hurt her, but to her horror she felt her body responding to his plunging, jarring vigor—responding as she did not want it to, and more than she wanted it to. What was more, he did not hurt her; he only exhausted her as he exhausted himself, and unwillingly she partook in some measure of the wet satiation in which he lay afterward. He whispered to her that she was as good at this as she was beautiful and shrewd. She did not answer. She lay silent, filled with the thought that this was only the first time and that he would expect to do this again and again indefinitely.

In fact, he did it to her again, less vigorously, before he picked her up and carried her to the cold bedroom and the cold bed.

If it had been her mission to kill Heydrich, she could have done it easily. Even the escape afterward would have been easy. He slept so soundly he was vulnerable. She tested him. She rose in the night and left the room, went to the couch and sat in the red glow of the dying fire and sipped brandy and revolved her thoughts through her head time and again. She returned after perhaps an hour, and he did not know she had been gone. The most dangerously clever man in Germany was a fool. He was so confident of her—meaning, of course, confident of himself—that he entertained no suspicion of her, took no precaution against her. Or maybe he perceived a risk and elected to take it. Either way he was a fool.

In midday, as they walked together on the mountainside, she raised the question with him. "What if some malcontent, some Jew, say, were in the woods with a gun? There must be people in Germany who would like to kill you."

Heydrich did not break his stride or glance down at her. "If a man is afraid," he said, "then he should not commit himself to a cause as I have done. On the other hand, if the commitment and all that goes with it denies a man every last moment of personal life and satisfaction, then his commitment is too costly."

They walked on, along a mountainside newly restored to lush bright green, both of them silent. The sound of a church bell leaped from the valley, so whole and vivid it seemed the church must be close, although in fact it was far below and only occasionally in sight as they walked.

"The Reichsführer is the kind of man I mentioned," said Heydrich suddenly. The thought had been turning in his mind as they walked. He was speaking of Himmler, of course—the Reichsführer SS, his superior. "He is afraid. What is more, he never enjoys a moment's personal life. He thinks of nothing but his work."

"An anti-Göring, you might say," she suggested.

Heydrich glanced down at her with a smile. He nodded.

On a shadowed bank behind the house, the snow still lay unmelted. In the afternoon Heydrich gathered buckets of it and brought it in to replace the ice he had flown in to chill their food and wine. He packed snow around green bottles of white wine in a wooden bucket. When they opened a bottle, the wine was crisp and cold. They nibbled white cheese and delicate pâtés spread on biscuit. Heydrich was in a relaxed, conversational mood. He slipped his hand up under her heavy black sweater and fondled her breasts as he talked. His touch was more affectionate than erotic; already he took the intimacy for granted. She resented the presumption, but she, too, relaxed and enjoyed the wine and food. It would have been pointless not to.

He talked about the SS. He told her the SS was building its own army and would put divisions into battle in the event of war. "Not just police divisions," he said. "We will have SS panzer divisions." It seemed to please him to talk about the SS army, which he called *Waffen* SS. She wondered if Churchill knew of this—or would care.

"I myself," he went on, "will not command troops in battle. I suppose I should regret that, but I was trained as a naval officer, not an army officer, and there will be no SS navy."

"Is all this secret?" she asked.

He grinned and shrugged. "No. But this is. We are working on the reorganization of all Reich security forces. We will establish an RSHA, *Reichssicherheitshauptamt*, with complete authority over all police and security organizations, intelligence, and counterintelligence. I will be the head of that."

"The Gestapo?" she asked.

"Yes, including the Gestapo."

"Foreign intelligence?"

"I am already involved in foreign intelligence. You know the names Tukhachevski, Uborevitch, Eidman, Primakov?"

"The Russian generals?"

He nodded. "The high command of the Red Army. Stalin shot them all. Do you know why? Because I saw to it that Russian spies in Berlin obtained documents proving the generals were guilty of conspiracy to overthrow Stalin. He shot every capable general he had."

Nancy looked up into his face and saw a caricature of self-satisfaction. He nodded, his thin, white lips twisted in a grotesque smile. She drew a breath. "And. . . ?" she asked. She sensed he wanted to say something more.

"The documents were forged," laughed Heydrich. "I fed Stalin a stew of lies, and he purged his high command. The purge went further than that. He decimated his officer corps. If he goes to war, his army will have to be led by commissars."

"You are a clever man, Reinhard," she said ironically. She pushed down her sweater, pushing away his hand; and she rose and stepped to the window to look down past the Alpine meadow, toward the valley.

Heydrich rose and followed her. He put his arm around her. "We have to prepare for war," he said solemnly. "To save the peace, you prepare for war. I need hardly tell you that."

"Who is interested in saving the peace?" she asked.

"I am," he said.

She glanced upward. The triumphant smile she had found so ugly was gone. He stared at the valley, where the last red light was fading into purple and gray—the Mongoloid slits of his eyes hiding the pale blue irises. He turned his head and looked down at her. "Because we'll lose," he said. "We can't win a major war."

He turned abruptly, for a moment giving his attention to the fire—poking at it, tossing in two more sticks of wood. What he had said was intensely interesting, and she followed him, hoping he would continue.

Heydrich sat on the couch. He looked up at her. "How far can I trust you?" he asked.

Nancy sat down beside him and picked up her glass of wine. "I don't know. You will have to judge that for yourself."

He stared at the fire for a long moment, visibly brooding. "The Führer," he said finally, "is an intelligent man: rational and shrewd. I need hardly point out to *you*, though, that there is in him, too, an element of the hysterical; he is also a mystic. There are those who encourage him in that and play on it. We, too, purged our high command. I myself had much to do with it. Now our military judgments are made on a mystic basis, not on the basis of cold calculation of comparative military strengths. The Führer consults his stars, or whatever it is he consults—something inside him. The *Anschluss* was easy enough, but Czechoslovakia was a reckless gamble. If the French Army had moved . . ." He stopped and shrugged. "We could lose everything we have achieved—our new Germany."

She sipped wine and watched the flames in the fireplace, keeping her silence to impel him to talk on toward whatever end he had in mind.

"What I fear most," said Heydrich, "is that we will blunder into a new world war."

His statement was disingenuous, she thought. She glanced at him, but still said nothing.

"I am not the only influential man in Germany who wants to

prevent an ill-considered major war. There are those who would attempt to overthrow the Führer, even to kill him, to head off war. It is my duty to frustrate their ambitions. And I will."

Nancy spread a biscuit with pâté. Keeping her eye on the biscuit and pretending it had much of her attention, she hoped to cover her determined silence.

Heydrich seemed not to notice that she did nothing but listen. He went on talking at the same pace. "We can anticipate and intimidate the generals," he said. "They count for little now. The Führer doesn't trust them. As for the would-be conspirators among them, I can handle them. They are not the problem."

He paused. She looked up from her biscuit, and their eyes met.

"The problem is with the old Party fighters around the Führer —Hess, Göring, Goebbels, Himmler. All of them—some of them much more than others—encourage him in his mystic tendencies. Hess, I am convinced, literally believes Adolf Hitler can make things happen, by exercise of his will. Goebbels will encourage the Führer to believe anything he wants to believe. Göring—why talk of Göring? And Himmler, the Reichsführer SS . . ." Heydrich shook his head. "He is myopic in more ways than one."

She could anticipate what he was about to say. She nodded, not to agree with him but to encourage him to go on.

"If I had the power," said Heydrich, speaking more slowly and more carefully, "I would—influence the Führer to keep the peace. In five or six more years of peace, Germany will be able to achieve its legitimate goals in the East without war. We have no ambitions against England, you know. Or France, for that matter. In five or six more years, Germany will be so strong that the Poles and Russians will have to cede us what we want. They won't fight. *But we need the peace!* Five or six more years."

Although his speech was disingenuous, what he was saying probably represented Heydrich's view of the world. He was far better educated than Adolf Hitler, but could be just as naïve. The West, he was saying, should stand aside and allow a rearmed Germany to expand to the east, by pressure short of war, until it achieved hegemony on the Continent. Göring, for all the contempt Heydrich had for him, said much the same.

"We must not gamble away what we have achieved: our New Order," Heydrich said dramatically. "Do you agree?"

She nodded. "I do, Reinhard," she said with a sigh. "And I assume the solution to your problem is for you to gain that influence—or power—you spoke of."

His cold eyes settled on hers, and his thin lips turned in a faint smile. "I told you at Salzburg," he said, "that we must not let the Philistines in our movement destroy what we have fought to save. The Philistines . . . the ignorant . . . the mystics . . ." He nodded. "You understand?"

"I understand. You want me to help you bypass Himmler and stand closer to the Führer."

Heydrich's smile widened. "Yes."

"In fact, you want more than that," she said.

His smile disappeared. "I do not offer you a partnership," he said coldly. "I offer you something short of that, with all the honor and privilege you could ask for. More than Adolf Hitler will give you. I want your loyalty."

"I think you are going to have it, Reinhard," she said. "But to what purpose? Precisely what is your ambition?"

"I intend to succeed him," said Heydrich. "I intend to be the next Führer."

❧ XIV ❧

Having held his huge black umbrella over Nancy as she stepped from the Paris taxi, the doorman of the Hotel Meurice hurried back to shelter Helmut as he paid the driver. Nancy stood waiting in the arcade of the rue de Rivoli. The May rain was torrential. The street was blurred in the wind-driven gray sheets. In spite of the doorman's umbrella, her blue hat and dress were spotted, and drops of rain glistened on her flushed face. Helmut's gray suit was quickly spotting with splashes the doorman could not help. She was not distressed. Before the rain began, they had eaten lunch on the sidewalk on the place du Tertre—where Helmut had never been before—and she was relaxed and for the moment happy.

"*Nancy!*" A high, English voice. "Nancy, for God's sake! In Paris! However are you?"

She turned. Her eyes flared, her jaw hardened. Then quickly she recovered. "*Freddy!*" she shouted. "Freddy, of all people!"

It was Binghamton, advancing on her with a beaming smile, hand out to seize hers. He reached her and grabbed her hand just as Helmut ducked out from under the umbrella.

"Helmut," she said. "Darf ich Ihnen meinen Freund Freddy Binghamton vorstellen?"

Helmut extended his hand to Binghamton. "Es freut mich," he said stiffly.

"Ein alter Freund," she said to Helmut. "Ein Engländer."

Binghamton turned a broad, toothy smile on Helmut as he pumped his hand. "A pleasure, General Bittrich!" he beamed.

"And, may I add, my congratulations! My congratulations to both of you!"

Helmut nodded skeptically at the Englishman. Binghamton could play the mindless playboy very effectively, as Nancy had seen before. "Thank you," Helmut said in English. He glanced toward the door of the Meurice. "Are you staying here, too, by chance?"

Binghamton grinned. "No, I'm afraid not," he said. "Nothing quite this luxurious for me, I'm afraid. I'm at the Regina, down the street."

"Ah," said Helmut. "Well, perhaps you would join us for some tea or a brandy." He glanced again toward the door of the hotel lobby. "We were going in. We've just gotten a bit wet."

"How very kind," said Binghamton. "I'd love to join you."

They sat at a small round table. A waiter served brandy with seltzer water. For a while they chatted. Binghamton said he had just "popped over" to the Continent for an extended weekend. He talked about people Nancy knew in England, including Bobo —Unity—Mitford, who he said was in Germany, having become a great admirer of the Chancellor, Herr Hitler. Helmut sat half-withdrawn from the conversation. He sent the waiter to the hotel desk to bring his mail, and the waiter returned with two telegrams from Berlin. Helmut read them casually and stuffed them into the pocket of his gray, double-breasted jacket. When Nancy asked him if he would mind going to their room and bringing her down dry shoes, he seemed grateful for a reason to leave the table and a conversation that did not interest him.

"Isn't this dangerous?" Nancy asked Binghamton as soon as Helmut was out of earshot.

Binghamton began to rub his nose with a knuckle, covering his mouth with his hand. "Probably not," he said. "It may be, however, if immediately on your husband's departure from the table your demeanor abruptly turns deadly serious. Smile. Also, talk with your head down or your hand over your mouth. There may be someone around who reads lips. What is more, when you see me on the street and I sing out 'Nancy!' do not respond by yelling 'Freddy!' The next time you see me, I may not be traveling as Freddy. Yell 'You!' or 'My God, I can't believe it!' or something like; and wait to see if I'm Freddy. We understand you're in Paris to see the Duke of Windsor."

She smiled. "Tomorrow," she said.

"Why?"

She reached across the table to take a nut from the bowl, and, with her face turned down, toward the bowl of nuts, she said: "It is at the personal request of the Führer. It's an idea of his and Heydrich's."

Binghamton leaned back and grinned as if she had said something witty. "Ah. Do tell me more."

Nancy nibbled the nut. She yawned and covered the yawn with a fist. "They want David—the Duke—to broadcast an appeal to England not to go to war. Hitler has taken note of Chamberlain's pledge to Poland. He wonders if David might not be able to turn English public opinion. Also, he knows the King and Queen are going to Canada, then to the States, and will see both Mackenzie King and Roosevelt. He thinks the purpose is to promote an alliance, and he'd like David to steal the spotlight and blunt the King's purpose by making an appeal to pacificism."

"You are to promote the idea of this broadcast to the Duke?" asked Binghamton.

"Yes. I can, of course, do it less than effectively. I can go back to Berlin and say I just couldn't convince David to do it. I assume the government does not want such a speech made."

Binghamton nodded. "The government very much do not want such a speech made."

"Then . . ."

"Get him to make it if you can," said Binghamton grimly. "You are far more important than any speech the Duke of Windsor might or might not make. Don't intentionally fail on the first mission Hitler sends you on. Anyway, if you demonstrate a strong influence over the Duke . . . Well, we might want to use that influence ourselves later on. The government is a bit nervous over what the Duke might do if war should break out. If Hitler can indeed use him to divide British opinion, we may call on you to neutralize him."

It was only in the taxi on the way to 24 boulevard Suchet the next evening that it occurred to Nancy to wonder what Binghamton might have meant by the word "neutralize." She had only a moment to wonder. Determined that Helmut should see as

much of Paris as possible during their brief visit, she had instructed the driver to take them up the Champs-Elyseés, circle
l'Etoile, and head for the Bois de Boulogne and boulevard Suchet
by way of avenue Foch. Helmut stared around him and asked
questions like any tourist, and she had no time to ponder on
Binghamton's word.

At 24 boulevard Suchet, a liveried servant took their coats and
led them to a small white and gold room, furnished with delicate
Louis XV chairs and small tables bearing vases filled with fresh
tulips and irises. They were not kept waiting. The servant had
hardly closed the door when another door opened and the Duke
and Duchess of Windsor entered smiling to greet them.

The Duke, wearing an evening jacket and a tartan kilt, welcomed Helmut in German, Nancy in English. The Duchess, in
a purple velvet gown, spoke odd, American-accented English.

"Der Frühling in Paris ist sehr schön, nicht wahr, Herr Generalleutnant?" said the Duke.

"For the brilliant opening gambit, David's conversation is un-
equaled," said the Duchess quietly to Nancy.

If the Duke heard, he pretended not to "Aber—das war ein
Platzregen gestern," he said—"that was a cloudburst yesterday."

Nancy had not seen him since his abdication. She had not in
fact had more than a formal word with him since he began his
affair with the Duchess. He had aged. More than that, he had been
wounded. It was evident in his eyes, which had always been
characterized by a certain hardness, or sharpness, that was now
gone. She hoped that by encouraging him to make his speech she
would not be urging him to do something that would hurt him
more. He deserved no more hurt.

"You're our only guests for dinner this evening," said the
Duchess.

"We are honored, Your Royal Highness," Nancy said. She saw
the Duke's eyes widen, and he nodded almost imperceptibly
toward her. She had known how pleased he would be if she used
the form of address the Duchess was officially denied.

"David wants to renew your old friendship," said the Duchess.
She said it graciously, without a trace of irony; yet Nancy could
hear in her voice that the Duke had told her something of what
the brief relationship had been. "Perhaps after dinner we should
go to a club and dance."

Another liveried servant entered, carrying a tray with glasses of champagne and sherry and two American martinis. Nancy and the Duchess took the martinis. It was not difficult to turn the conversation to the European situation, to the prospect of war. Men who had seen war, the Duke said—men who had fought on the western front—could not but chill with horror at the prospect of it happening again.

"I want to appeal to the men who bore that awful burden," he said. He spoke English now that he knew Helmut could understand it, for the Duchess was uncomfortable with German. "English. French. Americans. Yes, and Germans. If all the old soldiers would say 'No! No, there must not be another war,' then I think the governments might hesitate." His eyebrows rose. Deep lines formed across his forehead. His jaw dropped slack for a moment, and he shook his head. "For some reason the government opposes me. They don't want me to speak. I am being urged to keep quiet."

"Let me urge you to speak," said Nancy. "It is important that you do."

"I think so, too," said the Duchess. "After all, millions of English people never surrendered an iota of their affection for you. And—an appeal for peace. What could be more noble? What more fitting?"

The Duke shook his head sadly. "I don't know," he said.

"Sir," said Nancy, "you should not hesitate for a moment."

He tipped his head and looked at her soberly. "Do you think so, really, Nancy?" he asked ingenuously.

She nodded. "I do."

He spoke on May 8, a broadcast from the battlefield at Verdun, where, he said, he was conscious of "the presence of the great company of the dead." He spoke, he said, only for himself, "a soldier of the last war whose earnest prayer is that such cruel and destructive madness shall never again overtake mankind." He spoke chiefly to the United States, to which the broadcast was transmitted. His words were not broadcast in England.

Nancy was at the Chancellery in Berlin. Hitler had a translation of the speech. He had read it. So had Heydrich. "Good! Good!" Hitler laughed. "It's short, but . . . The new King is in

America, trying to bind Roosevelt to Chamberlain's promises to Poland. This," he said, tapping the typescript translation of the speech, "may be just enough to frustrate Chamberlain and Roosevelt in their purpose."

"The English newspapers reported it fully *Mein Führer*," said Heydrich. "Even if the BBC refused to carry the broadcast, Englishmen can read what the Duke said."

The papers of the typescript rattled as Hitler laughed and shook them. "It's good," he said again. "It was a good idea"—he nodded to Heydrich—"well carried out"—nodding to Nancy.

"We may obtain further services from the Duke of Windsor, *Mein Führer*," said Heydrich.

Hitler nodded. He looked at Nancy. "The English who want peace," he said. "And the English fascists like Mosley. Would they rally around this man?"

"I don't know, *Mein Führer*," she said.

"You should cultivate the friendship," said Hitler. "It may prove of great service to both your countries—both to England and Germany."

Heydrich did not sit a horse well. It was the only thing he persisted in doing that he did not do well. Although Nancy did not like horses, she rode well. Heydrich hoped he could learn horsemanship from her, and he arranged for them to ride in the Tiergarten, early in the morning on summer days. On the bridle paths they sometimes encountered General Franz Halder, now Chief of the General Staff, riding with Admiral Wilhelm Canaris, Chief of the Abwehr—Military Intelligence. Nancy wondered if Heydrich insisted on riding for the purpose of encountering Halder and Canaris. She dismissed the idea. He had better ways of keeping a watch on them.

She had no doubt he *was* keeping a watch on them. "Canaris," he sneered. "I'll hang him one day." He had already spoken to her more than once of his intention of bringing the military-intelligence function within his own jurisdiction, within his SD. Canaris, she supposed, stood in his way. "But he rides well, doesn't he?" Heydrich conceded grudgingly, with a faint smile.

On the morning of July 25, a Tuesday, while Nancy and Heydrich were riding, a small car suddenly sped down one of the

radial roads that left the circle where Hitler had now installed
the Victory Monument that had formerly stood before the
Reichstag. It pulled up near them, and an apologetic officer
hurried toward Heydrich to tell him he was urgently needed.
Heydrich took the car, leaving the officer with the horse. The
officer was unwilling to mount the horse and began to lead it back
to the stables. Nancy rode on alone. If she had no enthusiasm
for riding, she had less for walking her horse beside the red-
faced SS officer leading Heydrich's mount.

She had ridden only five minutes when she saw Halder, Canaris,
and two others she did not know. This morning, after they had
passed by and saluted her, one of them turned his horse and rode
back, to come up beside her.

"Good morning," he said. He was an army officer, in field-gray
uniform. "Allow me to present myself. Colonel Hans Oster.
Abwehr."

She nodded. She was cautious.

"You are Frau Generalleutnant Bittrich, I believe," said the
officer. "Lady Nancy Brookeford."

She nodded again.

Not confident of his horse, Colonel Oster tugged it awkwardly
into place beside hers; and for a minute, while he forced the horse
to keep pace with hers, he said nothing more.

"Heydrich's urgent summons was not a coincidence," he said
finally. "It was arranged."

She did not respond. She kept her eyes forward, away from
him. He, too, stared ahead.

"If our two countries go to war," he said, "the result will be
a disaster unparalleled in the history of mankind. I am one of
those who are determined to avoid that disaster. If you report
what I am saying to Heydrich, you will have destroyed the last
best chance our two countries have."

She glanced at him. She meant to keep quiet, to let him say
whatever he wanted to say; but she wanted an image of the man,
to judge him by. This was a trap. Not Heydrich's, she judged.
Someone else's. . . .

"I am going to give you a token of our good faith. It is more
than a token. It is a sacrifice."

The man was tense. *Abwehr.* She wondered if all its colonels
were as ill-suited to conspiracy as this one seemed to be. He spoke

with minimal movement of his lips, as if he thought someone watching might not realize he was talking.

"A joint French-English military delegation is going to Moscow for discussions with Marshal Voroshilov," said Colonel Oster in a voice hardly more than a hoarse whisper. "General Doumenc. Admiral Plunkett-Ernle-Erle-Drax. Communicate this to Chamberlain. Tell him we know."

Colonel Oster reined his horse aside and galloped off.

She had felt more secure in her role as an agent of British Intelligence, since she knew someone from MI-6 was watching her every day. Since meeting Binghamton in Paris, she could signal her need for a contact simply by wearing the blue dress and hat she had been wearing when Binghamton saw her on the rue de Rivoli in front of the Meurice. When she had returned her horse to the stable, she took a taxi back to the Markgrafenstrasse apartment where she and Helmut now lived, within walking distance of the Air Ministry. She bathed and ate, and in mid-morning she left the apartment again, wearing the blue dress and hat. She walked to the Air Ministry, stopping for half an hour to take coffee with Helmut in his office; then she walked on up Wilhelmstrasse toward Unter den Linden. Someone saw her signal. The contact was made that same day.

At first she did not recognize the contact. It was a call from William, Lord Euston, who said he was flying to Berlin the next day and hoped she and Helmut could meet him at the Adlon Hotel for lunch—reminding her they had done just that on January 30, 1933, the day when President von Hindenburg appointed Hitler Chancellor. Helmut could not leave the Ministry for a long lunch hour, so she met Willy alone, impatient by noon on Wednesday for her contact and never suspecting it was Willy.

"Freddy Binghamton sends his best," said Lord Euston when he had ordered white wine to precede their lunch.

"You . . . for God's sake?"

He nodded. "Just this once. I'm known to be your friend. Nothing suspicious in your seeing me. We're on the brink of war, you know. In another few weeks I won't be able to come to Germany anymore, and you won't be able to get out."

"Is everyone at home so pessimistic?" she asked.

He shrugged. "Not everyone. Have you really thought through the risk you are taking? You can still back out, you know."

Nancy sighed. "I don't want to talk about that, Willy."

"Very well. You gave the signal. Freddy said to tell you he hopes it's important."

"It is," she said. "I've been thinking about it. At first, even when I signaled for a contact, I didn't realize how important it was. Now I think it is of immense importance."

William nodded and listened.

"Yesterday morning I was contacted by a Colonel Hans Oster of the Abwehr—Military Intelligence. He said there are those in Germany who are determined to avoid war. Then he gave me a piece of information. He characterized it as a token of good faith. I think it's more than that. I think it suggests who he speaks for. His piece of information was that an Anglo-French military delegation is going to Moscow for talks with Marshal Kliment Voroshilov. The head of the British group is Admiral Sir Reginald Plunkett-Ernle-Erle-Drax. The French are sending General Joseph Doumenc. Did you know about the delegation? Is it known in England?"

Lord Euston shook his head. "This is the first I've heard of it."

"Ah. Then it's a secret."

"If it's true, it's a secret."

Putting fingertips together, she put her two hands to her nose and sighed between her palms. "If it's true . . ." she said. "If it's true . . ."

"If Hitler knows it, he will take steps to interfere," said Lord Euston. "Damn!"

"No, that's not the point," said Nancy. "The point is that the anti-Hitler group—if it's real—has access to information at the highest levels. This Colonel Oster rides with Admiral Canaris and General Halder. They—"

"But how do you suppose they found out?"

"That's another point. Obviously they have a spy inside the Foreign Office, if not indeed somewhere even more sensitive; and by telling me what they've told me, they have compromised him. That's their token of good faith: They've sacrificed an important agent."

"Why did they choose you for their contact, Nancy? Surely they took an immense risk."

"It makes me wonder if they don't already know I work for British Intelligence," she said. "If the man they've compromised is well enough placed, he might even know that."

"Then you're in grave danger."

"Maybe it's worth it," she said, frowning thoughtfully. A quick string of thoughts raced through her mind, and she tried to express them. "If they are trying to use me as the intermediary to stop Hitler and prevent the outbreak of war . . ."

"You're assuming a great deal."

She stopped, nodded, sighed. "Yes. But obviously I can't back away from it."

"Likely it's a trap."

"Set by whom? And why?" she asked. "Anyway, Willy, I think I can squirm out if I have to. If it's an Abwehr trap, Heydrich will pry it open for me. If it's Heydrich's, maybe Hitler . . . Anyway, I can't retreat. It's too important."

On Friday, July 28, 1939, the British Foreign Office announced the Anglo-French military mission to Moscow. Colonel Oster's information had been correct, including the identities of the heads of the mission; and Nancy now wondered if the Foreign Office had announced the mission because her message, sent back with Lord Euston, had convinced the government the secret was out.

Helmut came home to their apartment on Markgrafenstrasse that same evening with the news that he and she were invited—in effect, summoned—to Karinhall the next afternoon for a garden party being given by Göring. Helmut was to appear in uniform for the garden party but was to bring casual clothes for a dinner party afterward. They drove to Karinhall in the Mercedes that Göring had given them as a wedding present. It was an hour's drive, northeast from Berlin.

"It may be a destructive war," said Helmut. They were driving through green countryside, shining under a brilliant summer sun, and talk of war had an incongruity of which both of them were aware. "It may be destructive," Helmut said, "but it will not be a two-front war. Only if the Russians intervene on Poland's behalf will it be a two-front war."

"The British and French will intervene," she said.

"Yes, probably. But it won't be like it would have been in Czechoslovakia. We will go through Poland like a knife through butter. By the time the French have mobilized and the British have begun to move an expeditionary force across the Channel, we will have accomplished all our objectives in Poland, and the war will be over."

"Is your estimate based on German strength or Polish weakness?" she asked.

"Both," he said.

"The Luftwaffe is ready, then?" she asked.

"It is ready to support the army," he said. "Bomb London . . ." He shook his head. "No."

"Is war inevitable, then, Helmut?"

He frowned for a moment, then nodded. "It will be the end of life as we have known it," he said.

"Is no one opposed to it?"

"Yes," he said. "Göring."

At Karinhall, servants dressed as foresters led them to a bedroom in one of the wings off the huge central hall. Göring's estate had once been a hunting lodge—he had, in fact, bought it as a hunting lodge—and he kept it in the style of a movie set designed to film an operetta about boar hunting with wassail. She had been there many times before, and the Reichsmarschall often appeared in leather breeches and jerkin complete with feathered hat—in the uniform, in fact, of the Reich Master of the Hunt.

Uniform this afternoon, for the top officers of the Luftwaffe, was white silk with gold braid, and white patent-leather boots. Helmut buttoned himself into his with reluctance. Like most Germans, he liked wearing uniforms; he liked displaying his rank —particularly since he had attained high rank and was paid elaborate deference. Still, the white dress uniform embarrassed him. It was gaudy, and he knew Nancy thought it vulgar. On the lawn, among the umbrellas and tables, half a dozen others were dressed in the white dress uniform. Göring himself was wearing it, ablaze with the red and gold of his decorations.

"It is an extraordinary pleasure to see *you*, Frau Generalleutnant," Göring said to her, not without a trace of irony in his voice. "I shall look forward to some private conversation with you a bit later. The opportunity to do something to save the peace may be afforded us among our guests this afternoon, and I am sure you are as interested as I am in saving the peace. I speak in confidence."

"I am at your service, Herr Reichsmarschall," she said, measuring the irony into her voice as carefully as he had done.

Göring smiled broadly. He touched her arm. "I am sure," he said. "It is good to see you, Nancy."

The smoke from the roasting pits, where beef and pork were being turned over open fires, drifted on the shifting wind, driving knots of guests into hurried retreat. Waiters in skintight breeches and elkskin jerkins carried trays of champagne and cocktails across the broad lawn. The guests ranged from high-ranking officers and diplomats to a company of lightly dressed young women who looked suspiciously like prostitutes. Nancy knew many people. She was quickly separated from Helmut and drawn into conversations: with a Frenchman from the embassy in Berlin, with the wife of the American military attaché, with a Viennese film director, with a Swedish businessman. She could see no logic in the assembly of this heterogeneous crowd, no motive for the party.

The ashes of Karin, the first Frau Göring, were deposited in a small Grecian temple at some distance from the main house. Even though she had died in 1931 and he had remarried in 1937, Göring had named the estate for her. An aide found Nancy in conversation with a Wehrmacht general and told her the Reichsmarschall was at the little temple and would like to talk to her there. She found Göring alone, sitting on a marble bench, staring silently at the temple.

"The British and French are courting the Russians," he said to her quietly. "Ribbentrop is courting the Russians. If Ribbentrop is successful, we will find ourselves fighting the West instead of the Bolsheviks. Civilization will not survive. I do not exaggerate. Stalin will dance on our corpses—Germany's and England's. The Führer is determined to settle this thing with Poland. If the British and French will only hold their peace, we can settle with Poland and establish Europe's frontier against the Bolsheviks five hundred kilometers farther east."

"If the Führer will hold his peace," she said, "a compromise might be worked out—a rail corridor through the Corridor, for instance."

Göring shook his head. "Not enough. The Poles are murdering Germans in the lands given them at Versailles. There must be an overall settlement."

"Like with the Czechs?" she asked.

"Another Munich? No. Your Mr. Chamberlain will never take that route again." Göring's pudgy hands were clasped nervously in his lap. His face gleamed with perspiration. His voice remained low. "I have invited two Englishmen to meet with me this afternoon," he said. "Mr. Digby-Cobbs is a City broker. Mr. Jellip is a textile manufacturer. Do you know them?"

"I know their names," she said.

"I am going to say to them what I just said to you, with the understanding that they will report what I say to Chamberlain. I am trying to open informal lines of communication, you understand. I believe it would lend weight to my statement if you were present. At least it might diminish the tension in the meeting. I don't ask you to support my point of view, just to be present."

She nodded agreement. It might prove useful for her if Chamberlain and Wilson and Halifax heard that she had been present when Göring made a highly confidential appeal for peace. It would be evidence for them of her status in Germany. If her presence at the meeting did not lend weight to Göring's appeal, it might lend weight to her reports back to England.

In their room, while they dressed before going out to Göring's evening party, Nancy described the meeting to Helmut.

"I've never seen Göring so subdued," she said. "They were really quite rude to him. Digby-Cobbs told him neither honor nor good sense would allow England to stand by and watch Hitler rape another small country. I thought surely Göring would burst into a rage over that. But he didn't. He just picked up his own train of thought and went on as if they hadn't interrupted him with an offensive statement. He said he was devoted to peace and hoped the Prime Minister would realize that."

"Does the Führer know about this meeting?" Helmut asked.

"I don't suppose so," she said. "The Führer is in Bayreuth for the Wagner festival. Frau Göring is with him, in case you wondered where she is. Bobo Mitford is down there. They're all

chasing the spirit of the true Germany. I think the Reichsmarschall is acting on his own. I think he truly fears war."

Helmut shook his head. "I am sorry you went to the meeting
with the two Englishmen," he said.

"It was a disaster from the beginning," said Nancy. "We met in
the little study. Göring has hung the Rubens and the El Greco in
there—the ones he got after *Kristallnacht;* you know, Jews gave
them to him, hoping to win his assistance for their escape from
Germany. I think Digby-Cobbs and Jellip knew how he got
them—or suspected, at least. They sat there and stared at the
two paintings through most of the meeting, with the holier-than-
thou air of two men looking at stolen art."

"What did they expect to gain by treating him that way?"
Helmut asked.

Nancy shrugged. She did not tell him they had stared at her,
too, with unconcealed scorn. In their view she was an Englishwoman of prominent name who had befriended the Nazis and
now had even married one, on the eve of a repetition of the
world war. After they left, Göring had told her he was sorry to
have subjected her to them; he had not anticipated their irrational
attitudes.

Göring's dinner party, for a chosen few, would begin at nine,
after the lawn-party horde had driven back to Berlin. Returning
to their room late in the afternoon, they had found their invitation and its accouterments. The party was called a "Blue Angel"
party, and the invitation was printed over a photograph of
Marlene Dietrich in the motion picture by that name. With the
invitation, they found two top hats of glittering blue satin, two
evening canes, a pair of sheer black silk stockings, and two black
garters with blue rosettes.

"It seems," Nancy remarked as Helmut helped her pin the hem
of her skirt up six inches so she would show the black stockings
and the garters worn just above her knee, "that my long-faced,
war-fearing friend of this afternoon means to have a good time
tonight, whatever may be about to happen to the world."

"The Reichsmarschall," said Helmut, "loved the old times."

The great central hall of the Göring estate had been converted
for the night into the Blue Angel Club. Göring, himself dressed
in white satin tails, greeted his guests at the door and personally
pinned an orchid on each lady. He beamed. He looked like a

great, ruddy cherub. "Frau Generalleutnant, you look *extremely* charming," he said to Nancy. An attendant beside him handed each arriving guest a heavy gin drink.

A jazz band—including Negro musicians, imported from God knew where—played on a stage at the far end of the room. The band singer—dressed in top hat, black corselet, stockings held up with garter straps from the corselet, and jeweled shoes—was a male. He gestured with a cigarette in a long holder and sang in a tobacco-ravaged voice. Round tables for eight were set up around the room, each with bottles of gin and whiskey and a bucket of ice.

Nancy and Helmut moved slowly into the room, looking for their table. Some sixty guests were milling about, all wearing their blue top hats, all carrying their canes. Some of the women had done as Nancy had done; they had pinned their skirts a few inches above their knees, showing their black stockings and the garters with blue rosettes. A larger number stood about in various degrees of discomfort and embarrassment, in underwear they had not expected to show. The wives of the younger Luftwaffe officers in particular were working gallantly to lend the party the air the Reichsmarschall had made it plain he wanted. Some of them—probably at their husbands' urgent demand—were stripped to brassieres, panties, and garter belts; and their brave wooden smiles failed to cover their embarrassment. The young women Nancy had suspected might be prostitutes were in fact actresses from a Viennese motion-picture company—as Helmut had explained to her—and they wore black or blue corselets, much like that worn by the band singer.

Nancy recognized the film director who had brought the actresses from Vienna; Bayer was his name; Goebbels had introduced him to Nancy six months ago. A man sitting at a table with a husky blond woman was the playwright Ritter. The woman was a Berlin café singer whose name Nancy did not recall. A knot of people surrounded the Swedish actress Margit Birgus.

Finding their table, Nancy discovered she would be sitting beside the Swedish actress, at the Reichsmarschall's own table. Margit Birgus and the man with her—another Swede, named Karl Lagerkrist—seemed relieved to find someone else assigned to the table; both of them were uncomfortable in a crowd in which they knew no one except Göring himself. A moment's conversation established that the two Swedes had not even met each other before tonight. Margit Birgus was a striking woman: tall, with shoulder-length blond hair, her skin browned from exposure to the summer sun; she was wearing a black chemise.

Talking with the actress, Nancy caught a wisp of the conversation between Lagerkrist and Helmut—"Of course, Herr Generalleutnant, of course. Our government bought the American Northrup fighters, but we can, if necessary, manufacture the engines ourselves."

They were joined by a Luftwaffe colonel and his wife. The young Colonel was a squadron commander. His twenty-five-year-old wife was mercifully drunk, which had dulled her painful embarrassment at being publicly exposed in her tea-colored, lace-trimmed panties, garter belt, and brassiere. The Colonel's name was Jaeger. He commanded a squadron of Stuka dive bombers, he said. He said his squadron had recently been transferred from a field near Stuttgart to Schönefeld at Berlin.

Last to come to the table was Göring himself, escorting one of the Viennese actresses. By now he was drunk. His cheeks burned red, and the sleeves of his white tailcoat were smeared with the brownish makeup with which he covered the pallor of his face. He reintroduced everyone at the table and snapped his fingers for a waiter.

Nancy was to Göring's left. When he noticed Margit Birgus leaning away from Nancy to talk to Colonel Jaeger, he touched Nancy's arm and whispered in her ear: "Forgive me for seating you next to her. I'm paying her to sleep with Lagerkrist tonight. His company manufactures engines we could use. Helmut can explain."

Helmut engaged Colonel Jaeger's plump, inebriated little wife in animated conversation. The Colonel himself was obviously stunned to find himself at dinner not only with the Reichsmarschall but with the Swedish movie star Margit Birgus—and she handsomely exposed in a lace-trimmed chemise. He spoke earnestly to the actress. She smiled on him tolerantly. Karl Lagerkrist spoke past Göring, to open a conversation with Nancy.

He asked her if Britain would go to war over Poland. She said yes. "Tragic," he said. He shook his head.

"It's a matter of honor," Nancy said dryly, glancing into the eyes of Göring, who was listening.

"Honor . . ." Lagerkrist repeated. "Stalin and Hitler will divide Poland between them, and nothing Britain and France can do will stop it."

"*Stalin* and Hitler?" Göring asked excitedly. "What makes you think Stalin . . ."

Lagerkrist shrugged. "Is it a secret?" he asked.

"It is to me," said Göring indignantly.

An awkward moment was cut short as the jazz band suddenly broke into a rousing march—the "Horst Wessel Lied"—and the female-impersonating band singer began to strut up and down the stage, bellowing the words at the top of his voice. Many felt compelled to stand and sing. Eyes turned to Göring, who, surprised and unsteady, struggled to his feet and joined the song, swinging his arms. Helmut stood. Colonel Jaeger stood. His wife stood. Nancy—*die Engländerin*—stood and glanced around to meet the eyes of the people who were watching her. She picked up the rhythm and sang along with the rest—the anthem of the Nazi party.

Half an hour later, she left the table to go to the bathroom. She decided to walk into the wing of the house where their room was—hers and Helmut's. When she came out of the room, a young woman was standing in the hall. She was one of the Luftwaffe wives, apparently: half-dressed, wearing her blue satin top hat askew. She greeted Nancy and fell into step beside her on their way back to the party.

"I have a message from Colonel Oster," the young woman said.

"I am not acquainted with any Colonel Oster."

"Even so, this is the message: 'We know the specific terms of Admiral Drax's instructions for his conversations with Marshall Voroshilov. They are to prolong the talks as long as possible and to reveal nothing, commit Britain to nothing. This is a catastrophic error. The West has days, not weeks or months, to head off a nonaggression treaty between Hitler and Stalin. Heading it off is the last chance for peace."

"I don't know why you tell me this," said Nancy coldly. "You must mistake me for someone else."

"Ah. Perhaps I do," said the young woman as she straightened her hat and strode away into the crowd of the party.

❧ *XV* ❧

With Helmut, she walked to the Opera House to hear Hitler's speech. Since the burning of the Reichstag Building in 1933, the Reichstag had met in the Kroll Opera House. It was an easy walk from their apartment on the Markgrafenstrasse; but September 1 was a sultry, overcast day in Berlin—and besides, there was fear that French or English bombers might attack the city. Helmut had urged her a week ago to leave Berlin, to be on vacation in the Alps on September 1. She had refused to leave. Now he had suggested they drive to the Opera House. Nancy wanted to walk.

The streets were quiet, almost deserted. A few newsboys hawked the extras that she and Helmut had already read. Workmen—street cleaners, a construction gang, taxi drivers waiting for fares—showed no sign that this was any special day. Cafés were open. People did not huddle over the newspapers. They were apathetic.

"I don't understand how even the Poles can be such goddamn fools!" Helmut grumbled after walking for several minutes in silence. He was wearing his blue uniform for the session of the Reichstag, and two or three civilians had saluted him on the street. "They had to know the Führer was only waiting for such a provocation."

Nancy did not reply. For herself, she did not believe the Poles had attacked the German radio station at Gleiwitz. She did not believe that Polish troops had crossed the German frontier at various points, as the radio had been reporting all night. Like

Helmut, she did not believe the Poles could be such fools. More than that, she did not believe they *were* such fools. What she did believe was what the stations were now saying and what the extra editions of the newspapers reported: that the Wehrmacht, supported by the Luftwaffe, was engaged in a full-scale invasion of Poland.

What was difficult to believe, too, was that Hitler had started a war when no one seemed to want it. Göring, she knew, was frightened and resisting. Heydrich, when she had last seen him only a few days ago, had insisted he was appalled at the course events were taking. She had had more contacts from Colonel Oster, who insisted the army opposed the war. Could it be that Hitler himself, alone, was leading a reluctant nation into a major war, even a new world war?

She had learned in the past month that the Abwehr—Military Intelligence—was a center for the anti-Hitler conspirators. Colonel Oster had now gone so far as to assign an Abwehr agent to her, a young civilian pilot who flew for Lufthansa. His name was Hanskarl Ludeke. She had made his acquaintance before, and was surprised to learn he was an intelligence agent—although it was not unusual for German civilians with occasion to travel to foreign countries to be agents. It was easy for him to see her. Whenever she went to an airport, Hans could be there without being conspicuous.

"My people are patriotic Germans, you understand," he had told her over coffee in the lounge at Tempelhof. "It is not our purpose to reestablish the situation of 1918. We must have from Chamberlain assurances that he would not expect that of the new government that will replace the Führer."

"What will you do if he goes to war?" she asked him outright.

"The generals will move," said Hanskarl flatly. "We will overthrow him."

"Can you?"

The dark-visaged young pilot frowned and hesitated. Then he nodded. "We will take the risk."

She had seen little of Heydrich in August. He had told her over the telephone that in the event of war he would fly with the Luftwaffe, in combat. She had no doubt he meant it.

As the anti-Hitler conspirators drew closer to her, trying to use her as a channel of communication to London, she was relieved that Heydrich was not so close. Sometimes when he settled his cold blue eyes on her, she had the feeling he could read her mind.

She had dinner with him once during the month, on the day after the announcement of the Nazi-Soviet pact. He was brittle with excitement. "It was the last chance," he said. "The last chance to save the peace was in the possibility that the French, British, and Russians would confront the Führer with a solid alliance, a two-front war. The problem was, the British and French could not make up their minds whom they hated most: Hitler or Stalin. While they pondered, Ribbentrop scored a coup. It's all over now for Poland; and if England honors its commitment to Poland, we will be at war with England. Does Chamberlain understand *nothing?*"

"Do you still believe Germany will lose?" she asked.

His nostrils flared. He seemed to laugh bitterly under his breath. "Sooner or later," he said grimly, "we will have to settle matters with Stalin. We should be allied with Chamberlain against Stalin, not with Stalin against Chamberlain! Poland is nothing. The main issue is bolshevism. We have taken a fatal detour from rational policy."

"What now, then?" she asked.

Heydrich sighed. "Poland will fall within a month. The Führer will have a great victory and will be the hero of the hour. Then . . ." He shrugged.

Events seemed to have subdued him for the moment. Her last report to London, before September 1, said that Heydrich was in eclipse.

Seated in the gallery, she looked down on the Reichstag assembled in the Kroll Opera House. Helmut, as a Generalleutnant der Luftwaffe, lacked the rank to be seated on the stage with the ministers, but had the rank to stand behind the ministerial benches. He stood beneath the wreathed swastika that was clutched by a huge golden eagle that loomed above the podium. Göring, as President of the Reichstag, sat in the highest chair. Below him sat Goebbels, Hess, Funk, Frank, Ribbentrop, Halder,

Keitel, Jodl, Milch, and many others—almost all in uniform—the leadership of the Party and the Reich.

Hitler entered. The Reichstag rose to cheer. As Hitler strode to his place, the Chancellor's seat in the front row of the ministerial benches, the cheering faded and almost stopped. Hitler was wearing, not the khaki coat and black trousers in which they were accustomed to see him, but the field-gray coat of the Wehrmacht. They realized abruptly, dramatically, that he had come to announce to them that Germany was at war.

She had never heard him speak as he spoke that day—with a nervous solemnity she had seen in him before in private but never before in public.

"I am wrongly judged," he said, "if my love of peace and my patience are mistaken for weakness or even cowardice. . . . This night for the first time Polish regular soldiers fired on our own territory. Since 5:45 A.M. we have been returning the fire, and from now on bombs will be met with bombs."

The deputies of the Reichstag could not have been surprised, yet they reacted as if he had stunned them with news they had not dreamed of.

"I am from now on," he said soberly, "just the first soldier of the German Reich. I have once more put on that coat that was most sacred and dear to me. I will not take it off again until victory is secured, or I will not survive the outcome."

Göring rose and began to applaud, but the Reichstag remained stunned, and the applause was subdued.

"Victory will come!" Goebbels yelled. "There will never be another 1918!" He waved his hands in a wild gesture, demanding applause, and at last the Reichstag understood its cue and rose and began to cheer.

Göring encountered them outside. He seized Nancy's arm. "It is not too late yet," he said urgently to her. "Helmut . . ." he said. Helmut was set back; Göring almost always called him by title in recent years. "I need her. At the Chancellery."

She went with Göring in his car, leaving Helmut standing on the street before the Opera House. "There is a Swede," Göring said to her breathlessly in the car. "One you haven't met. Dahlerus is his name. He's been acting as a go-between. He has met with Chamberlain. He met with the British Ambassador this morning. I want him to see the Führer. You may be able to help."

By now there was a crowd before the Chancellery—an organized crowd, she supposed, whipped into place by the Ministry of Propaganda. Yelling policemen forced Göring's car through. Inside, the corridors of the Chancellery were filled with chattering Nazi functionaries. Göring led Nancy through. The crowd parted to make way for them.

Hitler was in his private study. General Jodl was with him, and they were looking at dispatches from the war front. Hitler was elated; the nervousness of his appearance before the Reichstag was gone. "Ah, Annchen!" he said to her warmly, using the diminutive for her name in front of others for the first time. "You may be proud to be a German now!"

Göring gave her no chance to respond. "*Mein Führer*, Birger Dahlerus is here. He is back from London. He conferred this morning with Henderson. England has not declared war, and our lines of communication are still open."

Hitler glanced at the Reichsmarschall as if annoyed that the fat man had pressed an unpleasant reality into his review of the good news from Poland. "Dahlerus . . ." he said absently. "I suppose I must see him."

Göring went out to fetch Birger Dahlerus, and Hitler spoke to Nancy. "I had no choice, don't you see?" He nodded for emphasis. Jodl slipped out of the room. Hitler rubbed his stomach as though he suffered indigestion. His elation, too, had disappeared, just as the earlier nervousness had done. He was mercurial, she knew. "I only pray that England will see . . . You understand, Annchen. *You* understand, don't you?"

She nodded. "Wolf . . ." she whispered.

"I will not make war on England unless England makes war on me. You can say that. You can tell Ambassador Henderson that. If you have any way to get through to Chamberlain, tell him that for me." He drew a deep breath. "I would not—I would not be so arrogant as to try to tell England what to do about Canada, so why should England try to tell me what to do about Poland?"

There was no point, she knew, in trying to answer. He did not want an answer to his rhetorical questions. He did not want argument, even from her. She had not seen him for several weeks. The tension of those weeks was marked on him. His eyes were with-drawn. He rubbed his stomach again. He looked down at the military dispatches lying on his desk. "The military operation," he said quietly, "is going very well. The damned Poles blew up the bridge at Dirschau this morning. Otherwise, it is all going very well."

He nodded. He picked up from his desk a pair of gold-rimmed eyeglasses—she had never seen him wear them before—and set them on his nose as he pored over the dispatches.

Göring returned. Hitler snatched off his glasses and extended his hand to the gray-haired Swede. The man was wearing civilian clothes, and Nancy realized he was almost the first man she had seen today who was not in some kind of uniform. Hitler intro-duced her to Dahlerus.

"Have you talked to Chamberlain?" Hitler asked bluntly.

"I spoke to Sir Alexander Cadogan, at the Foreign Office in London, within the hour," said the Swede gravely.

"Did you tell the Foreign Office that Poland attacked Germany during the night?"

"I told them that, Herr Reichskanzler."

"And?"

"They don't believe it, Herr Reichskanzler."

"Ahh . . ." murmured Hitler. The breath seemed to run out of him. He spoke to Nancy. "You see? The English government has decided for war. They don't want peace. They've not wanted it all along." His pallid face suddenly glowed pink. "All along, Annchen! All along they have been determined to fight me!"

Göring stood behind Dahlerus, who had sunk into a chair. Göring's face, too, was flushed. "*Mein Führer*," he ventured almost timidly, "Herr Dahlerus believes the English government would send a delegation to meet with someone of sufficiently high rank. Perhaps with me—"

Hitler stood with his backside pressed to his desk, confronting the nonplussed Dahlerus. "Poland!" he shouted. "They will fight me over Poland, will they? I tell you, Dahlerus, I will crush Poland and annex the whole country to the Reich before the English gentlemen can struggle up off their asses! Poland is their pretext for war. Well, I will eliminate their pretext before they can get their war started!"

Nancy had not seen him like this before. It was as if he were the madman some Englishmen thought he was. She opened her mouth to speak a calming word to him.

"If England wants to fight for a year, I will fight for a year!" Göring shrank. Dahlerus blanched and shook his head. Nancy stared in horror. Hitler waved his arms, and his voice rose to a scream.

"If England wants to fight for two years, I will fight for two years!" He glanced wildly at Nancy. "If England wants to fight for three years, I will fight for three years!"

"*Mein Führer . . .*" she whispered.

He doubled his fists and bent so low she thought he was going to pound the floor. He yelled at the top of his breaking voice. "*Und wenn es erforderlich ist, will ich zehn Jahre kämpfen!*" If necessary he would fight on for ten years.

She dined that evening at the Adlon Hotel, with Helmut alone. "He is insane, Helmut," she whispered hoarsely behind her hand. "I swear he has lost his mind."

"You mustn't think it, much less say it," said Helmut grimly.

"You must know there are those who want to overthrow him," she said.

"Yes, as your friend Heydrich well knows. What do you think he will do with them?"

"General Halder—"

"*Don't tell me!*" he hissed. "I don't want to hear about it. How do you know about it?"

"If England declares war—and France—he will face his dreaded two-front war. They will move. I hear they will move against him."

"That would be insane," Helmut snapped.

"The army . . ." she said. "The High Command."

He shook his head violently. "No! Don't tell me!" He lowered his head and shook it sorrowfully. "How can you know so much about this? Are you involved in some way? Your life will be worth nothing if . . . And what of me? What do you think they would do to me if my wife were found guilty of treason?" He looked up. "Nancy," he whispered, almost in tears. "You can go if you want. With the embassy. They will take you. It can be arranged."

She shook her head.

"You must not involve yourself in politics," he said. "It is not a game anymore. They will kill you. They will kill us both."

"Helmut," she said quietly but firmly, "where would you stand? If the army moves against him—if the army moves to save Germany from his insanity—where will you stand?"

"It won't happen," he said between clenched teeth.

"*If it does . . .*" she insisted.

His lips were white. The corners of his mouth turned hard down. "I have sworn an oath to him," he muttered. "He saved Germany from disgrace and weakness—and from the Bolsheviks. His rule has brought me to a position . . ." He shrugged and shook his head. "He has befriended and honored you. You chose to live in the Germany he has built. You accepted his friendship. Is it so easy to betray him? It is not for me."

Nancy's eyes filled with tears, and her throat tightened.

"Go home if you want, if you're so English," Helmut murmured disconsolately. "I will see you again when the war is over."

Nancy wept and shook her head.

❧ *XVI* ❧

Heydrich called on Tuesday morning, September 5. He was in Poland, he said, calling on an army line. "I saw your husband last night. He was on Special Train *Göring*. I told him I would call you today, and he asked me to send greetings."

"He's all right?" she asked. She had little doubt Helmut was not only safe but comfortable. He had left Berlin on Sunday—the day Great Britain declared war—on one of the three special trains carrying Hitler, Göring, Himmler, and many others to the Polish front.

Heydrich laughed. "He's a tourist," he said. "Although he said to tell you Colonel Jaeger was shot down and killed. The Poles are not altogether defenseless."

"My God," said Nancy dully. Jaeger, who had sat at their table at Göring's Blue Angel party—he was the first man she knew who was killed in the war.

"I understand Ambassador Henderson offered you a last-minute chance to leave Germany."

"Yes, on Saturday," she said. She had wondered if Henderson had understood that her telephone line was unquestionably listened to. She had wondered if he had not been giving her a chance to make a declaration for those who were listening.

"I am pleased you told him you are a loyal German now," said Heydrich.

"I am pleased you acknowledge that you listen to my telephone line," she said.

Heydrich laughed again. "Not to hear what you might say, my dear Nancy," he said. "To hear what someone might have wanted to say to you that last day or two before England went to war. He might have tried to tell you whom to contact in case you changed your mind and wanted to leave, and that would have been useful information for us to have."

"Sir Neville Henderson is not quite stupid, Reinhard," she said.

"No, no, I suppose not. It makes no difference now. Anyway, let me tell you why I called. I want you to fly out here tomorrow. There is a plane leaving Tempelhof in the morning to bring a group of my officers out here. I want you to come. I'll meet you at the field where it lands, in Poznan. I'll show you around a bit. You'll be back in Berlin for dinner."

"Reinhard—"

"Besides, I want to talk to you," he interrupted.

The Ju-52s she had flown had been marked as Lufthansa transports. This one was a Luftwaffe aircraft, painted dark green, although with dramatic splashes of yellow—the rudder, the engine nacelles, the wingtips—and mounted with an open machine-gun turret atop the fuselage. Her companions on the flight were five grim, silent, black-uniformed SS officers: an *Einsatzgrupp*, whatever that was. When they discovered she was the famous *Engländerin* and was to be met at Poznan by Heydrich, they told her they were going to Poland to coordinate police administration in the occupied territory.

Heydrich was exhilarated. It was almost as if he were drugged. He had flown to Poznan in his Storch. It was the same Storch he had always flown—the one with which she had almost collided the day she met him—but it had been repainted with larger, more emphatic Luftwaffe insignia and mounted like the Ju-52 with a machine gun in the rear.

"I want you to see what's happening here," he said. "You may never see anything like it again. The *world* may never see anything like it again. We'll have time for a late lunch alone together. Then I'll bring you back here, and the Junkers will return you to Berlin. We'll carry a gunner. We can't talk in front of him."

The gunner, a taciturn SS sergeant, climbed into the Storch

first and sat facing the rear. The machine gun pointed to the rear, through a mount in the Plexiglas. Extra canisters of ammunition were mounted inside the cabin. Nancy sat in the second seat. Heydrich sat in the front and flew the airplane.

He climbed to 500 meters and flew east, along the main road to Warsaw. Still the war was remote, something that had happened and was over for the land below. She saw vehicles lying along the road, shattered, burned out. She saw dead horses lying among them. Tent hospitals, marked with red crosses, sat along the road. Groups of German soldiers sat by the roadside, eating, resting; some of them waved cheerily at the Storch. The highway itself carried a moving chain of military trucks, all moving east.

"How far to the front?" she asked Heydrich, speaking to him through a hand microphone, for him to hear through his earphones.

"There is no front," he said. "There's never been one, really. The Poles are broken up. There's a unit here and there. They stand and fight at a river, in a town, in a forest. It's all local actions. We bomb them, shell them, then move up with the tanks."

He swung north of the highway. In the distance, to the northeast, she could see columns of smoke. He flew toward them. The countryside was pastoral, primitive; she saw huts and barns and pigsties and poorly fenced fields. She saw Polish peasants now, working on their fences, repairing. One farmstead was shattered. The hut and barn were black shells. The animals lay about, dead. Now ahead she saw five tanks moving across the fields. They overran the Polish fences and churned through the fields, throwing up dense clouds of red dust. Knowing now what the dust clouds were, she saw they were flying behind an advancing army of tanks, maybe a hundred of them, rolling toward some sort of battle.

"*Achtung!*" grunted the gunner into his microphone.

She glanced around. The gunner had told Heydrich they were being overtaken by a low-flying squadron of Stuka bombers. Heydrich dived. In a minute the Storch was skimming the treetops, no more than 50 meters above the fields, and not much higher the Stukas swept by, twenty or thirty of them. They were ugly, awkward-looking airplanes, with their inverted gull wings, their oversize wheel pants, their skimpy tails—each one carrying a big black bomb suspended under its fuselage. When they were almost out of sight, 10 kilometers or so ahead, she saw the flashes and upheavals, then the smoke, of their bursting bombs. Flying closer, Heydrich brought her to where she could see what they had bombed—a grove of trees on the near bank of a small river. The tanks, which were below them now, had stopped, and she could see them lurch from the recoil of their guns. They fired into the same grove. Heydrich climbed to give her a better view.

She watched closely, but she saw no return fire from the grove. As Heydrich circled at a safe distance from the action, half a dozen of the tanks moved out of formation and charged toward the grove. Not one was hit—that she could see—and they moved into the grove. After a few minutes they were followed by a company of infantry that trotted forward. The soldiers ran into the grove.

"There you are," said Heydrich. "Typical action. We'll clear that grove of trees, then cross the river."

She saw no Poles.

Across the river and to the north, a village was burning. This was the source of the columns of smoke toward which Heydrich had flown. From 1,500 meters' altitude, they had a view of the village five or six kilometers away. The church was burning; that was the biggest fire. Houses. She could see flame as well as smoke. On the road beyond the village, clouds of black smoke rose from two burning trucks and a burning car.

Again she saw no Poles, though here she was sure people were dying, and only distance separated her from the sight of horrible death.

As though he could read her thoughts, Heydrich spoke. "We bomb only the villages from which they fire at us," he said.

He turned southwest. They flew back over the grove where the tanks and infantry had just penetrated. The tanks were moving north along the river. Their dust obscured the river.

From 1,500 meters' altitude, she could see many columns of thick red dust, all across the Polish countryside. The horizon was vague in the billowing dust. She could see smoke. Heydrich was right when he said there was no front. It was a war of motion; and if the motion seemed confused to her, nevertheless it was all German motion, the Wehrmacht moving almost at will, relentlessly to the east. Heydrich was right, too, that the world might never again see anything like it.

He landed the Storch near the village of Pakosc on the Noteć River. The village was intact, and the SS had established a headquarters there. His Storch was met by a small armored car, which he took from the driver. Nancy saw a hamper in the back: Wine and a lunch had been provided for the *Engländerin* and the Obergruppenführer. He drove the car across the open fields toward the river. At the river she saw the ruins of a bridge, paralleled by a military bridge laid across a chain of boats. Teams of horses were dragging wagons across the floating bridge. The wagons were lined up on the dirt track approaching the bridge, and a Wehrmacht sergeant bellowed orders to the teamsters, to whip their reluctant horses onto the unstable bridge and hurry them across. The horses lunged and shrieked and tugged on the heavily laden wagons. Heydrich stopped and for a moment stared at the scene. "Napoleon must have moved across here much the same way," he said. He shook his head. "It has changed less than we think."

He drove the little armored car—it had an open top; the armor was only in the heavy steel of the body—along the river and into a copse of redolent pine. He stopped. The river was out of sight through the heavy green pines. So were the dusty fields behind. She could hear the sergeant shouting at the teamsters and the whinnying of the frightened horses, but the sounds were distant and diminished. The pine-scented air was fresh and cool. Heydrich took her in his arms and kissed her. She returned his kiss. He touched her breasts. He ran his hands over the heavy khaki twill of her jodhpurs.

"Everything has been made more difficult," he said. He twisted a corkscrew into a bottle of red wine. "At the same time, it has been made more urgent."

She nodded as though she understood. She meant to encourage him to talk.

"The Philistines are rampant," he said. "Their quick victory here entrenches them more deeply. Why couldn't Chamberlain have understood? He has written the epitaph of civilization!"

"Chamberlain has?" she asked skeptically.

"The Führer lives on vegetables and pills. Stalin, I am told, chews his pipestem to little bits of rubber, which he swallows, and declines even to scrub the accumulated filth out of his small-pox pits. And these two are allies! Allied against everything that humankind should cherish and sustain! We've given half of Poland to Stalin!"

"Half?"

"Of course. Within the week the Red Army will move into the eastern half. We destroy the Polish Army, and Stalin takes half of what we conquer. A little statesmanship by Chamberlain could have prevented it all."

"What could Chamberlain have done?" she asked

"What can he do now is the question!" Heydrich growled, hitting his palm with his fist. "And the answer is: *Move!* Get the French to move in the west. We are naked there. If they move, we will have to pull back here, hurry our army across Germany to defend the Ruhr, and the Soviet pact will be meaningless."

"Do you think the English and French don't know?" she asked. "I am confused. . . ."

"Of course they know! They lack the will! They are letting the lowest of the low win everything."

"You talk treason," she said grimly. She could not follow his logic and meant to encourage him to expand.

"Treason . . ." He smiled. He shook his head, and the smile disappeared. "I want you to understand that nothing has changed. What I have asked you to help me do is now more important than ever."

"Replace the Führer. . . ."

He nodded. "I have people who are loyal to me. I count you among them."

She nodded. She could not do otherwise.

Heydrich nodded. He poured red wine into cups.

"The general staff . . ." she ventured.

He nodded again. "Yes, but for themselves. They are as selfish as the gauleiters—and most of them no more cultured. Their *von*s mean nothing. Prussian farmers . . ."

"They have power."

He shook his head. "No. The political power has replaced the military. The day when the generals could overthrow the Führer has long since passed."

"They might be useful allies."

"No. I don't want them."

He savored his wine and the cold roast beef he had found in the hamper. She did, too; she was hungry. He caressed her face. His narrow eyes focused on her in unembarrassed appraisal. He touched her breasts. He said they must find a weekend for another tryst at his mountain house.

He had repacked the hamper and started the engine of the ·car when she heard an angry sound she had never heard before in her life. She did not know it, but it was the sound of an artillery round coming in. Heydrich threw her to the floor of the car, but the round burst well outside the copse of pine. Splinters of shrapnel and a cloud of earth roared through the tops of the trees. The sound had not subsided when the whine of another round threatened.

"Goddam!" Heydrich yelled. Holding her down on the seat with one hand, he jerked the car into gear and horsed it forward, lurching and rolling. "Poles! Goddam!"

The whine-roar of more shells followed in quick succession, and the explosions burst all around. It was plain he did not know which way to go to escape them. He spun the car when a shell burst fifty yards ahead, and spun it again when another burst even closer to their right and showered them with gravel and pine. The car hurtled out of the copse. Heydrich headed for the track leading away from the river.

The Wehrmacht Sergeant at the bridge stood atop a wagon that had been hit by a shell. The horses still writhed on the ground, spouting blood as if they were nothing but skins filled with blood. He saw the car. "*Heraus! Heraus!*" he screamed. He gesticulated wildly with both arms. "*Herr Obergruppenführer! Heraus! Gottverdammt!*"

Heydrich jammed the brakes to the floor and the little car skidded to a stop. Grabbing Nancy by the arm, he jerked her out of the car and dragged her across the ground. He shoved her into a ditch where half a dozen soldiers were already prone and cowering, and he jumped in after her. A shell burst nearby, and shrapnel whistled across the ground just above their heads. The windscreen of the armored car was swept away: an explosion of glass carried by a storm of shrapnel. A soldier in the ditch was wounded. He was screaming. He had been hit in the leg and dragged into the ditch by others, and a corporal was trying to work on his leg, to twist a bit of rope around it to stop the pulsing flow of blood. Another shell burst and threw up a ton of earth, much of which came falling into the ditch. The wounded man shrieked.

Then, as suddenly as the shelling had begun, it ended. The soldier's sobbing screams filled the silence. Men lifted themselves cautiously out of the ditch and beat the dirt off themselves. They looked around. Nancy could see fear in their eyes, and horror. Heydrich helped her up from the ditch. She was covered with dirt and dust. It was in her hair and clothes and on her face. Heydrich slapped at her gently, knocking some of the worst off. He was grim and angry but as much afraid as the rest of them. He could not conceal it.

The Wehrmacht Sergeant at the bridge was dead. His body was a huddled, bloody object lying beside a shattered wagon. The bridge was intact but blocked by broken wagons and dead and wounded horses. Stunned men stood staring.

Shards of the windscreen lay all over the inside of the armored car. Shrapnel had dented the armored body. Heydrich sat down dully in the glass and tried to start the engine. It came to life. The car was drivable.

"Come on," he said to her.

She began to clear the glass from her seat. He helped. From somewhere, a steady crack-crack of German high-velocity artillery began to answer the Polish barrage. She looked up and saw a Storch flying in circles beyond the river. It was a spotter plane, directing the fire. The crack-crack increased, and the rumble of explosions dulled all the nearer sounds—the screaming man, the yelling teamsters, the dying horses. Heydrich jammed the car into gear and pulled away.

The telephone rang while she was in the bathtub that evening, soaking the Polish dust out of her pores. She did not leave the hot water to answer, but two hours later it rang again. Hanskarl Ludeke was on the line. He said only that he was in Berlin, between Lufthansa flights, and wanted to ask if she was well, if Helmut was well, and so on; but as he talked he used a phrase that had been arranged between them, which told her he wanted to see her as quickly as possible. Half an hour later, although it was almost midnight, she left the apartment and walked along Markgrafenstrasse. In a moment a car pulled up at the curb. She got in with Hanskarl, and he drove purposefully to Unter den Linden, west into the Tiergarten, and on west toward Charlottenburg.

"Admiral Canaris wants to see you," he said.

"That may be a very foolish risk."

"Don't underestimate the Admiral," said Hanskarl soberly.

In his house in Charlottenburg, the Admiral sat behind a desk in a small library lighted only by a desk lamp with a green glass shade. He poured her a cup of coffee from a vacuum desk carafe and brandy from a flask and offered her a cigarette. He was a handsome man, with thick gray hair neatly combed across his head. His face was long and lined. He wore a gray civilian suit.

"Do not be deceived by what you saw today in Poland," the Admiral said to her, almost without so much as greeting her. "Heydrich wanted you to see how powerful is the Wehrmacht, what quick and thorough victories Germany is winning. He wanted you to see how we can march across Poland, almost as if the Polish Army did not exist. He wanted you to understand we can do the same in France."

Nancy only listened. She was not surprised that the Chief of Military Intelligence knew she had been in Poland. What was surprising was how little he understood of Heydrich's purpose in having her fly there.

"What you did not see," Canaris went on, "is the West Wall— the *so-called* West Wall. The French confront it with an army powerful enough to walk through it. Germany has no army in it! If the French will but move, the Führer will be forced to pull back in Poland and rush every division he can across Germany to defend the Ruhr. Did Heydrich tell you that?"

It was precisely what Heydrich had told her. This was the second time in twelve hours she had heard the same military appreciation, almost in the same words. It had to be true.

"Do the British have any idea of this?" asked Admiral Canaris.

It was a direct question. She had no answer. He waited for an answer. She sighed. "I wonder," she said.

Admiral Canaris leaned back in the leather chair behind the desk. He glanced at Hanskarl Ludeke, who sat outside the light from the lamp, on a chair with its back to the books that lined the library walls. "Do you know, Frau Bittrich, how Reinhard Heydrich came to leave naval service? He was booted out, because he had abused the confidence of a young woman. He is not a man of honor. Did you know he is the proprietor of a house of prostitution in Berlin? Not for personal gain, I admit. He arranges for foreign diplomats and others to go there, and he has them photographed and their voices recorded while they are visiting with the prostitutes. I am aware, Frau Bittrich, that your own relationship with him is most intimate. I am suggesting to you that he cannot be trusted."

"With word of this meeting, for example," said Nancy.

Canaris smiled woodenly. "With word of this meeting. More important, with word that you maintain a contact with your government—and by 'your government,' I mean the British government, for I am not for a moment deceived that you have transferred your allegiance since your marriage. I am sure you are still a loyal Englishwoman, with well-placed contacts in London. In fact, I will go so far as to say I suspect you are an agent of British Intelligence. If I didn't, I wouldn't be sitting here revealing all I am revealing to a woman who sleeps with Reinhard Heydrich."

"You take dangerous risks, Herr Admiral."

"As you do, my dear young lady," he said. "As you do."

Nancy sipped brandy and turned to look over her shoulder at Hanskarl, sitting tensely, watching apprehensively. She looked back to Canaris. "I sent your August messages to London," she said.

"They established my *bona fides*?" he asked.

"I should think so."

"But they did nothing," said Canaris impatiently.

"Nothing we know of," she said.

He lighted a cigarette. "What is your assignment?" he asked. "Who is your contact?"

"I have neither."

"You don't trust me."

"Not that far."

He laughed. "I understand you are an amateur. Even so, you are no fool. And thank God for that. Communicate the following to England: that Germany is weak in the West; that if the French move now, they can upset everything Hitler is doing in the East. It is imperative that they move *now!* If Hitler is defeated, we will overthrow him. There is no question of that. *But* . . . The French move must be a measured move. They must make enough of a move to compel Hitler to abandon the Polish campaign and move the army to the West. That defeat will destroy him. But if the French Army comes storming into Germany, Hitler will be strengthened, as the only national leader with the stature to save the nation from collapse and total humiliation. The French must use their army *politically*. If they do that, we will finish the work here. But they must move *now*."

"For whom do you speak, Herr Admiral?" she asked.

"I speak for the army," said Canaris solemnly. "The generals will want an assurance from the British and French that the peace we make will not be another like that of November 1918. We will terminate nazism, but we will not surrender our country to humiliation."

She had spoken the truth when she told Admiral Canaris she had no assignment and no contact. On Wednesday and Friday she wore the blue dress and the blue hat she been wearing on the rue de Rivoli in Paris when she was met by Freddy Binghamton. It was their signal that she wanted a contact; but now that the embassy was closed, she had no reason to think anyone saw it. Helmut returned from Poland. They dined with Goebbels and his wife. Goebbels was elated. Warsaw was surrounded, he said; its fall was imminent. The war was over. It was over before the French and British realized what was happening. Beginning on Sunday, Helmut spent sixteen-hour days at the Air Ministry. The transfer of the Luftwaffe to the West began.

On Monday, September 10, she received a call from Karl Lagerkrist, the Swedish manufacturer who had been at her table at Göring's Blue Angel party. He asked her to join him for lunch at the Adlon Hotel the next day.

"I was having lunch in this room," she said to him shortly after they were seated, "on the day when Hitler came to power. They announced it here, to the people eating at these tables. In fact, I was sitting at that table, there, with my husband and with a friend from England. The Generalleutnant was not my husband then, of course. I had, in a sense, run away from home with him, though. It was a romantic occasion."

Lagerkrist was a man in his late fifties, thin and erect and severe. She had wondered what he thought of Göring's having hired the actress Margit Birgus to sleep with him the night of the party. She recalled that he had carried on a very correct conversation with the woman that night—with no suggestion that he understood she had been paid to entertain him. He remained severe now, and a little uneasy. His conversation was stiff.

"Were you surprised at what happened in Poland?" he asked.

"No," she said. "I had heard it would be over quickly, and the people who told me knew exactly what they were talking about."

"Why should the world have been surprised, then?" asked Lagerkrist.

They talked about the war. They had little else to talk about. She wondered why he had invited her to lunch, and she waited to hear him say why; but they ate and lingered over coffee, and he said nothing that resolved the mystery. He was a pleasant companion: knowledgeable, yet reserved in his opinions. He was careful to say nothing that compromised his status as a citizen of a neutral nation.

"My car is waiting," he said when they left the hotel. "I will take you wherever you wish."

"I think I would like to walk a little," she said.

"Please," he said with a sudden note of urgency. "In the car . . . it is better to talk."

His Mercedes pulled up before the hotel. "Your chauffeur is to be trusted?" she asked quietly.

"Absolutely," said Lagerkrist.

They settled in the deep seats in the car, and Lagerkrist took some time cutting the tip from a cigar and carefully lighting it. The chauffeur turned the car into Tiergartenstrasse. Lagerkrist contemplated his cigar in silence for a long time, glancing at her, looking nervous. Finally the chauffeur stopped at the Swedish Embassy.

Lagerkrist smiled at Nancy. "Actually," he said, "it is my chauffeur who must speak with you. I will leave you here, and he will drive you where you wish." So saying, he left the car abruptly.

Before she could protest, the chauffeur pulled away from the curb. He glanced over his shoulder at her, then gave his attention to his driving. He was a dark-haired man, wearing steel-rimmed spectacles and a small black moustache. That was all she could see of him.

"Look here," she said. "Who are you?"

He stopped for a traffic light. He turned and looked at her and smiled.

"Oh, my God!" she exclaimed. He was Freddy Binghamton.

Ribbentrop made a whiskey and soda for her and one for himself. There were three cups with the teapot on the silver tray, but only Hitler would drink tea. She was accustomed to that. Others ate meat and drank alcohol in his presence, without hesitation. It was only smoking to which he might sarcastically object, and few lighted cigarettes in his presence.

"The war conferences are almost superfluous now," said Ribbentrop with an air of self-satisfaction. "The focus shifts back to the diplomatic front."

She had never liked the Foreign Minister. There was something unctuous about Ribbentrop, and that was a quality she despised in anyone.

"Oh," he said. "Your friend Miss Mitford has regained consciousness. She will survive."

"She's no friend of mine," said Nancy.

He referred to Unity Mitford, who had pursued Hitler around Germany for two years, fawning over him, embarrassing him— and yet flattering him by her attentions. When England declared war, she had shot herself in the head.

"I had supposed she was," said Ribbentrop. "I thought everyone who is anyone in England knows everyone who is anyone in England."

" 'Knows,' perhaps," said Nancy. " 'Friend of,' no."

"Ah," said Ribbentrop vacantly. He stood and walked to the window, abandoning the effort to make conversation.

After another minute or so, the door opened and Hitler walked in. Nancy stood. He strode immediately to her, took her hand and kissed it, and murmured, "Annchen. I am so glad you chose to remain in Germany, to see—"

"*Mein Führer,*" interrupted Ribbentrop energetically, "the news is good today again, is it not?"

Hitler's smile broadened until his teeth showed beneath his toothbrush moustache. "Excellent! Excellent!" he said ebulliently. He gave Nancy's hand a final squeeze and a pat. "Yes. Everything can move to the West now." He sat down in an overstuffed armchair facing the tea tray on the table, and he poured himself a cup of tea. He pointed to a chair for Nancy and another for Ribbentrop, putting her close to his side. "The army can refit and take up its new positions now," he said. "I couldn't be more pleased." He was wearing his field-gray coat and black trousers—the Iron Cross he had won in the last war worn prominently on his breast. With his cup of tea in hand, he settled back comfortably in his chair.

"Shall I proceed, *Mein Führer?*" asked Ribbentrop.

Hitler nodded.

"Frau Generalleutnant," said Ribbentrop, "I suppose you know the Duke of Windsor is in England?"

Nancy shook her head. "If the story has been published, I have overlooked it," she said.

"He is in England," said Ribbentrop. "He has seen the King. He expects to be appointed to a high military post. We have reason to believe his expectations will be disappointed. When he leaves England this time, his bitterness toward the present government may be deeper than ever. At the same time, the people of England have retained their affection for him. Indeed, an opinion poll recently taken in England demonstrates that the people hold him in exceptionally high regard. He has been welcomed back by cheering crowds. It is apparent that he could recapture the throne with little effort."

"No," said Nancy emphatically. "You misjudge the situation if you think that."

She glanced at Hitler. He held his teacup close to his face, and he was smiling faintly behind it.

"Perhaps for the moment, Frau Generalleutnant," Ribbentrop conceded. "But let England suffer one painful defeat—a naval disaster, perhaps, or a bombing, or a defeat for an expeditionary force landed in France—and dissatisfaction with the present government will grow to hatred. Then King Edward VIII might step forward, reclaim his throne, and negotiate a reasonable peace for his country."

She spoke to Hitler. "I don't think so," she said simply. "It misjudges English opinion; and probably, too, it misjudges David."

"Your good friend Heydrich thinks well of the idea," said Hitler.

He frightened her with that statement. What did he mean by "good friend Heydrich"?

"Yes," said Ribbentrop. "Heydrich has recommended the project we have in mind."

"What project?" she asked.

"Since you are a very close personal friend of the Duke of Windsor," said Ribbentrop, "you are the one who can deal with him. I believe the Führer has decided to call on you for your services in that regard."

"What services can I render?" she asked.

"You will act as the Führer's personal representative to the Duke—perhaps the future King of England. We will arrange a contact between you and the Duke. We will ask you to exercise your special influence over him."

"Consider," said Hitler, "how it might be if one day I send you as German Ambassador to the court of King Edward VIII."

"David renounced his throne," she said. "I renounced England for Germany and am regarded as a traitor by the English press, which is libeling me unmercifully every day. I am afraid the embassy would be a disaster, *Mein Führer*."

Hitler laughed. "One day England will be grateful to you," he said. "And to their King who has returned to make peace." He shrugged. "At any rate, it is worth a try, and I would be grateful if you would try."

She nodded at him. "Of course, *Mein Führer*," she whispered.

"Good," said Hitler happily. "Good!" He glanced up at his Foreign Minister. "Where are the cakes that go with this tea?" he asked jovially.

Nancy relaxed. It was a harebrained project, and probably nothing would come of it. If Heydrich really took it seriously, then she would report it to Freddy. Otherwise she would not even risk another contact with him. She watched Hitler. He was enjoying his triumph. Poland had fallen. The French Army sat stolidly behind the Maginot Line. The British had done nothing. Once more his judgment had been vindicated. Once more he had called the bluff of Europe, and he had won.

He was her assignment from MI-6. He was to be overthrown. She was to cultivate Admiral Canaris and improve her contacts with his group. She was to encourage Heydrich's ambitions. If MI-6 judged either Canaris or Heydrich capable of a putsch, it would lend support. If the putsch died aborning, or if it failed, then the assassination of the Führer would be considered as a less desirable but perhaps necessary alternative.

Freddy had told her something he was not supposed to tell her: that England had no other agent nearly as close to Hitler as she was; her position was unique and vital.

❧ XVII ❧

The Cathedral of Saint Stephen at Breisach was built in the fourteenth century. Standing high above the little city and the Rhine, it commands a view up and down the river and of France beyond. At a window in one of the towers, Nancy braced herself against a sharp autumn wind, pressed her binoculars to her eyes, and scanned the French side of the river. Colonel General Franz Halder stood beside her. He was Chief of the Army General Staff. She followed his promptings and identified two concrete domes with protruding gun barrels.

"Everything is deep underground," said General Halder. "The crews, the ammunition, their other stores. Tunnels interconnect the gun emplacements. Troops live in underground galleries. It is formidable."

"The Maginot line . . ." she said.

"Ja," said General Halder.

Heydrich stood at the next window, peering through his own binoculars. Like the General, he was dressed in field-gray, with a general's red lapels on his military greatcoat. Like the General, he wore a sword. To get a better view down the river, he moved to another window, around a corner in the tower.

"Is he toying with me?" Halder asked in low voice.

"He knows nothing," she whispered. "You were told he is my friend. It is only coincidence that he called you."

Halder was fifty-five years old, a stiff career officer, with bristling, close-cropped hair, a deep cleft in his chin, and a pair of penetrating, severe eyes behind the rimless pince-nez that bestrode his nose. She had met him several weeks before. He was committed—although Admiral Canaris had stated his commitment for him far more strongly than he had stated it for himself—to the overthrow of the Nazis and the establishment of a generals' regime that would make peace.

"I should rather have lunch with a snake," muttered the General.

"I assume you would be cautious in the company of a snake," she said coldly.

"Ja," said the General.

"Well," said Heydrich, his voice coming around the stone corner ahead of him, "it is obvious we can't cross here, but I assume they cannot either."

Halder nodded. "Our West Wall does not rely on emplacements like that," he said. "We will move divisions to meet them, wherever they try to cross."

"*If* they try to cross," said Heydrich with a wry smile.

"Yes," said General Halder. "If."

Heydrich raised his binoculars and gazed across the river for a silent minute. "Somewhere over there," he said then to Nancy, "your friend David may have his binoculars trained on us."

"I beg your pardon, Herr Obergruppenführer?" Halder said to Heydrich. He had not realized Heydrich's comment was for Nancy alone.

"I refer to the Duke of Windsor, Herr Generaloberst," said Heydrich. "He is a longtime personal friend of Frau General-leutnant Bittrich. We know he is attached to the British military mission to General Gamelin and that one of his duties has been to inspect the Maginot line. Did you know, Herr Generaloberst, that until they allowed the Duke to have a look at it, the French had consistently refused to let their British allies see their installations?"

"I did not know that," said General Halder.

Heydrich lifted his binoculars again. "That piece of intelligence was obtained by my Amt VI," he said.

"Ah," said the General noncommittally. Amt VI of the RSHA—Reichssicherheitshauptamt—was the foreign-intelligence unit of the SS. It was under Heydrich's direct command, and it was rapidly developing a bitter rivalry with Admiral Canaris's Abwehr, traditional military intelligence.

Through her binoculars, Nancy could see French soldiers

walking casually along the riverbank on the far side of the Rhine. They smoked. One drank from a bottle of red wine. They were within easy range of German guns, but no one fired on them. Indeed, the flaming red lapels on Halder's and Heydrich's coats might have drawn heavy fire—as had General von Fritsch's at Warsaw—if anyone on the French side had cared to shoot. It was difficult to believe no one over there had observed two generals inspecting this segment of the Maginot line from the cathedral tower.

She glanced at the General. He was a religious man, according to Canaris. During their meeting he had said to her what had now become a litany—that the generals would not overthrow Hitler simply to surrender, or to see Britain and France take advantage of the confusion to impose a harsh peace on Germany. He had said one other thing she had found intensely interesting—that the Canaris group had another contact with London, through the holy see in Rome. He seemed to want to play the Rome contact against her, as if she and the Pope were in competition to see who could obtain the most generous terms for Germany.

"It must be understood," General Halder had said somberly at their first meeting, "that the matter of Poland is now settled once and for all. It will not be reopened."

"Then," she had asked, "what is the difference, Herr General-oberst, between the peace you offer and the peace the Führer offers?"

Canaris, acutely uncomfortable with the conversation, had intervened to say there was indeed a difference, which he had then gone on to try to define.

"I am authorized by my friends in London, gentlemen, to say that England will enter negotiations with a new government and that the terms of the peace will not be punitive," she had told the group. That was the exact wording of her message from London, delivered by Freddy Binghamton.

"Which means what?" Admiral Canaris had asked.

"That is the extent of my communication from London," she had said.

"The deadline for an agreement is November first," Canaris had said.

"Why is that the deadline?" she had asked.

"Because," he had said, "the war will enter another stage on November fifth."

Two more deadlines had since been set. Her impatience with the conspirators was exceeded only by her impatience with London. If His Majesty's government wanted to see Hitler overthrown, it was stupid to let the war "enter another stage."

Heydrich lowered his binoculars. "Well," he said. "It's cold up here."

"I am prepared to offer a pleasant lunch, Herr Obergruppenführer," said Coloned General Halder.

They took their lunch early, and before one in the afternoon were at the field where earlier Nancy had landed her Storch. General Halder watched as Heydrich shed his military greatcoat and shrugged into a leather flying jacket. They were flying her Storch, not his. Hers still was not burdened with a machine gun and canisters of ammunition, so it could carry the weight of iced food and wine packed in insulated hampers in the back. The General looked around the airplane, inspecting it skeptically, as Nancy climbed into the cockpit and Heydrich took his place in the second seat. The General waved as she taxied away.

"The General is a fool, as I will have occasion to demonstrate," said Heydrich through her earphones.

Nancy did not comment. She swung the Storch into the wind, and when she pushed in the throttle it accelerated rapidly and immediately lifted into the cold air. She turned south, following the east bank of the Rhine, holding the airplane not more than 100 meters above the hills. It was barely more than 50 kilometers from Breisach to the Swiss frontier at Basel—a flight of a quarter of an hour up the Rhine, under wisps of gray cloud and with visibility of no more than 10 kilometers. Still, she could see the Maginot line across the river, and she flew with some apprehension that a Frenchman somewhere, with more aggression in his heart than most of them seemed to have, would fix his sights on the Luftwaffe-marked, slow-flying airplane and pull his trigger.

"Keep well clear of the Swiss frontier," said Heydrich.

He was watching the French side of the river through his binoculars and did not know how close to Basel she was when finally she shoved the throttle in, lifted the nose of the Storch, and climbed to gain enough altitude to turn out of the Rhine Valley. She climbed hard and cleared the hills to the east of the river. Heydrich turned and peered backward through his binoculars. He was still looking around with his binoculars, paying no attention to their course, when she crossed the Swiss frontier at Eglisau.

She flew 10 kilometers into Switzerland. She identified the Swiss city of Frauenfeld as they flew directly above it. A flash of sunlight on water, obscured in the clouds and haze to the south, was probably on the water of the Zürichsee. Alone, she could have made an abrupt southwest turn and in five minutes been on approach to a landing at Zürich.

Swiss fighter aircraft did not rise to intercept her. If the Swiss knew a Luftwaffe Storch was over their frontier, they did not react. She had wanted to know if they would react, and how. Another day it might be different; but for now, clearly, she could escape into Switzerland if she had to.

A freezing rain began to fall during the last ten minutes of their approach to Heydrich's mountain meadow. Cloud was settling into the mountain valleys. Afraid for the first time in many recent hours of flying in all kinds of weather, Nancy extended full flaps and settled the Storch lightly onto the mud. He carried her into the house and wrapped her in blankets on the big leather couch before the fireplace while he built a fire. When the fire was roaring up the stone chimney, he carried in the hampers of food and their gear from the airplane. He made coffee in a big pot that he hung over the fire, and he poured hot coffee and brandy. When the couch was warm and she was warm, he undressed her. She sat nude, with a blanket around her shoulders, tired and comfortable, almost able to be pleased with the place and the evening.

"It has begun to snow," said Heydrich. "We may be here a week."

"Your wife and my husband will send search parties up the mountain," she said. "They would anyway, if they knew which mountain to search."

"Would the Generalleutnant do that, really?" Heydrich asked.

Nancy closed her eyes for a moment. "No," she said quietly. "The Generalleutnant would not do that."

"Why not?"

She sighed. "Don't toy with my feelings, Reinhard," she said.

"I am curious about what your husband thinks," Heydrich persisted. "Perhaps I should know. Of what is he capable?"

"Of nothing."

Heydrich shook his head. "I don't think he is a cipher."

"Relative to you he is," she said crisply.

"Do you still sleep with him?"

"Yes."

"Would you if I asked you not to?"

"Yes."

Heydrich smiled as he reached for a towel and used it to lift the coffeepot from the flames. "I have another question," he said quietly. His smile faded. He looked up into her face.

"What?" she asked.

His eyes were narrow and pregnant with whatever he had in mind. "Uh—would you like some more coffee?"

"Yes, but that was not your other question."

He poured coffee into her cup and put the pot aside on the hearth. Crouched on the hearth, he looked up at her where she sat on the couch, and she watched him as his eyes moved over her bare breasts, her belly, her hips. "Nancy," he said softly. "I care for you, you know. If I asked you—let us say, if I asked you urgently—would you—use your mouth—I mean, give me oral sex?"

She shook her head. "No."

"If I told you it is important to me?"

"No."

He lowered his eyes for a moment. Then his smile reappeared. "I didn't think you would," he said.

"Annchen!" Hitler exclaimed. He strode across the room and threw his arms around her. "I thank Providence for this!" He laughed and bent down and slapped his knees with both hands. "An hour with you! I have wanted to talk with you. You have no idea how I long for an hour with you."

It was November 5, 1939. She was dining with him at the Chancellery, alone, in his private apartment. Two waiters in white jackets were lighting the candles on the small round table when she arrived. He himself had been adjusting the red roses in a bowl in the center of the table. He wore his field-gray jacket and black trousers. She noticed that he was a little pale and puffy.

He poured champagne for her, though as usual he had none himself. "Annchen," he said. He took her hand in his and pressed it to his mouth. "How grateful I am that you chose to stay in Germany."

"It is my privilege, Wolf," she said.

He kept her hand between his. "You know Lloyd George, I suppose?"

She nodded. "Dear old man."

"Yes. He came to see me once, you know, and I've been thinking of something he told me. He told me that in November 1918, if Germany had just held out for a few more weeks, it was the Allies who would have been compelled to sue for peace, not the Central Powers. Think of it! The man who was Prime Minister in 1918 told me that! *They* would have given up! They! If only Germany had not suffered a failure of courage at the crucial moment. It is a matter of *will*, Annchen. My generals told me I dared not enter the Rhineland, I dared not effect the *Anschluss*, I dared not demand the Sudetenland, I dared not retake what was ours from Poland. Now they tell me I dare not attack in the West. What do you think, Annchen?"

"I've seen some of the Maginot line," she said cautiously.

"I've seen the plans for all of it," said Hitler.

"I saw it at Breisach," she said.

"I know. With Halder and Heydrich. You and Heydrich . . . Are you sure he is not taking advantage of you? Heydrich is a man of strong will, you know."

"I am sure—"

She was interrupted by the two waiters, who entered with a cart and served her a meal of pheasant, wild rice, and fresh vegetables—Hitler the vegetables alone and a pot of mint tea. Hitler rose from the table, followed them to the door as they left, and latched it.

"You have been discreet with Heydrich," he said as he returned to her.

"It has always been my understanding that you knew of my relationship with him, which is not new," she said.

To her dismay, he did not retake his chair but knelt by hers. He bent his head down and kissed her legs below the hem of her skirt. Then he pushed her skirt back and kissed the bare skin of her legs above her stockings.

"I know, of course, you have marital relations with your husband," he said, nuzzling her legs. "And you have something of the like with Heydrich." He drew back and looked into her face. "If I were not who I am, if I did not bear the responsibilities I bear, I would be deeply resentful of any other man who touched you. But I am a sophisticated man, and I know you are a woman with womanly needs. I cannot and do not resent your relationships."

Pushing her skirt higher and pulling down the elastic waistband of her panties, he kissed her on the belly at the edge of her pubic hair. Then he pulled the hem of her skirt down to her knees, rose, and kissed her on the forehead. He sat down across the table, took the champagne bottle from the bucket of ice, and refilled her glass.

"I understood when you married Helmut Bittrich," he said, "that it was to please me, give you the status of a married woman, and make it possible for you to remain in Germany as a citizen of the Reich in the event of war. I like your husband. Don't suppose I don't. But he is no Reinhard Heydrich. Who but Heydrich himself is the match for Heydrich?"

"Wolf . . ." Nancy whispered. Her face was flushed, both from what he had done and from what he was saying.

"You are not pregnant yet, are you?" he asked.

"No . . ."

"You could do worse than to let Heydrich impregnate you. You yourself are Aryan—German and Anglo-Saxon—and Bittrich is a good enough German; but Heydrich is Nordic, the kind of Aryan who fathers perfect children."

"Wolf, please! You embarrass me."

Hitler's face colored. "My apologies," he murmured. "You know I want only the best for you. Anyone who keeps you close to me is my friend."

She slumped. "You are kind," she said dully.

"In September," he said, "I signed a decree reorganizing all the Reich security services. Do you understand what new powers I gave your friend Heydrich? He is chief of the Reichssicherheits-hauptamt. That makes him head of the Gestapo, the Kripo, and the SD—of all Reich security forces, against all our enemies. I formalized his foreign-intelligence powers, which he has exercised brilliantly. I will tell you frankly I gave Heydrich more power than Himmler wanted him to have."

Alerted, she drew a breath and asked, "Why, Wolf? Why Heydrich?"

Hitler took his first forkful of the vegetables. "Sooner or later the responsibilities I bear must weaken me, maybe kill me. In any event, I am fifty years old. Göring, who is nominally my suc-cessor, is only a little younger, and I need hardly point out to you what a toll life has taken on him. So . . . I must consider."

"But—*Heydrich?*" she whispered thinly.

Hitler raised his chin and smiled. "Just look at him," he said. "What a specimen of a man! And you of all people must know: Heydrich is not just a man of will and courage but a man who possesses that special ruthless self-confidence that makes things possible for him that are impossible for ordinary men. That's the kind of man . . ." He shrugged. "Of course, I haven't decided."

"If you've given him important new powers, haven't you in fact already decided?" she asked.

Hitler stirred his vegetables with his fork. "It makes the others very uneasy," he said. "Already they form combinations to thwart him."

Nancy forced a smile. "I see," she said.

Hitler pursed his lips and frowned. "If Heydrich has decided he wants to be the next Führer, maybe he will be whether I want him to or not. In fact, if I decide I don't want him, I might have to kill him to stop him."

She knew the Führer's habits. She knew after dinner he would go back to work. He might have a war conference. Keitel and Jodl might be waiting. He pressed a lingering kiss on her cheek, murmured in her ear that he wished he could sit and talk with her all night, and abruptly left the room. An SS adjutant appeared in the doorway and by gesture offered to escort her out. They had reached a public corridor of the Chancellery, and the SS officer had just said he would arrange for a car and driver to take her home, when they encountered Heydrich coming in.

"Ah, Günsche," said Heydrich. "I would like a word with the lady and will see to her transportation home. Thank you."

The adjutant saluted and walked away.

"Come with me," Heydrich said to her. "I think I can arrange for you to hear something interesting."

He conducted her a few paces along the public corridor, then opened a narrow door with a key and led her into a passageway that paralleled the corridor. They walked along the passageway, then through other doors and rooms, until he brought her finally to a small antechamber she had seen before; it was just outside the war conference room.

"Sit down," Heydrich said. He indicated a straight chair behind a small table. "I'll tell the Führer you're here if I can. If I can't, he won't object to your presence. Do you recognize the voice?" She shook her head, and he said, "General von Brauchitsch." He winked at her and passed through the door into the conference room.

Colonel General von Brauchitsch was Commander in Chief of the Army. His was another name used by Canaris, who had assured Nancy that von Brauchitsch, too, was committed to the overthrow of Hitler and the Nazis. She recognized another voice from the conference room: that of General Halder. For a moment she wondered if Heydrich had not brought her here to eavesdrop on an attempt by the generals to place Hitler under arrest—followed of course by a ruthless SS action to suppress their putsch.

The discussion in the conference room involved the date of the German attack in the West:

Von Brauchitsch: The field commanders are practically unanimous, Mein Führer, in saying an attack now would almost certainly result in a disaster. I have submitted a full report—

Hitler: I have read your report. It contains nothing convincing.

Halder: The meteorologists are in agreement that we can expect no better weather from now on.

Hitler: Our army cannot fight in rain and snow, but the French and British can. Is that what you are telling me?

Von Brauchitsch: We are planning a war of movement. If we can only move on improved roads . . .

Hitler: The French and English armies are south of the Belgian frontier. To counter our attack, *they* have to move. They will be moving in the same mud we are.

Von Brauchitsch: It will be better in the spring. . . .

Hitler: It *rains* in the spring! We have drizzle now, and snow, but in the spring we will have rain. Do the meteorologists promise ideal conditions in the spring of 1940? Do I have your promise you will not raise these objections then? No. I will hear excuses then, just as I hear them now.

Von Brauchitsch: Mein Führer, there is a factor I have been reluctant to mention.

Hitler: Mention it! I might as well hear it all.

Von Brauchitsch: I regret to say that reports from the commanders in the West tell of defeatism, insubordination, even of a spirit of mutiny in some army units there. One commander says the morale of his troops is as bad as he saw in 1918.

Hitler: From what units is this reported, Herr Generaloberst? Name units!

Von Brauchitsch: Mein Führer, I—

Hitler: What action has been taken? What discipline has been imposed in units where there is insubordination? Have death sentences been imposed on these incipient mutineers of which you tell me? *Has anyone been shot*, Herr Generaloberst?

Von Brauchitsch: No, Mein Führer. But—

Hitler: Name the officers who report bad morale in their units. They are to be relieved immediately! *Tonight!*

Von Brauchitsch: *Jawohl*, Mein Führer.

Hitler: *Tomorrow morning*, Herr Generaloberst. Tomorrow morning you and I will fly to the Rhine. I will see these units. They will see me. I will restore morale. If they do not respond to leadership, then they will respond to the gallows rope! Name the units, Herr Generaloberst.

Von Brauchitsch: Mein Führer, I meant to report a *general* want of proper morale, not incipient mutiny in any specific army units.

Hitler: Ahh . . . You—could—not—take me to—an army unit —that is not ready to fight. *Could you*, Herr Generaloberst?

Von Brauchitsch: A specific unit—

Hitler: The truth is—*the truth is* that the army is brave and well disciplined and ready to fight. It—is—the *generals* whose spines are made of rubber and whose will is made of jelly. But, gentlemen, I promise you, we *will* attack in the West. January 1! January 1, 1940! If you come to me with more dishonest arguments like those I have heard tonight, then I will find generals with the courage to lead. *I will find them!* If I have to promote lieutenants to field marshals, I will see my army led by *men! You may count on it!*

She walked beside Freddy Binghamton along Wilhelmstrasse, toward the Air Ministry. She was meeting Helmut there, and they would have dinner at the Adlon Hotel with Goebbels and his wife. Although the temperature was barely above freezing, it was raining lightly and she carried an umbrella. He wore his uniform as a chauffeur to the Swede, Lagerkrist.

"They might have impounded you for the duration," said Binghamton.

"And Heydrich?"

Binghamton laughed. "I suppose not. Anyway, you might have created an incident."

"But I didn't. And now we know. With an airplane like the Storch, we can fly into Switzerland. If it becomes necessary."

He nodded. "If it becomes necessary. I am glad to know you have an escape route."

"It's for you, too, if you need it."

"I'll keep it in mind."

"Now, as to the generals . . . It is apparent to me they do not represent even a possibility."

"For the moment there is no other possibility."

"Heydrich," she said.

"We want you to continue to cultivate Heydrich," he said. "We think it is so important that we almost decided not to tell you what I am about to tell you. It is proof of the high regard in which you are held in London that the decision was made to tell you. You will have to exercise an extraordinary degree of self-control in the presence of Heydrich from now on."

"Well, what is it, for God's sake?"

"Word has been leaking out of Poland that the Germans are rounding up every species of Polish leader—not just the politicians and army officers but the intellectuals, artists, musicians, religious leaders even—and summarily executing them. We have an authenticated report of the entire faculty of a university being rounded up in a raid, taken away, and shot. Needless to say, they are being especially careful to identify leadership personalities who happen also to be Jews."

"There is not even a rumor of that here," she whispered.

"No. My point to you is this: that it seems the organizer of this campaign is Heydrich. We have evidence enough to be certain, actually, that is who it is. He has death squads working in Poland—called *Einsatzgruppen*."

"*Einsatz—God!* On the plane I flew to Poland . . ."

"We are naturally interested in Heydrich's ambition to succeed Hitler and immediately sue for peace. We can't help but wonder, though, if he wouldn't out-Hitler Hitler. It's hard to think of a worse Führer, but . . . He's quite capable of killing Hitler. He's capable of killing you, it goes without saying. You must be extremely careful. Remember, your sole assignment is the removal of Hitler. Don't bring me any other information. I don't care about the January 1 date. We can learn that from other sources. I don't want to see you again unless it's absolutely essential. The generals have gone to ground for the time being, but they will stir again when Hitler suffers his first major defeat in the field. In the meantime, play the Heydrich line. We might decide to go with him. We just might."

❧ XVIII ❧

They did not eat at home. Rarely did they sit together at the
table in the small dining room in their apartment on Markgrafenstrasse for anything but a light breakfast. His hours were ir-
regular. She was an indifferent cook. Their social obligations
demanded their presence at someone's table three or four nights
a week. This spring evening Helmut had come home at seven,
and they had taken dinner in a small restaurant they favored,
where the food was good and the room quiet. They returned to
the apartment about ten.

She was in the bathtub when the telephone rang.

"It is Julius Schaub, calling for you," Helmut told her from
the bathroom door.

Schaub was Hitler's personal adjutant. She stepped out of the
tub, dried herself hastily, and, wrapped in a towel, went to the
telephone.

"I am speaking for the Führer," Schaub said. His voice on the
line was distant and hollow, as if he were not speaking from an
ordinary telephone. "The Führer orders you to report to the
Flight Operations Office at Tempelhof field at two A.M. You
should bring clothing sufficient for two weeks, including both
clothing appropriate for luncheons and dinners in the city and
that appropriate for flying and field operations. You should wear
the latter."

"He *orders*. . . ?" she asked.

"Ja."

"Where is this flight going?"

"I am not at liberty to say."

She returned to the bathroom to finish drying herself. Helmut came to the door, and she told him what Schaub had said.

"An order from the Führer," Helmut said quietly. "An *order*."

Helmut stood for a moment in the bathroom door, heavy with thought. He still wore his boots and breeches, half of the uniform he had worn to dinner, but above he wore an undershirt, and the pale flesh around his shoulders and armpits was loose and soft. The short, bristly hair at the sides of his head had begun to turn gray. He had worked hard all winter, through a winter that had burdened everyone in Berlin with cold, foul weather. His fortieth birthday was four days away—on Sunday, May 12—and he had said they would eat lunch on the shore of the Wannsee and rent a boat and row. He needed to see the sun, he said. He needed to use his body. She had agreed with enthusiasm and had resolved to decline every invitation. If it were too cold to row, she said, they would fly, in her Storch, somewhere. . . .

"I'm sorry, Helmut," she said. "I am, truly. Your birthday . . . Our plans . . ."

He backed out of the door, and she heard his voice from the bedroom. "Are you certain Schaub was calling for the Führer?" he asked. "Or is this some new escapade of Heydrich's?"

"He *said* the Führer."

"Two weeks. If it was the Führer, he has summoned you to watch the assault in the West. It can't be two weeks away."

"Schaub said the Führer orders me, Helmut. That is what he said."

She entered the bedroom. Helmut was lying on their bed, on his back, with a pillow crushed into a wad under his head. The room was lighted only by a single lamp in which a small bulb burned feebly. Helmut had taken very seriously the appeal to save coal by living with as little light and heat as possible—even if the Party dignitaries whose homes they visited conspicuously enjoyed being the victors so far in this war. Somewhat furtively, out of sight of the populace and the Führer alike, they had lived well in an austere, apprehensive city. She and Helmut had jumped back and forth between the two ways of life—being austere in their own home, sharing the sybaritic excesses of the likes of Göring and some of the gauleiters as their frequent guests.

"Maybe you will be a witness to history," said Helmut.

"Do you know the plan for the attack, Helmut?" she asked. "Do they know at the Air Ministry?" She had heard two versions —one from Canaris, one from Heydrich. Canaris had told her the German attack would be heaviest on the right, with the objective of capturing Antwerp and then moving down the coast, capturing the principal Channel ports and cutting off English help to France. Heydrich had said the plan was for an armored *Schwerpunkt* through the Ardennes, followed by a right turn and a race for the mouth of the Somme, so trapping the Allied armies between two German armies. "I've heard rumors," she said to Helmut.

Helmut's eyes seemed fixed on the ceiling. "The Führer does not confide in me as he does in you," he said. "And if he did, *I* would not confide in you."

She tossed her towel aside and picked up a white silk robe. "What do you mean by that?"

He dropped his eyes from the ceiling and looked at her face. "I entertain a distressing suspicion," he said quietly. "I suspect you continue to have contact with English friends. I am afraid you may be communicating things you learn, even from Heydrich, to someone in the English government."

Tying the belt of her robe, she did not look up. "If the chief of the Sicherheitsdienst does not suspect that," she asked, "why should you?"

Helmut filled his lungs with air and let it out slowly. He shrugged. "I think you loved me when I brought you to Berlin, years ago. Even then I understood how much your motives were mixed: that you wanted independence from your family as much as you wanted to live here with me. When you married me last year, I tried not to allow myself to be deceived. I think you loved me, in your way, and probably you do now. But you never act from an unmixed motive. I wasn't sure what your motive was. I thought it might be a romantic attachment to the trappings of our Third Reich, or maybe to the status you enjoyed here, the friendships you had, the flattery you were paid, the privileges you had; or, I thought, maybe you loved, too, the idea of being center stage in an immense drama that was building—with, of course, the understanding that you could withdraw if ever the game affected you too personally. I suspect now I was naïve and underestimated you. I suspect you had better motives than any of those. I have known you longer than Heydrich. I am capable of understanding you better than he does."

She stood. She did not approach their bed. "It is your duty to report what you think," she said.

Helmut shook his head. "No. For two reasons. It would destroy me as well as you. Anyway, I love you."

"Helmut . . ."

"Are you surprised. You shouldn't be. I am a simple man, you know."

She came to the bed and sat down beside him. "I love you, too, Helmut," she said. "I couldn't have married you otherwise."

Helmut smiled. "It *was* convenient, though, wasn't it?"

She lowered her head. "I don't love Heydrich, you understand," she said softly.

"You sleep with him for another reason."

She looked up. "Yes."

"And there is nothing I can do about it. I can't even send you away. I can't demand a divorce." He wiped his mouth with the back of his hand. "Because I am afraid of him," he said bitterly.

"Don't be ashamed of that," said Nancy. "Very few people are not afraid of him."

"You are not afraid of him."

"Oh, yes I am. More than you could imagine."

"I don't know what you are doing," said Helmut. "I would interfere, but I am afraid to—my meddling could cause disaster. Probably disaster is inevitable anyway. You don't even deny you are a spy." He shook his head. "And God knows what more."

"Are you afraid to be married to me? Do you feel trapped?"

For a moment he frowned silently. Then he shook his head.

Helmut drove her to Tempelhof, through the blackout-darkened streets of Berlin. Twice they were stopped. Respectful policemen saluted the insignia of a Generalleutnant and waved them on. In the operations office at Tempelhof, she was received curtly by SS officers who ordered her two bags put aboard the airplane outside and stood impatiently waiting as she kissed Helmut and promised to send him word as soon as she could. Two SS men escorted her to the Ju-52 standing on the ramp. She was shown to a seat inside and found herself in the company of half a dozen silent officers, none of whom could she recognize in the dark. One more passenger came aboard—a Wehrmacht colonel carrying a fat briefcase—and the airplane was taxied out to the runway. It roared into the air at 2:20 A.M.

It was an eerie flight. No one spoke. No one so much as lighted a cigarette in the darkness. She judged that the plane was flying generally west, but whether north or south of west she could not guess. The engines droned. From time to time she heard the familiar sharp splat of a glob of grease thrown from the middle engine and striking the windscreen or somewhere on the fuselage. She dozed. When a change in the sound of the engines told her they had begun a descent for landing, she glanced down at her watch. The time was 4:40—still about an hour before dawn—and the sky was still black, the stars still bright. As they approached the landing field, she saw a big river. It was perhaps the Rhine; she could not be sure.

On the ramp, cars waited. Drivers called out the names of the passengers they were meeting. She heard her own—"Frau Generalleutnant Bittrich, bitte!"—and identified herself to the driver. He recovered her bags and put them in the rear of a black Mercedes. As soon as she was seated behind him, the driver sped away from the airport.

For a few minutes she kept her silence, and the SS noncommissioned officer offered no word. When they sped onto a bridge and crossed the big river, she asked him where they were.

"Köln, Frau Generalleutnant," he said, pointing at a city spread out to the right of the bridge. Cologne.

The sky lightened to gray as they drove south from Cologne, on a country highway that passed through gentle hills, lightly wooded. The driver seemed in a hurry. He shot past what little southbound traffic they overtook. The countryside was wakening around them, developing a beautiful spring morning, when they sped into the village of Euskirchen. There as last she began to understand the reason for this journey. The Führer train was in the station.

She was not taken to the train. At the station the driver transferred her bags to the rear of a three-axled, open vehicle, a car capable of operating in the fields as well as on the roads. The SS man drove this car, too, but a Hauptsturmführer saluted her and sat down beside her in the back seat of the car. They drove on, but only for a few minutes. They entered a zone where the road was blocked by guards. They were checked three times within one kilometer. Finally, they began to climb a low, wooded hill. At the top, the driver pulled the vehicle off the road, into a copse where half a dozen like vehicles were parked. She recognized Schaub approaching, walking fast.

"The Führer," he said abruptly, jerking a thumb over his shoulder.

She walked out of the copse and over the crest of the hill. A modest fortification had been dug into the hill—an antiaircraft battery, she would be told—and at the edge of a small concrete bunker a little group of officers stood around Hitler. The conversation was intent if subdued, and she walked nearly up to them before anyone noticed.

Hitler saw her and stepped out of the group. He took her hands. "Annchen!" he exclaimed with a broad smile. "You are on time."

"I am to be a witness to history," she said soberly.

"I want you to be. However the fates deal with us."

"I am honored, Wolf."

He nodded, still smiling. He seemed ecstatic. With a toss of his head, he invited her to join the group of officers.

They did not welcome her. Jodl stared at his watch. Keitel's eyes were fixed on a distant hillside. Schaub stood on one foot and then the other. She did not know the other adjutants in attendance on Hitler. None of them looked at her.

The dawn was red. Birds were singing in the trees all around them. The fresh breeze was light with green spring. Nancy stood tense, filled with hard emotions all tied together. She felt a nervous sweat emerge on her back.

She began to hear the sound of engines. At first there were maybe a dozen, a kilometer or so away; then, in two minutes, hundreds of them were roaring, none close, but so many that the morning was blanketed with the sound. Trucks. Tanks, maybe. Hitler's adjutant, Puttkamer, emerged from the bunker and silently handed her a map. He pointed at the village of Euskirchen, then moved his finger south to another, smaller village: Münstereifel. The Belgian frontier was, perhaps, 30 kilometers to the west. Liège was 75 kilometers.

Puttkamer touched her arm and nodded toward Hitler. The Führer was staring at Jodl's watch. She glanced at her own: 5:35.

Artillery opened fire, all around them. From behind and ahead of the Führer's headquarters on the hill, the big guns built and sustained a continuing, pulsing thunder, and the ground beneath their feet shook with the repeated shocks. The white flashes of the guns were clearly visible, even on the cloudless morning sky. It was nothing like what she had seen in Poland. She could see nothing of where the shells were going. She could see no movement. It was all too far away, at the range of the heavy guns. A man dashed out of the bunker with a written message for Hitler. He glanced at it and handed it back. She could see his shoulders flex as he breathed heavily. His jaw was rigid. He did not react to a comment by one of the generals. Withdrawn inside himself, he stood and savored the sounds and shocks of his overwhelming barrage. Only when a flight of fifty Luftwaffe bombers swept over at low altitude did he break his reverie, look up, and say something to Jodl.

Nancy was housed in Münstereifel, in a house that had been taken over, as all of the village had been taken over, for the Führer's staff. One of his secretaries was housed in the same house: a young woman called Christa, whose last name Nancy never did discover. This Christa and an older secretary were the only other women in Münstereifel. Hitler did not come there. Nancy was driven to his hillside bunker, where apparently he ate and slept in a concrete cell underground, and had a few words with him each day. She was kept as well informed as anyone in Münstereifel, which meant she was better informed than almost anyone else in the world, but still she shared the agony suffered by everyone in the village, of hearing hourly appreciations compiled from the dispatches that arrived in a stream and still not knowing how the battle went.

She dared not ask Hitler. On the afternoon of May 11, she spent a few minutes with him. His huge situation map was spread out on a trestle table under the trees on the hill, and his adjutants moved around it, marking the positions of units on the acetate overlay. Hitler was in a somber mood. He had only a few units

across the Meuse. In spite of the weight of the attack, it seemed to
be going slowly. Another set of marks moving northeastward
from the Belgian-French frontier showed the French and British
moving up to meet the German attack with an army of a hundred
divisions.

"Your friend Mr. Churchill is Prime Minister now," said Hitler.
"Had you heard?" Aside from a murmured word of greeting
when she arrived this afternoon, these were his first words to her.
"Chamberlain has fallen."

"I had not heard that."

Hitler nodded, still staring at the map. "You know him, don't
you, Annchen? Better than you know Chamberlain?"

"Yes, I do," she said. It would make a difference to her, she
thought. Winston was decisive. "We cannot regard it as good
news."

Hitler glanced at her. "I do not so regard it," he said.

The next day, Sunday, she was able to send birthday greetings
to Helmut, through intervention by Hitler's secretary with a
headquarters telegrapher. She had tea with Hitler. They sat in
chairs outdoors, not far from the big map table. The artillery had
moved up, and the firing was only a distant muttering rumble
now. He was almost morose. She had read the maps and suspected
the battle was going ill. At Münstereifel there was worried talk
about bomber raids on German cities. Holland was defeated,
everyone said; but that would not change the strategic picture
much. The huge French Army was moving into place, along a
line Antwerp-Namur-Dinant-Sedan; with its right flank anchored
on the Maginot line and its left on the Scheldt Estuary, it seemed
to have stopped the German advance already. Preoccupied, Hitler
said little as they sipped tea. She excused herself when she could.

On Monday, the thirteenth, she did not see Hitler, and it was a
long, tiring day. Everyone had demanding duties but her. In her
twill jodhpurs, boots, and a white blouse, she walked from the
village to the Führer's command post on the hill, but she did not
see Hitler. The spring weather remained fine, and the artillery
had moved so far away now that its low rumble no longer over-
powered the song of birds in the woodland. In the afternoon,
when everyone was busy, she took over the bathroom in their

commandeered house and relaxed in a long bath. When she joined Christa and the others for dinner, all the talk was of Sedan. Units under General von Kleist had crossed the Meuse and taken the town where Napoleon III had been captured in 1870. General Guderian was across the river with infantry and a few tanks. Someone had drawn a thick black arrow across the Meuse on the map that hung from the wall in their dining room.

Sedan. The Ardennes. It was where Heydrich had told her the *Schwerpunkt* would occur.

She was summoned to dine with Hitler on the evening of the fourteenth. Dinner was set up on the hillside, under the trees, and the two secretaries joined the adjutants and generals Keitel and Jodl around the trestle table. The mood was different now. On the map table nearby, the breakthrough at Sedan was evident. The First, Second, and Tenth Panzer Divisions were across the Meuse. The French Fifty-fifth Infantry had been driven from Sedan in a headlong rout. The First and Second Panzer Divisions, under General Guderian, had turned west and were threatening the French infantry divisions defending other Meuse crossings, from the rear. What was more, the Seventh Panzer, under General Rommel—who as a colonel had come to London for the funeral of the Earl of Edham—had crossed the Meuse at Dinant. The French Ninth Army no longer held a line on the Meuse but had been driven back as much as 10 kilometers. Charleroi was threatened.

Hitler nibbled lightly on a big green salad and received the dispatches handed him by adjutants all through the meal. He read some of them aloud. The names of the towns were ominous: Saint Gérard, Antheé, Flavion, Revin, Flize. Obviously, the panzers were pouring through the Ardennes forest—on which the French had counted to impede the advance of tanks—as if it were no barrier at all.

She had no private conversation with him that evening, but Hitler spoke to her at the table when he said: "What I would not give to be able to go forward and see our army in battle! It is a burden of leadership to have to sit here, listening to the birds sing, when so much glory is being won."

A young colonel of panzers, slightly wounded at Dinant and brought back to give Hitler a personal account of the battle, talked to Nancy that evening when both of them wandered a little distance away from the table, where the headquarters staff were engaged in close, private conversations.

"It is strange," he said. He was a quiet young man, elaborately diffident in the presence of his Führer and the generals, diffident even to the *Engländerin*, of whom he had heard much and was shyly happy to meet. "We study tactics. We plan. And in battle it is as if we rushed ahead with no plan at all, no knowledge of strategy or tactics. The French are demoralized, apparently. Units fall back at the sight of us. But others fight like fanatics. I think the difference isn't a matter of plan, or even of leadership, but of chance."

"The Führer spoke of glory," she said.

"I will speak of that next year," said the Colonel.

She spent almost no time in Münstereifel after that. She spent her time—at Hitler's request—at the headquarters, an idle spectator in the midst of people working twenty-hour days, but always welcome to study the situation map, often favored with a word by Hitler. The generals came: Halder and Brauchitsch and Rundstedt. Halder avoided her eyes. Jodl and Keitel, perhaps because the tension was less, took moments to chat with her. The adjutants saw to it that she had food and drink, the modest amenities of the headquarters. It was plain to everyone that the Führer favored her, and they dared do no less.

On the map she saw the Allied front dissolve. The panzers raced for the Channel, as Heydrich had said they would. On the seventeenth, Friday, a week after the attack was launched, Jodl stood beside her in the morning as she was having her first look at the map that day. "You see, it is over," he said. "The war in the West is won."

If it was, Hitler did not believe so yet. The next day she heard him scream at Halder that Kleist's southern flank was suicidally exposed to a French counterattack, that the panzers had run too far west and had placed the entire campaign in immediate and mortal danger.

Even so, that same evening he led her away from the table after dinner, to a private spot at the edge of the woods, and there he told her it was time for her to return to Berlin. "But be ready. I may have an important mission for you in a few days. The war in the West may be won already. The time is near when we must begin to devote all our efforts to the peace."

"Heydrich is the only chance."

Binghamton lifted his brows and regarded her with lofty skepticism. "The Prime Minister doesn't think so," he said.

"Canaris gave me the plan for the attack in the West, fully expecting me to communicate it to London," she said. "And he gave me the wrong plan."

"Maybe he didn't know the real plan."

"*General Halder* didn't know? Come on now, Freddy. The truth is, the generals want to win the war. They want to overthrow Hitler, but they want to win the war."

"And Heydrich doesn't?"

"Heydrich did not want Hitler to defeat France," she said firmly. "With the fall of France, the war has taken on a new dimension. Britain will never negotiate a peace that leaves Germany occupying France. The Americans will come in. And sooner or later Stalin will switch sides again. This will be a war to the bitter, bitter end. Heydrich doesn't want that. He doesn't have the guts for it. He's afraid they'll lose."

"What advantage is there is replacing one fanatic Nazi with another?" Binghamton asked.

"Hitler is a charismatic leader," said Nancy. "He has a mystic hold on this nation. No one else will be as strong or as dangerous."

Binghamton chewed his lower lip. "Your orders are to continue your contacts with Canaris and the generals. I'll communicate what you say, but for now the PM still thinks the generals are the best hope. I see no reason why you should not continue to pursue the Heydrich connection. But don't forget how very dangerous he is."

Nancy sighed. "Tell Winston also that I'll be going to Paris as soon as it's safe—maybe even before. They want me to try to convince the Duke of Windsor to stay in Paris."

✵ XIX ✵

It was astounding. The taxi sped down the Champs-Elysées, swung around the place de la Concorde and into the rue de Rivoli, and Paris looked untouched and never so beautiful. Long-legged girls in summer frocks strode gaily along the avenues. People sat as always in the cafés, taking their aperitifs with Gallic insouciance. From the place de la Concorde you could see the white smoke rising over the Quai d'Orsay—clerks in the court-yard at the Ministère des Affaires l'Etrangères were burning documents—and still Parisians strolled and drank, and their children sailed boats on the ponds in the Jardin des Tuileries.

The news from the front was of debacle. Divisions of the German Nineteenth Armored Corps had reached the Channel coast. Boulogne and Calais were besieged or taken, depending on which dispatch you believed. If there was in fact a coherent army front between Paris and the rampaging panzers, it was on the Somme. In the north, five German infantry corps were driving the French Army and the British Expeditionary Force west to the sea. The German infantry were across the Scheldt in force. They had taken Ypres. The BEF was falling back on Dunkirk. It and the bulk of the French Army seemed trapped between three armored corps moving west and north and five infantry corps moving west and south.

This was the situation on May 27, when Nancy arrived in Paris. She had been briefed on it two days before in Berlin, and nothing she had seen or heard in France had contradicted the German appreciation of the situation. If Paris did not understand, Paris was deaf, dumb, blind, and numb.

At the Hotel Regina, place des Pyramides, she presented her British passport.

"You have not booked a room, mademoiselle?" the desk clerk asked, his brows raised, his lips pursed.

Nancy smiled. "Travel is a bit disorganized these days," she said in French.

"Ah, yes. Fortunately I can accommodate you. A room on the courtyard?"

"Please."

He began to fill out her police card. "This is still your permanent address? London? Yes. And may I know the purpose of your visit to Paris?"

"I am a journalist," she said.

An SS pilot, flying a Storch, had brought her to a field outside Dijon, where she was received by a French traitor and put on a train for Paris. The trip had been amazingly easy. Trains moving south were crowded, as were the roads. Trains moving north and west to Paris were almost vacant. Arriving at the Gare de Lyon, she had directed the driver to make the circuit of Montparnasse and bring her into the city past the Eiffel Tower and the Arch of Triumph and down the Champs-Elysées, that she might have a lingering look at Paris, in the fear she might never again see it as it was.

She had decided to come to France as Lady Nancy Brookeford. It was not likely that anyone at the Préfecture de Police would know the name, or would at any rate associate it with Frau Generalleutnant Helmut Bittrich. If anyone did, the British would be contacted, and she could count on His Majesty's government to extract her, one way or another, from any problem that might arise. All she needed do was avoid contact with English acquaintances—and in the circumstances, it was unlikely that many of them were in Paris.

Except one. David.

Heydrich did not like the idea. Admiral Canaris was not supposed to know about it, but did and did not like it. It was a scheme of Ribbentrop's, endorsed with enthusiasm by the Führer himself.

"Ribbentrop cares nothing," Heydrich had groused. "If the French . . . It means *nothing* to him. The French will be insane. If they lay hands on you, they will shoot you. In a moment."

"The Führer doesn't think so," she had said.

Heydrich had paused, frowning, sighing loudly through his nostrils. "Tell me," he had said, "will the Duke of Windsor ever again sit on the English throne—I mean, will he ever, absent our conquering England and putting him there? Will the English ever recall him?"

"No."

"Never? Are our plans for him unrealistic?"

"Entirely so."

"Have you told the Führer this?"

"Not in blunt terms."

"And he sends you anyway to Paris, to risk your life."

"He will do anything to achieve a peace with England."

Heydrich had paced the floor, glancing angrily out the window —this was in her apartment on Markgrafenstrasse. Abruptly he had stopped and taken her in his arms. "I care very deeply for you," he said. "May God go with you."

It was exactly what Hitler had said.

After a quick bath, she dressed in a spring dress of white and pink and took a taxi for 24 boulevard Suchet. In midafternoon she saw that Paris was not as untouched as it had seemed when she arrived. Limousines were moving south through Montparnasse, loaded with trunks and furnishings. Army lorries moved in the opposite direction, presumably toward the front on the Somme. The southbound traffic was heavy.

"Yesterday," her driver told her, "I drove two—you will excuse me—beautiful young prostitutes to Bordeaux. They paid me two thousand francs for the trip." He turned and grinned at Nancy in the rear seat. "In the last war, we drove soldiers to the front. In this war . . ." He shrugged.

"What if the Germans come?" she asked.

He shrugged again. "They will need taxis."

At 24 boulevard Suchet, she almost despaired of entry. She rang the bell five times before it was answered by an army major in khaki. When she told him she was a friend of the Duke's, he only shrugged and said the Duke was with the British Mission.

"Where is the Mission?" she demanded crisply.

"I'm afraid I can't say, really," said the Major.

"Can't? Or won't?" she asked. "Do you *know* where David is?"

He had begun to close the door; but when she referred to the Duke as "David," he hesitated. "You are . . ."

"Lady Nancy Brookeford."

His brows rose. "Indeed?"

"Tell the Duke I'm here," she said abruptly.

It was a chance shot, but it hit. The Major stepped back from the door and, with a nod, invited her to enter the house. He nodded her into the small gold and white room where she had met the Duke and Duchess when she was here before—a room in which now the furniture was covered, offering no place to sit. She stood there for five minutes, looking out the window onto the boulevard, not certain really if the Duke was there, wondering after a while if the Major had not gone to telephone the police.

The door opened. David entered. He was wearing a spring suit—gray, with a tiny check, double-breasted, with a light blue shirt, a bow tie. He stood for a moment inside the open door, frowning uncertainly. "They say you are a traitor," he ventured at last.

She lifted her chin. "Do you believe that, David?"

His jaw dropped, and his eyes hardened. He expected to be called "sir," not "David," by anyone except people most intimately acquainted, and for an instant his anger flashed. Then he stuttered: "Uh—uh—no."

"Where is Her Royal Highness?"

"Uh—at Biarritz."

She glanced around the room. "Have you any chairs that are uncovered?"

He swallowed. "Yes, of course. And, uh—uh, some champagne if you'd care for it."

He led her to the second floor of the house, to a study where his writing table remained uncovered. As they climbed the stairs, she saw servants carrying luggage down. He stopped one and told him to bring champagne to the study.

"But how *could* you, Nancy?" he asked emotionally as they sat down in his study. "How could you remain in Germany when we are at war?"

"My husband is German," she said. "Both you and I have German cousins, David."

He shook his head. "It is a tragedy," he whispered. "A war no one wanted." He stared downward, his face wrinkled with despair. Suddenly he looked up. "How does it happen you are in Paris?" he asked.

"I've come to see *you.*"

"Oh? To see me? Why?"

"The Reich Chancellor," she said, using a term she hardly ever any more applied to Hitler, "thinks you may be able to contribute to the making of peace. He sent me to see you."

"You are the envoy of *that man?*" the Duke asked distastefully.

"Hitler refers to you as King Edward, never as the Duke of Windsor," she said. "The same is true of the Foreign Minister, von Ribbentrop. France is defeated, David. I don't know if you realize that. The war is all but over. Hitler wants peace. He thinks you may be the man to make it. He thinks the English people will recall you to the throne, once they see the straits to which their present leadership has brought them. He envisions a treaty of peace, signed between him and King Edward VIII."

"He thinks *I* would preside over England's *surrender?*" the Duke asked indignantly.

"Over the making of peace," she said.

"A peace dictated by him? He *is* insane!"

"To avoid a tragedy," she said.

The Duke's face hardened. His thin lips whitened. "He thinks he's defeated France, does he? Well, I tell you—and you can tell him—France is in a better position now than it was in 1914. You think the war is over? I tell you, the French Army will hold on the Somme. If not on the Somme, then it will hold on the Marne. If not on the Marne, it will hold on the Seine. I tell you, it is Germany that is defeated, not France."

"David—"

"*Don't call me that, God damn you!*" the Duke snapped furiously. "You *are* a traitor. You're in the employ of the Nazis, and you've betrayed the King and the King's people." He stood.

"Please leave. If you remain here another minute, I shall call the French authorities."

She could have been proud of him. She could have if she had not wondered where all the luggage was going that his staff was carrying down the stairs, and if she had not learned shortly that he had left Paris that same afternoon, within the hour in fact, for Biarritz—abandoning the British Military Mission, his duty, and the war.

Anyway, she could be grateful to him. She could report to Hitler that he had thrown her out. If he had given her the slightest encouragement, she would have faced a distressing problem.

She had come to Paris without either a German or a British contact arranged. What was more, she had no arrangements to return to Berlin. Heydrich, who was responsible for her through his Amt VI, had told her to wait for her contact; it would come in due time. He had assumed she would need time in Paris—time to talk to the Duke, to convince him. No one had anticipated that her mission would be over a few hours after she arrived. When she returned to her hotel, she ordered a bottle of champagne brought to her room, stretched out in a hot bath, and lay smiling and comfortable, genuinely and deeply amused by the course fate had taken.

She slept well, in spite of the alarms of the night—two air-raid alerts accompanied by much banging of antiaircraft fire but no sound either of planes or of bombs. In the morning she took breakfast in the breakfast room of the hotel and went out for a walk, to the Champs-Elysées and all the way to the Arch. When she sat down with a newspaper for a morning aperitif, the news was of the surrender of Belgium.

When she returned to her room at the Hotel Regina, she found on the settee a lady's black umbrella. She picked it up. It had broken ribs. As she was looking at it, frowning over it, a card fell from it. "Les reparations des parapluies. 114 rue Jacques Rousseau."

It was within walking distance. On the rue de Rivoli she saw a convoy of trucks, carrying away either records from the Ministère des Finances or art treasures from the Louvre. Other trucks were loading at the Banque de France.

The umbrella shop was small and shabby. The window frame was painted a light blue, but the paint was chipped and dirty. She looked in before she entered. An old man sat on a stool behind the single counter, before a wall of umbrellas, all hanging from hooks. Others hung from the ceiling. Though black predominated, the umbrellas were of every color.

For a moment, when she put the umbrella down on the counter, the old man seemed not to see her. A stub of a cigarette burned hazardously close to his thick, yellow-stained moustache. He took spectacles from his vest pocket and carefully placed them astride his thin nose. He peered then at the umbrella.

"Madame Bittrich?" he asked.

"Non. Je suis Mademoiselle Brookeford."

"Wie Sie Wünschen," he said. As you wish. "Ich bin Pierre Augustin. Ich habe eine Botschaft für Sie." He had a message for her.

"Eh bien," she said. His German was wretchedly accented and she wanted him to speak French. "Qu'est-ce que c'est?"

He spoke French. "I can send and receive messages for you," he said. "You need only check here with me. My present message is only that your friends wish you well and are anxious for a report."

"Send this," she said. " 'Our friend adamantly refuses to co-operate. He has abandoned his post and gone south. Shall I return?' "

The old man nodded. "It is not safe for me to visit your hotel. Call tomorrow. I will have your umbrella fixed."

Outside the shop, she stood for a moment on the sidewalk and stared at the old man behind the counter. He was a French traitor. He was despicable. He was what her friends in England thought *she* was.

But not everyone in England thought so. Back at her hotel, she found a man sitting in the lobby, waiting for her. His name was Bascombe Dunbar, and he was an old friend of her father's, whom she had seen only once or twice and whom she remembered only vaguely.

" 'Twas a tragedy to lose the Earl," he said to her as they sat at a table facing the fountains before the Comédie Française. "I'm not sure his children know what a fine man he was."

Dunbar was conspicuously the English aristocrat—tall, ruddy-faced, dressed in a dark blue suit and white shirt, wearing a black bowler, carrying a tightly rolled brolly. "It's perfectly all right for you to be seen with me," he had said to her at the hotel. "I was in point of fact a friend of your father's, and that's known. Anyway, I'm with the embassy, and the French let us know these days whenever any prominent British subject arrives in France."

"My father spoke of you often," she said distractedly.

"I haven't been told what you're doing, but I'm relieved to know you're not a traitor," he said.

"Thank you."

"The Germans judged the risk correctly when they sent you here. The Préfecture sent us notice that you are in Paris. They did not identify you except as one of half a dozen London journalists who arrived yesterday."

"The French government is hardly functioning, I suppose," she said.

"It's not quite that bad. But if the French forces cannot hold on the Somme—and there is every reason to doubt they can—then the German Army will be in Paris within a month."

Nancy nodded. "Such is my impression, too."

"I am instructed to ask how long you will be in Paris."

"I don't know. I may be leaving very soon, as soon as tomorrow, or . . ." She shrugged.

"If you have to leave abruptly, try to telephone me from a public telephone kiosk. Here is the number. Otherwise, we will be keeping watch, and you may have another contact in a day or so."

She ate alone again, this time in the hotel. The French newspapers complained that evening that the British Expeditionary Force was being evacuated through Dunkirk, leaving France to stand alone against the Nazi attack being prepared north of the Somme. Her waiter believed it. He was rude. She heard the sirens again that night, and the antiaircraft fire; but once again she heard no planes, no bombs. In the morning the traffic was heavy. More Parisians were leaving.

At the umbrella shop that afternoon, the old man had a message for her. "You are to remain in Paris. If your friend returns, try to renew the contact. He may change his mind as the situation develops. In any event, it is not safe for you to try to return by the way you came. You will receive a further message." He looked at her over his glasses. "I may add personally, mademoiselle, that if you should find it necessary, I will be glad to provide a safe hiding place for you here, above my shop. I mean, if there is fighting . . ."

"Merci, monsieur," she said curtly. "Merci."

Remain in Paris. A new contact from England, perhaps. Another message from Berlin sometime. Not safe to return the way she came. Maybe fighting in the streets. The BEF leaving France, leaving the French to hate the English. The most beautiful city in the world losing its spirit as she walked its streets. It was inconceivable that it should have become painful to walk the streets of Paris in May. She walked. She had nothing else to do. She walked, with an ominous sense that she might be seeing it for the last time. She sat in the sidewalk cafés and sipped coffee and aperitifs. She ate well, in restaurants that still served well, in spite of all.

She had arrived in Paris on Monday. She called at the umbrella shop for the third time on Friday. No word from Berlin. Walking back to the Hotel Regina, she was stopped on the rue de Montpensier by a young woman who asked her for a light for her cigarette and then said quickly in English: "Have dinner tonight at Venegende, boulevard Saint-Germain. If you are not contacted by ten, walk to the Church of Saint Germain des Prés."

She reached the restaurant at eight, allowing two hours for dinner. The place was small, a turn-of-the-century restaurant specializing in seafood. The fish was good. The wine was excellent. Whoever had chosen it for a rendezvous knew something of good eating in Paris. When the waiter presented her bill, he told her, "Votre voiture attend, madame." On the street, a car was indeed waiting for her. She entered the car, not knowing if this was a contact from Berlin, or London, or maybe even the French, placing her under arrest.

"Good evening, Lady Nancy."

She peered into the darkness inside the car. The voice was English. The man sat in the far corner of the back seat, only two feet from her."

"We have but a short drive," the man said crisply.

"To where?" she asked. "And why?"

"It is a secret," he said. "You understand, of course, you have nothing to fear. We are MI-6."

The car made quick turns and sped through short streets. It was a small black car, nothing conspicuous. Two men sat in front. Shortly she had no idea where she was, except that it had to be somewhere in Montparnasse. When the car stopped in a dark, narrow street, she could not name the street, nor the street from which they had turned—which was undoubtedly what they had wanted. Two of the men showed her to the door of a modest, stucco-fronted house. The car drove away, leaving them.

One man opened the door with a key. When they were inside a dim, dusty hallway, he trotted up the stairs alone, while she and the other man waited. In a moment he came to the top of the stairs and beckoned them to climb up. He held a door open. He bowed to her as she passed through, and he closed the door behind her.

"Nancy. Please forgive the cloak-and-dagger routine. It's as distasteful to me as it is to you."

Winston Churchill! He sat at a table covered with an ornate fringed cloth. He was slumped wearily in a formidable old armchair upholstered in tattered red plush. He held a coffeepot in one hand, a cup and saucer in the other, and he poured black coffee.

"Please." He nodded at another chair much like his own. "Coffee. And . . . Cognac." He put down the pot and cup and took up a bottle and glass, to pour her a generous amount of Cognac. "I've spent some hours with the French: Reynaud, Pétain, Weygand . . . It's been one of the most discouraging days of my life."

"They're beaten, aren't they?" she said.

The yellowish light from a small bulb burning in a frosted tulip-shaped globe cast deep shadows from Churchill's brows down over his eyes. His lower lip shot forward defiantly, but he nodded. "Yes. As soon as Hitler gathers his forces, he'll break through again. We will be alone, Nancy. Very shortly, we will be alone."

"The United States?" she asked.

He shrugged. "Someday. Maybe."

"What can we do?"

He drew a breath. "A thousand things," he said. His chin came up, and he nodded. "A thousand things."

"Do you want me to kill Hitler?" she asked bluntly, abruptly.

Churchill frowned. "Can you?"

"Yes."

"At the cost of your own life."

"Yes."

"How soon could you do it?"

Nancy swirled the Cognac in her glass and watched the dim light play in it, amber and gold. "I don't know," she said quietly. "When the opportunity comes. That's all I can say. When I'm alone with him. It could happen next week. It might not happen for two months. Anyway, I do see him alone, and they don't search me."

Churchill drew a deep breath and sat contemplating her, his frown deep, his mouth working. She could guess his thoughts. She was a girl to him, a little girl he had seen grow up, as if she were a niece or cousin of his own. He didn't know this svelte, confident, aristocratic young woman as well as he had known the girl; it had been easier to know her. Here she was, offering to commit the assassination that could change the world more than the one at Sarajevo had changed it. She was calmly offering to sacrifice her own life. She guessed he wondered if she could really do it. Had she the courage?

"I should rather someone did it for us," said Churchill. He took a small sip of his Cognac. He nodded. "Much better."

"You cannot count on the generals, Winston," she said. "Even if they had the courage, which they do not, they wouldn't do it—not while they are winning. They wanted to rid themselves of him because they were afraid he would push them into a war they would lose. If he wins . . ."

"What if he should lose a major battle?"

"When is he going to do that?"

Churchill smiled bitterly. "When, indeed?"

"The generals will never overthrow him, I tell you," she said grimly. "*Never.*"

"You are for Heydrich, then?"

"He is motivated. He is ruthless."

"Granting that, what advantage?" Churchill asked.

"Several. The generals are troubled in their consciences whenever they contemplate moving against Hitler—because they swore an oath of loyalty and obedience to him. They swore none to Heydrich. Heydrich is not the demagogue Hitler is. The Germans who know him only fear him. He will not inspire their loyalty. He—"

"You contemplate a putsch and counterputsch, internal struggles, confusion. . . ?"

"Probably. But even if Heydrich wins out and becomes Führer, there is advantage."

"Why, if he is the ruthless man you say and the bestial killer we hear told?"

"He is not a fanatic," she said. "Hitler is a fanatic, also a mystic. So is Hess. So is Himmler. Göring isn't. Heydrich isn't. You could make a rational deal with Heydrich or Göring. Heydrich is a practical man. He wants to enjoy the rewards of power. He doesn't want to fight on, making more and more enemies, until Germany is overwhelmed. You could negotiate a peace with him."

"I doubt that."

"He would make concessions Hitler will never make."

"Nancy . . ." Churchill said tentatively, softly. "I may in the end have to order you to kill Hitler. Let it be understood that the death of Hitler—or his overthrow—is your sole mission in Germany. You are not to gather intelligence. What is more, you are not to kill the Führer unless you receive my specific order. You are not, on your own initiative, to sacrifice your life. I leave you no personal discretion in that. You are to do it only on my order—which will be the most difficult order I have to give in this war."

"Give it if you have to, Winston," she said. "When others are dying in thousands, I . . ." She shook her head.

"I will give it, if I must," he said firmly.

"That's *your* duty."

He nodded. "Yes. Now, as to the generals, I'm afraid I can't accept your judgment entirely. Continue your contacts with them. Let them know your reports to London are brought directly to me. What you hear through Binghamton will be direct word from me. Tell them we will negotiate a peace that is not punitive. But tell them, too, if they think they can digest their conquests and establish permanent German hegemony on the Continent, we will fight them till hell freezes over.

"As to Heydrich—well, you can't tell him anything of the sort, because he does not know you work for the government. If he should find out—and you survive—you can say the same to him. I'm not sure how we can encourage him to kill Hitler, but if we can, do it. I accept your judgment that we could benefit from his doing so."

She closed her eyes and nodded.

Churchill put his hand on hers. "We have no more important agent in Germany," he said. "If we lose you, I will see to it that you have every honor. Besides me, a few others know what you are doing and at what sacrifice. You are considered a traitor in England now. I'm sorry we cannot tell your family, at least, that you are not. The time will come when everyone will know you are a heroine."

She smiled wryly. "I hope I'm there to see it."

"May God grant that," said Churchill fervently. "And now—one more thing. I have something to give you." He reached deep into his coat pocket and took out a small brass cylinder, a little smaller than a lipstick. He unscrewed the cap and shook a smaller cylinder of soft black rubber onto the table. "Inside the rubber there is a vial of the most deadly poison," he said solemnly. "Cyanide. If you bite down hard on the rubber, you will break the glass vial. Your teeth must also pierce the rubber. I'm told you have to bite hard and chew on the thing to release the poison into your mouth, so it's safe to carry it in your mouth in time of hazard. If you swallow it, it will pass through without ill effect. But if you bite and release the poison in your mouth, you will be dead within the minute. They are capable of brutal torture, you know. . . ."

"I understand."

His hand tightened around hers. "I treasure you, Nancy," he growled. He lifted his Cognac. "To the day," he said, "when you and I laugh at this ugly thing"—nodding at the brass cylinder—"and return it to the men who invented it. May a benevolent Providence grant us that day."

PART III

1941–42

Only because the room was dark could they open the curtains to the June night. It *was* dark, and they stood at the open window, watching the air raid. Nancy was nude except for a pair of white panties. She flexed her shoulders to rub her back against the scratchy wool of Heydrich's uniform. "Damn buttons are cold," she whispered. He nuzzled her neck. His hands cupped her breasts. She could feel his erection against her buttock. He had just arrived. He had taken her robe and tossed it on the sofa, and he had led her to the window.

"The flak tower," he said. He was looking at a sustained, pulsing red flash, standing over the rooftops to the north and east. A group of antiaircraft towers was being built in the zoo, on the southwestern corner of the Tiergarten. One of them was in operation already. The Ministry of Propaganda said the towers, when complete, could lay a blanket of antiaircraft fire over the center of the city, and that this summer—the summer of 1941— would see an end to the nuisance raids of the RAF. Almost half a minute passed before the flash was followed by the staccato roar of the guns mounted in the tower. The house was in Friedenau, five miles from the zoo.

She did not see the bombers. She never did. They were British, of course, Stirlings or Halifaxes. She had flown the Messerschmitt 110, the twin-engine night fighter hastily developed to go up after the night bombers. She had accompanied Göring and Goebbels and even Hitler himself to view the wreckage of British bombers shot down. She had heard Hitler's fury and Heydrich's scorn, directed at the embarrassed Reichsmarschall, whose Luftwaffe had failed to keep the bombers away from Berlin. She had taken part in the interrogation of British aviators, captured after their bombers crashed. But she had never seen the bombers, flying 4,000 or 5,000 meters overhead, opening their bellies and disgorging loads of bombs.

It all had a certain futility. She knew from figures Helmut had brought home that—contrary to what the propaganda said—the fighters and the flak were bringing down only about two percent of the bombers sent over Germany. On the other hand, the bombing was ineffective. Here in Berlin, the bombs had fallen in the Wannsee, in the Grunewald, in the Grosser Müggelsee—in the waters and woods, in other words—and on houses and roads and athletic fields, and on shops and churches and into the canals. Few bombs had fallen on factories or on the railroads or on military installations. She had seen it personally, what they had hit. The aiming was bad. All it was doing was stiffening the German spirit.

Sent by Hitler's personal orders to talk to English fliers, she had actually encountered men she knew. "You can tell your friend Adolf his slaughter of innocent men and women in London has only made us stronger," one man had said to her—Wing Commander Robert Gibson, a man married to a friend of hers. She had shaken her head sadly. "And what more will bombing Berlin do, Bobby?" she had asked. He had sneered. "You don't see the difference, really, do you?" he had asked.

"Ah!" said Heydrich, pointing up. A flash of flame high over the center of the city told him a bomber had been hit.

Helmut had given up the apartment in Markgrafenstrasse and moved their home to this small stone house in Friedenau, in the thought that it would be removed from the center of the city, which would be a target for the English bombers. It was a pleasant house. She liked it. The stone was covered with ivy. The windows were leaded. They had a fireplace, in which they could burn wood in the winter. It had two stories, plus a cellar, which Göring had stocked with cases of French wine. Hitler himself had come for the housewarming.

Helmut was at home no more than two nights a week. He telephoned from the Air Ministry every afternoon, usually to say he would not be home. Heydrich slept here as often as Helmut did, when he was in Berlin.

"Enough," said Heydrich. He closed the window and the curtains. "*Danke*, Herr Meyer." Göring had said they could call him Meyer if ever an English bomber reached Berlin, and Heydrich was by no means the only one who commonly called him that now. "Have you anything in the house to eat? I've flown in from Vienna."

He switched on a lamp. He had tossed his driving gloves on a table, and now he tossed his cap there.

"I can serve you a banquet," she said.

He sat on the sofa. "One of the most charming things about you, Nancy—one of the things I most admire—is that you have absolutely no domestic talents. You can't cook, you can't sew on a button, you have never vacuumed a carpet in your life, and God forbid you should ever be called on to wash clothes. You are a true aristocrat."

"If that's the index of aristocracy, I am indeed," she said. "I was taught to speak flawless French and German, to ride a horse, to know *how* a table should be set but never to set one, to spend money but never to make it . . . et cetera: everything the parasitic leisure class understands."

"Plus one more thing," he said. "To make the most brilliant conversation of any woman—or man, for that matter—I've ever heard."

"I'm told I talk too much," she said.

"Never."

"Anyway, Reinhard, would you like a bottle of Herr Meyer's Bordeaux?"

He nodded. "I'll fetch it. And open it. Have you anything at all to eat?"

They sat on the sofa, facing the low table before it, with the wine and some sandwiches she had cut in the kitchen, some soft French cheese, a bunch of grapes. He had undressed in the bedroom and wore only a white silk robe. She was still naked but for her tight, sheer panties. He was hungry. He ate all the sandwiches but the one on which she nibbled.

She had had her hair trimmed shorter and thinned. It curled softly under her ears. She was still slender. In the close, warm air inside the heavy blackout curtains, her body glistened with light perspiration. Heydrich lifted a drop of it off her nipple with a fingertip, and he switched off the lamp and opened the curtains and windows. The air raid continued. The flak tower erupted intermittently with a sheet of flame. Spotlights worked the sky. If there were bombers, they were unseen and silent, and it was difficult to believe they were up there.

"You know about the Bömer affair?" Heydrich asked.

She shook her head, then said, "No," realizing that in this low light he probably had not seen.

"A drunk. One of Goebbels's drunks. He talked too much at a reception at the Bulgarian legation, talked about Barbarossa, said we would finish Russia in four weeks and he would become Undersecretary to the Governor General of Russia. I can't tell you how angry the Führer is. He ordered me to find evidence of treason against the man; and when I couldn't find it, he sent the man before the People's Court anyway."

"Barbarossa is compromised?" she asked.

"I wish it were," said Heydrich. "I wish it were, even though I doubt it would make any difference."

"The two-front war," she said.

"Yes," said Heydrich. "No matter what."

"There is no way to stop him?"

"Short of killing him, none."

"You recall how Bismarck maintained what he called his 'reptile fund'?" Goebbels asked Nancy as he handed her a glass of champagne he had just taken from the tray of a passing waiter.

"I am afraid my education in German history omitted that one, Herr Doktor," she said.

Goebbels glanced around the room, at the assembly of journalists gathered in the great reception hall of the Ministry of Propaganda. He smiled slyly at her. "It was his secret fund for bribing newspapers," he said, his smile widening.

She laughed. "Surely it isn't necessary in the Third Reich," she said.

Beaming, he lifted his eyebrows. "Lots of foreign ones here today. Be careful of the Americans. Snakes. Lizards."

"I'll avoid them."

"No, please. Since they will not see the Führer, whom they expected to see today, you are an attraction. Be yourself. That will be quite enough."

She nodded.

He touched her arm lightly. "I appreciate your coming here today. I hope you and Helmut can join Magda and me for a simple dinner at home after the reception."

The American correspondents—their country still neutral—smoked, drank champagne, and conspicuously ignored the functionaries of the Ministry who handed out press releases and tried to guide them to discussions with selected soldiers and fliers who were there to be interviewed.

"Bob Tyler, INS," said a balding, pipe-smoking American to Nancy. "You're Lady Nancy Brookeford, aren't you?"

She nodded at the American. "Ich bin Frau Generalleutnant Helmut Bittrich," she said.

"Yes. Would you mind speaking English? My German is passable but not much more."

"Berlin is a strange assignment for you, then, isn't it?" she said in English.

He chuckled. "Yes, I suppose it is. It's temporary. I'm on my way home from Moscow."

"Do you speak Russian, then?"

Tyler laughed. "My dear lady, *no one* speaks Russian. After listening to the Russians for three months, I'm not convinced they speak it to each other."

She smiled. He was not entirely illiterate.

He looked around the room. "They won't talk about what I want to talk about," he said.

"Which is?"

"Russia. London and Washington think Hitler's about to invade Russia. Moscow says no. Berlin won't talk about it."

"I shouldn't think that would surprise you," she said. "If the Führer means to invade Russia, I hardly expect he'll give advance notice to Tyler of the INS."

Tyler chuckled, pursing his lips in the peculiar way of a pipe smoker, and he pushed the pipestem into the corner of his mouth. "Is there anything we can talk about? I mean, is there anything you can comment on?"

She shrugged. "Anything you want."

"Is Hitler going to invade Russia?"

"No one has said so to me. I see no evidence of it."

A billow of white smoke issued from his mouth. "What about

the sinking of the *Bismarck?* The story on you is that you're close to Hitler. How'd he react to the sinking?"

"He was sorry to lose a fine ship and many brave men."

Tyler nodded. "Hell of a defeat."

"No."

"The world thinks so."

"Tell me, Mr. Tyler," she said, "would you trade a battleship for an island—say, the *Bismarck* for Crete?"

"What's the point?"

"The Admiralty sent eight battleships, no less, in pursuit of the *Bismarck*—not to mention two aircraft carriers and I don't know how many cruisers and destroyers. Many of those ships were pulled out of the Mediterranean, out of the battle for Crete."

Tyler shook his head and chuckled. "An interesting rationalization."

"It's my own. It's not the official position. But we English understand something of naval strategy, you know."

" 'We English,' " he repeated. "Maybe you're the best story here. You still consider yourself English?"

"English and German," she said smoothly. "My husband is German, you know."

"I wouldn't plan on ever going home," he said. "They'll hang you. Have you seen any of the London newspaper stories on you?"

"People spare me that."

"The Blitz, you know. The English have developed quite a capacity for hating. Have you heard of the 'Thanks, Nancy' signs?"

"No."

"They stick them up on bombed-out houses. People know what they mean."

"How kind of you to tell me," she said thinly, looking past him at Goebbels, hoping to catch his eye and be rescued from this man.

"Give me an interview and I'll write your side of the story," said Tyler.

"I had supposed *this* was an interview."

"I mean a *real* interview. Say over dinner. Are you and your husband free for dinner?"

"My husband works eighteen-hour days at the Air Ministry. He sleeps there."

"Well, I guess it wouldn't be improper if you and I had dinner without him."

"I have a tentative engagement to have dinner with a friend."

"Bring her along. Or him. It's okay by me."

"Mr. Tyler, my dinner engagement is with Reinhard Heydrich."

"Oh, Jesus! Jesus, lady, you *are* a Nazi, aren't you?"

"He'll be your contact now. He's thoroughly trained. He knows precisely what he's doing. It will be simpler for him."

Freddy Binghamton sat on her sofa. The new man, Gordon Aherne, stood by the window, nervously peering out into the night between the blackout curtains he had parted with elaborate caution. He wore the field-gray uniform of the Wehrmacht. He was wounded—his right leg had been taken off below the knee. He was in fact a physician, trained in Vienna, and his papers identified him as Klaus Diekermann, army surgeon. He would work at Abendliche Hospital in Berlin.

"The Prime Minister speaks extremely fondly of you and sends his warmest regards," said Aherne to Nancy. He spoke English with the cultivated accent of a Cantabrigian, German like a Viennese. "I saw him only Monday."

"Close the curtain, will you please," she said.

He did, and she turned on the light. She wanted a better look at him, and one at Freddy as well. Aherne was her own age, though he looked younger. He was blond and pink-faced. He had lost his leg on the beach at Dunkirk and had nearly bled to death on a pitching little boat in the Channel. Since then, he had spent half the year recovering and half in training with MI-6. He was a sad, badly hurt young man.

Aherne was less interesting to her than was Freddy Binghamton, who in the same year had been ravaged by the stress of living as a British agent in Berlin. He carried his rubber-encased vial of cyanide in his mouth almost all the time. In fact, he had swallowed it once; and because he did not have another, he had taken his bowel movements on newspaper until the vial passed and he could recover it. She was glad he was so fanatically careful. He worked several other agents besides her, and she knew he had lost at least two—one of them a woman who had been tortured to death at Spandau Prison. She could be sure he would crush his vial if he were captured. No one would ever torture his secrets out of him. But he was thin, graying, haggard.

"I must establish my ability to fly, even with my wooden leg," said Aherne. "That will be our reason for seeing each other."

"*Morgen,* Herr Doktor Diekermann?" she asked.

"Tomorrow?"

"Have you ever seen a Storch?"

"I'd love to fly one of those," said Aherne.

"You will, tomorrow. We will call it therapy for you, recovering your ability to fly."

"You will run into Heydrich sooner or later," said Binghamton. "I cannot overemphasize the importance of being careful in the presence of that man. He is extremely intelligent, totally ruthless, and immensely dangerous."

Gordon Aherne nodded. "I understand," he said quietly.

"He sleeps with me, Gordon," said Nancy. "You have to understand that, too. And he's jealous."

"I understand."

"What you don't tell him, he can't check. Be vague in your conversation with him," said Binghamton.

Aherne nodded.

Nancy rose. "The tea should be ready," she said.

The concussions from the flak tower were rattling the windows when she returned with the tray.

"Do you think there is any possibility at all that the Russian invasion won't come off?" Binghamton asked her. "Could it be a feint? Is there any possibility he means to come across the Channel instead?"

She shook her head. "No. They're moving everything east."

"That's what we believe," said Binghamton. "He's not taking any particular pains to disguise his intentions."

"What are your sources of information?" Aherne asked Nancy.

"General Halder," she said. "Chief of the General Staff. Plus Heydrich. Plus my husband."

"Halder again?" asked Binghamton.

She nodded. "And Canaris. This time they say they are prepared to kill him to stop him."

"They're looking for encouragement?"

"Yes. They want to know what kind of peace Winston would

consider if they remove Hitler and offer to negotiate. I've never had the least confidence in them, but this time they are better organized and more deeply motivated. They believe he's courting final disaster."

"The invasion can't be more than a few weeks off," said Binghamton. "He's got to go in early summer. Can they move against him in time to stop him?"

"If Winston sends the right word, they might," she said.

Binghamton lifted his cup and sipped the hot tea. "Well," he said, "the 'right word' will not be forthcoming. Don't give them the slightest encouragement."

She nodded. "Winston's decision, or—"

"The Cabinet's. His own, for the most part, I should think. It's a damn tough bit of statesmanship. Is Heydrich under control?"

"Not at all. He's talking about assassination."

"Is it serious? Is he apt to try it?"

"He's far more likely than the generals, and he doesn't need any encouragement from London," said Nancy.

"Can you read him? Can you be sure of what he's doing?"

"I can't read everything, but I don't think he'll try this one without trying to involve me. I'm still the one who can carry a weapon into Hitler's presence. I'm not sure he can. Anyway, if he's to succeed, he'll want to put a little distance between himself and the actual assassination."

"I have a new order for you from the Prime Minister," said Binghamton. "If Heydrich tries to remove Hitler before the invasion of Russia, you are to stop him any way you can. You are to kill him if you have to. It takes precedence over removing Hitler. We'll return to that project after. For now, nothing is to interfere with the invasion."

"Have I missed a step somewhere?" asked Aherne. "I find it hard to believe what I'm hearing."

Binghamton glanced at Aherne. "We *want* Hitler to invade Russia, of course," he said coolly. "Isn't that obvious?"

Aherne looked at him, jaw dropped, frowning. "I—suppose so," he murmured.

"Yes," breathed Binghamton. "Call it cynical if you want. It may be our salvation." He looked at Nancy. "Do whatever you have to do to prevent any serious interference. Betray the generals to Heydrich if you have to. Betray Heydrich to Hitler. Or whatever. *Hitler must invade Russia.* After he does, we'll return to the project of getting rid of him."

"*Mein Führer!*"

"Annchen!"

He put one arm around her waist, the other over her shoulder, and he kissed her on the mouth. It was a quick, almost brotherly, kiss, but the other guests were stunned; when she looked past him, she saw them stiff and gaping.

The other guests were Jodl, Hewel, Raeder, and Himmler—gathered at the Berghof as the rain poured on a warm June Saturday afternoon. Frau Jodl was in the house, Nancy knew. Heydrich had been due to arrive at noon and was late.

Hitler held her close to him for a minute. "I am glad you are here, Annchen," he murmured.

When he released her, she shook hands with each of the others —Generaloberst Alfred Jodl, SS Gruppenführer Walther Hewel, Grossadmiral Erich Raeder, and Reichsführer SS Heinrich Himmler. Jodl was as ever the professional soldier, courteous to her because she was the Führer's friend, otherwise not interested in her. Hewel was from the Foreign Ministry and was an honorary SS general only; he was superficially warm, smoothly correct. Raeder, who had never seen her before, could not conceal his curiosity. Himmler showed her his characteristic smile—cool, awkward, unnatural—and he settled on her an introspective, appraising gaze.

It was with Himmler that she found herself alone after a moment. "The Führer is in a fine, warm mood," he observed.

Since officially she did not know why the Führer was in a fine, warm mood—that he was about to launch Barbarossa, the culmination of all his plans and dreams for twenty years—she could only smile and nod.

Himmler took a glass of tomato juice from a tray. Without asking what she wanted, he also took a glass of sherry and handed it to her. "We were privileged last night," he said, "to hear the Führer talk at some length about the parallels between our crusade and the expansion of Christianity through the agency of the Roman Empire. People who don't know the Führer well would be astounded by the depth of his knowledge and understanding of history. He could discuss Germanic history with the most learned professors, and they could learn from him."

"He has a remarkable mind," she said.

"We should regard ourselves as extraordinarily fortunate to have lived in his time," said Himmler.

In the hallway on her way to her bedroom, Nancy encountered Eva Braun. Eva lowered her eyes, murmured "Guten Tag, Frau Generalleutnant," and hurried on. Nancy unlocked her door and entered her room, expecting to take a quick shower and relax on her bed for a few minutes before rejoining Hitler and his guests for the midafternoon lunch. But in her room she found Heydrich.

He switched on the radio. Norddeutsche Rundfunk was broadcasting Wagnerian music. The sound would overpower the microphones that were almost certainly hidden in the room. He put his finger to his lips. "Bormann . . ." he said quietly.

He led her to the window and parted the curtains. The rain was pouring steadily in sheets that moved lazily on a gentle wind. The nearby Alps were hidden in rain and mist.

"The twenty-second," Heydrich said soberly. "Sunday. Barbarossa. The first scene of the last act. On the very anniversary of Napoleon's invasion. Isn't *that* tempting fate?"

Heydrich's face was hard. His cold blue eyes were narrow, and his lips were pressed tight together in scorn.

"He is euphoric," she said.

"Exactly. He is totally irrational."

Nancy sighed. "I wonder if the defection of Hess didn't unhinge him at last."

"No," said Heydrich. "Barbarossa was planned long before. Its origin is in his ignorance."

She looked up into Heydrich's grim face. "You yourself, Reinhard, tricked Stalin into purging his officer corps."

"To cripple the Red Army against making war on us, not to encourage the Führer to invade Russia," he said with bitter emphasis.

"He might win again," she said.

"Impossible," Heydrich snapped. "We are strong enough to hold the Bolshevik hordes out of Europe. We can hold the line from Istanbul to the Gulf of Finland, but every kilometer we advance into Russia spreads our forces thinner over a longer line. Who could hold a line from Murmansk to Baku? And that's what he wants—the Caucasus and everything west."

"A grandiose ambition," she said.

Heydrich nodded. "He is ready to sacrifice the Third Reich to that ambition," he said. "And no one can stop him—as long as he's alive."

"Reinhard. . . ?"

"I intend to kill him," said Heydrich. "We have only a week."

❧ XXI ❧

Heydrich smiled and placed the small, gold-plated cylinder on the white linen tablecloth between them. Anyone in the restaurant could have seen it. "It has your initials engraved on it, you see," he said. "It has a clip like a fountain pen. But it is no fountain pen." He picked it up. "You arm it by twisting the cap to the left—so. Then you point it toward his face, and you lift the clip—so. It makes a little pop. He will gasp, drawing the gas into his lungs. In two minutes, he will be dead, with the precise symptoms of a heart attack. Only a very careful autopsy could find a trace of the poison, and the chief of the Reichs-sicherheitshauptamt is telling you there will be no careful autopsy."

He held the cylinder and turned it over and over, examining it closely. She stared at it. The thing gleamed warmly in the light of the candles on their table. They were in the restaurant on Kurfürstendamm, at the very table where they had first dined together, in December 1938. Ribbentrop was sitting two tables away. Heydrich was confident Ribbentrop would not watch their table, and would not see anything suspicious in the little gold cylinder if he did.

Heydrich shoved the cylinder back into his jacket pocket. "You may be sure I'm not risking your life," he said. "Even if you breathe the gas, it won't hurt you. You will have an antidote in two parts: pills to be taken in advance and a counteracting gas to be sniffed from a smelling-salts bottle." He smiled. "I would not risk anything so beautiful."

Not suspecting he would tonight ask her to assassinate Hitler, she had innocently dressed to please him, in something she knew he liked—a simple black silk dress that left her shoulders and knees bare. She had brushed out her hair as far as she could and let it tangle playfully in the strings that held up the dress. The silk flowed in a smooth, shiny cascade over her body. She never wore anything under it.

He put his hand on hers. "I would do it myself," he said. "I wouldn't ask you. But I have two small matters to attend to."

"What?" she asked quietly. She was deeply distressed.

"I will rid us of Himmler myself," he said. "Another man will shoot Sepp Dietrich, but I cannot leave the RSHA until I hear his report that it is done. Then I will come immediately to the Chancellery and assume command of the government. I will do it by stages, taking command first of the investigation into the death of the Führer, then ordering nationwide security measures, then the postponement of Barbarossa, and so on. Himmler and Dietrich are the only ones close enough, who might act fast enough, to interfere. Others will want to, but they will be too late. By the time they understand what has happened and organize their thoughts, I will be firmly in control."

"What of Göring?" she asked. "He is, after all, heir apparent."

"I'll give him two minutes to issue a public statement of loyalty to me."

She sighed. "Goebbels?"

"As soon as he sees the situation, he'll stumble over himself in his haste to join the new government."

Nancy picked up her champagne glass and for a moment looked away from Heydrich. The air-raid sirens were wailing outside—their sound muffled almost to extinction inside the restaurant—but no one showed the least inclination to leave his table and descend to the shelter in the wine cellar. If Heydrich felt the least uneasy, either about the raid outside or, more significantly, about his scheme, he showed it only by pushing a silver spoon forward to the tips of his fingers, then pulling it back, then pushing it forward again. . . . With him, confidence and arrogance were inseparably mixed. So were his ruthlessness and intelligence. In the restaurant he was the only man besides Ribbentrop who was not in uniform—certainly he was the only one with the bravado to appear in an imported, tropical-weight, white dinner jacket. He wore no insignia, no decoration. Everyone knew he was Reinhard Heydrich.

She turned her eyes back again to his face. "What of the army?" she asked. "The generals?"

He smiled hollowly. "You would know better than I."

"Why? Why do you say that?"

He put his hand gently on hers. "Nancy . . ." he said softly, yet firmly. "General Halder places more confidence in you than he does in the Führer, much less in me. So does Oster. And so does that sneaking little weasel Canaris, of whom you should be more careful."

"*Reinhard* . . ." she whispered hoarsely. She was frightened, and involuntarily her hand closed around his. The candle flames swam before her eyes, and her body weaved. "*Reinhard* . . ."

His hand closed around hers, and he put his other hand on top. "The Führer trusts you," he said. "He believes you—so much that, if you were to betray me to him, he would destroy me instantly, probably on your word and little more." Heydrich nodded, and his cold, narrow eyes attached themselves to hers. "I have placed myself at your mercy. But you have never had enough confidence in me to tell me you are an agent of MI-6. I have waited for you to tell me. I wish you had."

She trembled. She felt cold. Her mouth felt as though it were filled with her tongue. She recaptured her wits for an instant and muttered, "I wish I had, too, Reinhard. . . ."

He shrugged. "Well, you are, after all, heir to a tradition of military intelligence. It's difficult for you to take a man like me into your confidence. I understand. I admire your discipline. Fortunately for us both, the interests of your country coincide almost perfectly with the true interests of mine."

"To—make peace?" she asked weakly.

He nodded. "Before the final bastion against the Bolshevik-Asiatic horde is so weakened in a useless war that we can no longer stand. In defense of Western civilization."

Nancy nodded, too. "Yes," she whispered.

Heydrich's smile returned, and he tightened his hands on hers. "*Tomorrow*," he said. "Thursday at the latest. When Hitler is dead, you can tell Binghamton to signal Churchill."

"Binghamton?" she whispered.

He grinned. "When you met with Canaris, my suspicions were aroused. When you met with Binghamton, *I knew*."

"Vladimir Dekanozov has asked for an interview with Weizsäcker. Do you understand the significance of that? The Führer is trembling."

Göring stood by a window in the Chancellery, talking quietly to Nancy. Dekanozov was Stalin's Ambassador to Berlin. Weizsäcker was State Secretary at the Foreign Ministry.

Göring shook his head. "Is Stalin sending a message, saying, 'Führer, I know what you are about to do and warn you not to do it,' or what?"

"Suppose he did," said Nancy.

"The Führer will not cancel Barbarossa," said Göring. "But what if Stalin wants to propose a conference? What if he proposes to make major concessions? The Führer fears he will try to confuse the issue. Everything is settled. The Führer wants no confusion."

"Let us then hope there is none," she said.

"When you are with him, try to settle his nerves," said Göring. "It is nerve-racking, the most nerve-racking thing in the world, to be on the *brink* of a great operation. When it really starts, he will be calm. But now . . ."

As she nodded distractedly, Göring bustled away to engage Jodl in another tense conversation.

She was carrying a little purse. In it was the gold-plated cylinder and the tiny bottle of antidote. She had taken the pills. The cylinder was loaded now, with the deadly gas. She had been summoned to see Hitler at 10:00 P.M. Heydrich was at the RSHA. As soon as he received word that Hitler was dead, he would kill Himmler, then he would satisfy himself that the man detailed to kill Dietrich had done it, and within the hour he would arrive at the Chancellery. He had not told her all the elements of what had to be an elaborate plot. If she survived the first hour after Hitler collapsed and died in her presence, she might learn the rest of it.

She might, if Heydrich was not lying about the poison and the antidote. She could visualize a variation on the scene in which he had rehearsed her. In that variation, an adjutant entered to find *two* people dead—both the Führer and Frau Generalleutnant. She could imagine many variations on the scenes Heydrich would play next.

No matter that the need was desperately urgent, she had not dared to contact Freddy Binghamton. She had not dared contact the new man, Aherne, either. Binghamton was compromised. Maybe Aherne wasn't. The first thing she needed to tell Binghamton was to stay away from Aherne.

She did not need to hear Freddy emphasize the Prime Minister's appreciation of the situation and his cynical order to let Hitler live for now. She knew more than Churchill did: that in four days Hitler would throw 146 German divisions into Russia. The weight of the war had shifted heavily to the East, and in four days it would be committed there beyond recovery. Probably Churchill did not know how much the pressure was about to be lifted from England. Hitler's survival, until he had flung the majority of his military might into the vasts of Russia, was perhaps England's last chance.

What would Heydrich do when he learned she had not killed Hitler? The next few hours might see an ironic twist on the commitment she had made to Churchill.

"Frau Generalleutnant." Speaking to her was the Christa she had met in Belgium a year ago—one of Hitler's secretaries. "The Führer will be a few minutes late in keeping his appointment with you. He asked me to show you to a more private and more comfortable place to wait."

The tall, dark-haired young woman led her to a room with which Nancy was familiar, an anteroom to the Führer's private office. She poured coffee for Nancy and, with a smile, left her alone. Nancy sat on a comfortable couch and sipped the coffee.

In her purse with Heydrich's small cylinder was the brass cylinder Churchill had given her in Paris, the one containing the tiny rubber-covered vial of potassium cyanide. It was the first time she had carried it. Maybe this was a good time to slip the vial into her mouth.

A door opened. "Frau Generalleutnant." It was Admiral Canaris, leaving Hitler's office. He glanced around to see the door close behind him; and when he saw it had, he bowed to her and stepped closer. "Do our friends know what is about to happen?" he asked quietly.

She nodded.

"Shortly they will have their last chance to help us," he said. He turned his head and nodded toward the door to Hitler's office. "If he wins or he loses, either way our friends stand to suffer. But he can be stopped before he does either."

"I'll convey the message," she said dully.

Canaris settled a short, skeptical look on her before he bowed and turned toward the exit door. He glanced back. She had not concealed her tension.

"Annchen!"

Hitler came out and led her into his office, where he had maps of western Russia tacked to the walls. He looked drawn, tired, apprehensive. He sat down heavily on a couch and beckoned her to sit beside him. He sighed. He put his hand firmly on her knee, sighed again, and nodded.

"How old are you, Annchen?" Hitler asked.

"Thirty-one," she said quietly.

"I am fifty-two," he said. "All my life I have dreamed of the day that is about to dawn. I have committed my life and the life of this nation to a great and noble crusade. We march on Sunday, Annchen! You know. You have been entrusted with the information. We march to save Christian Europe from the Bolshevik Slavic horde. It is a battle our civilization has fought since the invasions of the Mongol khans. It is my dream that this shall be the final battle. It is my dream to be remembered in history as the man who eliminated the Asiatic-Slavic threat to Europe, once and for all."

"If you win, you will be the most powerful man the world has ever seen," she said.

Hitler nodded. "Yes. I have never wanted power for the sake of power, you understand. What I want is to reorder the world."

Nancy's fingers found the gold-plated cylinder through the thin fabric of her purse. She wondered if Churchill had considered the possibility that Hitler might win in Russia.

"This is the greatest of all risks, you know," Hitler said. "We may win in Russia as readily as we did in Poland. Or we may encounter the strongest enemy we have ever faced. It will be an

ideological war. We will have to destroy Russia. We cannot make
a peace as we did in France. We dare not leave the Russians with
much. And they understand that as well as we do. This will be
no gentlemanly war."

"What if you lose?" she asked.

"They will destroy Europe. The Czar was in Paris in 1815.
Stalin will be there in 1945 if we lose. Our only chance of pre-
venting that, if it should come to it, would be a magnificent
alliance: Germany, England, and America. Because Churchill
and Roosevelt are blind, I am forced to commit Germany alone
to this crusade, to bear alone the burden that should be shared
by every nation that is heir to the Christian civilization of Western Europe." He frowned deeply. "If—if it goes badly in Russia,
I may send you to England, Annchen—to speak to Churchill for
me. That may become your great mission."

"I would be honored to be entrusted with such a mission," she
said. She knew her voice sounded dull, with no edge. She did
not know how to participate in conversation so far removed from
reality. His hand on her leg distracted her, too. He had begun to
push her skirt up, to stroke her leg.

"Where is your husband?" he asked.

"At the Ministry," she said.

"He is not, in fact," said Hitler. "He is at Wildpark—Luftwaffe
headquarters."

"He spends many of his nights on duty," she said.

"As do I," said Hitler. "*All* my nights, in fact. And on Monday
I go to my new eastern headquarters—*Wolfsschanze*—to live as
a soldier during this new campaign. I don't know how long it
will be before I see you again, Annchen."

"Not long, I hope, Wolf," she said. She put her hand on his—
on the hand that had now pushed her skirt above the tops of her
stockings.

"Annchen . . ."

Her heart seized. He was going to do what she had dreaded for
years—tonight of all nights. She shuddered.

"I have never asked you this before," he said. "But I ask you
now. I ask you not to leave me tonight. I want you to stay—to
spend the night with me."

"Wolf . . ." she whispered. She closed her eyes. "It will change
—what you and I are to each other."

"As I have always wanted," he said.

She licked her lips. "Of course, I can't refuse you."

"You can," he said. "It is not a Führer order. I am just a man— asking you."

She had anticipated this moment. She had prepared herself for it, with reasons, justifications—bright, brittle phrases, carefully calculated not to offend, yet to say no finally and permanently. Right now, carrying in her purse the weapon with which she was supposed to kill him, the easy words would not come. Emotionally they would not come. More than that, she sensed vaguely that his offer might present a way out of the dilemma Heydrich had put her in. She was not sure how, and there was no time to consider it; but it might be her escape from Heydrich's anger and from the loss of his trust. Besides . . . what else might she be able to accomplish overnight?

She put a hand on his cheek. "I don't refuse, Wolf," she said.

It was more than three hours later before she retired with him to his private apartment within the Chancellery complex. They had spent the intervening hours over a late supper with Göring, Ribbentrop, and Arthur Seyss-Inquart, the Vienna lawyer who had become Hitler's viceroy for the Netherlands. The talk was dull and slow and endless. Hitler talked of Turkey; of Russia; of strategies and tactics; of Christianity and bolshevism; of the old days of the Party, when he despaired of ever attaining the power he would need to launch his great crusade; of Roosevelt and Churchill . . .

Ribbentrop dozed off at one point. Hitler seemed not to notice. The others remained dutifully attentive. Hitler sipped mint tea and nibbled sparingly on little sandwiches of soft white cheese, but he encouraged everyone else to eat—to take more of the poached salmon, the cold roast beef, the caviar, the several wines, the strong black coffee. Seyss-Inquart, who had no idea who Nancy was, settled a curious eye on her whenever he could without being conspicuous, and seemed after a while to accept the idea that she was the Führer's mistress. Göring favored her with small, sly smiles and a raised eyebrow. Hitler's hand was never anywhere but on hers, or on her leg or hip; his schoolboyish anticipation was not subtle, but it was diluted by his obviously being in no hurry to be alone with her.

It was almost three before they closed the doors to his private suite and he turned the key in the lock.

He took her in his arms and kissed her. "Annchen," he breathed. "What I would give for a second lifetime—in which I could be a private citizen and have you for my wife."

She had tried to build her courage for the rest of this night by drinking more of the vintage Bordeaux he had offered than she would have otherwise taken, and she was half-euphoric. "You were destined for a better purpose, Wolf," she said.

He held her two hands in his, and he extended his arms and looked at her. "Will you undress, Annchen?" he asked.

She nodded. "Of course, Wolf."

"The—bathroom is—there."

He turned to a little desk. Surprised, she went to the bathroom.

Nothing about his private suite was luxurious. The furniture was bourgeois, much like that at the Berghof: comfortable, a reflection of a lower-middle-class boy's dreams of a rich man's elegance. She undressed alone in the bathroom, wondering if she was supposed to find a robe there and emerge into his sitting room still covered. She studied his toiletries. He shaved with a straight razor. He bathed with French soap. He splashed himself with a German cologne she had smelled on him for years. And here was the Führer's toothbrush—worn to a frazzle, long since in need of replacement. Here, too, was an assortment of pills and capsules. They were not labeled, though all were obviously prescription drugs. It would have been valuable if she could have reported to MI-6 what drugs the Führer took—valuable, that is, if she still had a contact to whom to report.

When she was naked, she stood in the bathroom doorway. It was this element of her duty that she hated most: the necessity of offering up her woman's body, first to Heydrich, now to the Führer himself. She had to acknowledge that she had developed a degree of affection for Reinhard Heydrich, as a man, isolated from what he was; but for Hitler it was more difficult. It was not inconceivable that she might have allied herself voluntarily with a man *like* Reinhard Heydrich—intellectual, sensitive, aristocratic (or at least able to maintain a credible pretense), and, above all, *effective:* a man who performed what he purposed. Hitler . . . He was another case. Whatever he might be, he was imprisoned in his lace-curtain, crocheted-antimacassar background, and he would never escape it. Heydrich was roast beef with claret. Hitler was fish and chips with beer. The line could never be crossed.

"Wolf . . ."

"Ah! Annchen . . . You are exquisite!"

He rose from his desk and stepped toward her. She stood while he kept apart from her and marveled over her.

"Annchen, I have loved you from the day I met you."

"I am flattered. I love you, too, Wolf." Her eyes settled for a moment on the purse containing the poison gas with which she was supposed to kill him. She wondered if the pills that were the first element of the antidote were still effective. "It is an honor to have the love of a man like you."

"There are very few in the world like you and me," he said. "I recognized that the first time I met you."

"You had already achieved enough for me to recognize it in you, too, Wolf," she said.

He nodded. "Yes." He glanced over his shoulder, toward the desk. "I—I want you to read something," he said.

He turned to the desk and picked up a sheaf of papers. He handed them to her.

She read:

> German soldiers! You are entering upon a harsh and demanding fight—because the fate of Europe, the future of the German Reich, the existence of our nation now rest on your hands alone.
>
> May the Lord God help us all in this struggle.

"It is my proclamation to the Wehrmacht," he said.

There were more pages, many more pages. She could not imagine the simple soldiers of the army reading and digesting so many words. She scanned the pages. On the other hand . . . it *was* a proclamation of the Führer, and maybe they would eagerly absorb every word.

"What do you think?" he said.

"I am trying to recall," she said, "the proclamations Napoleon issued to his armies on the eve of great battles. Probably you have read them."

"Ahhh . . ." he said quietly, lifting his brows. He had never heard of them.

She handed the papers back to him.

"I would like to review this with you, Annchen," he said. "I do so much respect your judgment."

The sun rose outside the Chancellery and was visible through the blackout curtains ·before they had finished editing his proclamation—he wearing gold-rimmed glasses and scowling over the sheets of typescript, she sitting naked and apprehensive beside him, impatient and bored but feigning patience and interest as he worried over every sentence, striking words with a pencil, writing in new words, erasing the new words and writing others, reading aloud, listening as she read, erasing and writing again. Although he caressed her constantly, his attention was monopolized by the proclamation.

When at last he noticed the sunlight, he took off his spectacles and rubbed his eyes. Although he still was not satisfied with the proclamation, he pushed it to the back of the desk. Then he turned to Nancy and smiled.

His bedroom was Spartan. It was furnished with a bed; a chest; a small, square telephone table; one chair. A portrait of Frederick the Great hung on one wall; the locked case containing the nude of Nancy by Ziegler hung on another. Hitler opened all the blackout curtains. The suite filled with white morning sunlight. He pointed at the telephone. "I can order coffee— before—if you like."

"No, thank you."

He went into the bathroom. She sat on the bed. She heard water running. After a while he came out. He had taken off his clothes and was wearing only a suit of underwear, of ribbed cotton. He pulled down the bedclothes. His eyes did not meet hers as he nodded toward the bed.

"Annchen," he murmured.

She lay down on one side of the bed, taking one pillow. He lay on the other and pulled the sheet up over them.

He was on his back, and his hand closed around hers. "You see how my life is," he said. "I have not slept before this hour any night for a month. Even now the dispatches are coming in, piling up, and there will be a thousand difficult matters waiting my attention when we waken. Greece . . . Yugoslavia . . . Crete . . . Spain . . . Egypt . . . Syria . . ." He sighed.

"And Barbarossa," she said, staring at the ceiling.

"Above all."

"Yes," she said. "Barbarossa above all."

"From it will emerge a new world," he said. "Free of the centuries-old threat."

"Free of Jews, too?" she asked.

"*Judenfrei*," he said—Jew-free.

"What will you do with them, Wolf?" she asked.

She felt his whole body stiffen. "Alles was notwendig ist," he said in a harsh, hoarse whisper—Whatever is necessary.

"Kill them?" she asked quietly.

"Wenn es notwendig ist"—If necessary.

"By the millions?"

He turned his head and looked at her. "Nothing of that sort will be necessary. We will relocate them—resettle them somewhere where they will be harmless. For the present, we are herding them into ghettos and moving many of them east, into Poland. We will move them on, to the new lands we capture."

"I hear that many are dying," she said.

"Some resist. Some are proven criminals."

"Heydrich—"

He interrupted. "Heydrich has won my gratitude. He has undertaken difficult work, in which the world accords a man little honor, and he has done it well, without complaint. I am taking him off it now. He is going to the eastern front, to fly with the Luftwaffe over Russia as he did over Poland. When he returns, I am giving him a better assignment."

"Does he know this?"

"No. I haven't told him. I am sending him to Prague, to govern Czechoslovakia as my viceroy. It is an immensely important assignment. There are important armaments works in Czechoslovakia, and we have experienced labor problems. If Heydrich can solve our problems there, I will know I have been correct in my assessment of him—which is that he is too good a man to remain a policeman."

Too good a man to be left in Berlin while the Führer was absent from the city for a protracted stay at his eastern headquarters, she thought. "We will miss him in Berlin," she said.

"Berlin will not be the focus of events for a time," said Hitler. "Many of us with larger duties will be elsewhere."

"May I tell Heydrich what you have decided?" she asked.

"Yes. He will understand it is a major promotion. I am preparing him for the day when I may call on him to succeed me."

Hitler's voice had weakened. He turned on his side, facing her, and gently caressed her cheek, then her neck, then her breasts. She turned her head toward him. He smiled at her, but his eyes were heavy-lidded and he yawned. They were close. She could smell the cologne he had used in the bathroom: a sweet, heavy odor. He put his arm over her and pulled her closer to him, until their bodies touched. He kissed her on the throat, but his breathing was deep and rhythmic. He closed his eyes. He sighed contentedly and went to sleep.

Heydrich strode purposefully toward her along a corridor in the Chancellery. She stopped. He shrugged off an aide who was dogging him and strode up to her alone.

"When I entrusted you with an historic assignment," he said crisply but with a small smile, "I should have remembered you are shrewd, meticulously careful, and independent. I could have spared myself the loss of a night's sleep."

"It was impossible last night, Reinhard," she whispered shrilly, glancing around to see that no one was near enough to hear. "I could not carry it out. *I could not*."

"I heard all that happened," he said. "You were not alone with him until three o'clock this morning. I was afraid you might go ahead with it, though I should have known you wouldn't. If you had . . ." He shook his head. "Himmler had gone home and was beyond my reach. Dietrich had shaken my man. Besides, the antidote pills had worn off by then, and you would have died. I *thought* your judgment was good enough not to go ahead at that hour. I should have been confident that it was. I could have relaxed in that confidence. Instead, I have spent a bad night."

"So have I, Reinhard," she said.

"Ah. I can imagine. I'm sorry. I'm afraid I do have one bit of bad news for you."

"Oh?"

"A pair of SD men picked up Binghamton last night. He chose to take poison. He collapsed before they even got him to their car. Efforts to revive him failed."

She must have looked as though she were about to faint, because Heydrich put his hand under her arm and supported her. For a moment the corridor did spin slightly and the floor seemed to heave under her feet. She closed her eyes and shook her head.

"Nancy," said Heydrich. "I am sorry. I didn't order it. I didn't intend it."

"Let me ask you one question," she whispered. She swallowed. "The other night—over dinner—you mentioned his name. If I had pretended I didn't know the name, would you . . ."

"I didn't order him arrested. I swear. It was a quite separate counterintelligence operation. You were not, after all, the only MI-6 operative on his string. We may thank God he swallowed his poison and died before they had the chance to interrogate him. He might have compromised you before I could have interfered. And I *would* have interfered, you may believe. I would not risk losing you. What is more, I suppose you are now left without a contact."

"Another one will be provided," she said dully. She stood slack, her shoulders dropped, drained. "That is, if you allow it."

"Of course," he said. "I wouldn't have touched Binghamton. It is essential to me that you have a contact."

She nodded. "I suppose so."

"No one but me knows, Nancy," he said. "I have too much at stake—too much personally—to have entrusted to anyone the information that the exquisite *Engländerin* is an agent of MI-6. You are quite safe."

"As long as I work for you," she said bitterly.

"As long as we work together," he corrected her with a smile.

❧ *XXII* ❧

"I do not trust Canaris," said the General with the wrinkles around his eyes, the hard jaw, the turned-down mouth. "Not his character, not his judgment."

He was General Ludwig Beck, Halder's predecessor as Chief of Staff. Nancy had seen him before but had never met him. Iron-gray, stiffly formal, he sat erect and now punctuated his comment by taking a swallow of whiskey from a glass that had been ready on the table beside him.

Colonel Oster—the man who had first approached Nancy on horseback in the Tiergarten, on behalf of Canaris—was now a general. He was second to Canaris in the Abwehr. The others looked to him, expecting a response to Beck's comment. He only shrugged.

"In any event, we don't need him," said Field Marshal von Kluge.

"We need his neutrality, at least," said General Halder.

"That will be easy to assure," said Beck scornfully.

The house at Spandau, where they were meeting, belonged to a Colonel Rühling, who was not present. Another colonel was: Colonel Albrecht von Hindersin, a man much younger than any of the generals.

The four generals—Beck, Halder, von Kluge, and Oster—and the Colonel made up the party Nancy had been summoned to meet. The call had been from Oster himself.

"He is opposed to assassination, I may tell you," said General Oster. "The Admiral favors a change in government—"

"Without assassination, there can be no change in government," said Beck sharply.

"That is unhappily true," said Field Marshal von Kluge. He was a handsome man of aristocratic bearing, with striking blue eyes. "The apparent victories in Russia have made the Führer more popular than ever."

" 'Apparent' victories, you say, Herr Generalfeldmarschall?" Nancy asked.

"Frau Generalleutnant," said von Kluge, "you should report to Churchill that Germany is suffering a military disaster in Russia."

This was the first she had heard of anything but complete success in Russia. Four weeks after the launching of Barbarossa, the Wehrmacht had advanced 200 miles into the Soviet Union, destroying whole armies, taking prisoners by the tens of thousands, capturing and destroying tanks and guns enough to supply entire armies. Heydrich—with whom she had spoken only briefly since June 22, since he was in fact flying with the Luftwaffe—had reported without enthusiasm that it appeared the Führer had won the war. Göring thought so. Gordon Aherne, in the character of Dr. Klaus Diekermann, said London thought so, too. It had been a dreadful time for her, watching a new *Blitzkrieg* destroy the Red Army and Nazi Germany absorb still another British ally. She wondered if Winston felt as she did: that they had erred in failing to kill Hitler before he invaded Russia.

"Every report is to the contrary, Herr Generalfeldmarschall," she said.

"And the Frau Generalleutnant has access to official reports," said Halder dryly.

"Considering the extent to which we have so far trusted her," said Beck, "we would be fools indeed to withhold from her what we know about operations on the eastern front. Indeed, we cannot ask her to communicate to Churchill anything less than everything we know. Otherwise, he will not believe us."

"You may tell Churchill we have captured or destroyed more than *ten thousand* tanks," said von Kluge.

"How is that bad news?" Nancy asked.

"It is bad because it is more than twice as many tanks as the Führer believed they had," said von Kluge. "It is bad because, having captured or destroyed ten thousand, we still encounter them in as great numbers as at the beginning. We now have no idea how many tanks the Russians have. Certainly they have many times the number we had supposed."

"And the industrial capacity to make them," added Oster. "That, too, we didn't know they had."

General Halder looked at her grimly through his round, gold-rimmed spectacles. "We went to war on the assumption the Red Army could commit no more than one hundred and fifty-five divisions to combat," he said. "Our commanders in the field have identified three hundred and sixty divisions opposing them."

"Our own army is one hundred and forty-five divisions," said von Kluge.

Oster had explained to her why the generals wanted to meet her. Convinced they could not win the war in Russia, and deeply afraid of a Russian onslaught into Central Europe, they wanted to communicate an appeal to Churchill to reach an accommodation in the West, freeing the entire German army for battle in the East.

"Do you understand the significance of what we are telling you, Frau Generalleutnant?" Oster asked. "Not only do we encounter three hundred and sixty Russian divisions, we encounter them immediately, mobilized and ready, in western Russia. We have overrun forward airfields, only a few kilometers from the frontier. Some of their tanks are heavier than anything we have ever seen before. Do you understand? There is no question—*there can be absolutely no question*—but that Stalin meant to attack us this summer. In one thing the Führer was right: If we had not attacked, Stalin would have. We can only thank God we struck first."

"The evidence is incontrovertible," said Beck stiffly. "For five years at least, it has been Stalin's unwavering intention to attack Germany. If we had gone to war with France and England over Czechoslovakia, he would have attacked us then. He would have attacked last year, when our armies were committed in Belgium and France; but he wasn't ready, and our quick victory surprised him. This year he was ready. This year he would have attacked. His ambition is to defeat Germany, overrun it, and Bolshevize it. Has Churchill considered the menace of a combined German-Russian Bolshevik state? If he had that, what would stop Stalin short of the Channel? What will stop him even there?"

"You have made this argument many times, gentlemen," said

Nancy. "The Führer makes it. Ribbentrop makes it. It was made in 1939."

"We understand that Churchill will not make peace with Hitler," said Oster. "The prospect of leaving him in command of the Continent appeals no more to Churchill than does putting Stalin in command of it."

"Indeed with a choice between the two . . ." Nancy said. She shrugged, and reached for her coffee and Cognac.

"We know," said Oster. "But that will not be the choice. We are going to offer a different choice."

"You are going to kill Hitler," she said with cold skepticism.

Oster nodded.

"As soon as Churchill assures you he will allow Germany to hold its conquests intact," she said. "We have heard it before."

"No," said Beck curtly. "We can't wait for Churchill to make up his mind. We are going to eliminate Hitler now. Immediately."

"The situation has changed, Frau Generalleutnant," said Halder. "Hitler might have won the war in Russia, but it is clear to us now that he didn't. Not only that but his amateurish interference in the command of military operations in Russia assures a disaster. We will be unable even to extricate ourselves so long as he remains. We will kill him whether Churchill wants it or not."

"Then why have you called me?" she asked.

"We want to communicate propositions to Churchill," said Halder. "We will open negotiations."

"How and when are you going to kill him?" she asked.

The generals exchanged glances. They were grim, gray-uniformed men, all in their late fifties or early sixties, all wearing the red-and-gold collar tabs of their rank with assurance and pride, and none of them was ready to hear skepticism and argument from a slight, thirty-year-old woman.

Beck's lips tightened and wrinkled. "Colonel von Hindersin is going to kill him. As soon as he can."

"You can explain it to her," said von Kluge to von Hindersin.

"We'll blow him up," said the young Colonel. "That's all."

"It won't be easy," she said. "He is well protected."

"I am prepared to die in the attempt," said the Colonel blandly.

"The Colonel, we should advise you, believes the Führer is the antichrist," said Oster.

"He who persecutes the one true Church is the enemy of God," said Colonel von Hindersin in the same bland voice. His face, too, was fixed in an expression that showed nothing, like a badly drawn portrait. "I am an expert with explosives. I have access to the Führer occasionally."

"He is on my staff," said von Kluge.

"The best opportunity would be when he flies," said the Colonel. "We had one such opportunity, but Guderian was aboard the airplane, and we did not want to kill him."

"General Guderian is not one of us," said Halder, "but he will be a useful man in the new government."

"What do you want me to communicate to London?" she asked. "I must warn you, I lost my contact a month ago. I may have some trouble effecting efficient communication."

Halder glanced around his circle. "I will speak for us," he said. "In return for an armistice that frees us to concentrate all our forces in the East, we will withdraw from France, Belgium, the Netherlands, Luxembourg, Denmark, and Norway."

"What of Poland?" she asked. "What of Greece?"

"When the war with Russia is over, we will negotiate as to the future of those countries."

"North Africa?"

"Oh, yes. We will bring home the Afrika Korps."

"What of the Jews?"

Halder shrugged. "We'll repeal the Nuremberg Laws. We have nothing against the Jews."

"We cannot settle all outstanding questions at a stroke," said Beck testily. "We will eliminate Hitler, seize the government, and root the Nazis out. We will make major concessions to England, unilaterally, asking for nothing but the armistice. The problems that remain will have to be the subject of negotiation."

"Emphasize," said von Kluge, "that those negotiations will not be with Hitler but with *us*. We are men of honor, in whose word he can place his confidence without fear."

The radio transmitter and receiver was built into the false bottom of a worn black medical bag—one of two externally identical bags carried by Dr. Klaus Diekermann. It was open now, the power cord plugged into the outlet in his tiny sitting room. He pushed the little earphones over his head and frowned and listened.

"I never transmit from here," he said. "You needn't worry that my flat is watched."

Even so, she stood at his window, watching Abendlichstrasse below. She had taken some care to shake anyone who might have been following her when she came here, and she was sure no one had outwitted her. If, on the other hand, they were watching Aherne . . .

"Ah," he said. He began to write words on a piece of paper, and she stood beside him and watched.

HOUSE SOCIETY M 342 BEAR ANCIENT NN PETER LIGHT CLEO PJR CALIBRE CULTURE 60 RUN HAWTHORNE TELL BOTTLE 566 CLOCK GREEN GARBO 222 AUGUST HISTORY THOMAS MIDNIGHT SCOT TURN PHOTO 782 VOYAGE BB LIGHT CLEO . . .

It went on and on. She watched him with little patience. He had suggested she be here at six, and she had not realized he did not expect to receive the message before then, that he wanted some time to talk with her. This was one of those rare nights when Helmut would be at home, and she was anxious to return to Friedenau. She wanted to be there when he came in.

Aherne took off the earphones and folded them into the bag. He unplugged the radio, rolled the cord, and stuffed it in. He took out a small book and began to leaf through it, decoding.

"Do you recognize yourself there?" he asked, nodding at the jumble of words on the paper. " 'Garbo.' That's the code word for you. 'Garbo.' "

"I am flattered," she said. She looked down again from the window. It had rained. Tonight it would rain again, from the looks of the weather. Maybe tonight the bombers would not come.

"I sent something vitally important to London on Tuesday," he said without looking up from his decoding. "I can't believe I was compromised with Binghamton. Surely they wouldn't let something this important go through if they knew and could prevent me from sending it."

"What was it?"

He looked up at her, frowned and hesitated, then he said: "Hitler has had a message from Guderian. The Second Panzer Army is exhausted. The equipment is breaking down. Guderian says that he alone needs three hundred new tank engines."

Nancy sighed. "Maybe that's what they want us to believe."

Aherne said nothing and bent again to his decoding.

She glanced nervously at the street and sky. She was not as confident as Aherne said *he* was that he had not been compromised by his contacts with Freddy Binghamton. Apparently Heydrich had had Binghamton under surveillance for some time. Likely he knew everyone who had been in contact with him. If Heydrich knew that Dr. Klaus Diekermann at Abendliche Hospital was in fact a British agent, operating a radio transmitter for MI-6, why would he not leave him untouched and under surveillance while one British agent after another came to him?

Indeed, it was not outside the realm of possibility that Aherne was not from MI-6 at all but was an agent of the RSHA. Binghamton had died very soon after Aherne appeared, and she did not know what Binghamton's word from London about Aherne had been.

She had transmitted to London, through Aherne, word of the generals' conspiracy. She had no doubt that Heydrich knew of it anyway. She had not sent word that Heydrich knew she was a British agent. If Heydrich learned she had reported that, he might regard it as the ultimate betrayal. On the other hand, if she did *not* report it, he might take it as the ultimate evidence of her commitment to him.

As a test, she had sent a cryptic message to Churchill:

ARMY READY TO CARRY OUT OPERATION WE POSTPONED IN JUNE. YOU WILL UNDERSTAND CONDITIONS, WHICH ARE HOW- EVER MORE INTERESTING THAN BEFORE. SHALL WE CONTINUE TO POSTPONE? YOUR WORD IMPORTANT AS ALWAYS. WHAT COLOR WAS CHAIR?

Aherne was aware of her impatience. He glanced up from his work two or three times, and when he was finished he handed her the message almost sullenly:

LAUNCH THE ATTACK BUT KEEP WELL TO THE REAR. LET
SOLDIERS DO THEIR JOB AND DO NOT RISK YOURSELF. I CAN
GUESS CONDITIONS. YOU MAY EXPRESS MY INTEREST. THE
CHAIR IN THE ROOM WHERE WE HAD COFFEE AND COGNAC WAS
THREADBARE AND RED.

She relaxed a degree. Even if Heydrich knew about Aherne,
he had not written this message. It could have been written by no
one but Winston Churchill, whom she had last seen in Paris,
where he had sat in a tattered red plush chair and drunk coffee
and Cognac while they talked alone.

"It is to be understood, Herr Admiral," said Nancy angrily to
Canaris, "that my husband knows nothing of any of this and is
not to be in any way involved."

Admiral Canaris turned and looked over his shoulder, across the
room, to where Helmut stood talking with another Luftwaffe
general. "A pleasant dinner, my dear lady," Canaris said with a
little shrug. "How does this involve him in anything?"

Helmut had taken two hours from his desk at the Air Ministry
to join Admiral Canaris and Nancy for dinner at the Adlon Hotel.
He would have to return to the Ministry shortly, and even now
his dinner had been interrupted, as were, inevitably, his rare nights
at home. He was aging under the strain. His face was drawn. He
was turning gray. She watched him with the General he was
talking to. He had a little notebook in hand and was making a note
of the conversation.

"The problems," said Admiral Canaris, "of trying to keep our
shattered Luftwaffe supplied with replacement aircraft, fuel,
ammunition, and all the rest would exhaust the energies of ten
supermen. Generalleutnant Bittrich is invaluable, but even he is
losing ground every day."

"He was as reluctant to see this war begin as you were," she
said quietly. "Now he is sacrificing himself as much as any soldier
on the eastern front."

"He is a reproach to any man who dilutes his loyalty, hmm?"
said Canaris with an artificial smile.

The lights in the dining room went out. It made little difference since scores of candles burned on the tables all around the room; and after a moment's murmur, people laughed nervously.

"I am not interested in reproaching anyone, Herr Admiral," she said.

Helmut returned to their table. He sat down without a word and picked up his glass of wine.

"Ill news, Herr Generalleutnant?" Canaris asked.

"Western defense has counted two hundred and fifty English bombers crossing the coast," said Helmut. "On their way to Oschersleben and Halberstadt apparently. Probably some will continue on to Berlin. They are two hours away."

"Can't we stop them?" asked Canaris ingenuously.

"Of course," said Helmut. "If we withdraw all our air forces from the Mediterranean and the eastern front and use them to confront the English bomber flights, we can stop them."

"It's not worth it, for the little damage they do, as I understand it," said Canaris.

"You know as much as I, Herr Admiral," said Helmut. "I have suffered some serious interruptions of production."

"Stalin begs Churchill to invade," said Canaris. "Indeed, he demands it. Churchill responds by sending more bombers."

"We hear our pilots shot down behind the Russian lines are being murdered," said Helmut.

"Not just pilots," said Canaris grimly. "Prisoners of war generally. We don't know how many."

"*Barbarians!*" growled Helmut. "The Führer has always been right about Russia," he said to Nancy. "The war we are fighting against them is simply an obligation of civilization."

Canaris lifted his wine. Nodding over the glass, he murmured, "Hear, hear." He sipped. "I agree, Herr Generalleutnant."

Helmut ate hungrily. Nancy knew he missed meals; and when he ate, often all he had was skimpy and tasteless. The room was filled with officers, most of them of lower rank than he. Whenever she went to dinner, she saw officers in uniform, eating well, drinking French wine, looking sleek and comfortable. She wondered how many of them had applauded Hitler's decision to go to war in 1939.

He knew she was an English agent. She had watched him learn to measure very carefully what he told her. He treaded what had to be a difficult line: not to betray his wife and not to betray his country. He talked freely of things he supposed she knew from other sources. He expressed his opinions. He never disclosed information he thought she did not have. He asked no questions. She had not told him what Heydrich knew. She had emphasized to Heydrich that Helmut did not know what she was.

"I must ask you to forgive me," Helmut said. He would leave before the coffee. "Please leave the center of the city before the English bombers are due," he said to Nancy. He looked at his watch. "In an hour, say."

She rose and kissed him. He held her for a moment, then extended his hand to Canaris.

"It will be my personal responsibility, Herr Generalleutnant," said Canaris, "to see she is at home in the suburbs before the bombers arrive."

When they sat down again, Canaris summoned the waiter and ordered coffee. "I will suggest we leave as soon as we have coffee," he said to Nancy. "We can talk more freely in the car or at your home."

He stopped at the telephone on their way from the dining room. He learned from his office that fifty English bombers were indeed crossing the Elbe and would be over Berlin in thirty minutes. He dismissed his chauffeur and drove himself, west through the Tiergarten. The city was blacked out now, and he drove slowly, relying on the dim light of his hooded headlamps.

"Von Kluge," he said, "is back at the eastern front, where his duty demands. Halder is with the Führer at the Wolf's Lair. Colonel von Hindersin is with von Kluge. He carries his explosives with him, waiting for his chance."

"You know it all," she said.

"Oster is no fool," said Canaris. "Neither are you. Allow me to suggest you be extremely cautious."

"They told me what they are going to do," she said. "They didn't ask anyone's approval or consent."

"They are naïve," said Canaris. "They dream of the restoration of the old aristocracy. While the Kaiser lived, they thought of bringing him back. I have disassociated myself from their conspiracy because I think it will fail."

"Do you have an alternative?" she asked.

They drove around the tall Victory Monument, long since

moved from its old position before the Reichstag to the center of the Tiergarten. To their left and ahead they could see the black silhouettes of the flak towers, barely perceptible against the dark gray sky. The sirens began to sound. Canaris switched off his headlamps.

"It might be better if we stopped here," he said. "The bombers seem to be flying with a tail wind. They are here sooner than we thought."

"They will hardly bomb the Tiergarten," she said.

"If they know what they are bombing," he said, as he pulled off the road and onto the grass to one side.

The windows were rolled down, and they could hear the night sounds of the Tiergarten—crickets, small frogs in the ponds, animal sounds from the zoo. The city was silent. Berlin lay under the air-raid alert, quiet and waiting.

"I could wish I were stopped here with you in different circumstances," said Admiral Canaris. "You are surely one of the most attractive women in the world."

"Thank you, Herr Admiral," she said with studied blandness, to fend off his tenuous essay—if that was what it was.

Canaris drew a deep breath and stared out his window at the night sky, which remained quiet. "Do you remember," he asked, "the old cliché, which perhaps I do not quote precisely but which goes something like this: 'If you would assault the King, be sure you kill him'?"

"I remember."

"That's what's wrong with the generals' plot," he said. "They think killing Hitler kills the King. But it doesn't. He is not the King. The movement is the King—the whole Nazi movement. If you kill their Führer, they will only replace him and remain in power. Your conspiracy has to be big enough to displace the whole thing. Otherwise . . ."

"Isn't the army big enough for that?"

"No. Not anymore. It's not unified. Beck and Halder and von Kluge will risk death to overthrow the regime, and twice as many others will risk it to preserve it. Keitel, Jodl, Rommel—"

"Rommel?"

"He's Hitler's man, body and soul. Don't forget, he commanded Hitler's headquarters before he went to France in 1940. He swore an oath to Hitler, as did all the others, and most of them will not violate it. Anyway, if the generals manage to assassinate Hitler, who succeeds him? The generals think they will. I tell you it will be Bormann or Heydrich or Himmler. Of the three, your friend Heydrich is most likely. And what will the generals have gained?"

"What of the war?" she asked.

"The war was lost before it began," said Canaris.

"Then what do you want of me?"

Canaris stuck his head out the window and listened. The roar of aircraft engines was on the air now, distant but real. "I . . ." he said, distracted. He sighed loudly. "You should tell them to hold. Tell them Churchill doesn't want them to kill Hitler. Tell them he wants them to wait until there is a coordinated plot, to rid Germany of Hitler and all the rest of them. There is a growing movement in Germany. Soon it will be strong enough to do all that must be done. What they propose is premature. Let winter come. Let the army be defeated in Russia. Then see what happens. Hitler may fall of his own. For the future of this nation, for the future of Europe, that is to be desired."

"What if the Russians overrun Germany?"

"It is a delicate balance we must strike. Maybe when Churchill sees that happening, he will come to his senses."

The roar grew. It was impossible not to cower. The sky seemed filled with the sound of engines, as if the bombers were in every quarter of the sky and there were no place to hide from them. The roar increased, with a nightmare quality—it grew until they were as if immersed in it. Then abruptly the flak towers opened fire, and the Tiergarten was lighted by the flashes. Birds, stirred from the trees, fluttered confused into the night sky. The roar of engines continued low under the higher-pitched, staccato roar of the batteries in the towers. The sky over the city was dotted with orange bursts. The steeple of the Kaiser Wilhelm Memorial Church was clearly visible to the left of the flak towers, lighted by the gun flashes as vividly as if the church were on fire and casting an orange glow on the stones. It was impossible to know where the bombers were—except as the bursts overhead seemed to concentrate to the north and east. Another flak tower, north of the Tiergarten, was firing, too. But some of the bursts were overhead, and shards of shrapnel began to fall around the car. It was inevitable that some of it would hit the car, and three pieces did—two on the roof, one on the hood.

Canaris sat behind the wheel, stiff and grim. She could see his face. He was a small man and generally regarded as handsome, but now he was pale and afraid. She was afraid. When the shrapnel hit the car roof, some of her dinner boiled up from her stomach, and she spit it out the window.

As abruptly as they had opened fire, the flak towers ceased firing. The roar did not straggle off; it stopped. The sound of the aircraft engines remained distinct, but it was fading. They had seen no bombs fall, heard no explosions. The flashes were gone, and it was again dark.

"It is more frightening than dangerous," Canaris muttered. "I will get out and see if the car is damaged."

She sat waiting, her head down, regaining her self-control, as he left the car and walked around it. He got back in. He started the engine.

"We should stay here," she said, "until you can use the head-lamps. If we run over sharp bits of shrapnel, it might burst the tires."

"Ahh . . ." he said. He switched off the engine.

Nancy sat, still trembling slightly, conscious of the labored rhythm of her breath.

"Do you still have a means of communicating with Churchill?" Canaris asked.

"Don't you know?"

"I assume your contact was Binghamton. If you have a new man, I suggest you be very careful of him. Binghamton was a professional, but the RSHA knew about him for six months before he died. He must have compromised half a dozen British agents. I know that two the Abwehr was watching disappeared."

"How long did you know about Binghamton?" she asked quietly, staring ahead into the darkness.

"We at the Abwehr did not learn of him until after the RSHA disposed of him. Heydrich's people did some crowing about it."

"How did they 'dispose of him'?" she asked.

"Their story is that he took poison immediately on being arrested. It was crude of them to let that happen."

"He was, as you say, a professional," she whispered.

"You may be the only British agent still operating in Berlin," said Canaris. "I can arrange communication for you, if you need it."

"Through a double agent . . ." she said dully.

Canaris sighed. "My dear," he said, "*you* are a double agent. How else would you define a British agent who lives and operates in Berlin with the knowledge and consent of the chief of the Abwehr—and, for all I know, with that of the chief of the RSHA? I will ask you directly: Does Heydrich know?"

"Reinhard Heydrich is not that subtle, Herr Admiral," she said. "I would be long since dead—or locked up in a cellar somewhere —if Heydrich knew."

"Don't forget, Lady Nancy," said Canaris, "that I know Reinhard Heydrich very well. He was under my command for two years, during his service as a young naval officer. I know his charming wife, too, incidentally."

"You are unsubtle yourself, Herr Admiral."

"You are my best channel of communication to Churchill," said Canaris. "That is why ordinarily I keep my distance from you. That is why your file at Abwehr headquarters is free of anything compromising. I am troubled, I will tell you frankly, by General Oster's attempt to use you independently of me. I really would prefer that you communicate through me."

"Your man has the necessary codes?"

"Definitely. He is an agent of MI-6. They supplied his codes and his radio."

"A traitor," she remarked dryly.

"A double agent."

"Very well," she conceded.

"You should understand," said the Admiral, "that the generals have another means of communicating with Churchill. They have a contact at the Vatican. They do not rely on you entirely. They suspect you are not sufficiently enthusiastic about their cause and that you advise Churchill to withhold unqualified support. What is more, they don't like to rely on a woman."

"I suspected as much."

"I would like you to advise Churchill to disregard what he hears through the Vatican contact."

"Discredit a rival," she said.

"Yours and mine."

She sighed. "Herr Admiral," she said, "I will communicate what you want. I must ask you not to ask me the meaning of some code phrases I insert in my messages to Churchill. They are his guarantee of authenticity, since he knows I have to use various means of communication."

"Agreed," said Canaris.

"How do we explain my transmitting through a different agent?"

"Simply say, 'Bernhard has contacted me.' MI-6 will understand."

"If you have an electric torch, I will hold it for you, and you can take down a message, Herr Admiral."

She held the torch, shielded by her cupped hands, while Canaris printed her message to Churchill on a paper he held on his knee:

LITTLE GIRL. RED INDIANS. ON BASIS OF INFORMATION AT HAND I DISTRUST THE SOLDIERS' VATICAN CONTACT. I AM KEEPING WELL TO THE REAR. VATICAN CONTACT MAY HAVE DONE IN FREDDY. COFFEE IS GOOD IN A GREEN CHAIR. BERNHARD HAS CONTACTED ME. WILL TRANSMIT THROUGH HIM HENCEFORTH. BIG GIRL. BIG GIRL.

❦ XXIII ❦

She had not flown a Ju-52 for several years, but the cockpit was comfortably familiar and it was good to sit again behind the big wheel and feel the great, solid airplane throbbing under the vibrations of its three engines. Even its idiosyncrasies were welcome, and when a blob of grease plopped on the windscreen, she smiled at Heydrich and nodded. He was in the right seat, flying as her copilot. He acknowledged she had more experience with the Junkers than he, and he had been glad to take the right seat.

"Tausend meter," he said.

She eased back on the throttles and let the airplane settle into cruise. They had taken off from Tempelhof and were flying to Rastenburg in East Prussia, site of Hitler's Wolfsschanze—Wolf's Lair—headquarters. It was some 500 kilometers northeast. The late-September day was fine—white, billowy clouds in a blue sky, a pleasantly cool temperature, smooth air. The Ju-52, in Luftwaffe colors, was armed with machine guns, and alert gunners squinting into the sky. They were carrying as passengers five SS officers accompanying Heydrich, two Wehrmacht colonels, and two couriers carrying bags of dispatches to the Führer.

"I read a report before I left for the airport this morning," said Heydrich. "Something unbelievable. The Russians are using dogs against our panzers. Dogs!"

"How?" she asked.

"To carry explosives. Apparently for months these dogs have been fed only under tanks or tractors with running engines. They

bring the dogs to the front, starve them for a few days, and when
our panzers approach they strap explosive charges to their backs
and turn them loose. The dogs run under the panzers, looking for
food, and the detonators brush the bottoms of the tanks. They've
destroyed only a few tanks this way, but we've had to issue orders
to look out for dogs with saddles strapped to their backs."

Nancy shook her head. The image was disturbing.

"The Russians . . ." said Heydrich. "It's cant to call them subhuman, but truly there is something about them that curdles your
blood."

Heydrich had been summoned to the Wolfsschanze. Hitler had
sent her a handwritten note, suggesting she fly there with
Heydrich. Hitler was returning to Berlin to speak to the German
people in a few days—a major speech from the Sportpalast—and
his note had suggested she could return to Berlin on the *Führer*
train. As was usually the case with Hitler's invitations and sum-
monses, she had only a day to make ready. Heydrich had returned
to Berlin. She had spent time with him over the past two weeks.
They had had dinner together last night.

Heydrich had said nothing about her meeting with Admiral
Canaris. Apparently he didn't know about it. The Admiral's
double agent had transmitted her message to Churchill and had
received one in return, which Canaris had sent immediately to her.

LITTLE GIRL. HAD NOT SUSPECTED WHAT YOU HAVE REPORTED,
WHICH MAKES YOUR REPORT DOUBLY VALUABLE. WE WILL
CONTINUE TO USE CONTACT OF WHICH YOU WARN BUT WILL
TREAT ALL WE RECEIVE FROM THAT SOURCE WITH APPROPRIATE
SKEPTICISM. GREEN CHAIR COFFEE HAD MILK AND SUGAR. BLUE
TURK. PM.

Canaris was apparently satisfied with the exchange. Certainly
Winston had understood it. She was grimly pleased that she had
exposed the double agent. She wondered if Heydrich would have
been so naïve as to let her do anything of the kind to him.

Heydrich had been moody, almost disoriented, since his return
from his Luftwaffe duty. He had begun to believe Hitler was
winning the war against Russia, and he was uncertain how he
should react. "He may succeed in destroying bolshevism after all,"
he had said to her over dinner. Then—"Suppose we had killed

him. . . ?" His confidence in himself was shaken. He wondered if
he had not miscalculated. His assumptions had been shaken, and
he was not flexible enough to shift. She was surprised. She had
thought better of him.

The radio operator came forward and handed Heydrich a
message. Heydrich read it and dismissed the operator without
sending a reply.

"Will you come to Prague?" Heydrich asked. He knew that
on this visit to the Führer he was to be appointed Reich Protector
of Bohemia-Moravia.

"Of course," she said.

He nodded, and resumed his forward, unseeing stare.

She had never seen anything like it. The Wolfsschanze was
entirely unlike the headquarters on the western front in the spring
of 1940. Security Zone One, in a grove of trees, lay under a
camouflage net spread over the treetops. It was a cluster of
wooden barracks and concrete blockhouses, all built hurriedly
on marshy ground—depressingly ugly. She had never passed
through a security check like that required at Security Zone One.
Even Heydrich was searched from the skin out, by humorless
officers who ran their hands over his body, rubbing, patting,
feeling for any kind of weapon. She was searched no less closely.
They passed through two separate gates. The search was repeated
at the inner gate.

As she walked along one of the paths under the camouflage net
and trees, toward one of the low bunkers, mosquitoes found her.
They settled on her arms and neck. She slapped. They buzzed
around her ears.

The bunkers—one-story concrete buildings dug into the
ground; proof, she judged, against concussion but not against
direct hits by bombs—were scattered among the trees. Each one
had a few small windows, but ventilation was provided by some
kind of mechanical system that hummed and rattled on the roofs.
The leaves had begun to fall. Wet leaves lay over the sodden
ground. Pools of water stood among the trees. Electric wires were
strung on poles and hung low throughout the zone. The headquarters had more the air of a detention camp for incorrigible

boys than the site from which a nation's leaders conducted a major war.

An SS Hauptsturmführer approached deferentially. "Herr Obergruppenführer, your presence is requested at the situation conference," he said to Heydrich. "Frau Generalleutnant, allow me to show you your quarters."

It was like walking down into a root cellar: A narrow corridor a meter below ground ran between ranks of doors. The ventilating system rattled and blew a draft along the corridor, but pools of water stood on the concrete floors. Her tiny room was like a prison cell. The narrow cot had a straw tick for a mattress. The dampness seeped through the wood panneling that was supposed to hide the concrete walls and the green slime that grew on them. The lights glared. The ventilation blew a damp wind through the room. A washbasin was folded against the wall. Like a hotel bellboy, the Hauptsturmführer switched on the radio before he left the room.

"The Führer invites you to join him at five. Anyone outside can show you the Führer bunker."

She had sat on her bed for a minute only, listening to a news broadcast from Berlin on the shortwave radio, when, after a single abrupt knock, her door opened and a man stepped in.

"You remember me?"

She nodded. "Of course."

He was Colonel Albrecht von Hindersin—the man who was going to assassinate Hitler with explosives.

"I have what I need," he said. "Stay away from him as much as you can. I will try to do it when you are not present. Also, I will try to do it when Heydrich is with him. To kill both of them is more than we could have dreamed."

"The generals. . . ?"

He smiled. "Will be elated," he said.

Bormann and Himmler, as well as Heydrich, were with Hitler when she entered his bunker at five. Two of his secretaries were also present—handsome young women wearing fall dresses as though they were taking coffee and pastry in a café on Kurfürstendamm instead of in a cramped room in a damp concrete bunker in a marshy forest in East Prussia. Their eyebrows rose at her twill jodhpurs, boots, and long-sleeved flying jacket, which she had decided to wear against the damp and the mosquitoes. The coffee was waiting on a hot plate, and two large round trays were covered with Viennese pastries. Bormann and the secretaries were eating. Hitler was sipping tea. He was seated at a trestle table, spread with a huge map of western Russia. Heydrich and Himmler stood behind him, frowning over the map.

"Annchen!" The Führer rounded the table and drew her into his arms for a fervent kiss—astounding the others, except for Heydrich. "Frau General. I have sent orders to Göring to promote your husband. Helmut Bittrich, General der Luftwaffe. How does that sound?"

"Wolf . . ." she whispered as she kissed him on the ear. Then, drawing back, she said: "Wonderful, Mein Führer. I am grateful."

"Ah!" he said with enthusiasm, patting her affectionately on the rear—again to the shocked dismay of all but Heydrich. "Have coffee! Have a cake! We must attend to a bit of business. Then, dinner. It is good to have you here, Annchen!"

She took a cup of coffee, poured by Bormann, who looked at her curiously with a cold gaze. She met his eyes. "*Danke*, Herr Bormann," she said.

The room was five times as large but otherwise not unlike her cubicle in the sleeping bunker. The wood panels did not stop the chill damp from the walls. The light was harsh. The ventilating fan rattled. The mosquitoes had entered through the loose-fitting screens on the two narrow windows. One of the secretaries held a flyswatter in her hand and watched a large mosquito circle the ceiling.

"Generalfeldmarschall von Kluge," said Hitler, "has sent a man to brief us on his operations. I believe he is waiting."

Bormann stepped outside, and in a moment he returned with Colonel von Hindersin.

"Herr Oberst," said Hitler crisply. "What of Typhoon? Is the Generalfeldmarschall entirely ready?"

"*Jawohl*, Mein Führer," said von Hindersin. He stepped to the map table, carrying a fat briefcase.

Nancy pressed her back to the wall. She supposed von Hindersin carried his explosives in the briefcase. As he stood at the map table

and put down the briefcase, he ignored her, as if he had no idea
who she was. In one small room he had Hitler, Himmler,
Heydrich, and Bormann. He was entirely prepared to sacrifice his
own life, as he had said, and she had no notion that sparing hers
was motive enough for him to spare the lives of these four. She
had offered her life to Churchill, to England. She wondered now,
as she stared at the black briefcase under the edge of the table, if
the offer had been realistic, if she had really known what it meant
when she made it. Sweat trickled down her back. She wondered
if he had set a timer or if he had to stoop and work the detonator
by hand.

Hitler slapped at a mosquito. He laughed. "It is the Luftwaffe's
job to defend us against enemies that fly," he said to Nancy. "Will
you tell Herr General Bittrich when you see him that the anti-
mosquito defenses here consist of nothing better than flyswatters
and that we need better security against these enemies?"

Nancy forced a smile and nodded.

Heydrich squinted toward the ceiling. "These mosquitoes have
little red stars on their bellies," he said. "That means they are
Russian Bolshevik mosquitoes. Haven't you noticed, Mein
Führer?"

"Ah!" laughed Hitler. "You are right, Herr Obergruppenführer. In that case—they being infiltrators—they are the responsibility of the Reichsführer SS. Will you see to it, Herr
Reichsführer?" he said to Himmler.

Himmler smiled wanly. "Techniques that rid us of rats and Jews
should prove effective," he said.

The exchange, abrupt in its inception, was abrupt in its end.
Hitler bent over the map. Nancy could not hear his conversation
with Colonel von Hindersin.

Heydrich's eyes were on hers. It would be easy to warn him,
with a subtle lift of the eyes, of what might be in the Colonel's
briefcase. She would not even have to explain how she knew; he
would take care of that. She looked at the briefcase. She looked
into her coffee cup.

Hitler, Himmler, Heydrich, and Bormann—all in one explosion.
She had no right to interfere. The explosion would change history.
For the better. For humanity. She closed her eyes and sipped her
coffee. . . .

"*Danke*, Herr Oberst."

She looked up. Hitler had dismissed Colonel von Hindersin, and he was picking up his briefcase and leaving the *Führer* bunker— smiling, lifting his arm in salute, murmuring something quietly to his Führer. In a moment he was gone, out the door with his briefcase.

"Have more cakes, girls," Hitler said to the secretaries and to Nancy. "If we do not fly them all the way from Vienna, anyway we fly the baker who makes them. They are one of our few luxuries here."

The pastries were excellent, but Nancy had heard that they were followed almost immediately by dinner. She took another, but she only nibbled at it.

". . . an *Autobahn*," Hitler was saying when again she focused on the conversation. "From Berlin to Moscow. Another from Berlin to Baku and then maybe on to Teheran. Let our people drive through their new colonies and they will prize them more and be more willing to fight if necessary to keep them. In their Volkswagens . . . through their new lands . . . God! If I could live to see it!"

"But you will, Mein Führer," Bormann hurried to assure him.

"Ahhh . . ." Hitler shrugged, dismissing the assurance.

He looked haggard. He was grayer than she had seen before. His flesh was soft and white. His eyes were cloudy. He looked down at the map, and his hand slapped it nervously. He nodded spastically. The others looked away—not so much to spare him embarrassment, she thought, as to spare themselves the sight.

"Dinner . . ." said Hitler. "A quarter of an hour."

On a path she encountered von Hindersin.

"Why not?" she whispered through clenched teeth.

"Were you prepared to die?"

"If not, I'd have denounced you."

His jaw trembled. "It was too sudden. I wasn't ready."

Hitler, Himmler, Heydrich, Jodl, Bormann, Seyss-Inquart, Frank—with Nancy and the two private secretaries, this was the company for dinner in a barrack dining room called Number Two Dining Room. They sat on benches at a trestle table—the Führer seated no better—and he sipped mint tea while they drank before-dinner wines and whiskeys. The room was hung with maps. The mosquitoes prowled. A cold, damp breeze blew in through the open windows of the wooden building.

"We expect the first heavy frost here within the week," said one of the secretaries to Nancy. "It will kill the mosquitoes, they say. You noticed, I hope, that your room is supplied with an electric heater. You may need it tonight."

Nancy nodded. The young woman was extraordinarily handsome. In any other headquarters, she would have been someone's mistress; the Wehrmacht did not carry women otherwise. With Hitler she was a companion, an ear for his talk when everyone else was too dull to hear. Nancy understood that well. She had heard that the secretaries had almost nothing to do, but that Hitler would not permit anyone else to call on them for secretarial services.

It was certain that von Hindersin was not prowling outside, planting an explosive charge under this wooden building as the sun set. She had discovered that the tight security she had personally experienced coming in was redoubled inside Security Zone One. Lean young SS men were everywhere—staring, unsmiling, dutiful blond animals: chilling in their dull sincerity.

Hitler kept the hours he had always kept. At three in the morning she was finally alone with him, in a room again very much like her own: a cubicle in a concrete bunker, where the fan blew damp air across his rude cot and the wood paneling was rotting only a few months after it had been installed.

"You see," he said. "I keep your picture here, as I did in Berlin."

The case containing the painting of her nude was fastened to the wall.

"Whoever chose this site for the Wolfsschanze," he said, "must have been a bureaucrat intent on saving money on the purchase of land. My soldiers in the field do not live like this. I will have it preserved as a historical monument, exactly as it is. Let future generations see how I lived as I directed the last great battles."

She sat on his cot, beside him. There was no other furniture in the cubicle. His hand lay on hers. With her free hand she scratched the mosquito bites on her neck. "They are the last battles, Wolf?" she asked quietly.

He nodded. "If not, we will be destroyed."

"After so many victories."

He sighed, shrugged. "The only victory that counts is the last," he said.

"Helmut will be grateful for his promotion," she said.

"And Heydrich?" he asked.

"He, too, I am sure."

Hitler nodded. "Annchen . . ." he whispered. "I am not deceived. You are much more intimate with Heydrich than you are with your husband. I have always known. It is with Heydrich's career that you will reach the heights."

"Wolf . . ."

He squeezed her hand. "I am like Moses," he said. "I will lead my people to the Promised Land, but I myself will not see it."

"Wolf. . . ?"

"I am dying, Annchen."

"Wolf!"

He nodded. "My heart. Dr. Morell is shooting heart stimulants into me every day. And other medicines. But a year—two or three at the most—that's all I have."

He had a capacity for self-dramatization, which she had often seen; but she had never seen it used this way. It was impossible to doubt he believed what he said. It was impossible, too, not to experience a tug of sympathy for him. He was human now, as he had not been in the dining room or before, when he talked about superior peoples and inferior peoples and racial necessity. She hoped he died in the explosion of a bomb detonated by von Hindersin, not of a heart attack.

"You and Heydrich . . ." he whispered emotionally.

"Wolf . . ."

"You are alike. You could be brother and sister. He will shed his wife, and you will shed Bittrich. . . . You will have with him what I could not give you."

He nodded convulsively. Then suddenly he dropped his head into her lap and began to sob.

At 23.30 hours, October 2, 1941, the Führer train pulled away from Rastenburg, on its way to Berlin, where Hitler was to address Berlin and the nation. The Führer train was drawn by two locomotives. The first car was a flak car, bristling with antiaircraft guns. Two coaches followed, filled with SS guards. The secretaries

and adjutants had compartments in the next car—as did Nancy.
Then came the Führer's car, and after that came a car with compartments for Bormann, Jodl, and other officers. There was a
dining car with galley. Finally, the last car was a second flak car.

At 05.30 hours that morning, Operation Typhoon had begun,
and all day everyone at the Wolfsschanze had huddled around
situation maps, trying to comprehend the dispatches coming in
from 500 miles to the east. Fourteen panzer divisions, eight
motorized infantry divisions, and forty-six infantry divisions
were in motion. Their objective: Moscow, to capture Moscow
before the snows began. In his proclamation to the army—which
he had read over and over to Nancy later that night in his personal
quarters—Hitler called Typhoon "the last mighty heave necessary
to smash the enemy before winter breaks upon us."

Over lunch Hitler had brooded, frowning over the reports that
this division had advanced 6 kilometers, that unit 4; that one
division was encountering stiffer resistance than expected; that
another was moving forward against nothing. "The only thing
that could save Timoshenko," he said, "would be an English
invasion of the Continent. I know Stalin is begging for it. What
do you think, Annchen? You alone know Churchill personally.
Will he throw himself into a battle that is bound to be a disaster
for him, only to save Moscow?"

Conversation around the lunch tables had stopped, and everyone
looked at her. None of them was accustomed to hearing him refer
to her as "Annchen," and the secretaries in particular continued
to be shocked at his intimacy with her.

"I cannot know his mind, Mein Führer," she had said quietly,
"but I can't imagine he would make such an attempt at this
season. The Channel is a rough crossing and often foggy this time
of year."

Late in the afternoon, she'd had her bags put aboard the Führer
train. She took a shower in the communal shower in the sleeping
bunker. She intended, as soon as the train pulled away from
Rastenburg and its mosquitoes, to put on one of the dresses she
had brought. She had walked through Security Zone One with
Heydrich—along the gravel paths between the barracks and
bunkers, under the trees. He would fly on to Prague tomorrow in
the Ju-52 they had flown from Berlin.

"Everything depends on Typhoon," he had said to her.

She had understood. His conspiracy against the life of Hitler was suspended by success. If Typhoon resulted in the capture of Moscow and the war ended in another immense victory, his calculations would have proved wrong, and he had not yet made new ones. If Hitler failed, then Heydrich was once again his most dangerous enemy.

Heydrich's conversation had suggested to her that Hitler had not confided in him about his coronary sclerosis. The opportunity to tell him did not arise, and she had decided in any case to withhold that information until she evaluated it.

A final meal had been served to them in Dining Room Two, just before the departure of the Führer train. Hitler had been exuberant: The reports from the front were encouraging. Heydrich had sat beside him. Nancy sat to the other side. Hitler toasted Heydrich's new assignment—in mint tea. Heydrich toasted Operation Typhoon—in champagne.

The train was comfortable, and she had changed into a black dress as soon as she was aboard. Heydrich had come to her compartment and kissed her. He promised that they would see each other again before the month was out. He helped her fasten a strand of pearls around her neck; and as she stood at her mirror, brushing out her hair, he told her he would arrange a special trysting place for them in Prague. "It is a romantic city," he said. "We will enjoy it."

She had gone with him to the Führer car, where he meant to speak a final word to Hitler before the train pulled out. They had stood on a step between the car and the platform, looking for Hitler at last to approach. The platform was dimly lighted, and crowded with security guards and soldiers. She saw a man coming, hurrying along the platform, carrying a briefcase and a valise. He stopped to inquire, and a guard directed him to the car behind the Führer car. He bustled aboard. He was Colonel von Hindersin.

The run to Berlin would take fourteen hours. Although a supper had been served immediately before the train left, Nancy was invited to the dining car as soon as the train was moving. Walking through the Führer car and the following car on her way to the dining car, she saw Colonel von Hindersin in his compartment. He was smoking a cigarette and staring out into the darkness. The briefcase and valise were overhead. He did not see her, and she did not speak to him. At the next open compartment door, she encountered Jodl, who came out and said he would walk to the dining car with her.

After the Wolfsschanze, the train was luxurious. The dining tables were laid with heavy silver. Candles burned in silver candelabra, weighted on the bottom against overturning as the train moved. The dining car was filled with the delicious odor of coffee, and a table was laden with pastry; but wines and champagne were open also, on a table they shared with trays of hors d'oeuvres. Hitler was not there, and the secretaries and adjutants were smoking. They were relaxed and obviously happy to be away from Rastenburg, even if only for a short time.

Nancy sat down with General Jodl, and the steward served him coffee and brandy; her, champagne.

"That Colonel, two compartments from you," she said to Jodl. "I thought he was with von Kluge. What's he doing on the train?"

"He told the Field Marshal he was sick and asked for leave," said Jodl.

"A nice time to plead illness, just when every man is needed."

"We don't need von Hindersin," said Jodl. "I don't know why von Kluge tolerates him. He's a religious fanatic, an incompetent."

She sipped champagne and looked out the window behind her, into the night. The window was streaked with rain. Not a light was to be seen, not even a signal light on the railroad. The train was moving fast, swaying gently.

Colonel von Hindersin opened the door and entered the dining car. He bowed stiffly toward Nancy. "Frau General," he said. "Herr Generaloberst." He moved on to the coffeepot and poured himself a cup of coffee. He took a plate of pastries and sat down alone. He closed his eyes and seemed to mumble a prayer over his food. He ate then, sitting alone. No one went near him.

He was followed very shortly by Hitler. People quickly crushed cigarettes. Someone opened a window to let the smoke out. He smiled at all the people standing, gestured to them to sit down, and himself sat down with Jodl and Nancy. The steward brought him mint tea, and he accepted a small pastry.

"Fourth Panzer has broken through," Hitler said to Jodl. "They've taken Dmitrovsk-Orlovski and are moving toward Orel. They're twenty kilometers behind Yeremenko's line. The Russian Thirteenth Army has cracked."

"More than we could have hoped for," said Jodl.

Hitler nodded. He looked at Nancy and nodded again.

Von Hindersin's eyes were on Hitler—brooding, hating. For a moment she wondered if he did not carry explosives strapped to his body, if he might not stand up and move behind Hitler and detonate a charge. When he killed Hitler—if he did—it would not be to save Germany but because he hated Hitler, hated him personally. Hitler persecuted "the one true church"—whichever one that was—and von Hindersin would kill him for it and die a self-satisfied martyr himself. The generals knew their man. They had been cynical in their choice.

Hitler conspicuously enjoyed the train. Here, in this paneled private car, he was surrounded with what he knew as luxury—fine wood gleaming in candlelight, thick carpeting, comfortable furniture, silver on white linen, good food—and if his conscience troubled him, it was comforted by the fact that he was doing something: moving on leadership business; he had not, even for a moment, given himself up to pleasure. He was ill. She could see it. He was tired and sick. But here, for a few minutes, he sat with his tea and pastry, satisfied that an operation was going well, able to be content.

"We will not march into Moscow, you know," he said to Nancy. She looked at him curiously, and he went on. "No. They will have the city thoroughly mined. Anyone who goes in will be at hazard of his life. We will leave a gap in our lines, to the east, so the civilians can leave. And we will warn them to leave. Then we will sit outside and level the city with artillery. I don't intend there will be a city there in the future.

"The same for Leningrad. We will build new cities for the Germans who will settle these territories. We will drive the Slavs and Jews behind the Urals. I will let Stalin rule them there. There is enough land there to feed them. They won't starve. They will be a nation of peasants, working their land. They should be quite content; it's consistent with their character. The Jews, of course, won't be content with that fate, but no one said they should be. I promised the Jews they would be sorry for this war."

He began to talk about the new cities Germany would build in Eastern Europe, the railroads, the highways, the new "Grossdeutschland" that would benefit not just the German people but all the people of Western Europe. Colonel von Hindersin, who overheard some of this, rose; bowed to Hitler, Jodl, and Nancy; and left the car.

"Here and there," said Hitler, "there are Communists left in Germany, I suppose. I wish I knew who they are. I would send them into Russia and let them see how people have been living."

Nancy accepted a brandy. If Colonel von Hindersin returned with his briefcase, she would say she had to go to the toilet and would leave the car. If he didn't . . . then where *would* he plant his bomb?

An adjutant came to hand Hitler a message. Hitler put on his gold-rimmed spectacles and read it, then handed it to Jodl. As he stuffed his spectacles back into his pocket, he sipped tea and said to Nancy: "A human being, you know, cannot live without bacteria. They bring disease and death, of course, and we are at much pains to control them; but they also contribute to the digestion of food—indeed, we couldn't digest it without them—and without them we could not live. Some people thought it was that way with Jews. We know they are vile, but some supposed a nation needed them in some way, as the human body needs a subhuman species living in its guts. I have proved we do not need them. That is the greatest blow I have dealt the Jews. I have proved that the world does not have to tolerate them; we can live and prosper without them."

She had learned how to cope with this kind of talk. She simply directed at him the blandest gaze she could manage and never said a word. He understood she scorned his anti-Semitic outbursts, but, because she never commented on them or even looked scornful, he had nothing against which to argue. He changed the subject. He told her about the huge tanks the Russians had. They took point-blank shots from the panzers and still rumbled forward. If they had many and knew how to use them, he said, they could be a real threat.

Dawn would be late at this time of year. They would not sit in the dining car, staring at the dark windows streaked with rain, and wait for it. Hitler became restless and began to heave loud sighs by 3:00 A.M. He sent a man to the radio room to inquire after the dispatches. The man returned saying there was nothing but the routine. Hitler accepted a glass of champagne, but sat with it in his hand, taking no more than a sip from it. It became warm and he put it aside. The train at last passed lights. They sparkled momentarily in the drops of water on the windows and then were gone. Hitler was restless, but she knew he dreaded going to bed. He did not sleep until he took a drug, and he did not want to take a drug. One of the secretaries and one of the adjutants were asleep at the adjacent table. He looked at them, half-resentfully, half-enviously.

"Annchen," he said to her, very quietly, at about 4:00 A.M. "Maybe . . ."

She nodded. She supposed he meant to ask her to go with him to his private compartment.

He rose. He glanced at the tired people in the dining car with a wan smile, a bobbing series of nods, and he took Nancy's arm and left the car.

"When I was a boy," he said to her as they walked along the car between the dining car and the Führer car—the car where Jodl, Bormann, and von Hindersin, among others, had compartments—"I used to watch trains passing, and I used to think it would be the greatest privilege in the world to board one of them and travel to some far-distant city."

Bormann was sitting inside the open door of his compartment, working over some papers. Nancy knew his kind; the world had plenty of them. He would sit there until Hitler passed by and saw him still working; only then would he close his files and go to bed.

He looked up. "Mein Führer. Frau General."

Hitler nodded at him and walked on.

"In my mind's eye all trains were like this. I was Führer before I ever saw a train like this."

Jodl's compartment door was closed. Von Hindersin's was closed.

They passed between cars and entered the Führer car. It contained, at the rear, a radio room and a compartment for the two radio operators. The rest of the car was given over to the Führer's suite—a tiny parlor, a study, a bedroom, and a bathroom. He led Nancy along the corridor to the door of the suite. Inside, they were in the parlor. The bedroom and bathroom were to the left, toward the front of the train, his study to the right, toward the rear. The parlor was not as luxuriously appointed as the dining car was; it had a table and three overstuffed chairs. The door to his study was open and she could see a desk and chair like one might find in the orderly room at an army barrack. He put his cap on the table in the parlor and turned and opened the door to his bedroom. It was a compartment only a little larger than her own. His bed, where apparently he expected her to sleep with him, was narrow; a bunk attached to the wall of the compartment.

He took a step into the room, then abruptly he turned. "Ah," he said. "We should check the radio room once more. Something important may have been received."

She walked out of the suite with him. With his arm now around her waist, he led her along the narrow corridor of the car, toward the radio room.

With a hard shock, the floor seemed to drop from under her, and she felt that sudden sickening certainty that she had lost her balance and was falling. From some instinct she looked back toward the Führer suite, in time to see the wooden walls that divided the car dissolve in the fire, smoke, and boiling debris of a violent blast. The blast roared up the corridor, and in an instant she was thrown by it and submerged inside it.

"Ich bin verletzt. Ich bin verletzt"—"I am unhurt. I am unhurt."

"Und du, Annchen? Und du?"

She was in a shower. What she most needed, she thought, was to wash the dust and the stench of the explosion off her body and out of her hair. Her ears rang and she was unsteady on her feet inside the tiny metal shower stall; and she could still hear the broken, guttural voice of Adolf Hitler muttering "Ich bin verletzt." He must have said it a score of times, to the succession of solicitous people who hovered over him in the half-hour after the explosion. An SS doctor had examined them both, first him and then her, and had found no injury. They had walked out of the Führer suite and perhaps twenty feet along the corridor before the blast. His sudden impulse to check for radio messages had saved both their lives.

The explosive charge had been set in Hitler's sleeping compartment. It had been rigged to the door, apparently, and fixed to go off ten or fifteen seconds after he opened the door—long enough for him to come inside and perhaps sit down on the bunk, where probably the charge had been located. It had torn the car apart, ripping off the roof, blasting the outer wall away into the night, leaving a jagged hole in the floor. On the theory that the train was under attack, the trainmen had jammed in their throttles and run at top speed for ten minutes before at last they stopped and let the SS troops swarm over the cars.

By that time, the single attacker was dead. Everyone had heard the pistol shot. It came while the SS doctor was manipulating Nancy's legs, checking for fractures. Colonel Albrecht von Hindersin shot himself in the head, in his compartment—probably without knowing whether or not he had succeeded in assassinating the Führer.

As she stood under the hot water, soaping herself, gingerly examining the two small cuts she had suffered, the train began to move again.

"Annchen. . . ?"

Hitler had come in. He was standing just outside the curtain of the shower stall. She looked around the curtain. He stood there in his dusty, torn clothes, his face still deeply flushed. He had left his cap on the parlor table, where the explosion had undoubtedly torn it to shreds, and he stood bareheaded, his disheveled hair white with dust and bits of wood and paper.

"Can you hear me?"

She nodded. His own ears rang, and he spoke loudly.

"I must ask you to do me an important service," he said.

She turned off the water and reached for the towel. He picked it up and handed it to her. He stood with his back to the wall of the compartment and watched her dry herself.

"Annchen . . . It is extremely important that no word of what has happened tonight ever be spoken to anyone who was not here to see it. I ask you to understand and to comply with my request that you keep the matter a complete secret, even from your husband, even from Heydrich. Will you do that for me?"

"Of course, Wolf."

"We will shunt the damaged car off on a siding in Pomerania, where it will be taken in charge by the SS. Heydrich will indeed probably find out, sooner or later. But it is vital that the story not spread. The rumors it could generate could be extremely damaging. They could give encouragement to Stalin and to God knows who besides. The man who did it was a religious fanatic and an idiot. There is no reason to think he had any confederates at all—though of course we will investigate thoroughly. You are not hurt. I am not hurt. Once again Providence has intervened to save my life, and I am grateful it saved yours, too. I am convinced beyond any question that we were saved because I am on the threshold of the greatest victory, the greatest service to mankind, ever achieved by any leader anywhere. How could I doubt it?"

❈ XXIV ❈

It was a cold but bright-blue December day, and she had flown the Storch from Berlin to Prague, landing at the airport near the village of Lidice, west of the city. Heydrich had met her there, and he was driving her into Prague in his own car, alone, with neither escort nor guards. A Schmeisser machine pistol lay within reach on the rear seat and was his only concession to security.

"I've given them what their own government never gave them before," he told her. "Retirement on a pension for every worker when he's sixty-five. Free medical care and a pension for himself and his family if he's injured on the job and unable to work. The kind of thing Bismarck did in Germany sixty years ago. The nation is grateful to me."

"The Führer is grateful," she said.

Heydrich drew a deep breath. "There were dissidents here," he said with a frown. "Saboteurs. I will be frank with you. I executed four hundred. Now I have a peaceful, productive people, working in the factories, turning out what we need—and they like me; this nation has accepted me."

"Reich Protector of Bohemia and Moravia . . ." she mused.

He nodded. "My work will be finished here in a few more months. Has the Führer told you what is next for me?"

"No."

He smiled. "Reich Protector of France. All of France, including Vichy."

"And someday," she said, "the next Führer."

He shook his head. "There will be no 'someday,' " he said.

"It has gone bad, hasn't it?" she asked. She was uncertain of what was happening in Russia. She had not spoken with Hitler since October, nor with Heydrich; if Göring knew, he would not say, and Helmut came home from the Air Ministry exhausted and uncommunicative, insisting he did not know what was happening. She avoided Aherne when she had no message for him to send to London, and the one time she had spoken with him he had been as ill-informed as she was. The newspapers and broadcasts continued to crow about magnificent victories, but they had a newly hollow ring that was sensed by everyone. "I mean, in Russia. It's gone bad."

Heydrich nodded. "Would you believe you can't even operate a German steam railway locomotive in the Russian winter? The Russians build them with all their pipes inside. We build them with outside piping, and even the steam pipes freeze up. Even our gunpowder doesn't burn right. The offensive has bogged down. We're freezing to death and bleeding to death. And we have reliable information that the Russians shoot our prisoners of war and eat them!"

"Reinhard—"

"Our intelligence is still effective. We know what Marshal Timoshenko told the Supreme War Council in Moscow. He said Russia has won the war. *Has* won it! With our army fifty miles from Moscow, he says Russia has won the war—and he may be right. They're doing to us exactly what they did to Napoleon, and the results will be the same, too. You can signal Churchill for me: If the Russians destroy the Wehrmacht the way they destroyed the Grand Army, Stalin will celebrate a triumph *in Paris*, just as the Czar did. Only, there will be a difference. Stalin will not share his triumph with his allies."

"Does this revive your determination to kill Hitler?" she asked.

Heydrich pointed a finger ahead. "Hradčany Castle," he said. "Where we're going. I want you to see it."

They were driving along the river—the Vltava, which the Germans called the Moldau. Ahead, the castle loomed over Prague —an immense complex of palaces, churches, houses, standing on a hill above the river and above the city.

"It's a beautiful city," she said.

"Yes. I thank God we did not have to bomb it in 1938."

To their left, a funicular climbed through a wooded park. Many tall church spires rose around the castle.

"The Führer," said Heydrich abruptly. "He is responsible for the catastrophe: first, for bringing it upon us; then for interfering in military matters and making it impossible for the army to win the war. He will never acknowledge defeat. He will make war until we are all destroyed. I shudder to think what we will have to concede to Stalin and Churchill to end this war, but it has to be done. Germany must have a leader who is ready to make peace."

"I doubt I could get near him with a weapon now," she said.

"With the poison gas, as before, I think you could," said Heydrich. "Even so, I am thinking of a different way."

"When?" she asked.

"In the spring."

"Why not now?"

His eyes settled on her for a moment. "The Russians will mount a winter offensive," he said. "You may be sure of it. Our army must hold. If it breaks and a retreat begins, it may not stop short of the Rhine—short of the Channel coast. I do not exaggerate. In spite of every suffering, the common soldier must hold his ground this winter. That's the key: the common soldier, not the generals, not the Führer even. It's a question of morale. The common soldier doesn't know how badly Hitler has blundered. He blames it on the generals. We read their letters. You should see what they say: They hope the Führer will punish the generals. If we take their Führer from them this winter, they might crack."

"And it will be different in the spring?"

"In the spring we will be able to go on the offensive again. We will win some victories probably—though likely only small ones. The soldier won't suffer the sense of desperation he suffers now. Then, if the Führer suddenly dies and is replaced by—by someone they trust, they will hold in place until peace can be negotiated. Absent the Führer's unreasoning recklessness, the army can hold western Russia on a defensive line, while we talk peace."

"That is your plan."

"Yes. You can tell Churchill."

* * *

He installed her in a suite of rooms in one of the seventeenth-century houses within the precincts of Hradčany Castle. The suite was small but exquisitely luxurious. The leaded glass of a dozen small windows faced a courtyard of the castle, the view blurred and colored by the uneven surface of the old glass. The floors were of rough, pegged oak, worn smooth where centuries of footfalls traced tracks across the rooms. The beamed ceilings were low. Light was from candles. Heat was from two small fireplaces, one burning wood and one coal, attended by servants who entered unasked and unannounced. The furniture was elaborately carved. The brocade upholstery was worn but still vividly colored. The only concession to the twentieth century was a small bathroom, built unobtrusively into a room that probably had once been a dressing room. Only there did an electric bulb burn.

Heydrich explained that he had work in his office that would require an hour, after which he would drive to his villa outside Prague, where his two sons were staying for a few weeks. He would return by eight, he said, and they would go to dinner.

She settled into her suite with an uneasy sense of confinement. She had no telephone here, no car, no access to the street except through the courtyard of the castle. The people around spoke and understood no language she could speak or understand. The SS guards in helmets and black uniforms, who stood outside the door of the house and at every exit from this courtyard, might have orders not to let her leave. She was reluctant to try them, for fear of the panic she would feel if they stopped her.

For the past several months, in fact, she had been reluctant to test her limits: for example, to fly, as she had once done, across the Swiss frontier a few kilometers, just to see what reaction it would produce. Heydrich knew now that she was an agent of MI-6—although maybe he had known it that day when he sat in the rear seat of the Storch and offered no objection as she had followed the eastward turn of the Rhine and flown almost within sight of Zürich. She was utterly dependent on him now. If he entertained the least suspicion of her, he would destroy her. She could not understand why he seemed to trust her as much as he did. The only reasonable explanation she could find was that he expected to use her, that she was an important element in his scheme to dispose of Hitler and take power in his place.

She bathed and dressed in a dark-green silk dress Heydrich had given her—a gift from Paris, where it had been selected for her by one of his SD agents, a man of excellent taste, it appeared. She had shoes and lingerie and perfume from the same source. Servants entered the suite even while she was dressing. They attended the two fires and began to set a table with white linen, silver, candles, and flowers. It seemed she and Heydrich were not leaving the suite for dinner.

He arrived in the black and silver uniform of the SS, complete to the gleaming boots. "I want to know exactly the extent of your involvement with Canaris," he said abruptly when champagne had been poured and they were sitting at the table nibbling biscuits with caviar.

It was a test. She decided to tell him. "I am afraid the Admiral knows of my London connection," she said as casually as she could, "just as you do."

"As I surmised. He, too, wants to communicate with Churchill."

"He already communicates with Churchill," she said. She decided to risk a gambit that might anger Heydrich or might cement his confidence in her more strongly than ever before. "He is using a double agent—MI-6 and the Abwehr."

"If so, then what does he need with you?"

"*His* double agent does not have access to the Führer."

Heydrich smiled. "A nude portrait of his double agent does not grace the Führer's bedroom wall."

Nancy nodded. "I doubt it."

The smile disappeared, and Heydrich sighed. "But he does have his own contact, hmm? God knows what he tells Churchill."

"It makes no difference what he tells him," she said.

"Why not?"

"Churchill knows the Admiral's man is a double agent. I reported it to him."

Heydrich frowned. "How?"

"Canaris demands that I communicate to London through him only. I sent a message to Churchill. I phrased the message so Churchill would understand that the agent who transmitted it was a traitor."

"And you think Churchill understood this?"

"I *know* he understood it. He confirmed he did."

Heydrich laughed and lifted his glass to toast her. "My darling

Nancy, you are a *jewel!* Canaris could have been a problem. But with this we can throw him off completely. Churchill will co-operate—whether he knows he is or not." Heydrich grinned and chuckled. "I am glad you are on my side."

"You would hate to have to kill me," she said, lowering her eyes and taking a bit of biscuit.

He ignored that. "Did you know what Colonel von Hindersin was up to? Was he working for Canaris?"

"Not for Canaris. For the generals."

"You knew?"

She looked up into his eyes. "If I had known, Reinhard, I'd have kept a few feet more distant from Hitler."

His brows rose. "Yes . . . He came dangerously close to de-priving us both of the Führer and of the *Engländerin.* The Führer will not allow himself to believe that von Hindersin had even one confederate. He will not allow himself to suspect von Kluge. For myself, I suspect von Kluge . . . Halder . . . Beck. I suspect Canaris, though you say I shouldn't. Oh yes, one more—Oster. Is that the list?"

"You are a remarkable man," she said quietly. It was not flattery. He *was* a remarkable man. Amoral. Dangerous.

"I have two assignments for you," he said. "First, you are my liaison with Churchill. Second, you will be my liaison with the generals. I have decided to ally myself with them—up to a point."

The little Berlin restaurant was modestly decorated for Christmas.

"Mein tisch ist reserviert, nicht wahr?"

"Jawohl, Herr Doktor. Nah dem Fenster."

The proprietor led them to the table reserved for Dr. Klaus Diekermann, near the window. It overlooked the airfield—Tempelhof. The blond, boyish-looking Aherne lowered himself a little awkwardly to his chair. Nancy sat opposite him and looked out at the field, where a Condor was landing.

"I decided this is less dangerous," said Aherne. "If they see us together in public, there's a chance they will not be suspicious. If they see us meeting secretly, there is no chance they won't."

"I hope you're right," she said. "You made the decision. You left me no choice."

"It was Binghamton's intention that we seem to have a personal relationship," he said. "You were going to teach me to fly."

She nodded. That was before she knew Heydrich understood she was a British agent. Up to then, she had accepted his assurance that she was not closely watched. "We should set to work on that," she said. "In the spring."

"Yes. I would like it. You can still get gasoline?"

"If General Bittrich or Obergruppenführer Heydrich can't get gasoline, there is no gasoline."

"Considering the failure of the Wehrmacht to capture the Caucasus oil fields, you may have described exactly what the situation will be in a few months," said Aherne. "Now the Americans . . ."

"Yes," she said grimly. "Let us thank God for the Japanese. It will be months before the Americans can be ready to contribute much, though; and I imagine we must expect them to concentrate on the Pacific at first."

"I feel better about it all, though," he said. "We are not alone anymore."

"You and I are," she said quietly.

"Hmm?"

"In Berlin."

"No. There are others."

"Beware of one called Bernhard. He's a double agent, working for Canaris."

Aherne shook his head. "I haven't heard of him."

"He has his own radio, transmits to MI-6."

Aherne sighed. "I'll watch." He glanced around the room. "I have a message for you. That's why I arranged this meeting. It's from the Prime Minister."

"What is it?"

"I couldn't write this down, as you can understand. He tells you to move as quickly as you can to accomplish your chief mission. It is imperative to go forward as quickly as you can. Then there is a code sentence—I suppose it confirms the identity of the sender. I memorized it. It says, 'I had come from a meeting with the old marshal.' Does that make sense?"

"Perfect sense," she said. The night she had met Churchill in Paris, he had come from a meeting with Marshal Henri Pétain, among others. Churchill was continuing to use the circumstances of that meeting as a code. "Tell the Prime Minister I will do what I can as quickly as I can, but that it is unlikely I will be able to accomplish the mission before spring, when I will have the help of Heydrich. For a code, add, 'And I from a meeting with David.' "

" 'And I from a meeting with David,' " Aherne repeated with a shrug. "You don't quite trust me, do you?"

"I do, entirely," she said. "Because with you I'm getting correct exchanges. I didn't with Bernhard, and that's how I know he's a double agent."

Aherne nodded nervously. "All right," he said. "I had no right to suggest you don't trust me—or to ask you to trust me, for that matter. Do you agree, though, that it's difficult to live without any open, straightforward personal relationships?"

"I do agree. Of course."

He sighed. "It would be good if you and I could have one."

"Yes," she said. "But very, very dangerous."

"If not for that . . . ?"

She smiled. "Perhaps."

"Could I entertain a hope? I mean, if it could be arranged without unacceptable risk?"

Nancy frowned and drew a breath, surprised and dismayed.

"A man without a leg," he said quickly. "Could you face that without shuddering?"

"I would not shudder, Gordon," she said firmly.

"Then?"

She sighed. "Have you forgotten that I am a married woman?"

"You sleep with Reinhard Heydrich," he said bluntly, almost petulantly.

"That is a bit different, isn't it?" she asked coldly, biting off each word. "You've lost a part of your body in the line of duty. I've lost a part of my self-respect."

Aherne lowered his eyes. He drummed his fingers on the table. "What kind of man is he?" he asked. "I mean, if you weren't married, and if it were not in the line of duty . . ."

"Then there would be another impediment," she said. "He admitted to me he has put to death four hundred Czechs to pacify his protectorate. God knows how many others he's killed—Jews, among others."

"And if not for that?" Aherne persisted.

She lifted her chin and shook her head. "Then he would be a fascinating, romantic man, with whom any woman could fall in love. Is that what you wanted to hear?"

"It's going to be a bleak Christmas," Helmut said morosely. He stood at their bedroom window looking out at the streams of fire from the flak towers. "The English seem to have gotten a second breath. The bombing is heavier, and it's beginning to hurt. They sent over four hundred bombers one night last month."

She sat on the bed in the dark, looking intently at his slumped figure silhouetted against the orange fire in the sky. This was Sunday night of the first weekend he had spent at home in more than a year. He had slept many hours, and today they had taken a long winter walk in the Grünewald. Except for that, they had not left the house.

"That's not what's hurting most," she said.

He glanced back over his shoulder. "No. The losses in Russia are extremely heavy—and of men and equipment that are irreplaceable."

"The war is lost," she said.

"It *can't* be lost. We'll be overrun, destroyed, enslaved. We have to fight on. We have to use our every resource."

"Heydrich thinks it's lost," she said. "Canaris thinks it's lost. "Halder and Beck and von Kluge—"

"A lot of important people confide in you," said Helmut dully.

"More than you know," she said. "It's time we talked about it, Helmut."

He turned. "I don't want to know," he said firmly.

"You *have* to know," she said. "It affects you."

"I think I know too much already," he said. "I carry that with me every day. If I said what I think—"

"I would be put to death," she interrupted. "Or maybe I wouldn't. I am an agent of British Intelligence, just as you suspect. But Heydrich knows it and has known it for a long time. Canaris knows it." She paused and sighed. "Of course, Hitler doesn't. Himmler doesn't."

"I have not heard you," Helmut said through clenched teeth.

"You *have* to know," she said gently. "My life is at stake. And so is yours."

She could not see his face. It was in the dark. She could only see him standing with his back to the window.

"Helmut . . . I work for the Prime Minister. Directly. I have only one assignment: to kill Hitler. Once I nearly did. Heydrich knows. Heydrich wants to kill him, too. So do the generals. Probably it is going to happen. When it happens, probably it will be known that I am involved. I am your wife. You will be involved. You cannot escape it."

"*Why?*" Helmut whispered. "What good will it do?"

"For Churchill, it is an element of making war. For Heydrich and the generals, it is a prerequisite to making peace. They want to end the war, before Germany is overrun, as you yourself just said must be prevented at any cost."

"The Führer is essential," said Helmut. "The nation cannot survive without him. Whatever reservations I may have had about him once, I know now that he is our only chance of avoiding catastrophe."

"He is the *origin* of the catastrophe, Helmut. In 1938 and 1939, you feared war, because you thought Germany could not win. Hitler led the nation to war anyway. Now he has led it into the two-front war that every German statesman and general since Bismarck has dreaded. What is more, the generals say he interferes in military operations. The army did not want to invade Russia; but having been committed to it, they could have won, they say, if only he had let them. He has compounded the catastrophe at every step."

"So you assassinate him and plunge the nation into confusion."

"Churchill and Roosevelt won't negotiate with him, Helmut. Germany's only chance now is a negotiated peace, and those negotiations have to be conducted for Germany by someone other than Hitler."

Sighing, Helmut turned and stared out the window again. "He has treated you like a queen," he said despondently.

"Do you understand why Churchill and Roosevelt will not negotiate with him?" she asked.

"Because he lied to Chamberlain at Munich, I suppose."

"No. Because his administration of the conquered nations has been inhuman. We don't know how many have died. They are trying to move all the Jews out of Western Europe, into Poland or Russia; and thousands of them are dying. Hitler admits it.

They're killing thousands of people, Helmut. For no reason but Nazi ideology. You took a major risk to help me when I tried to save Ernst Leinberg. An element of what I'm doing now is trying to save the lives of God knows how many."

"In alliance with Reinhard Heydrich," said Helmut bitterly, with a touch of sarcasm in his voice. "How many have died at *his* hands?"

"I wish I knew," she said.

"He wants to kill the Führer. I suppose he wants to succeed him."

"He is the chosen successor."

"What? He says that?"

"Hitler says it. He said it to me himself."

"Churchill will negotiate with Heydrich?"

"He hasn't said he won't."

Helmut stepped away from the window at last. Gesticulating helplessly, he shook his head. "*Why Heydrich, of all men?*" he asked plaintively.

"Because he is the man who can do it, quite simply," she said.

"It won't be easy, if that's what he thinks. He'll be opposed. Göring . . . Himmler . . . And in the army, Jodl and Keitel . . . and Rommel. They are loyal."

"Himmler will be killed," she said. "You won't mourn him, I suppose? Göring hasn't been effective for years. You should know that. Jodl and Keitel will be at the Wolfsschanze. Rommel will be in Africa. Some others will be killed, I am sure. I don't know all the details, but you may be sure Heydrich has them all firmly in mind. He's no fool, Helmut."

"Does Heydrich want something of me?"

"No. *I* want something of you."

"What?"

"I want you to survive."

✖ *XXV* ✖

On Sunday, January 18, 1942, Gordon Aherne took the risk of coming directly to her home, not even calling first to learn if she was there or if Helmut was there. Almost trembling, he handed her a message from Churchill:

COLONEL DOBBIE AND MR. SHERWOOD WILL REPRESENT ME AT MEETING PROPOSED BY YOUR FRIEND. I BELIEVE YOU ARE ACQUAINTED WITH COLONEL DOBBIE, WHO SERVED WITH YOUR FATHER IN FRANCE IN 1917. THEY WILL STATE MY VIEWS. REGARD YOURSELF AS MY REPRESENTATIVE ALSO. I CANNOT OVERSTATE THE IMPORTANCE OF REACHING A REASONABLE ACCOMMODATION. STRESS THAT MAJOR MILITARY CONCESSIONS BY GERMANY, INCLUDING TOTAL AND UNCONDITIONAL WITH-DRAWAL FROM OCCUPIED NATIONS, ARE A PRECONDITION TO NEGOTIATED PEACE. BEST OF LUCK AND BEST PERSONAL REGARDS.

An exchange of messages had taken place during the preceding week. She had told Churchill that Heydrich proposed an alliance between himself and the generals but that Heydrich required of Churchill an assurance that he would negotiate with the government they would establish after they had overthrown Hitler. Churchill had replied that he would negotiate with that government. She had then told Churchill that Heydrich proposed a meeting. He asked that Churchill send representatives to meet with him and with Generals Halder and Oster. The meeting was to be held at Heydrich's mountain house in Bavaria, to which the representatives of both sides would fly in secret.

She could not doubt that Churchill had reached conclusions not too different from Heydrich's. Stalin's army had proved monstrously big and strong. The Wehrmacht was all that stood between it and the Channel coast, and the Wehrmacht was dying in the ice and snow of Russia. A negotiated peace was urgently necessary if all Europe were not to fall under the domination of Stalin. But Churchill and Roosevelt could not deal with Hitler.

She had been in Prague a week ago, at Hradčany Castle. Heydrich had said, "It's not the army at the front I need worry about; everything will be decided and finished before the generals at the front even hear of it. It's the garrison I'm concerned about. I may need the Berlin garrison to help me take Himmler. I can count on Halder, Beck, and von Kluge. Von Rundstedt will stand aside and do nothing. So will Guderian now that he's dismissed in disgrace. Rommel will be in Africa. Göring and Goebbels are ciphers. I will have to kill Bormann and Himmler. Dietrich, if he's where he can interfere. My little friend Müller of the Gestapo. Maybe Kaltenbrunner."

He had not entrusted to her every detail of his scheme. He expected to have Hitler killed at the Wolfsschanze—how and by whom he had not said. He himself would be in Berlin. He commanded thousands of SS troops, of whose loyalty to him he had no doubt; but he confessed they could not stand against both Himmler's troops and the Berlin army garrison.

She was essential to his plot. She was his channel of communication with Churchill. She was his liaison with the generals. She was an element of his deception of Canaris.

Through the little Admiral's Bernhard, she had sent another message to Churchill:

MOVEMENT GAINING STRENGTH THAT WILL REMOVE SUBJECT BY POLITICAL MEANS. SUGGEST NO ENCOURAGEMENT TO THOSE WHO PROPOSE OTHER MEANS. MOVEMENT WILL SUCCEED DURING 1942. AM IMPRESSED AND ENCOURAGED.

Churchill had replied:

PLEASED WITH YOUR ASSESSMENT. WILL TAKE IT STRONGLY INTO ACCOUNT BEFORE REACHING ANY DECISION.

Both messages closed with small misstatements of fact about the circumstances of their 1940 meeting in Paris, so both understood the messages were not to be believed.

Admiral Canaris professed to be pleased. In token of his *bona fides*, he gave her for transmission through Bernard some details of the new radar being installed in the Kammhuber line—the new defense line being built against English bombers. Unhappily, she had no way to tell Churchill that this information was probably correct, so it was doubtful Churchill placed any more credence in it than he did in anything else Bernhard sent.

She had not seen Hitler since October, the night of the explosion on the Führer train. He had been in Berlin for a week in December, when he made his speech to the Reichstag, declaring war on the United States; but he had not called for her. She knew why. He faced a major crisis. Even as he was declaring war on yet another powerful nation, on December 9, a Russian counteroffensive had broken through the German lines on a 30-mile front. Though the gap was ultimately plugged, the Führer was condemned to unrelenting, punishing labor to hold his command together and stave off an immediate collapse along the whole front. Even Halder, who was conspiring to kill him, expressed grudging admiration for Hitler's leadership in that hour.

Out of touch with Hitler, Nancy had no counterweight against Heydrich. She was his captive. He issued orders to her, in the same way he issued them to any subordinate. He lodged her in luxury in Hradčany Castle, he treated her to elaborate candlelight dinners, he lavished on her frequent gifts of clothing, perfume, and jewelry, and he made love to her; still, it was plain he expected his orders to be obeyed. He listened to her judgments and seemed to respect them; still, he plainly made the decisions. He let her see his enthusiasm. His conspiracy was developing rapidly. He meant to be führer within six months.

Her duty now—on January 24—was to fly General Halder and General Oster to Bavaria, to the meeting on Heydrich's mountain with the two men being sent by Churchill.

In black overcoat, with black hat jammed down on his head against the wind, General Halder was without his military bearing and dignity. General Oster's coat was brown and his hat was gray. Both of them stood in the gray light of winter dusk beside the Storch, Halder eyeing it with nervous skepticism, Oster feeling its fabric body with one unsteady hand. Nancy, in boots and jodhpurs and a leather flying jacket, stood on a ladder and, with a flashlight, peered down into one of the fuel tanks to be certain the tank was full.

"It is not snowing south of a line Erfurt-Dresden," she said to the two generals. "I had a call confirming it not more than ten minutes ago."

"Five hundred kilometers in this weather," said General Halder, hunching his shoulders and glancing around at the swirling snow. "Do you carry enough fuel?"

"Yes," she said as she screwed the cap down on the gas tank. She did not add the appropriate word—"barely."

"Are you confident you can find this mountain field in the dark?"

"We will have light when we need it," she said.

Heydrich had assured her the ground was frozen and that there was as yet no snow on the meadow. He was landing there himself before dark, and on her signal he would light flares to identify the meadow for her. He had not said it was without hazard; he had only said he was confident she could land there.

She had had the machine gun and its mount removed from the Storch. Without them and without canisters of ammunition, the plane would be light enough to take off in this cold air. By the time they had reached the mountains to the south, where the ability to make a quick climb might be crucial, the Storch would have burned more than a general's weight in gasoline.

Nancy glanced around the field one more time, judging the swirling snow, the gusty winds, the low visibility over the field. The Storch was not equipped for blind flying. She would have to fly beneath the low cloud cover, fairly skimming the treetops until she was south of the storm. Then it would be dark. If the storm did not end where the meteorologists said it did, if it was moving differently from what they thought, if the snow was falling more heavily to the south, if the winds . . . If not for the fact that the English plane carrying Churchill's two representatives had not by now already taken off on a far more dangerous flight, she would have postponed.

The storm was in fact more severe than the meteorologists had understood. The snow was heavier. For an hour she had to fly staring at her wavering, yellow-lit gyroscopes and altimeter, struggling every second to keep the pitching, rolling little plane upright and flying somewhere near the correct heading—while the two generals sat in the rear, stiff and silent with fear. When at last they emerged from the storm, they found themselves flying over a blacked-out landscape, under a thin moon, blown off course and lost. They worked together, she and the generals, peering at landmarks dimly visible in the moonlight, speculating about what they might be, until finally General Halder recognized the Ludwig Canal that joined the Main River to the Danube and she was able to recover her course by following the canal to Kelheim. As they flew east of Munich, the city was bombed by the RAF, and they saw the searchlights, then the antiaircraft fire, then the bursts of bombs, from only 50 kilometers. The bombers flew above the Storch as they made their wide turn to the northwest for their flight back to England.

The mountain landmarks south of Munich were clear and familiar. The last half-hour of the flight was almost easy. Though she had never landed on the meadow at night, she had flown there so many times that she could find the place in the moonlight, except for the final approach to the ground. Heydrich had anticipated that. Now, following his instructions, she set the radio to the frequency he had given her, pressed the button on the microphone, and whistled the initial phrase from the "Horst Wessel Lied." In a moment a white flare shone on the ground ahead. After a minute another flare shone, red. The white flare was her touchdown point, the red the end of the meadow.

The mountainside stood above her on her right as she lined up on the red and white flares. She could see a faint yellow light inside the house, also to her right. With her throttle back, the nose high, flaps down, she eased the Storch down, almost feeling with its long landing gear for a touchdown in the forgiving grass of the mountain meadow. Only at the last moment, when the white flare was immediately ahead and below, did she switch on the bright landing light under the wing. She could see Heydrich then, standing to the right, watching her put the airplane delicately down.

She was high. The white flare passed beneath; the red flare was a hundred meters ahead. She let the Storch settle as if it were groping for the earth. With the red flare rushing toward her, still the wheels did not touch. She shoved the throttle forward and the engine roared. The Storch struggled upward.

She came around for a second try. This time she let the airplane settle lower, well ahead of the white flare. When it disappeared under the long nose of the Storch, the wheels touched.

"Herr Generaloberst. Herr Generalmajor." Heydrich greeted the two generals. He was dressed in the field-gray of the Wehrmacht but with the insignia of the SS.

"Herr Obergruppenführer," said Oster.

Halder saluted but said nothing.

"I must ask you to help me drag the aircraft off the field and under cover," Heydrich said. "Our English friends are due."

The two generals helped him tug the Storch into the edge of the wood and to throw a cover of canvas and freshly cut branches over it. His own Storch stood beside it, similarly covered. Without comment or complaint, Halder, who was fifty-eight years old and Chief of the General Staff of the army, put his shoulder to the airplane and labored to move and hide it.

The mountainside was cold. The moon was behind the bulk of the mountain and the landing field was dark. Heydrich suggested they go in the house, warm themselves, and eat, while he waited for the English airplane. Nancy shook her head and chose to stay outside. The generals stayed, too.

"The raid was to their advantage," said Heydrich to none of them in particular. "In fact, it may have been sent to cover them."

Nancy stood in the meadow, all but unconscious of the cold. She scanned the sky, straining to hear the sound of an aircraft engine, caught in a surprising tension of anticipation. In a few minutes, perhaps, she would meet Englishmen and could speak English comfortably and in confidence. She had not expected to be moved by the idea. Even on the flight down here she had not thought of it. Now, looking for their plane, she found herself thrilling to the simple proximity of friendly countrymen.

"They had to stop and refuel somewhere in France, I imagine," said Heydrich. The radio on which he would hear their signal to light another set of red and white flares sat on the ground. He glanced at his watch. "Even so, they are due."

Another quarter of an hour passed, and the generals had gone to the house to warm themselves, before a tiny red light on the radio came on to indicate it was receiving a signal. Heydrich leaped to switch on the speaker. The whistled notes were clear and distinct, repeated twice over. He lit the white flare and ran to light the red one, and still they heard no engine sound. A skilled pilot had cut his engine and was gliding silently out of the night. They didn't see the airplane at all until, no more than a hundred meters from the white flare, the pilot lighted two intense spotlights in the wheel fairings, looked at the meadow for a moment, then switched them off again. The plane—Nancy recognized it as a Lysander, painted black and carrying a huge, ungainly extra fuel tank between its landing gear—touched down precisely on the white flare, shattering it, and rolled to a stop just at the red flare.

Colonel Giles Dobbie, smartly turned out in the uniform of the Coldstream Guards, saluted the two German generals hurrying toward him as he stepped from the Lysander. He nodded curtly to Heydrich, then pulled off his leather gloves and took Nancy's hands in his. "The Prime Minister will be pleased that I can report you are looking fit, Lady Nancy. We will have time for some private talk, I trust."

Though Churchill's message had said he was a friend of her father's, she did not recognize Colonel Dobbie, either by name or face. Neither did she recognize Mr. Arthur Sherwood, the civilian with briefcase who jumped down from the airplane after Colonel Dobbie. He was younger; his moustache was dark brown, and the Colonel's was gray.

Heydrich looked to Nancy to help him serve champagne, salmon, pâtés, and caviar; but Colonel Dobbie made a point of sitting beside her, a little apart from Sherwood and Heydrich and the generals, to talk while he nibbled with studied casualness on a cracker spread with caviar.

"I saw your mother only ten days ago," said the Colonel. "Regretted I could not tell her I would see you soon. Regret that I cannot go back and tell her I've seen you."

"I've heard nothing from my family since 1939," she said.

"They're all fit: your mother, your sister, your brother. Your brother took a commission in 'thirty-nine; he's on Malta, I believe."

"I have to acknowledge I don't remember you, Colonel."

The Colonel smiled. "I saw you last at your father's funeral. You don't remember me then. No reason you should. You were a very little gull when I used to visit Edham House. I went out to Australia immediately the First War was over and didn't come back till 'thirty-five. My wife is Australian."

"Did Freddy Binghamton leave a family?" she asked.

"Yas. A sister. Gordon Aherne has a wife, an Australian gull he met in Vienna; and they have two children. They live at Winchester. The man Admiral Canaris calls Bernhard is a Dutchman who made his way across the Channel to England in 1940. We're grateful, incidentally, that you put us on to him."

The meeting went on all night. Heydrich wanted assurance that Churchill would accept him as head of the German government after Hitler was killed. The generals wanted assurance that Germany's western frontier, as it was in August 1939, would be guaranteed. They spoke of an understanding that their withdrawal from France was not to be taken as a surrender but as a shifting of forces to the east to meet the greater threat. Sherwood insisted Germany must withdraw from Czechoslovakia. Significantly, he did not insist on withdrawal from Poland. Colonel Dobbie insisted the Afrika Korps must be brought home. Greece, it was agreed, must become once again self-governing, but the terms on which that would be accomplished would be left to later negotiation. With bright sunshine on the mountain, they took a break of four hours to sleep.

Heydrich walked with Nancy outside the house. They looked first to the three airplanes. The English pilot, who had slept all night, was out, carrying cans of fuel from a cache of drums behind the house to the Lysander.

"I think it is settled," Heydrich said to her when they had walked some distance away. "Churchill will negotiate with me."

"That is my understanding," she said.

"Now the generals will propose to you that they don't need me. They will ask you to communicate to Churchill an amendment to the understanding: that they will recapture Germany for the honorable generals of the old army, ridding Germany and the world of the despicable Nazis. In this they will be joined by Canaris."

Nancy drew her leather flying coat more tightly around her. A wind had begun to blow, ripping plumes of snow off the peaks above them. She nodded. She, too, anticipated an attempt to exclude him from the process of peacemaking.

"Now comes the test of your commitment to me," said Heydrich.

She nodded again. "I know," she said quietly.

"I have let you operate as a British agent inside Germany," he said. "I've left your radio man alone, though I could probably find him easily enough. I've done it partly out of my warm fascination with you as a woman. My better reason is that you are my link with Churchill. Without you, I could not have gotten those two Englishmen here. By getting them here, I've won the grudging agreement of the generals to work with me for our joint purpose—even though they will make one more attempt to betray me. When Hitler is gone and we are actually negotiating the terms we have sketched out in the last hours, you will play a major role. For the immediate future, I have a small but vital task for you."

"I know what it is," she said.

"Yes. When the generals and Canaris ask you to communicate to Churchill a small amendment to the terms agreed to by Colonel Dobbie and Mr. Sherwood—an amendment to exclude me, for Churchill to treat with the army alone—you must accept the message, even help them to draft it if they ask you, *and then not send it*. You must bring it to me, and you and I will draft Churchill's reply to them. By making them see that Churchill will deal with me, we have brought them this far. By making them think that Churchill will not deal with them without me, we will put an end once and for all to any dreams they may have of seizing the government exclusively for themselves."

Nancy walked on over the frozen ground, staring down, silently nodding.

Heydrich trudged beside her, holding his chin high as he seemed to sniff the wind and scan the sky. "It is in England's interest as much as Germany's for us to achieve this accommodation," he said. "The generals cannot establish a regime stable enough to effect the big changes we are talking about—not if the Nazi party remains powerful in opposition. I control the police. I will control the Party. Unless the generals try to fight me, I can hold the country together while we bring the army home and shift it to the eastern front."

"That seems to be the Prime Minister's appreciation, too," she said. "Something like that."

Heydrich smiled. "I agreed to another point last night," he said. "It was not difficult to agree to. I agreed that you will be returned safely to England as soon as Hitler is dead. Churchill has made that almost a condition of negotiating peace. He values his *Engländerin* as much as the Führer does—as much as I do."

❧ XXVI ❧

Nancy woke to the ringing of her doorbell. She squinted at her bedside clock, in a room filled with the red light of dawn. It was 5:00 A.M., and the mid-April sun was rising over Berlin. She rolled over and swung her feet to the floor. My God, why. . . ? Could the Air Ministry have been hit? The bombers had been gone three hours. She lived in dread because Helmut spent every night in a building that had to be a prime target. He assured her he went down to the shelter and remained there through every raid, but she did not entirely believe him, and, in any event, she was not confident he would survive in the shelter if the building were hit and fell on top of it. She had had nightmares of someone ringing her doorbell to bring her word that Helmut had been killed.

Barefoot and wearing a white silk nightgown, she hurried down to the door. "Wer sind sie?"

"Polizei."

Oh, God! With what word? She fumbled with the lock and jerked the door open.

There were two of them: one in a black rubber raincoat and a black hat, one in a yellowish-gray trench coat and rain-spotted gray hat. Gestapo.

"Frau General Bittrich?" said the one in the rubber raincoat.

"Ja."

They stepped inside the door. "Sie sind allein?"

"Ja." She was alone in the house. They knew that.

Peering around inside the house, they began to take off their coats. The one in the trench coat closed the door and switched on a light in the entrance hall. He put his coat and hat on the tree. He was tall, gray, and wore steel-rimmed spectacles. He gestured toward the living room and moved toward it and toward her, in a way herding her ahead of him. The other, younger, with a broken nose, hung his raincoat and followed. In the living room, Spectacles switched on a lamp.

It was plain they had not come to bring news of Helmut. This was something very different, something terrifying. She glanced toward the stairs and sought some reason to tell them she had to go up to her bedroom for a moment. She wanted to put her cyanide capsule in her mouth.

"Uh—mein Kimono . . ." she murmured, with a flutter of her hands to suggest she was embarrassed to be seen in her clinging white silk nightgown.

"Setzen sie sich," muttered Spectacles, pointing to a wooden armchair.

She sat. Spectacles stepped to one side of the chair and Broken Nose to the other, and, in quick motions they seemed to have practiced, they seized her arms, pulled them under the chair arms and back, and in an instant she felt the pinch of handcuffs on her wrists.

"Warum?" she whispered weakly.

They did not choose to tell her why. Broken Nose leered at her for an instant as she squirmed in the chair, trying to relieve the painful twist of her shoulders; but Spectacles was already busy looking into the drawer under the telephone.

They were quick and methodical. Spectacles went upstairs shortly. Broken Nose worked in the living room, dining room, and kitchen—never more than a moment leaving her out of his sight. He tossed on the sofa anything he seemed to consider suspicious—a few books in English, a notepad with telephone numbers written on it, a bottle of Scotch whiskey. Upstairs, Spectacles was pulling out drawers, pulling apart the bed; she could hear him.

This could not be routine. No one would dare do this, except on very high authority. She had to believe that Heydrich, too, was under arrest—or, more likely, dead. If not, who short of Himmler would order this? Even Himmler would not risk the Führer's anger by laying hands on *die Engländerin*, unless he were in possession of firm evidence of Heydrich's treason and her connection with MI-6. On the other hand, if he had that evidence, he would strike like a snake. If he had what he needed, likely he was on his way even now to the Wolfsschanze—accompanied, like as not, by Göring and maybe Goebbels; and in the confrontation with the Führer, he would have as allies, not just them, but also Bormann. If he had seized Halder and Beck, Oster and von Kluge, he would confront them with Dietrich and Keitel and Jodl and maybe even Rommel and Guderian and Manstein, summoned from Africa and the eastern front to assure a sufficiently powerful combination. If Heydrich's plot had been discovered and someone strong enough to move against it was moving, she was only an afterthought—and two crude Gestapo agents were enough to ransack her house and bring her in.

Her breath came hard—because of fear and because of the posture into which she was locked by the handcuffs. She hung her head. Her hair fell around her face. If only she had the capsule . . . Freddy had crushed his and died to save his secrets. She would do the same if she could, rather than endure what they would do to her.

Broken Nose was silent. She tossed her head to flip back her hair so she could see him. He was sitting on the couch, looking at her books, and he raised an eyebrow and smiled faintly at her.

"Wie heissen Sie?" she muttered—surprised at how her voice came out hoarse and broken.

"Kriminalinspektor Schumbacher, Geheime Staatspolizei," he said curtly.

"Herr Kriminalinspektor," she whispered from her throat. "Meine Schultern und Handgelenke tun weh. Bitte, können Sie nicht diese Handschelle losmachen?"

Broken Nose grinned and shrugged. "Ich habe den Schlüssel verloren." He had lost the key.

Nancy sighed and again hung her head. She rocked back and forth, trying to ease the ache in her shoulders. She pushed the cuffs down her wrists to shift their pressure.

Except for the pain she suffered and expected, she found herself oddly detached, regarding everything in the past tense. She was confident the truth would be told in England; all the promises to her would be kept. She could not save Helmut; she regretted that. When the pain became bad enough, she would betray

Gordon Aherne; she had no delusions about her own courage. She had done what she could. The failure was not hers. She hoped only for an early release. It would be at the end of a rope. She was thirty-two years old.

Spectacles returned. He carried the pistol Heydrich had provided her many months ago: a 7.62-mm automatic she had kept in her nightstand. He tossed it on the couch beside the things Broken Nose had piled there. "Offnen Sie den Mund," he said sharply to her.

She opened her mouth. It made no difference; the cyanide capsule was in her purse upstairs, and apparently he hadn't found it. He thrust his finger into her mouth and felt around—belatedly, she thought bitterly—for a capsule. She gagged. When he took out his finger, he wiped off her saliva on his trousers.

He went to the dining room and returned dragging a chair, which he pulled close to hers. He sat down facing her. "Wo sind Sie geboren?" he asked.

She sighed. He knew the answer well, but it was the opening question of what had to be a prolonged routine. "England," she muttered.

Spectacles put two hard knuckles under her chin and lifted her face. "Wo sind Sie geboren?" he asked again.

She looked into his pale, scornful face. She sighed. "Ich bin in England geboren," she said.

"Ah. Und wie alt sind Sie?"

"Ich bin zweiunddreissig Jahre alt."

Broken Nose had a pad on his lap and was making notes of her answers. Spectacles asked his questions in unhurried sequence: Where in England had she been born? When had she come to live in Germany? At what addresses had she lived in Germany? Who were her family? Where did they live? . . . When he asked her of her friends, he was not moved by the names she mentioned: Hitler, Göring, Goebbels, Heydrich. He insisted she face him with her eyes open. When she squirmed on her chair to relieve the pain in her back, he waited patiently until she was still and looking at him before he asked another question.

He had asked questions for half an hour, she guessed, before he asked: "Seit wann sind Sie eine Spionin?"—"How long have you been a spy?"

Out of some irrational instinct, she felt she had at least to try to resist. "Ich bin keine Spionin."

Spectacles sighed and turned down one corner of his mouth. He nodded. "Bitte entkleiden Sie sich bis zum Gürtel," he said crisply.

Obviously she could not strip herself to the waist, but Broken Nose could strip her, with enthusiasm. Spectacles got up and left, and Broken Nose came to her and roughly jerked down her nightgown. Not satisfied with exposing her breasts, he pushed it down further, until her belly was naked, too. Spectacles had left the house, apparently to go to their car, and he returned carrying a square, leather-covered box by its handle.

"Schöne kleine Brüste," he muttered as he eyed her breasts. He knelt by the box and opened it. "Schade."

The box was an electrical transformer. He plugged its cord into the receptacle on the floor. Then he uncoiled two long wires and stretched them toward her. They had alligator clips on them. He squeezed the clips and they opened, exposing springs and teeth by which they would grip anything they clamped down on. Spectacles stood. He lifted her right breast and put one of the clips to her nipple.

"*Nein!*" she shrieked. "*Ach, nein, bitte!*"

The sharp steel teeth of the clip pinched shut on the sensitive flesh of her nipple. Nancy groaned. "Nein . . . Nein, bitte . . ." He applied the other clip to her other nipple.

The pain was sharp. The springs in the clips were not strong enough to break her skin, but the teeth bit into her nipples, and she shook her head and moaned. The wires hung from her breasts and reached to the box on the floor. Broken Nose knelt by the box. His hands were on two controls.

With eyes wide, she shook her head. "Nein . . . Bitte, Herr Kriminalinspektor!"

He closed the switch. The pain coursed through her in an excruciating spasm. From deep in her throat she vomited a convulsive, guttural scream, and she jerked wildly against the handcuffs. She felt herself falling and thought she had overturned the chair.

She felt cold water hit her face like a slap. She knew what it was, but it seemed to hit for an instant only, then disappear.

She felt it a second time, then a third. She looked up. Her breasts ached, and Broken Nose stood before her with an empty saucepan. "Aufwache!" he muttered angrily.

She looked up. Spectacles was at the door, talking to a man who stood in the red light outside. Broken Nose watched him, frowning deeply. Spectacles stepped back, as if to let the man come in; then he seemed to take a little jump, and he toppled backward and fell. The man in the doorway aimed a pistol at Broken Nose and shot him, too.

Heydrich had pulled down the sheet and looked at her breasts. Now he put it gently back in place.

"You have nothing to fear," he said. "It is over."

She lay in the bed she had learned to think of as hers, in the suite she had learned to think of as hers, in Hradčany Castle. She had been sedated for some time and was not sure what time of what day it was. She remembered being treated by uniformed SS doctors, then being helped into the cavernous rear seat of an old dark-blue Daimler; and she remembered a young woman who sat on the jump seat, facing her, as they drove for hours through the night and day. The young woman had applied a cream to her breasts several times, and had given her tablets: the sedative.

Nancy glanced around the room. It was small and warm and reassuring. She let her head settle more deeply into her big pillow. "How much did they know?" she asked Heydrich.

"Too much," he said. "About you."

"How?"

"The more senior of the two men who hurt you was a man named Gotthard Richter. He held the rank of Regierungsrat in Amt IV of the RSHA—the Gestapo. He was also an Obersturmbannführer in the SS. You had met him before. I suppose you don't remember."

"No."

"You encountered him in 1938, on *Kristallnacht*. You were on the street—doing what, I would like to know—and you were questioned briefly by a Gestapo detail. The man you spoke with was then-Kriminalinspektor Richter. You had a man with you.

You called him Captain Henke; but when Richter checked later, he found it could not have been Captain Henke.

"Richter could not touch you, because you were the Führer's *Engländerin*, but the way you lied to him aroused not just his suspicion but also his resentment. He opened a dossier on you, and over the years he added to it until it became a very fat dossier. He connected you to Freddy Binghamton. His dossier says you were contacted by a British intelligence agent when you were in Paris in 1940 to meet with the Duke of Windsor. He knew you were on the train when von Hindersin's bomb nearly killed the Führer. Worst of all, he knew you flew General Halder out of Berlin in the middle of a snowstorm in January—although, thank God, he didn't know where you flew him. He had been watching you for a long time, very quietly, very methodically building a dossier. He was a professional policeman."

"Then why...?"

"Think of the coup for him when he could confront Himmler and the Führer with incontrovertible evidence that the famous *Engländerin* was a British agent, involved in an army conspiracy to assassinate the Führer. Think, on the other hand, of what would have happened to him if the Führer had found his evidence insufficient."

"Think of the coup," she suggested quietly, "if he could connect you to me."

"Precisely," said Heydrich. "Oh, he knew a lot about our personal relationship—another reason why he was careful and hesitant. As he dug into that and discovered how much you and I are together and in what circumstances, a bigger suspicion dawned. That is when, for the first time, he went to a superior. That is when his long investigation turned into a conspiracy."

"There were others?" she said.

"Three others. Professors."

"Professors?"

"Intellectuals who volunteered for police work after 1933. One called Krüger was a doctor of law. He was Richter's immediate superior in Amt IV. He was typical of his kind. More Catholic than the Pope, as they say—that is, a late convert to the Party and more Nazi than the Führer. His ambition was based on his egomaniacal notion that his rank should match his intellectual capacity."

"Reinhard—"

"If a man like Krüger thinks I don't know about him, he's wrong. I *did* know."

"Reinhard . . ." she whispered again. Heydrich's voice had become thin, almost shrill.

Heydrich sighed. "Even within the RSHA . . ." he admitted wearily. He sighed again and straightened his shoulders. "When Richter and Schumbacher came to your house, my man reported immediately."

"You've had me watched, then."

"Damn lucky I did, hmm? My man reported. I was called. I sent two men to rescue you, others to move against Krüger and his two confederates, and my most trusted man to capture the dossier."

"You have it?"

"Not any longer. I burned it, of course. By the way, who *were* you with on *Kristallnacht?*"

"Freddy Binghamton."

"You lie. I thought you might say that. Binghamton was in England."

"All right. I was with Ernst Leinberg. Do you know who he was?"

"No."

"A Jew. I was trying to save his life."

"Did you succeed?"

"No."

"You should have asked for my help. And the contact in Paris?"

"I met with Churchill in Paris."

Heydrich laughed. "I might have thought of that. Of course. Churchill was in Paris to meet with the French government. You were important enough for . . . I've allied myself with no inconsiderable woman."

"I suppose you know who my present English contact is," she said dully.

"If I were the incompetent fool you seem to think I am, Richter would have burned the tits off you, filmed your confession to be shown to the Führer, and disposed of you with an injection that would have made it seem you had died of a heart attack. Aherne? Dr. Diekermann? Don't worry. I won't touch him. I want you to send a message to Churchill through him."

"Saying . . ."

"May first. At the latest May second. Hitler will be dead May first."

"Why not sooner? It's important—"

"It's important that the spring offensive in Russia be under way," Heydrich interrupted. "The morale of the army will then be able to sustain the shock of the loss of the Führer. May first."

She nodded. "Very well."

"You will see the Führer once before then. He is making an important speech to the Reichstag on April twenty-sixth. After that, he is going to the Berghof for a few days' rest before he returns to the Wolfsschanze on April thirtieth or May first. You will be summoned to the Berghof. You will have to keep tight control over yourself. Don't allow yourself to become emotional over seeing the man for the last time before his death. You and I will be in Berlin when he is killed. We will talk to Churchill directly then, by telephone. I want you to arrange that."

Nancy could not tell if the Führer car had been restored or if another had been built just like the one damaged by von Hindersin's bomb. She boarded the train at the Anhalter Station and was taken directly to the Führer car and to Hitler's small private sitting room.

In the past hour she had learned why Heydrich would not move against Hitler before May 1. Sitting in the gallery of the Reichstag, she had heard the Führer demand and the Reichstag obediently vote the ultimate in dictatorial powers. From now on, there was no limit whatever on the powers of the Führer—whoever might hold that title and office. Hitler's successor might experience difficulty in seizing those powers, but once seized they would be beyond the reach of any man or institution.

The Führer's sitting room was small but comfortable. Iced champagne was ready and was poured for her when she entered. Fresh flowers—they were yellow roses—lent a clean fragrance to the room.

They would be on the train all night, and she expected Hitler would want her to sleep with him. She dreaded being asked to undress. Her nipples remained bruised and swollen. Worse than that, her wrists were circled with dark bruises—still, a month after she had jerked against the handcuffs so hard she had torn her skin. She could explain away the swelling and discoloration of her breasts as the result of a minor aircraft accident throwing her against the instrument panel; but the circles on her wrists would be difficult to explain. She wore a long-sleeved blouse as well as a linen jacket and hoped she could somehow discourage Hitler from requiring her to undress.

"Annchen," he said simply when he entered the sitting room. He carried a bundle of file folders stuffed with papers, which he dropped on the table. An aide quietly deposited another bundle and withdrew.

"Wolf . . ." she said.

He sat down gingerly, as if in pain; and when he clasped his hands before him on his lap, she saw them tremble. White hair now softened the color of his hair and moustache. His jaw moved as if he were nervously nibbling on his tongue.

"I—have sent an order to General Bittrich," he said. "He will join us at the Berghof on Tuesday. Mussolini will be there. I want General Bittrich to take part in the meeting. You will be my guests at the dinner for the Duce."

"Thank you," she said. "We are honored."

"The strain of war has—marked you, Annchen. You have aged. I am dismayed to see it, but in another sense I am grateful that you have chosen to share our burden to such an extent. I understand you spend a great deal of time with Heydrich. He tells me you contribute useful ideas. He tells me you acquainted yourself thoroughly with his problems in Prague and helped him choose his measures to cope with them."

"He gives me too much credit," she said.

"I have here," he said, tapping the stack of files on the table, "some recent reports from England. I would like you to tell me where the truth lies. You saw the Berlin crowds cheering me this afternoon. Do you think crowds of Londoners gather to cheer Churchill after he speaks to the House of Commons?"

The train began to move. Hitler opened one file folder after another, showing her confidential intelligence reports from the Abwehr, from the RSHA, and from the Forschungsamt, the office for the interception and decoding of foreign communications. He was torn between two policies, he said—and he had intelligence reports supporting each: first, to strike England as hard as he could wherever he could, in the hope of knocking it out of the war; second, to eschew his most destructive options, in the thought that a negotiated peace was still possible. He did not want her advice as to his basic choice; he wanted her reaction to specific intelligence reports—Did the English really think this? Did they actually believe that? How would they react to this? Would they understand the significance of that?

"Lübeck," he said as she was eating the meal brought to the sitting room—and he was nibbling without interest on a tiny sandwich. "Churchill bombed Lübeck. Why? It was of no military or industrial significance. All he did was knock down and shatter the irreplaceable Medieval stones. *What if I bomb Canterbury Cathedral?* It's vulnerable. It's within easy reach. What would the English think, Annchen? Would it teach them to hate me? Or fear me? Or both? Would the war be shorter if I destroyed Canterbury Cathedral? Or longer?"

"It would severely damage the chance of a negotiated peace," she said.

"Ah," he said. He nodded. "So what does Churchill expect to gain by bombing Lübeck? Suppose I sent bombers over Canterbury and they dropped nothing but leaflets—leaflets saying, 'You see, we did not bomb this great monument to Western civilization; we spared it as you did not spare a similar monument of ours.' How would the English people respond to that?"

After midnight he asked her if she knew Admiral Sir Louis Mountbatten. She said he had been a close friend ten years ago; she had hardly seen him since. Even so, Hitler questioned her for an hour about Mountbatten. Who were his closest friends? What was his attitude toward his Battenburg ancestry? Was he capable? Did he drink heavily? Did the English generally like him? There was reason, said Hitler, to believe Mountbatten would command the cross-Channel invasion—if ever there were one.

He did not spare her—or himself—one file. The intensity with which he scanned documents and discussed them with her did not diminish. At 4:00 A.M. he closed the last file.

"If a man wants to be Führer," he said abruptly, "he should understand what it costs."

Startled, Nancy caught her breath. She frowned, nodded. "I have seen what it costs," she said quietly.

He changed the subject. "Annchen, I want to make you a promise. I promise that someday you will go home to England, to be honored for what you have done during this war. They think you are a traitor now, but they will learn better. I promise."

"Thank you, Wolf," she whispered.

He rose and stood unsteadily in the swaying railroad car. "I have a few more things to do," he said. "I am meeting the Duce today. I will bring him up the mountain tomorrow. You should rest today. You look tired."

Mussolini looked defeated, distracted. His smile still came readily enough, but to his mouth only; his eyes looked inward and shifted furtively. Hitler placed Nancy at the Duce's side at dinner, apparently to talk with him while the Führer took the opportunity to talk intently with his own generals, some of whom he had not recently seen. The Duce knew who Nancy was. He said he himself flew and enjoyed flying. He spoke a little of England. He said the late spring snow that covered the Obersalzberg was beautiful and he was surprised at how bitterly the Führer had complained of it. He suggested that in Russia the Führer had learned to dislike snow.

When Mussolini and the generals had retired, Eva Braun appeared. Albert Speer, Hitler's architect, remained. Bormann went out briefly and returned. Hitler gathered them around him and began to talk about Russian railroads—how he would rebuild them to a different gauge after the war, so that they would not match the gauge of the old Russian railroads that would remain east of the Urals, so assuring the economic separation of the Asiatic Russia from the new German Russia. Japan would occupy Russia's Pacific coast, he said. Stalin's rump Soviet Union would have no access to the world's oceans or to sources of economic and military power.

Helmut, who had spent the day with the Führer and the Duce in conference about the coming summer campaigns, sat close to Nancy, his hand touching hers, his fingers caressing her palm. During the day, he had told her a little earlier, Hitler had set impossible goals for aircraft production for the balance of the year. In a brief private meeting outside the conference, Hitler had roared his outrage over what he had called the "incompetence and cowardice" of the Luftwaffe generals; but as they returned to the conference, he had taken Helmut by the arm—had, in fact, balanced himself with a firm grip on Helmut—and told him he did not include him among the cowards and incompetents.

As soon as she could—after an hour of listening to Hitler's monologue—Nancy excused herself and Helmut, and they retired to their room.

"We cannot talk in our room," she warned him on the way. "I am sure Bormann has microphones installed everywhere. I would be surprised if he does not listen to Hitler himself."

In the room, Helmut said loudly and distinctly: "I feel the need for a little fresh air. Could we walk for a few minutes on the terrace?"

The new snow had already begun to melt. The cold air had a taste of spring in it: the odor of fresh green vegetation growing even under the snow, the odor of new pine growth. The SS guards on the terrace recognized them and silently nodded to let them pass, away from the lighted room where Hitler and his court still whiled away the night, away from the dark rooms where, likely, the generals lay awake.

"Your—health?" Helmut asked when they were at the edge of the terrace, touching the stone wall, looking down toward the valley. He knew what had happened to her. His anguish at seeing her hurt had drawn her closer to him. It had been genuine, unaffected; it was a human emotion, undiminished by calculation.

"I am all right. The pain is almost gone."

Helmut glanced backward, toward the lighted windows. "He thinks he is going to win the war this summer. Rather, he knows he *must* win it this summer, or it is lost."

"Can he win it?"

Helmut shook his head. "It is impossible, unless the Russians are on the verge of collapse as he believes. I spend my days and nights searching for gasoline—then allocating what little I can find. What is more important, tanks or fighter aircraft? Or bombers? Or submarines? Or road transport? We do not have oil enough for them all. What is more important, shells for antitank guns, or shells for the panzers? Or for heavy artillery? Or should we put the explosives in bombs? Or torpedoes?" Helmut shrugged. "Oil. Explosives. Steel. Aluminum. Rubber. Men, women. We are short of them all. But the Russians seem to have them—men and women, particularly—in endless supply. Now come the Americans. He says we will win because German soldiers are brave. The Poles were brave. Has he forgotten?"

"We have a little time, Helmut," she said. "This is Tuesday. If Hitler dies Friday, then what?"

He nodded curtly. "Then what?"

She looked out across the night, toward the shadowy white mountain. "No matter what Heydrich does," she said, "I do not want to stay in Germany."

"What do you want me to do?"

"I want you to get us a Messerschmitt 110."

"An airplane for two," said Helmut. "And for 'us.' You and I? I haven't said I'm going."

"If you're not, then I want a Focke-Wulf 190. I'll take the added eighty kilometers per hour."

"But I am going, Nancy," he said. "I hope you understand what agony it is for me."

"I do."

"Do you want to know why?"

"Yes, of course."

"They have built a nation in which two policemen can come to a home and subject a woman to obscene torture—and no one would object. It is common. I know. And Heydrich will not make it different."

"More than that, Helmut," she said. "Two other men came to the same house and killed the two policemen. No one has asked why. No one has asked anything. No one will."

"Where do you want the airplane?"

"Berlin. Gatow Airfield. If you had an alternative or two on other airports, it might give us more chances."

"You must promise me," he said, "that you will fly to England without me if you must. It may not be possible for us to go together."

"It will not be possible for us to go otherwise," she said.

❧ *XXVII* ❧

The assassination of Hitler was definitely set for May 1, as Heydrich had promised. The *Führer* train would carry Hitler back to East Prussia, to the Wolfsschanze, on that day; and on its arrival in Rastenburg station, it would be attacked by a squad of SD men dressed in Russian uniforms and carrying Russian equipment. Hitler's security would be compromised by others of Heydrich's men, working as guards inside the train and in the station. As soon as Hitler was dead, the word would go to Berlin that the Führer had been killed by Russian paratroopers—an eventuality that had long been feared by those responsible for his security. In Berlin, Halder would move to take control of the Armed Forces High Command. Beck would seize the Berlin garrison. Heydrich's SS and SD squads would move to kill Himmler and others marked by Heydrich for quick elimination. As soon as Heydrich was firmly in control, Nancy was to join him in a direct, personal telephone call to Winston Churchill. Nancy had sent word to Churchill to expect the call.

May 1 came and went. The *Führer* train was delayed in Poland and did not arrive at Rastenburg until late that night, by which time it was too late to put the complex plan into effect. What was more, it was too complex simply to be moved forward a day. Heydrich postponed everything to Tuesday, May 5. He flew back to Prague.

On Sunday evening, May 3, he telephoned Nancy. "Your generals are procrastinating again," he said bitterly. "Beck wants to meet with me. I told him he'll have to meet with you, at least for now. A man of mine will come to your door within the hour. He will call himself Willi Rost. He will take you to meet Beck."

She tried to telephone Helmut at the Air Ministry, but was not able to get through before Heydrich's man came to her door. For a week she and Helmut had been in touch almost hourly. He had two Me-110s ready for their escape, one at Schönefeld Airfield, one at Gatow. She and Helmut were counting on an hour of frenzied activity and confusion when word of Hitler's death reached Berlin. Heydrich would be totally engaged in seizing power. By the time he looked around for Nancy to join him in his call to Churchill, she and Helmut might be beyond his reach, in a fast airplane streaking for the Channel.

General Beck waited for her in a small room in a shabby little hotel above a café—a room in which, he complained, "ten thousand sordid assignations have undoubtedly taken place." He sat gingerly on the sagging, creaking bed, allowing her the only chair. He was rigid and severe as always, dressed as a civilian in a gray suit with vest. She noticed that his hands trembled as he frowned intently over the lighting of a cigarette.

"Are you and the Obergruppenführer aware, Frau General," said Beck, "that General von Manstein opens a major offensive in the Crimea day after tomorrow? Kleist launches another major attack next week. These operations are critical. It is the wrong time to kill the Führer."

"Will it always be the wrong time, Herr Generaloberst?" she asked. "Can Germany never spare him? Have you changed your minds entirely?"

"No," snapped Beck. "But to kill him at a critical point, just as the spring offensives are launched, is poor timing."

"When the offensives are moving, it will still be poor timing," she said.

Beck drew an impatient breath, stiffening. Plainly he did not wish to negotiate with a woman. "I am directed by my colleagues to offer an alternative plan," he said. "Will you convey it to Obergruppenführer Heydrich?"

"Of course."

"On June fourth, Marshal Mannerheim will observe his seventy-fifth birthday. The Führer will fly to Finland to meet with him and the President of Finland. He will fly in a Condor from Berlin to Helsinki. Even though he will be escorted by fighter aircraft, he will be far more vulnerable in the air over the Baltic than he could ever be in East Prussia. Please convey this information to the Herr Obergruppenführer and tell him Generals Halder and von Kluge concur with me and urgently ask him to reconsider his plan."

"It is not as foolish as it seemed at first," Heydrich said to Nancy as he spread the Baltic chart on their bed in her suite at Hradčany Castle. "Look. The distance from Berlin to Helsinki is eleven hundred kilometers. That's within the Condor's range, easily, as you well know. But it is beyond the range of the fighter escort. The Condor will be escorted from Berlin by four Focke-Wulf 190 fighters. They will stay with it to about fifty-six degrees latitude, then will break away and fly east to Königsberg. Four others that took off from Königsberg will intercept it there and accompany it on to Helsinki. On the way back, they will reverse the process: The four that fly southwest from Helsinki will break away about the same point and make for Königsberg, replaced by four that flew out from Königsberg to intercept."

"Why don't they fly escort with Me-110s?" she asked. "They have the range."

"They are too slow for daylight missions," said Heydrich. "At night they are formidable. With their radar, they find bombers and shoot them down. In daylight they are no match for Spitfires or Yaks."

"That's a tricky rendezvous operation, over the water," she said.

"Exactly," said he with a faint smile. "And there lies the key to shooting down the Condor."

"That's the new plan?" she asked.

He nodded, and pointed to the chart. "Two other 190s take off from Danzig. They intercept the Condor's course ten minutes southwest of the point where the rendezvous is supposed to be made. They transmit the proper identification codes, so it is supposed they are simply two members of the replacement, a little early. The 190s from Berlin are short of fuel by now, so two of them break away for Königsberg. The two from Danzig are now part of the escort, and the opportunity to shoot down the Condor will present itself immediately. They shoot it down and turn away. The two original 190s are unlikely to try to pursue. They are out over the Baltic and short of fuel. They have no choice but to make for Königsberg. The two 190s from Danzig will return to Berlin, where the pilots can give me their personal assurance they saw the Condor hit the water. We have two opportunities: one on the northeast flight, one on the southwest. And it's a very clean operation. If it doesn't work, no one need know it was even attempted. We will, of course, say the Condor was shot down by Russian pilots flying German-marked FW-190s captured on the eastern front."

Nancy shook her head. "It's hard to believe the Führer is taking such a risk."

"There's little risk," said Heydrich. "His security does not lie with the fighters that escort his airplane. It lies in the fact that his flight is a secret. Also, not until he has taken off from Berlin will we know the time of the flight. You know him. You know how on impulse he changes schedule. But I will have agents observing his takeoff. We will know its time precisely, so will know when the 190s should take off from Danzig. For us the only risk is in missing the rendezvous. I am glad we have two chances."

She turned away from the chart. It was late afternoon, and in the fading daylight in the room the details on the paper were not visible anyway. She had flown the Storch down from Berlin in gusty weather and was tired. "Who are your pilots?" she asked.

He began to fold the chart. "Why not you?" he asked.

"Reinhard, I couldn't. I've never flown a 190. Even if I had, I've never fired the guns on any airplane. Anyway, I assume the escort pilots will be experienced fighter pilots. For a few minutes anyway, someone is going to have an aerial fight on hand."

"No," he said. "Point by point—you've never flown a 190, but you have flown a Messerschmitt 109 and a Messerschmitt 110; it isn't that much different. Firing is easy enough; I can teach you in an hour. You won't have a dogfight, because what you will do is turn away and dive for the Swedish coast. The other 190s are no faster than you and won't be able to catch you, and they will have to break off pursuit after a few minutes at most because they will be so short of fuel. Nothing will happen that will be beyond your abilities as a flier."

"In any event, if I'm shot down I'm expendable," she said.

"Did Churchill tell you you would survive the assassination of Adolf Hitler?" Heydrich asked coldly. "Did you tell him you would not do it if you had to risk your life? I doubt it. Of course there is risk, but I'm telling you it is minimal. I wouldn't send you if I thought otherwise. I need you."

"But don't you have many other pilots who—"

"No. I don't. I have access to many skills. Pilot skills are not among them. I have recruited two young men to fly the mission. You are better than either of them. You have a far better chance than either of them of making the interception. It is going to be a tricky problem in navigation: five or six thousand meters' altitude; a hundred kilometers or so out over open water; the Condor approaching at three hundred kilometers per hour; you coming at five hundred. I want you to lead one of my young men to the rendezvous. He will shoot down the Condor. He is so dedicated he will ram it if he has to. Probably you will not have to fire a gun. The other escorting 190s may think he alone has lost his mind and attacked the Führer's plane. I know I can rely on you to use your head, not to panic, and to do what you have to do."

The Focke-Wulf 190 was new. Very few of them were in the squadrons, and squadrons that did have them were experiencing engine troubles. The young pilot who introduced Nancy to it warned her that at full throttle the engine might burn out its valves. Anyway, with a BMW radial engine rated at more than 1,300 horsepower, it was the fastest and fastest-climbing airplane she had ever flown. She had a sense she was simply riding a huge engine that pulled her wildly into the air and hurtled her toward a bank of clouds so fast she would be inside them before she could turn. She did turn the airplane and found it was responsive even to a light pressure on the controls. She flew it for an hour over the Czech mountains that first day and returned to an easy landing on the airfield at Lidice.

The next day she fired two short bursts from the guns; that was all. If she had to fire on Hitler's Condor, she was to move in close and fire until her guns overheated. It was better to hit the wings, with the fuel tanks and engines, than the fuselage. She could fire a longer burst coming up on the Condor from below than she could diving on it from above. When she joined the escort, she should, if she could, position herself behind and below, to the right. To attack, she would initiate a climbing left turn, bringing her nose and her guns across the wings and body of the big Condor. Surprise would assure the success of the attack, as it would assure her escape. Having fired her burst, she would roll the 190 to the left, into a power dive. If one of the real escort pilots elected to pursue her, he would have to react in seconds. Diving away from him, she would be out of the range of his guns in five or six seconds, and there would be nothing he could do to close the distance.

She had decided she would fire on the Condor, not just lead the other pilot to the rendezvous and witness his attack. She had risked too much and endured too much, and too much was at stake, for her to sit passively a hundred meters away and watch someone else attack Adolf Hitler.

Helmut arrived in Prague, ostensibly on his way to an inspection of the Skoda works. Heydrich met him at the airport, where together they watched Nancy fly a roaring, high-speed pass over the field; and the three drove to Hradčany Castle in Heydrich's open car. Heydrich installed Helmut in Nancy's suite in the castle and told them his car would call for them at six, to bring them for dinner to his villa outside Prague.

One of Heydrich's sons was at the villa—a tall, handsome, blond boy. Nancy had never seen the villa or any member of Heydrich's family before. Heydrich was dressed for the occasion in black and silver uniform, and white-jacketed SS orderlies served dinner.

After dinner the son was dismissed, and Heydrich invited Helmut and Nancy to take their coffee in the twilight on a terrace. They sat on thick-cushioned metal chairs, watching the light change on the distant northern mountains.

"My wife," said Helmut, "has taken me into her confidence relative to the mission over the Baltic."

Heydrich saluted Helmut with his glass of brandy. "I am pleased to hear that," he said.

"I am going to contribute something," said Helmut. His voice was dull. His face was bland. "The choice of Focke-Wulf 190s for the Führer's escort was a political decision, Herr Obergruppen-führer. There are those who want the Führer to look out the windows of the Condor and always see those new fighters—very reassuring—flying as his escort. Not Messerschmitts, you understand—Focke-Wulfs. Someone wants the Führer to see them and have a good impression of them. And he will—so long as nothing requires a maximum effort from their engines. If they have to fly with throttles wide open, the valves may overheat and stick. If my wife has to fly into a power dive after she fires on the Condor, she will be in grave danger. So will the pilot of any other 190 who flies that maneuver. But the defect can be remedied. The valves can be replaced with new ones, machined from a different alloy containing more nickel and chromium. We will retrofit all 190s with these new valves, in time. The two for the Baltic mission can be retrofitted now."

"So our two 190s will be superior to all others," said Heydrich with a pleased smile.

Helmut sipped his brandy. "I can't promise you that Göring or Milch won't order a similar retrofit of the eight 190s chosen for the escort," he said quietly.

Heydrich glanced at Nancy, then nodded at Helmut. "I am very pleased to have your assistance, Herr General," he said. "You may be sure I will remember it."

"You are welcome to share this, if you like it," muttered Göring as he lifted to his nose a small quantity of white powder on a tiny gold spatula. He inhaled abruptly, and the powder disappeared up his nostril.

Goebbels watched in pinched, disapproving silence. Helmut and Nancy pretended to ignore what they saw. Göring had also provided cheese, fruit, and wine; and Nancy picked up a morsel of delicate white cheese. They had been summoned to this meeting in Göring's office in the Air Ministry and were seated on leather couches, facing an inlaid low table of vaguely Oriental design. Göring wore white uniform. Goebbels, in an unpressed double-breasted suit, slumped inside the wrinkled gray fabric and looked as though he might slip down inside it and disappear. Berlin had been raided last night. Goebbels, as he had remarked a moment ago, had spent the day in the bombed neighborhoods, showing the government to the people, as he put it.

"Bormann," grumbled Göring. He nodded. "Martin Bormann."

"Bormann again," sighed Goebbels.

"Herr General," said Göring to Helmut, "I am sorry if this embarrasses you, but it is known that that your wife has a close and personal relationship with Reinhard Heydrich. My own relationship with him is quite distant. I am calling on you to help me establish a dialogue with Reinhard Heydrich."

Grim and solemn, Helmut drew a deep breath. "Bormann," he said. "You mentioned Bormann."

Göring nodded. "Herr Doktor Goebbels agrees with me that if something is not done to establish a counterweight to Martin Bormann, he will assume power second only to the Führer himself and will be his successor."

"So," said Helmut coldly, "you want my wife to...?"

Göring glanced at Nancy. He had not wanted Helmut in this meeting, but she had told Helmut of her own invitation, and he had insisted on accompanying her.

"Herr General," said Göring, "we are establishing a small circle of people who are interested in blocking the further acquisition of power by Martin Bormann. If Heydrich—"

"Let us be frank," said Goebbels. "We want Heydrich to kill him."

"Well, not necessarily," said Göring. "We want—"

"You want me to convey to the Obergruppenführer an invitation to join your circle," said Nancy.

"How do you think he would react?" asked Goebbels.

"Specifically," interrupted Göring, "do you think he might go to Bormann and tell him?"

"I can assure you of only one thing he will not do," said Nancy. "He will not go to Bormann and tell him *I* brought him an invitation to join an anti-Bormann cabal. For any assurance more than that, you will have to look to your own knowledge and judgment."

"Are you, in any event, willing to present the question to him?" asked Göring.

She nodded.

Ten minutes later, as they walked through the corridors of the Ministry toward his own offices, Helmut glanced at her and said: "Bormann is going with the Führer to Helsinki."

They sat down in his office, an untidy working place filled with stacked files, the walls covered with graphs, charts, and maps. He had been gone only half an hour, but a dozen telephone messages waited. Anxious officers had greeted her with superficial smiles, dismayed to see that General Bittrich was going to spend time in his office with his wife and would not be immediately available to them.

"The two 190s have been fitted with the new valves," said Helmut. "Do you think Heydrich is really happy about that?"

"Why not?"

Helmut sighed heavily. "Your specific instructions are to fire a burst at the Condor and then escape by throwing your 190 into a maximum-power dive. Hasn't it occurred to you that Heydrich knew perfectly well that is exactly the situation in which the engine valves were likely to overheat and seize up? What a neat way to rid himself of two people who are going to be an embarrassment to him."

"He needs me to talk to Churchill," she said.

"So he's told you."

"I guess the world is littered with the corpses of people who have trusted him," she said.

Helmut nodded. "Do you remember Karl Lagerkrist?"

"The Swede? Of course."

"I have had occasion several times to visit his corporate offices in Stockholm," said Helmut. "I will be there on Thursday, June fourth. I am flying there myself, in a Me-110, on the pretext that I want to test some new radar equipment we are installing in the 110s. I will have a pilot with me, since the 110 is a little too much airplane for me. I will meet with Lagerkrist and return that night. I—"

"Helmut," she interrupted. "When Lagerkrist was in Berlin, Freddy Binghamton worked for him as a chauffeur. Since they know Freddy was an agent of British Intelligence, I am sure there is a fat dossier on Lagerkrist. A visit to him might be regarded with—"

"Suspicion," said Helmut. "We still buy engine parts from him. He travels to and from Berlin freely. In any event, he is not involved in what I am telling you, except as my excuse for flying to Stockholm. Heydrich doesn't know I'm going, since I haven't announced it around here and have made arrangements very quietly. He will find out on June fourth, of course, but I think we may assume he will be a very busy man that day."

"You are suggesting I fly to Stockholm?"

"After you have shot down the Führer and made your dive toward the Swedish coast to elude the escort, instead of turning south and flying to Berlin, you continue north and land at Stockholm. It is a neutral country. You explain to the Swedes that your 190 has developed engine trouble and you have made an emergency landing. Then you discover, to your amazement, that your husband is also there, with another airplane. We tell the Swedish authorities that you will return to Berlin with me in my plane, and that my pilot will remain to fly the Focke-Wulf back to Berlin as soon as it is repaired. England is entirely within the range of a fully fueled Me-110. Coming across the North Sea in a single German night fighter, we can hope the Spitfires won't shoot us down."

She reached across his desk and put her hand on his. "Are you sure you want to do this, Helmut?"

He lifted his chin. "I will return to Germany when it is a nation in which we can resolve political differences otherwise than by murdering each other."

❧ *XXVIII* ❧

Heydrich lowered his violin. For some minutes it had been apparent that his mind was on something besides the music. He looked at Nancy. "Tell me," he said. "Be frank. What do you plan to do with the rest of your life? I mean, assuming all we have planned turns out as we hope, do you want to go home to England and live again as a wealthy English aristocrat? Or—"

"I am far from wealthy," she interrupted. "In fact, I am virtually penniless. In England I am dependent on an allowance from my brother, which he cut off when I married a German and remained in Germany in 1939."

Heydrich laughed. "We will send you to England as ambassador extraordinary and plenipotentiary. *You* will present me to the King. You will be a heroine honored with medals and titles from both countries. As for your brother, well, if he wants you to receive him, we will make him pay dearly for the privilege. Maybe we can get them to make you a duchess. But—do you really want to return to England?"

"For a visit at least," she said.

Heydrich nodded. "It is difficult for you, I am sure, not to have seen your country or your family for so long. I would think less of you if I didn't see how that affects you."

He put his violin aside, on a table by a window, beside a tall china vase of Holland tulips. He sat down and began to tug off a boot.

They were in her suite in Hradčany Castle on May 28. They had dined in the city, and when they returned she had found the suite alight with dozens of candles, champagne cooling in a bucket of ice, his violin on the table, and two gifts waiting for her in gaily wrapped packages. One of the gifts was the negligee she was wearing now: a long, deeply pleated skirt of sheer, pale yellow silk, with a bodice of delicate yellow lace cut in a scoop under her breasts, leaving them bare. The other gift was an Albrecht Dürer watercolor of a nesting bird.

Heydrich dropped one boot and began to tug on the other. "Do you want to remain married to General Bittrich?" he asked.

"Why not?"

"Why not, indeed. It is obvious he is devoted to you. He is suddenly quite protective of you."

"I couldn't conceal from him what the Gestapo did to me."

"Yes. I suppose the most phlegmatic of us becomes emotional when he sees his woman abused. He is an honorable man."

As he began to unbutton his tunic, she poured herself another half-glass of champagne. She glanced around the warmly lighted room, at the exquisite old furniture, the intimately low ceilings. She knew she would never see this room again. Tomorrow Heydrich was leaving Prague, and he would not return. He would be in Berlin a short time. He would meet with Hitler at least once. Hitler had already indicated that Heydrich's next assignment was France, where he was expected to rule as he had done here. He would be in Berlin on June 4, when Hitler made his quick trip to Finland for the birthday of Marshal Mannerheim. On that day, she would be in Danzig.

"I am sorry we can't fly back to Berlin together," said Heydrich. "This time I really can't spare the time to go with you in the Storch."

"I'll leave about noon," she said. "The forecast is good."

He put aside his black and silver tunic. "I will have to leave you early in the morning," he said. "I must drive out to my villa and pick up some documents I wouldn't want to entrust to anyone else. I am afraid it will be late afternoon before *I* can get away for Berlin."

He continued to undress, and she stepped to the mantel and studied the Dürer. She admired it very much, of course, but she wondered how it had come into his possession, whether from a

museum or from someone's home, whether someone had felt compelled to give it to him or if he had taken it. She wondered if she
could ever return it.

"We will of course see each other in Berlin," said Heydrich. He
stood and slipped down his underpants. Naked, he lifted the bottle
from the bucket and poured himself a glass of champagne. "You
leave for Danzig on Tuesday. I will make an occasion for us to be
together before then."

It had come to this: that he could be almost casual about being
quite naked in her presence in a fully lighted room, not a bedroom. He saluted her with his glass, sipped champagne, then bent
down and kissed her. "Sit down with me," he said quietly.

They sat together on a small upholstered bench that faced the
cold fireplace. He kissed her breasts lightly. He guided her hand
to his crotch, and she began to do what she knew he wanted: She
caressed his genitals with her fingertips. He put an arm around her
and held her close to him.

"Are you dissatisfied?" he asked. "Do you think I am using
you?"

She glanced up into his face, then lowered her eyes and nodded.
"I understand you are using me," she said. "In some sense, I am
using you. Our purposes are the same."

"Our motives are the same," he said.

"Our motives are different. Let's not discuss that."

He chuckled. "You are shrewd. You are perceptive. You are
brave. What is more, you are very much like me. I know you
don't regard that as a compliment, but you are; you *are* like me.
You are young, but if you had one of these"—he reached down
and flipped his penis—"you would be in the government in
England; in ten years you would be Prime Minister: another
Lloyd George, another Churchill. Or you might have become a
Marlborough or a Wellington. I do not flatter. I am not toying
with you. I am sincere. I believe it."

Nancy sighed. "If you had lived in England, Reinhard, you
might have turned your exceptional talents in another direction
and—"

"And be successful and powerful in England?" he asked with a
little smile.

She nodded. "And been successful and powerful in England."

He bent over and kissed her. "That's a marvelous compliment," he said. "Maybe you understand after all how little different I am from other men like me, who live in England or America."

She nodded, but her thought was that he seemed not to realize how little different he was from Adolf Hitler, the man he scorned so violently.

"I don't believe in what they call 'fate,'" said Heydrich. "I am a rationalist. Still, it is hard to explain, rationally, how two people from backgrounds as widely separated as ours could ever meet, understand each other so readily and so well, and be somehow drawn to work together in what is the most important thing in both of our lives. I confess to you: I am emotionally joined to you and committed to you. I have never before in my life placed so much confidence in a woman, or so much trust. It is irrational, and I have done it on an emotional basis. Do you have any such feeling for me at all? Be honest. If the answer is no, say no."

She frowned and stared downward at his flat belly, muscular legs, and big, half-erect penis. "The answer is not 'no,' Reinhard," she whispered.

"Truly?"

She looked up. "Truly." She was not lying. She did not love him, certainly, but she had always been fascinated by him, attracted to him—even now, when she had heard him confess to murder and when she had good reason to suspect he meant somehow to rid himself of her as soon as she had served her purpose to him. She could kill him, too, willingly, if Churchill ordered it; but she would regret it; it would be like smashing a grotesquely flawed porcelain, yet regretting the necessity of destroying the elements of beauty its flaws distorted.

"I have been meaning to ask you something," he said. He kissed her lightly on the forehead. "When this is over—when we have done what we have to do—when I am the new Führer of the German Reich and we have begun the negotiations to make peace with England—then would you consider—I mean, would you allow me to make you pregnant? Could you and I omit the precautions until you were carrying my child? I can think of no greater honor I could have, nothing that would make me happier, than for you to become the mother of a child of mine. I would honor it and you." His face gleamed pink. "I have thought of this for a long time. I could not be more sincere."

A plump young SS Untersturmführer named Hausser was her driver when she was in Prague. He was to pick her up at eleven and drive her to the airport. She was ready at eleven. She had brought little and had little to pack or carry. She had carefully wrapped the Dürer. The yellow negligee was in her one small traveling bag. She was impatient and soon annoyed when Hausser was late. The weather was sunny. She wanted to take off for Berlin while it remained that way.

There was no telephone in the suite. The nearest telephone she knew of was in the SS guard station on the courtyard below, where the grim and officious men on duty had never been cordial. Anyway, she would not know where to call Hausser. She had no choice, really, but to wait. She stood at the leaded window, watching the comings and goings in the castle courtyard. It was no ordinary morning, Heydrich's last morning as Reich Protector, and several cars moved into and then out of the courtyard at high speed. She suspected Hausser's duties were heavy that morning. Driving her to the airport was probably a time-consuming nuisance for him.

It was 11:46 when the gray BMW she recognized as the car assigned to Hausser sped into the courtyard and squealed to an abrupt stop under her window. Hausser squirmed out and trotted to the door below.

"Frau General!" he coughed when she opened the door and saw him running up the stairs toward her. "Frau General! Something horrible has happened! The Obergruppenführer has been injured in an explosion, an attempt to murder him! At the hospital—he is asking for you!"

It was difficult for them to enter the hospital. Half a dozen times Hausser had to insist that Heydrich was demanding to see her, that he himself had been sent for her with express orders to bring her directly to Heydrich. The hospital was surrounded in depth by SS troops. It was being evacuated of Czechs, even the sick and injured being carried away in wheelchairs, on stretchers, and in ambulances. Inside, regular hospital personnel stood about in confusion in the corridors, their offices being occupied by SS and Gestapo men, using their telephones, shoving the work off their desks to make room for their caps and weapons and their radio sets. Officers' holster flaps were open. On a landing off the main stairway, a light machine gun had been set up and a crew of three sat ready to sweep the entry hall and adjacent corridors on command.

Hausser was stopped finally at a guard station improvised by dragging desks into a corridor, so blocking it that the very few men who were being allowed to pass had to climb on a desk and jump down on the other side. The Hauptsturmführer on duty refused to let either Hausser or Nancy pass. He refused to believe Heydrich wanted to see this woman, whoever she was.

"Herr Hauptsturmführer," mumbled Hausser through his teeth and under his breath, "Sie ist seine Maitresse."

The officer picked up a military field telephone on a box on one of the desks. He spoke with someone, and in a moment he climbed onto the desk and offered Nancy his hand. He helped her up, then jumped down and helped her down. Without a word he led her along the hospital corridor to the door of a room. He nodded at the door and stood aside as she entered.

Heydrich was sitting on an examining table, his booted feet dangling. He was stripped to the waist, and two doctors were working on his back. He was pale. He was obviously in some pain.

"Ah," he said weakly when he saw her. He extended his hand. "I feel better now."

"Reinhard," she whispered. "I was afraid . . ."

"They had killed me?" He shook his head. "They tried."

"A bomb?"

"A Sten gun, but it jammed. Then they threw a grenade. It fell in the back seat, but the explosion . . ." He glanced over his shoulder. "I have some holes behind, some fragments inside. The doctors want to operate. I am waiting for some specialists."

The two doctors had continued to work on his back, and now one of them deposited a bit of metal—it looked like a two centimeters of wire—in a white-enamel pan.

Heydrich winced. "Doctors, will you allow the lady and me a moment's private conversation, please?"

The doctors stepped outside and closed the door to the corridor.

"Nothing is changed," said Heydrich. "I have a week to recover sufficiently to carry out our project. It will be enough."

"Are you certain?"

He nodded. "I have a broken rib. They think there is a grenade fragment in the spleen. Those two doctors are German, but a surgeon is being flown down from Berlin. I have already had a call from Himmler, who is sending the surgeon and other doctors. I will ask you to remain in Prague. For a few more days anyway. So I can see you."

She nodded. He took her hand and squeezed it. He closed his eyes and weaved back and forth on the table. She hurried to the door and summoned the two doctors.

"We have met, Frau General." Speaking was Karl Hermann Frank, Gruppenführer SS, Heydrich's second-in-command in Prague. She had indeed met him once. He was a thin, tall man with a funereal face. He was waiting for her in the hospital corridor when she climbed over the desks again and jumped down.

"Yes," she said. He walked beside her, with Hausser falling in behind.

"The condition of the Obergruppenführer is more serious than he admits," he said. "It is more serious, probably, than he knows."

"I was afraid of that."

"The explosion drove fragments deep into his body—bits of the grenade itself, bits of the automobile seat: leather, horsehair, spring wire. When I was first called, I was told he had little chance to live. The doctors are more optimistic now, but his wounds are grievous."

She nodded. "The surgeons will be here soon?" she asked.

"Not until this evening. The surgery should proceed, but he insists on waiting for the surgeons from Berlin."

"Who did it? Do you know?"

"Jews," said Frank. "Trained in Moscow."

Returning to Hradčany Castle, her car was escorted by an armed motorcycle patrol, and an SS trooper with a machine pistol sat in the front seat beside Hausser as they sped through streets

that were almost deserted. Soldiers were nailing a curfew proclamation to poles and doors. The few Czechs who were on the street
watched sullenly, and when she met their eyes from the window
of the car, they turned away. On the street approaching the gate
where they would enter the castle, Hausser had to drive slowly
among four tanks. Inside the courtyard, the number of SS guards
had quadrupled since she left two hours ago.

"Frau General," said the officer of the guard, "because of the
tension in the city at this time—in fact, the danger on the streets—
we must ask you not to ask to leave the castle. My orders are to
see that all your needs are met but to require you to remain in
your suite unless an escort is sent to take you elsewhere."

"May I have access to a telephone?" she asked. "For instance, I
would like to call my husband in Berlin, to tell him I will not be
returning there today."

The officer nodded curtly. "The telephone at our guard station
is at your service."

Once before she had had a sense of being a prisoner here. Now
she *was* a prisoner. They brought her meals. No one came to her
door but the man who brought the table and later came to take it
back. No one brought her news. She did not know if Heydrich
had undergone surgery or if his condition was worse or improved.
The day passed, and the night, and the morning of the next day.

It was after her lunch table had been taken away that she heard
a knock on her door and opened it to find a young SS officer, who
asked her to accompany him. He took her across the courtyard
and through passageways of the castle until they came to a
building she recognized as Heydrich's Prague headquarters. She
had never been inside. The officer led her in, through a series of
guard stations, and finally to a luxuriously furnished suite. He
knocked on a door, then opened it.

"Frau General Bittrich," said the man who came to the door and
welcomed her into the big inner office. "My name is Kurt Daluege,
Gruppenführer SS. I regret we have not met before. I was sent
to Prague by the Reichsführer, at the direction of the Führer, to
assume command in Bohemia-Moravia during the convalescence
of the Obergruppenführer."

"How is he?" she asked. "Have they performed his surgery?"

"Some surgery. It will require more. The Führer himself is

sending Herr Doktor Morell. The Obergruppenführer's condition is quite serious."

"He will be in hospital. . . ?"

"A month, at least."

"He was so confident yesterday," she said hollowly.

"Yes. His courage has always been a source of inspiration."

Nancy sat weakly, shaking her head. In a week Hitler would fly to Helsinki. . . . No. She could not carry out the mission. Even if the FW-190s were still ready in Danzig without Heydrich's influence, he had not yet obtained the identification signals that had to be transmitted to the Condor and its escort. The attempt to assassinate Heydrich had ruined the last best chance to assassinate Hitler.

". . . as you may wish," Daluege was saying. She realized he was offering her a flight to Berlin.

"He—Reinhard—the Obergruppenführer asked me to stay, to visit him at the hospital," she said distractedly.

Daluege nodded. "As you wish," he said. "He is at present under sedation. I doubt he would know you."

"I will stay," she said. "For a few more days, anyway."

Daluege nodded again. "I regret that I will not be able to be your host for a pleasant dinner, at least not for a week or more. We have not yet apprehended the criminals who tried to murder the Obergruppenführer, and I will devote every energy to that until they are brought to justice."

She sighed, nodded. "Jews, Gruppenführer Frank said."

Daluege smiled. "It is convenient to say so," he said. "Actually, the Obergruppenführer was attacked by a Czech murder team, trained and flown here by British Intelligence. It was an operation of MI-6, Frau General. Your countrymen. I am sorry, your *former* countrymen."

The suite, however much she had once loved it, was a plush prison; and she learned it was impossible to make a prison comfortable. Friday passed, then Saturday and Sunday, and Monday was June 1. The guard station insisted it was not able to complete a telephone call to Berlin. On Wednesday, the day Heydrich was attacked, she had been able to reach the Air Ministry, though not Helmut himself, to leave the message that she would remain a few more days in Prague. On Monday, for the first time, they brought no wine with her dinner. She took it as dramatic evidence of the transition of power from Reinhard Heydrich to Kurt Daluege—or to Heinrich Himmler behind Kurt Daluege. The number of guards in the castle courtyard had returned to normal. That was all she could see of Prague, of what was happening; it suggested they had caught the partisans, if that was in fact what they were, and the city was under tight control once again.

She did not believe what Daluege had said about MI-6. British Intelligence would not support an effort to kill Heydrich when it well knew Heydrich was within two weeks of killing Hitler. MI-6 might have its reasons for wanting Heydrich dead, but it would not work at cross-purposes with Churchill's plan to eliminate Hitler and negotiate some significant change in the situation in Europe. That Daluege had dared suggest to her that MI-6 had sent killers to eliminate Heydrich was more evidence of what was happening inside the RSHA: Daluege and others were moving rapidly to gather up the shards of Heydrich's broken power. A week ago Heydrich had been coldly contemplating the deaths of Hitler, Bormann, and Himmler—among others—and now they were playing the ghouls over his still-warm body. Helmut wanted to live in a society that did not countenance such brutality. So did she.

She paced the floor of the three rooms of her suite. She had at least a deep bathtub in which she could soak and muse. She had unwrapped the Dürer again, and it stood on the mantel. Otherwise she stood at the window and watched the traffic in the courtyard —a prisoner as much as if she had been locked inside a cell.

On Tuesday, very early in the morning, someone knocked on her door. It was Hausser.

"He wants you. The Obergruppenführer. He has been asking for you."

The streets of Prague were gray and quiet—and absolutely deserted under the curfew—at dawn as Hausser drove her to the hospital. He was haggard and silent. The hospital was quiet. The number of security stations had been reduced. Armed men were about, but not conspicuously. A floor was reserved for the Reich Protector of Bohemia and Moravia, and in a white room, lying pallid on a hospital bed, in the ruddy light of a spring dawn, she saw Heydrich and knew he was dying.

She took his hand. "Reinhard—"

"Listen," he said, with a trace of the old peremptory voice. "In minutes they will be in here with another shot of whatever it is they are using, and then I won't be able to talk. So listen."

She squeezed his hand and nodded.

"The men who tried to shoot me and then threw the grenade were probably Czechs. I don't know," he muttered weakly. "But they didn't kill me. Someone else is doing that. Not Czechs. Germans. Do you understand?"

"I'm not surprised. Daluege has taken your office."

Heydrich nodded. "Himmler . . ." He paused, drew a noisy breath. "At least it's easy—overdoses of morphine, I think, one after another. Himmler doesn't know about you. But in time he will learn what we were going to do on Thursday. Too many know, and someone will talk. Escape, Nancy! Get out of Germany as quickly as you can. They're bringing on the Götterdämmerung! No one will survive. No one who stays. Get out! *Get out!* Please!"

His eyes were dull, the pupils dilated; he could not see her, she suspected. He stank of infection and of the failure of bodily functions. His bed was not clean. No one had so much as sponged his face, and streaks of discolored saliva had dried from the corners of his mouth to his jaw. What they were doing was perfectly plain—keeping him quiet with morphine while the unchecked infection in his wounds slowly killed him. She put the back of her hand to her eyes and pressed out tears.

"Don't imagine you can accomplish anything more," he muttered. "I won't be able to help you the next time the Gestapo arrests you."

"If I need help . . . is there anyone I can trust?" she whispered.

"Bittrich."

"No one else?"

"Hausser . . . But only for another hour. Make him take you to the airport. Don't go back to the castle. Tell him I order him to take you to the airport."

She glanced toward the door. No one was outside—no one, at least, that she could see. "Could I get word to Hitler of what they are doing to you?"

"Too late. Anyway, don't try to fight my fight; you will only be defeated. Just *go! Run!* Save yourself. That's all that's left for you to do."

Again she squeezed his hand. "Thank you, Reinhard," she whispered. "For the warning. For—your friendship."

Heydrich smiled weakly. "The Führer has had my respect for one quality anyway. He was perceptive enough to see in you the matchless woman you are. Now go. I will see you in heaven."

She touched his forehead. It was hot with fever. She stood, bent over him, and kissed it. Then she turned and walked to the door.

"*Nancy!*" His whisper was hoarsely vocal and urgent. She returned to his side. "Nancy . . . Not Aherne. Don't trust Aherne."

❧ XXIX ❧

At the end of the bridge over the Vltava, a turn left was a turn toward the airport, a turn right a turn toward the castle. As Hausser drove onto the bridge, Nancy was tense. He had said nothing when she told him Heydrich ordered him to drive her to the airport. He had simply nodded and driven away from the hospital, into streets still deserted though the sun was now high and white. Now, on the bridge, he glanced over his shoulder and spoke for the first time. "How did you find the Obergruppen-führer this morning?" he asked.

She had to pretend to receive the question casually. She was looking at the wisps of morning mist lying on the green surface of the river, and she withheld her answer as the car crossed the bridge. "I was surprised," she let herself say finally. "He was alert. He said he believed the medication was finally taking effect. He said he felt a little improved."

"That is good," said Hausser blandly. He turned left.

She had minutes only before they would reach the airport. In that time she had to analyze the situation somehow, to prepare herself to act decisively and with apparent confidence when she walked out onto the ramp to take the Storch. She had to believe Daluege knew nothing of Heydrich's scheme to kill Hitler. If he had had even small evidence of that, the conditions of her imprisonment in the castle would have been very different and she would not have been able to leave with Hausser this morning. Likely he had detained her only because he did not know what to do about her and was waiting for orders from Himmler. It seemed likely, too, that Heydrich was right about what was happening to him. An assassination attempt by the Czechs—for their own very good reasons—had delivered Heydrich into the hands of Himmler's SS doctors, who could in total secrecy eliminate the cold threat he had come to represent. No one would tell Hitler how Heydrich had died; no one would dare. The secret would be kept very close. It was possible not even Daluege knew what was happening—otherwise Hausser's repeated insistence that the Obergruppenführer wanted to see this woman would not have got her out of the castle and to Heydrich's bedside.

By this analysis, she was witnessing a vicious power struggle within the Nazi hierarchy—and no more. They would have to regard her as a very minor factor, and therein lay safety. But that safety, if it existed, would last only as long as it took for word to reach Himmler that she had spent some minutes with Heydrich alone and then taken off in an airplane for Berlin. Himmler would suspect Heydrich had told her how he was dying, and he would suspect she was carrying the word to Hitler. He would kill her to stop her, beyond any question.

How long would it take? Who had seen her? Would Hausser himself feel obligated to report to Daluege that he had complied with Heydrich's order to bring the *Engländerin* to the hospital? When Daluege found out, would he think himself obliged to report to Himmler? He would when he learned she was gone, had escaped. Himmler would know in—what? An hour?

"Do you know the motto of the SS?" Hausser said to her, interrupting her thoughts.

"What?" she asked, not understanding what he had said.

" 'Loyalty is my honor,' " he said. "That is the motto of the SS. We are sincere about it. We live by it." He glanced over his shoulder. "I have been loyal to Obergruppenführer Heydrich. Now I fear for his life."

"He said he was improved this morning," she lied.

"You are his friend," said Hausser. "You are a friend of the Führer and of Reichsführer Himmler. You can tell the Reichsführer what is happening."

"Tell him what?"

"Gruppenführer Daluege was sent here to perform the Obergruppenführer's duties while he is recovering. Instead he is assuming the power for himself, and the doctors he brought are not giving Obergruppenführer Heydrich the treatment he needs to insure his recovery. You must tell Reichsführer Himmler. He will listen to you. I myself do not dare try to communicate with him. But you can."

She nodded. "I will," she said. "As soon as I arrive in Berlin."

An SS Hauptsturmführer—a captain, outranking Hausser—was in command of a small security force at the airport, and an SD man in civilian clothes watched Hausser tell the Haupsturmführer that Heydrich had ordered clearance for Frau General Bittrich for a flight to Berlin. It became apparent that no one at the airport had any idea of Heydrich's condition. As she checked over the Storch in preparation for takeoff, she tried to watch the two security officers, to see if they were making a call to Hradčany Castle. They watched her, too—closely, skeptically. They watched her skirt ride high on her hips as she climbed the struts and swung into the cockpit of the Storch.

For a moment the thought occurred to her that maybe the Storch was sabotaged, that maybe Himmler and Daluege were ridding themselves of her by letting her fly away in an airplane that would fail in the air. She dismissed the idea. If they were doing that, they would not have risked letting her talk to Heydrich first.

The engine started easily, and oil pressure came up on the gauge immediately. Fuel tanks were full. She looked at the SS man and the SD man, standing a few meters away, and saluted them. Hausser stood apart. She waved at him. She taxied away from them.

She took off. A hundred meters off the ground, she banked and turned to the north, toward Berlin. She flew on that way for a minute, climbing another two hundred meters. Then she turned to the right, crossed the Vltava River and flew east, across the northern limit of Prague. Still climbing, she turned south. She passed Prague to the east and swung around to the southwest. She found the Vltava again, south of the city, and began to follow it, climbing slowly as she approached the higher country of southwestern Czechoslovakia.

If they set a trap for her, it would have to be in Berlin. At least it would have to be where they could find her. She was in the air, in a highly maneuverable, capable airplane, with full fuel tanks and 500 kilometers' range, and for the moment anyway they did not know where she was. When they began to look for her, they would assume she was on her way to Berlin.

As she flew south, she formed a plan. Salzburg was within easy range. No one expected her there. She had landed there before, and maybe they would remember her at the airport. Maybe from Salzburg she could get a call through to Helmut.

She continued climbing. Her altimeter showed 500 meters, while the airplane remained no more than 200 meters above the ground. Keeping a low altitude made it less likely she would be seen or tracked on radar. East of Pilsen she saw a Me-109 pass above, maybe a thousand meters higher. It was unlikely that the pilot saw the Storch or that he radioed its position if he did. The Storch was painted olive green on top, which made it difficult to see from above, and it was marked with Luftwaffe insignia.

After she left Salzburg, she could probably reach Switzerland on the fuel she would have left. She was not sure how the Swiss would react. Technically, she had dual citizenship. Probably Germany would denounce her as a spy and demand her return. Whether the Swiss would resist the pressure, she was not certain. Maybe they would intern her for the duration of a war that looked likely to continue for years. Anyway, Helmut could not follow her there, and it was possible they would threaten to harm him to motivate her to return. Switzerland was an alternative only if she could make no better escape.

Flying to Stockholm in the Storch, to meet Helmut there on Thursday, was out of the question. The Storch would require at least three refuelings. What was more, it could not make the direct flight over the Baltic. It had no more range than the Focke-Wulf 190.

Once it was understood she had not flown to Berlin but was missing somewhere and trying to escape Germany, they would set a watch on Helmut. She had no idea how she could meet him. If only she could meet him and the Me-110 somewhere, they could fly to England as they had planned to do from Stockholm.

She wondered if Heydrich was still alive. She reminded herself that Himmler was doing to him nothing but what he had expected to do to Himmler two days from now. She would be a fool to waste sympathy on the likes of Reinhard Heydrich. She could regret his death, just the same. Without him, she could not carry out the mission on which Churchill had placed such emphasis. Without him, she was naked of protection. Göring had warned her that an alliance with Heydrich would be extremely dangerous. It had proved so.

The air was stable, fortunately; only a few updrafts pitched the Storch. She held the stick between her knees and spread her charts. There were two peaks ahead that rose almost 1,500 meters. Flying between them would keep her on a course for Salzburg. If she could not refuel at Salzburg—and she had to wonder if she could, considering the new restrictions ordered by Hitler himself—she had only another 250 kilometers' range. That limited her to Munich, Innsbruck, a few other small airports in Germany or northern Italy. Vienna was out of range, almost. In Switzerland she would be unable to reach an airport but would have to come down on some mountain field just over the frontier.

But she had a source of fuel. Suddenly she remembered.

"I am Frau General Helmut Bittrich. I require a secure military telephone line to the Air Ministry in Berlin. It is vital that I speak with my husband, the General, immediately. I have information he requires—as does Reichsmarschall Göring."

The Luftwaffe Major frowned and pursed his lips. "It is an unusual request."

"It is not a request, Herr Major," she said. "When you have my husband, or the Reichsmarschall, on the line, you may inquire if I am authorized to use such a line."

The Major glanced at the Sergeant who had met her as she taxied the Storch to the ramp and had escorted her to this office. "I believe we have met before," he said to her.

"I have been here before, with Obergruppenführer Heydrich. We landed here in a Heinkel 170."

"Ah, yes. You are—the English lady," the Major said. "The line—I will try to put the call through. Will you require fuel as well?"

She smiled at him. "That's in short supply, isn't it? I have enough to fly on to Munich, where probably they have more. But have you any real coffee? And maybe an Austrian pastry?"

He required fifteen minutes to put the call through. She was confident he was putting it through, not calling the police. As she sipped the coffee and ate the pastry—her first food of the day—

a man in SS uniform entered the little office and introduced himself.

"Friederich Gebhardt, SD, Frau General," he said. SD— Sicherheitsdienst, Heydrich's own security police force. "I am honored to meet you."

She nodded. She was not sure she could control her voice.

"The Major says you've flown in from Prague. May I inquire if you know anything of the condition of Herr Obergruppen-führer Heydrich?"

How much did he know? Why did he ask? "I—am afraid he may be dead," she said. If Gebhardt knew he was, that was the right answer. "He said he felt better, but he looked very weak and ill." If Gebhardt knew nothing, *that* was the right answer.

"God save him," said the SD man, shaking his head.

She nodded. "Yes. He is irreplaceable."

"Thank you," he said.

He left the office, leaving her wondering if an agent of the SD was capable of an ingenuous inquiry into the health of his chief, or if it had been a ploy to give him a look at her before he began to wire questions to Berlin.

"The line is ready, Frau General."

The instrument was a heavy, steel, oversize telephone in the Operations Office of the airport. Three men left their desks to give her privacy on the line. Helmut was on the other end.

"Helmut, do you have any confidence this line is not tapped?" she asked first.

"It is not tapped here," he said. His voice was distant and metallic. "I don't know what they do there."

"We have to take the risk," she said.

"What is happening?" he asked. She could hear the anxiety in his voice, even over this imperfect connection.

"Heydrich is dying," she said. "He may already be dead. The Czechs failed to kill him, but the SS doctors are killing him. Everything is compromised. We have a few hours maybe, to get away. I can't reach Stockholm."

"Why are you in Salzburg?"

"They expect me in Berlin. I flew the other way."

"Can you reach Switzerland?"

"Yes, but I want to fly with you, to England."

"Impossible."

"Do you still have the 110 available, with a pilot?"

"Yes."

"Then listen. I am overdue in Berlin now. Soon they will be searching for me. They will learn I landed in Salzburg, and they will learn I did not take on fuel here. They will limit their search, then—at least for a while—to a radius of two hundred and fifty kilometers from Salzburg: as far as I can go on the fuel that's left after my flight from Prague. But I know where there is a secret cache of fuel. I can land and refuel, and no one will know. I can meet you at the airport in Stuttgart, or Frankfurt, or even at Cologne. They won't be looking there."

"Where is this fuel?"

"You should know. You remember what I told you about Heydrich's mountain house and his meadow landing field? He keeps drums of aviation gasoline there."

Helmut's choice of a landing field surprised her: He told her to fly to Strasbourg. His choice of an hour surprised her: He told her to land there as 4:00 A.M. By that time, he said, the English bombers would be out of German skies and the interceptor squadrons would be standing down, their pilots exhausted, their planes in need of fuel and repair. She could take off from Heydrich's field a little after 2:00 and keep to a westerly course along the northern edge of the Alps, a little north of the Swiss border, and well south of the bomber targets. For himself, Strasbourg was only an hour from Berlin for the Me-110. Another 110 flying west between 3:00 and 4:00 A.M. would not be much noticed. If their rendezvous was successful, they would have less than 90 minutes' flying to make the English coast.

That ninety minutes would be the most dangerous. Many things could go wrong. She could not be sure there was fuel at Heydrich's chalet. There had been several hundred liters of it left after the last time she refueled there, but she could not be certain Heydrich had not been there in the interim and used it. The meadow might be soggy. The house might be occupied. The night flight to Strasbourg would be tricky. And finally Helmut, unaccustomed to intrigue, might fail to escape from Berlin.

It was not yet noon when she left Salzburg, and only a little after noon when she made a low pass over the meadow to judge the surface and then turned back for a landing. The wind was

gusty and variable in direction. She would have trusted no airplane but the Storch to land here. It settled gently onto the grass
of the meadow and rolled to a stop. She jumped out and ran to
the rear of the house to check the drums. She had to break into
the house to find a wrench to unscrew the caps. She found
gasoline in plenty.

She found a little food in the house—some tinned beef, some
tinned stewed tomatoes. She found an axe, and she spent most of
her first hour there chopping branches and arranging them over
the wings and tail of the Storch. She was not strong enough to
drag it into the edge of the pine wood as Heydrich and the
generals had done in January, but she did the best she could to
hide it from the air. When the search for her began, the searchers
would not overlook the possibility that she had landed on a field
somewhere, not at an airport.

Inside the house, she sat on the leather couch, facing the cold,
dark fireplace, and ate from the tins. The house was dead silent
and smelled damp. After she ate, she wandered through the
rooms. She wished she had left clothes here, flying clothes
especially; the white linen skirt and pink silk blouse she had worn
when she left Hradčany Castle this morning were ill-suited to
flying. But she had left nothing, and neither had Heydrich. She
loaded a dozen white candles into the Storch; they might have
some use. She found a pistol under the bed where she had slept
with Heydrich: a 9-mm Luger with a loaded clip. She put that
in the Storch.

Then she began the heavy labor of transferring gasoline. First
she had to insert the hand-crank pump into a drum and screw
it into place. Then she had to turn the crank at high speed to
start the gasoline coming through the hose. She could carry only
one 20-liter can at a time, around the house and down the slope
to the plane. She had to climb to the top of the wing to pour
the gasoline into the wing tanks of the Storch, hauling up the
heavy can, unscrewing its cap, and pouring the sloshing gasoline
into the tank. In an hour she carried only five cans.

She stopped after the fourth can and waited until a flight of
biplanes passed by and out of sight. It was impossible to guess if
they were looking for her, but they flew past the mountain at
low altitude, two men—probably a pilot and an observer—in
each plane.

Although her arms ached and the cans seemed heavy enough to separate her elbow joints, she carried two more. While she was atop the Storch, pouring the second of those, a Messerschmitt 109 flashed over the mountainside. He almost outran his sound, diving at a speed well in excess of 500 kilometers an hour, and she could not jump down from the Storch before he passed by so close she could make out the stripes painted on the propeller spinner and could see the figure of the pilot clearly in the cockpit. Apparently he did not see her. She jumped down and ran for the woods, in the fear he would return for a second pass, maybe even strafing. But he did not return; she saw him climb out of the valley and make a wide climbing turn to the north.

She carried out the eighth and ninth cans. That made 180 liters of gasoline. It was enough. The tanks were nearly full.

Exhausted, stiffening, she lay down on the leather couch in the house. It was late afternoon now, and she wondered if she dared sleep for a while. If anyone knew she was there and was on the way up the mountainside, she could do nothing about it. It would be futile to flee into the woods. She thought of going to the Storch and bringing the Luger back to the house. She knew she would rather die than be taken to a Gestapo prison.

At midnight she went out and threw all the pine branches off the airplane. The night was quiet. She heard nothing but insects and animals. By starlight she saw a mist begin to form below and to creep up the mountainside. She planned her flight out. If by two o'clock the mist had risen above the house and meadow, she would take off anyway, holding a compass heading of 170 degrees and putting the Storch through a maximum climb until she was above it. If the mist developed into an overcast over the mountain range, she would have to try to find her way to Strasbourg by flying a compass heading. She had no weather forecast. She had no idea what lay to the west—clouds, storms, winds, anything. For a while she sat in the cockpit of the airplane and studied the chart with a flashlight.

Not long after midnight, she saw an orange glow to the north. Munich, 50 kilometers away, was under attack again.

The yellow glow of a rising moon appeared on the horizon to the east. Alone in her room in Hradčany Castle, she had been asleep by eleven the past few nights and had not realized the moon was rising after midnight. She stood by the wing of the airplane and watched it appear over the mountain crests to the east. By one o'clock the meadow and the mountainside were painted in shades of cold moonlight gray.

She marched up and down the meadow, pacing the ground over which the Storch would make its short takeoff roll: A gopher hole or new rainwater gully could bring disaster. She was afflicted with a distressing loneliness when she was away from the airplane and the house. The darkness had hidden the world and made it seem small, but in the moonlight she was alone on a vast mountainside. As the yellow moon turned white, its light was colder and the night was more forbidding.

A dog barked. It seemed far away, and she remembered how sounds echoed up the mountainside from the distant valley. Even so, she hurried to the airplane. Standing by the Storch, with a foot on the wheel, she heard the bark again. It *was* distant. But it was repeated. It was not so distant as the bottom of the valley. It was on the mountainside, maybe a hunter's dog—or maybe a dog coming up with a patrol.

The Storch was not in position to take off. It had to be taxied back and turned; and of course once the engine was started, any patrol below would know immediately that an airplane was moving above. She had to decide what to do before they came too close. It was 1:30, too early for her takeoff. Even so, she strapped herself in position in the cockpit and made the Storch ready to move. She peered out, and she listened. She heard the dog again. She believed she heard two dogs, in fact.

She cracked the throttle and engaged the starter. The propeller turned over four times, and the engine did not catch. She tried again. It did not start. The dogs were barking incessantly now, and they were not far down the mountainside. She advanced the throttle and engaged the starter. The engine coughed and sputtered. Again. It fired. Again. It started. Now she could see movement below. Lights. It was no single hunter. She swung the Storch around and taxied northward, the wheels at the end of their long struts bumping over the rough ground.

A shot was fired. The vicious crack of the rifle was unmistakable. She heard then a dull thud, and in a moment a brilliant white parachute flare burst into flame a hundred meters down the mountain. A hundred meters beyond she could see the patrol. The soldiers, of course, could see her. They began to fire.

She hadn't all the takeoff run she needed, but she hadn't time to taxi for more. Swinging the Storch abruptly around, she shoved in the throttle and roared wildly over the meadow. A bullet shattered the glass behind her. She was sure others were whipping through the airplane's fabric body. It bounced into the air, banged down again, then awkwardly wallowed upward. She swung the nose to the left and let the airplane glide downward at full power over the slope of the mountainside, sweeping along only 4 or 5 meters above the ground but rapidly gaining speed because it did not have to climb. It passed by the flare, which by now was lying on the ground, still burning. The patrol was directly ahead. She switched on the landing light. The Storch roared directly toward the soldiers, its light glaring in their faces. She could see them flattening themselves on the ground. She felt a terrifying shock as a wheel hit one of them, but the airplane hardly staggered. It continued downward, bouncing as the other wheel now touched the ground. The patrol was behind her. She eased the stick back. The Storch floated out over the valley, still gaining speed, and she switched off the light and banked into a steep right turn.

Landmarks were few, and it was difficult to identify anything, even in the bright moonlight. She flew as low as she dared, never more than 200 meters above the ground. She had taken off half an hour too early, so she flew with the engine throttled back. It was well. It was quieter that way. She identified the Starnbergersee and the Ammersee a quarter of an hour after takeoff. They were easy enough. Then for almost an hour she saw nothing. There were north-south rivers, several of them—all looking alike in the moonlight. She saw towns. They, too, looked alike. The key was the Badensee—the Lake of Constance. If a north wind blew her south of the lake, then she would unintentionally fly into Switzerland, and she would be so far inside the Swiss frontiers that a Swiss patrol would almost certainly herd her down—if it did not shoot her down. If she did not find the lake in an hour, then probably she was flying into a headwind and would need to advance her throttle and try to gain speed.

She flew on anxiously, peering endlessly to her left, hoping the lake was to her left. When she saw it, she was almost over its shoreline. It looked like an expanse of flat gray, nothing more. The surface was covered with fog, and the moon was not reflected on it. She adjusted her course a little to the north. Her next goal was the Rhine.

It was 3:00 A.M. If Helmut had been able to reach an airport and commandeer a 110, he should be taking off now. The 110 would fly more than three times as fast as the Storch, and his pilot could probably fly a straight course.

Her own course brought her northwest over the Schwarzwald —the Black Forest—and she dropped as low as she could, flying barely a hundred meters above the ridges. The towns were blacked out. The roads were a meaningless tangle from the air at night. She held a compass course of 280 degrees.

She reached the Rhine about 3:30. Dropping into the valley, she headed downstream. Immediately she caused an alert. Over a town—she did not know what town—the spotlights suddenly flashed all around her. She dropped lower over the surface of the river. The lights probed above, and shortly they were behind her, and then they went out.

She watched the right bank for Saint Stephen's Cathedral at Breisach, where she had stood with Heydrich and Halder in the autumn of 1939 and scanned the Maginot line across the river. She knew she would recognize the cathedral; and when she did not see it, she knew she had reached the Rhine north of Breisach. She was therefore less than half an hour from Strasbourg. The sky was lightening to gray, but the sun would not rise soon. She would land at Strasbourg in the gray of predawn.

She saw the city. She saw the Rhine bridges and the single spire of Strasbourg Cathedral. Her chart showed the airport was close to the city and to the southwest. No lights would be showing. She crossed the shoreline and approached the city along the road and highway. She switched on the navigation lights, then the landing light of the Storch, hoping the gunners around the field would not fire on a plane making its presence so conspicuously known. She spotted the field and swung the nose toward it. As she eased the Storch to the ground, she saw an Me-110 sitting near the hangars.

✕ XXX ✕

The interceptor squadrons that flew the twin-engine Messer-schmitt 110s were allowed to indulge a fancy: They painted red and white the mouth and teeth of a shark on the thin nose. This one was so marked, and she noticed immediately, too, that it had been stripped of the array of radar antennas that made it an effective night interceptor but reduced its speed. It was painted light gray and green in a random pattern—camouflage. Helmut stood beside it, with his pilot.

Nancy taxied the Storch to the side of the Me-110.

"My wife and I will use the 110 to return to Berlin," Helmut said to the Luftwaffe Captain who had brought a clipboard with a sheaf of papers to the side of the airplane and was making a record of their flights. "Major Weilhelm, my pilot, will bring the Storch."

"Very good, Herr General."

"Will you please show Major Weilhelm to the Operations Office and secure a weather forecast for us?"

The Captain saluted and led the Major away, down the line of hangars.

Helmut stood silent beside Nancy until the Major and the Captain were out of earshot. He was wearing full, booted uniform, with all insignia. He watched thoughtfully as the two men walked away, then he reached for Nancy's hand and squeezed it. "The gods have been with us so far," he murmured quietly.

"Does it have enough fuel?" she asked, nodding toward the 110.

"Yes."

"Then let's fly it," she said.

The cockpit of the Me-110 was long and narrow. She settled into the deep front seat, where she was surrounded with instruments and controls. Helmut, in the rear, took the radar observer's seat and was surrounded by the electronic gear, even though the antennas had been removed. The 110's advantage to them was its long range. Its disadvantage was that it was substantially slower than the Me-109s or FW-190s that might be sent in pursuit.

"The guns are loaded," Helmut said.

She nodded as she studied the array of controls and tried to remember the engine-starting sequence she had followed the one time she had flown a 110. It was armed with cannon that fired through the nose, machine guns that fired through the wings, and a movable machine gun the radar observer could use to fire to the rear. It might have been better if they had carried no ammunition; the reduced weight would have given them speed. It was too late to think of that now.

Holding down the brake pedals, she engaged the starter for the left engine. It fired immediately and settled easily into an 800-rpm idle.

"Nancy—" Helmut's voice was sharp. He tapped her on the shoulder and pointed, and she saw a small gray automobile speeding toward them, its lights blinking. The driver ran it directly in front of the 110, blocking them from taxiing. He got out. He was a civilian in a dark brown suit and hat, and he walked around the spinning propeller of the left engine, waving, signaling with a turned-down thumb that she was to stop the engine.

"We have no option at the moment," said Helmut.

She stopped the engine.

"Step down, please," the man called up.

They climbed down from the airplane to confront him. His face was flushed, though his gray eyes were cool. His brown suit fit him ill, and it was stained on the lapel. He tipped his hat at Nancy, extended a Nazi salute to Helmut.

"I am Hans Weiss," he said. "RSHA Amt IV."

"Gestapo," said Helmut.

The man nodded. "By coincidence entirely, I happened to be on the field this morning when Frau General Bittrich arrived. It seems there is some irregularity in her flight from Prague and

Salzburg. I am afraid I cannot permit you to leave here until that is resolved."

"Any irregularity can best be resolved in Berlin," said Helmut.

"I regret any inconvenience, Herr General, but it will be resolved here. I cannot in any event allow you to take off in this airplane. I have orders not to."

"Orders from whom?" Helmut demanded.

The man's eyes shifted to the holster in which Helmut was carrying an officer's sidearm, and he reached to a holster inside his jacket and pulled out a small automatic. "You may consider yourselves under arrest," he said. "We will walk to the Operations Office." He gestured with the pistol.

Despondent, diminished, Helmut turned away from the airplanes and obeyed the man.

"For your investigation you will require the papers given me at Prague when I took off," said Nancy. "My authorization. They are in the Storch."

The man glanced at her and at the Storch, then at Helmut and his holster. He moved the muzzle of his pistol toward Helmut. "You may get them," he said to her.

As always when she climbed up the struts to the cabin door, her skirt rode up her legs. She glanced back at the Gestapo man. He was looking. She leaned into the cockpit. The Luger she had found under Heydrich's bed was lying on the floor beneath the seat. She reached for it. She studied it for a moment. The word *Sicherheit*—"safety"—was engraved in the dark gray steel on the side. It was under the safety lever. She pushed the lever up and it covered the word; the safety was off. Holding the Luger to her body, she extended her leg and, with her foot, sought the little metal step on the strut. She shrugged and helped her skirt to creep up. When she glanced around at the man, her white silk panties were fully exposed, and he was staring hard. She turned, aimed the Luger, and fired.

"Move the car!" she yelled at Helmut as she jumped down from the Storch.

The Gestapo man, hit in the stomach, was doubled over on his knees on the ground. His pistol had fallen beyond his reach, and as she ran past him she gave it a hard kick and sent it skidding away from him. She climbed into the cockpit of the 110 and initiated the start sequence on the right engine. Helmut moved the

Gestapo man's car out of the way, and as he climbed to the cockpit the right engine was turning. The left started easily. She advanced the throttles and released the brakes. The 110 lunged forward, and she turned it to the right, toward the taxi path for the airport's single runway.

Men were running from the hangars and the Operations Building. She could see that some of them carried short automatic rifles. She swung the 110 into the runway short of the end and pushed the throttles full in. The 110 was lively but heavy, and it accelerated slowly. She could see soldiers kneeling to take aim. She put the stick forward. The tail rose, and the rate of acceleration increased. They were firing. She could see the yellow fire on their muzzles. She eased the stick back to encourage the airplane to take off, but it did not yet have the speed, and the end of the runway was less than a hundred meters ahead. The soldiers were not used to firing at such a fast-moving target, and they were missing. Suddenly the 110 was flying, and immediately she retracted the wheels. She held the airplane down, made it fly just above the last few meters of runway, and only as trees loomed ahead did she let it climb enough to clear them.

She continued to hold it down, clearing the treetops and rooftops by no more than 20 meters. As the airplane accelerated rapidly, approaching 500 kilometers an hour, the sensation of speed was sickeningly vivid. The fields and villages ahead rushed at them so fast they seemed to dissolve in a blur as the 110 passed over them. She eased back the throttles a little; she knew the engines would not stand ninety minutes of flying wide open. She glanced at the magnetic compass—she had had no time to set the gyrocompass—and set her course west.

"How much fuel do we have?" she shouted at Helmut.

"Two hours," he shouted.

"I am thinking of flying to the south of Paris, then turning north for the Channel. They won't expect that. Also, it avoids some of the heaviest defense concentrations."

"They'll find us with their radar."

"Maybe not, if we fly this low all the way."

"We're terribly vulnerable at this altitude," he shouted.

"Any fighters that find us will shoot us down," she replied. "They are less likely to find us down low."

"All right. I accept your judgment."

"You must navigate for us. I can't take my eyes off what's ahead. Give me a heading."

After a minute or two, he leaned forward and put his hand to her ear. "Two-six-zero," he said.

She nodded. She was already flying 260 degrees.

The country was hilly. She had to climb a little, then suddenly put her nose up and climb sharply to cross a ridge that rose ahead. Beyond the ridge, she let the airplane settle back to the altitude she had been flying before—still only 25 or 30 meters above the ground. She glanced at the airspeed indicator. The 110 was capable of higher speeds at higher altitudes, but here it was holding at 520 kph, more than 8 kilometers a minute. She had to keep her eyes fixed ahead; a very few seconds' inattention could bring her to collision with a high tree on a hill, a steeple, a power-line tower. It all rushed toward her at a speed that was beyond comprehension.

The sun had risen behind. The gray land was turning red. Shadows appeared. On the horizon to the north she could see columns of smoke, probably from the factory stacks at Nancy. This was Lorraine, French countryside in which she would find friends if she had to make a crash landing—if only enemies did not find her first. The rivers below looked alike, but one would be the Moselle.

Helmut tapped her shoulder and pointed to the north and above. She glanced up. He had spotted fighters, four of them, high—maybe 6,000 meters—and 10 kilometers or more to the north. Maybe they were looking for the 110. More likely they were not. It made no difference. Either way they had to see the 110, though at best it would be difficult to see: a camouflaged airplane speeding at more than 500 kilometers per hour over rural countryside and only a few meters above the ground. She glanced at them from time to time as they held their position far above and gradually passed on to the north and west; but she had to hold her attention ahead.

She glanced back at Helmut. "Had Heydrich died when you left Berlin?" she asked loudly.

He leaned forward. "I had no word about him after I talked to you in Salzburg."

"Did you have difficulty getting away?"

"No. But I noticed the bullet holes in the Storch."

She ran her eyes over her engine gauges. All was normal. She
let the airplane climb a little, so it was flying maybe 50 meters
above the ground. She thought of the man she had shot. She
shuddered and put the thought out of mind. She glanced back at
Helmut again. He had taken off his cap and was staring above
them, looking for fighters. When he saw her looking, he smiled
faintly.

The country below was lower, flatter, more open. Farmers were
in the fields, with horses. Small lorries moved along the roads,
some of them obviously military traffic. They passed over an
airfield where planes with Luftwaffe insignia stood in ranks on
the flying line. A truck was refueling them. A man waved happily
as the 110 roared overhead.

Helmut tapped her shoulder. He pointed to a river. "Seine!"
he shouted. He pointed right. "Two-seven-zero."

She shifted course 10 degrees to the right. Thirty minutes out
of Strasbourg, they had reached the Seine southeast of Paris, and
he was telling her to shift to the due-west course, which would
take them by Paris to the south. It would take them also, as both
of them well knew, into an area far more heavily defended. She
eased the airplane down, to the lowest altitude she dared fly.

She recognized nothing. France was awake in early morning.
Wisps of white smoke rose above small houses on the farms. She
saw a crowd of children walking on a road. The sun was bright
now, and high, and she had to readjust her perception of the
height of trees and buildings to take account of shadows. She
glanced repeatedly to the north for a sign of Paris, perhaps of
industrial smoke lying on the horizon; but from this altitude she
saw no farther than she would have seen standing at the window
of a tall building, and she saw nothing of Paris. She saw signs of
Paris in the wider roads running north and in the double-track
railroads. She knew it could not be far.

She was staring at something on the horizon ahead, and had
decided it was the cathedral at Chartres, when Helmut slapped
her shoulder hard. He pointed up. Two Me-109s were above and
ahead, no more than a thousand meters above them; and as she
watched, both of them altered course and dived toward her.

She watched them, helpless, as they appeared to grow. There
could be no question but that they had seen the 110 and were

diving for it. She could see their spinners and their guns. Outlined against the sky, they looked like sleek glass bottles riding on slender wings. Except that they grew rapidly and the sight of them became more vivid, she had no sense of their speed. She steeled herself to hold her heading until she saw the flame from their guns. She knew no defense against their attack but to turn sharply when they opened fire. That tactic might save her once. After that, she did not know what she could do.

They were huge now, looming ahead as if they were going to collide with her. She tensed on the stick and pedals, ready to turn. But abruptly the two 109s flattened their dive and passed overhead without firing. The pilots had realized almost too late, apparently, that the 110 they were attacking was only 20 meters above the ground. If they had dived past her, they would have gone into the fields below.

"Turn!" Helmut yelled.

She made a shallow turn to the right. She glanced back, but could not see the 109s. In their dive, they had passed by her at more than 600 kph, and, combined with the speed of the 110, the closing speed had exceeded 1,100 kph. They would need half a minute to pull out of their dive, climb back to a maneuvering altitude, and turn in pursuit. In that time the distance between them and the 110 would grow to more than 10 kilometers. It gave her a chance. They would have to guess whether she had changed course, and they would have to guess which way. Then they would have to spot a camouflaged airplane moving over the variegated French countryside at 500 kph from as much as 10 kilometers away. Any wrong turn they made would increase the distance. She turned northeast toward Paris. She would be less visible, she thought, over buildings and roads than over open farms.

Helmut tapped her shoulder and pointed. The 109s, flying low, were over Chartres and speeding west. They had been eluded, but they were on the radio now, beyond any doubt, broadcasting the alarm.

Versailles and the outskirts of Paris were below now. She increased altitude a little. She turned east and flew over Saint Cloud, streaking just above the rooftops. Parisians jumped from a trolley car as the 110 roared over the length of a brick street only 30 meters above the pavement. The airplane was well below the tops of factory stacks. She saw them and flew between them. Turning left, she crossed the turns of the Seine and flew over Argenteuil. She crossed the Oise River and turned to 300 degrees. It was a direct course for the Channel.

The fields of Normandy were below. The Channel coast was ten or fifteen minutes away. She could see airplanes above. What they were she had no way to know. Again she passed over an airfield, where FW-190s were lined up ready to take off: a dozen of them, grim and gray and no doubt in the charge of veteran fighter pilots. These were the pilots who went up to challenge the British bombers every night. She hoped they were asleep. The villages were handsome, as they always were in Normandy; she had spent summer days there, years ago. She skimmed the hedgerows at 20 meters.

They crossed the coastline just north of Dieppe. Over the Channel she climbed to 100 meters. If there had been pursuers, she had lost them, or the pursuers did not choose to follow over the Channel. More likely she had lost them, she thought.

The Spitfires came out. As soon as she saw them, she began to rock the wings. They came down and fell in beside her on both sides. Helmut in the back seat waved a white handkerchief, first to one side and then the other. The Spitfires, six of them, led them across the English coast at Beachy Head and to a landing field near Haywards Heath.

Incongruity was his forte. Winston Churchill wore a blue-gray coverall suit, zipped from the collar to the waist and cinched by a broad fabric belt with a military buckle. Under it he wore a white shirt, and gold cuff links gleamed at his wrists. His fat cigar, unlighted, was between his index and forefingers, and his half-spectacles were between the next two fingers. He shook Nancy's hand, then Helmut's, and nodded toward two ehairs.

"My very heartiest congratulations," he said to Nancy.

"On our escape?" she said uncertainly.

"On the DSO," he said. "You will receive it from the hands of the King. Haven't you been told?" He glanced at Helmut, who obviously did not understand. "The Distinguished Service Order," he said. "A high honor in Britain."

"I am grateful," she said.

"I am grateful to see you alive," he said. "We supposed you were dead. Your signals stopped six months ago."

Nancy glanced at Helmut. She frowned deeply. "Winston . . ." she said. "When *was* your last message from me?"

"January," he said. "It was your message through Bernhard, saying the anti-Hitler movement was growing and likely to displace him. Since it came through Bernhard, we discounted it of course and replied noncommittally. Before that, I had a signal from you in December, the last communication we had through Gordon Aherne. Is he alive?"

"He worked for Heydrich," she said. "That was Heydrich's dying word to me: not to trust Aherne."

Churchill smiled wryly. "A ploy, probably. If Heydrich condemned him, all the more reason to trust him. I hope we receive signals from him again."

"If you do," said Nancy, "ask him what he did with the messages I sent you since January. More important, ask him the origin of your replies."

"You received signals from me since January?" Churchill asked, peering up skeptically from under his brows.

"Five or six all obviously composed by Heydrich," she said.

"Well," said Churchill with a nod. "You can congratulate me for having disposed of the late Herr Heydrich."

"If congratulations are due, Winston, they are due to Himmler. That's who killed him," she said flatly.

Churchill shook his head. "He was killed by Czech resistance fighters, trained and equipped and dropped into Czechoslovakia by us."

"They only wounded him, Winston. I saw him in hospital two hours after the attack. His wounds were serious but not fatal. He was killed by SS doctors."

Churchill frowned for a thoughtful moment, then shrugged. "Ah, well," he said. "He is dead anyway, died yesterday. That's what we wanted."

"Oh, Winston . . ."

"Didn't we want it? Isn't it worth something to have rid the world of Reinhard Heydrich?"

"But," said Helmut, "if he had lived a few more days, he would have killed Hitler."

Churchill glanced back and forth between the two of them. "Do you believe that, really? *Heydrich*—would have killed *Hitler?*"

"*I* would have killed him, actually," said Nancy. "And Heydrich would have seized the government."

Churchill rubbed his upper lip with the tip of his index finger. "It sounds—a bit fantastic," he muttered.

"Tell me something," said Nancy. "Did Hitler fly to Helsinki and back yesterday?"

Churchill nodded.

She sighed and closed her eyes.

"It was arranged," said Helmut, speaking ponderously in his accented English. "It was arranged in every detail. Nancy would have shot down the Führer's plane over the Baltic. Generals were involved: Halder, Beck, von Kluge . . . others. The plan collapsed with the attack on Heydrich, Herr Prime Minister. He was the key."

Nancy nodded. "If you had held off your damned Czechs another two weeks, we would have killed Hitler and . . . Heydrich wanted to make peace."

"I knew nothing of this," said Churchill.

"What then of Colonel Dobbie and Mr. Sherwood?" she asked, almost in tears.

Churchill shook his head. "I know of no Colonel Dobbie, no Sherwood."

"They, too, were Heydrich's men, then," said Helmut to Nancy.

Nancy swallowed audibly, nodded. "Then probably he had no plan to make peace," she whispered. "He used me and the talk of peace to draw the generals into cooperation with him."

"He was using you," said Helmut.

"He never denied it," said Nancy dully.

Churchill stood up and walked to a window, parted the curtains to look out into the spring sunshine, and spoke with his back to

Nancy and Helmut. "Herr Heydrich outsmarted himself, it would seem," he said. "After the death of Freddy Binghamton, Heydrich controlled your transmissions and kept his own name out of them. If I'd had any idea he was involved in your effort to kill Hitler, I would indeed have held back the Czechs. But . . ." He shrugged. "I had no idea, no way to know. He himself prevented my knowing."

Nancy spoke softly, half whispering. "It has all been futile," she said softly. "In the end, it has all come to nothing."

"Ach, nein!" Helmut protested. "Wir haben—"

Churchill swung around and interrupted Helmut. "Nancy," he said through curling lips, "your bringing me General Bittrich has been a major service, worth all your risk and sacrifice. The information he has already volunteered is invaluable. What he knows about German production, about its vulnerability . . . Nancy, I cannot overstate its worth to us. You returned to Germany in 1939 to strike a blow against Hitlerism. Well, you have struck it! You have served your country with courage and distinction. Your heroism is its own justification and does not require success to justify it; but if it did, your mission to Germany has been more than a success; it has been a triumph, for which you will have our gratitude and our highest honors."

The Times, November 6, 1981—

LADY NANCY BROOKEFORD DIES IN MOTOR ACCIDENT

Lady Nancy Hilary Alexandra Brookeford Bittrich, DBE, DSO, MP, died shortly after midnight of the injuries she received in a motor accident on the M1 in the vicinity of Stony Stratford. The accident had occurred less than an hour before and involved only the automobile driven by Lady Nancy, which struck a bridge abutment at high speed. Lady Nancy was alone in her automobile at the time.

Lady Nancy Brookeford was born in 1910, the younger daughter of General Sir Henry Brookeford, tenth Earl of Edham. Lady Nancy was educated privately, by tutors at

Wickstone, the family seat of the Earls of Edham, and at Edham House in London. She was married in 1939 to General Helmut Georg Bittrich, who preceded her in death in 1979. She is survived by a son, Frederick Bittrich, a barrister, and by a daughter, Mrs. Hayes Hawthorn.

Lady Nancy was an accomplished aeroplane pilot, having learned the skill in the early 1930s. She continued to take the controls of aircraft and even to fly solo until the very last few years. She was the recipient of honors for her skill and daring as a pilot.

Lady Nancy served as an intelligence agent during World War II. She had lived in Germany prior to the war and remained there, ostensibly as a friend of Adolf Hitler and nazism, after the outbreak of war on September 1, 1939. The records of her services will remain sealed until the year 2000, but she was awarded the DSO immediately upon her return to this country in 1942. In further recognition of her services, she was created Dame Commander of the Order of the British Empire in 1951.

Her husband, General Bittrich, served in the German Air Ministry during the war and escaped to London with Lady Nancy in 1942. A recognized authority on aircraft design and on the management of aircraft production facilities, he acted as a consultant to many British and American firms until the time of his death.

Lady Nancy used the name Brookeford in her political life. She was elected Member for Norton in 1955 and served that constituency intermittently until the time of her death. An outspoken advocate of an aggressive space and aviation policy, she was one of the original sponsors of the Concorde.

The body of Lady Nancy Brookeford Bittrich will lie in state in Westminster Abbey tomorrow, after which it will be carried to Wickstone for burial beside her husband in the family plot by Wickstone Old Church.